D0783837

48p

£2-50
HdB

The
Tangle
Box

By Terry Brooks

THE SWORD OF SHANNARA

THE ELFSTONES OF SHANNARA

THE WISHSONG OF SHANNARA

The Heritage of Shannara

THE SCIONS OF SHANNARA

THE DRUID OF SHANNARA

THE ELF QUEEN OF SHANNARA

THE TALISMANS OF SHANNARA

The Magic Kingdom of Landover

MAGIC KINGDOM FOR SALE—SOLD!

THE BLACK UNICORN

WIZARD AT LARGE

THE TANGLE BOX

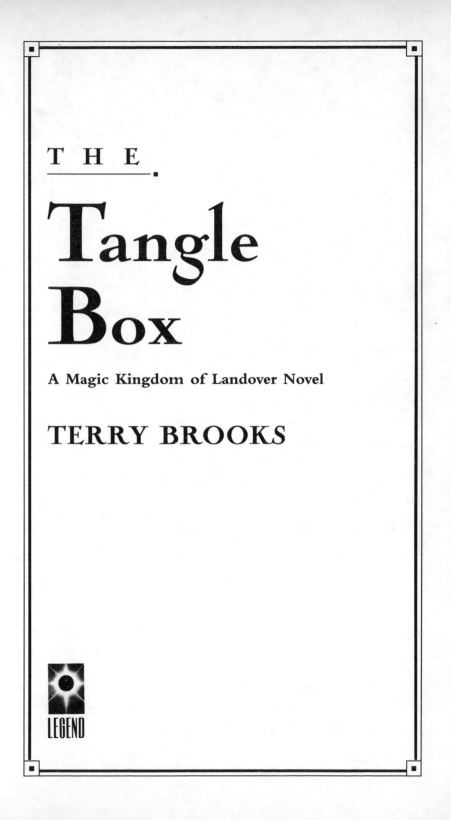

THE.

Tangle
Box

A Magic Kingdom of Landover Novel

TERRY BROOKS

LEGEND

Copyright © 1994 by Terry Brooks

All rights reserved

The right of Terry Brooks to be identified as the author of this work has
been asserted by him in accordance with the Copyright, Designs and Patents Act 1988

First published in Great Britain in 1994 by
Legend Books
Random House UK Limited, 20 Vauxhall Bridge Road, London SW1V 2SA

Random House Australia Pty Ltd
20 Alfred Street, Milsons Point, Sydney, NSW 2061
Australia

Random House New Zealand Ltd
PO Box 40–086, Glenfield, Auckland 10
New Zealand

Random House South Africa (Pty) Ltd
PO Box 337, Bergvlei 2012, South Africa

The catalogue data record for this book is available from the
British Library

Printed in England by Clays Ltd, St Ives plc

ISBN 0–09 931431 2

For Chris, Denny, Gene, Phil, Scott, Stuart,
and somewhere out there, Larry.

Old friends who knew me when
and left me the better for it.

"One evening coming in with a candle I was startled to hear him say a little tremulously, 'I am lying here in the dark waiting for death.' The light was within a foot of his eyes. I forced myself to murmur, 'Oh, nonsense!' and stood over him as if transfixed.

"Anything approaching the change that came over his features I have never seen before, and hope never to see again. Oh, I wasn't touched. I was fascinated. It was as though a veil had been rent. I saw on that ivory face the expression of sombre pride, of ruthless power, of craven terror—of an intense and hopeless despair. Did he live his life again in every detail of desire, temptation, and surrender during that supreme moment of complete knowledge? He cried in a whisper at some image, at some vision—he cried out twice, a cry that was no more than a breath:

" 'The horror! The horror!' "

Joseph Conrad, *Heart of Darkness*

Contents

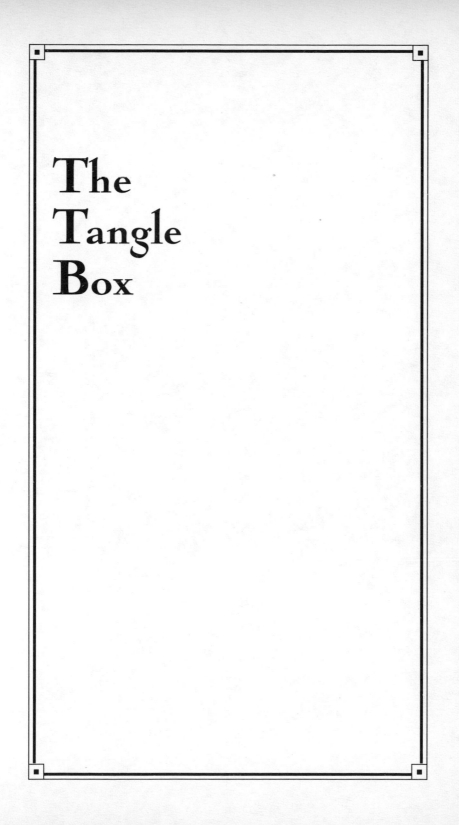

The
Tangle
Box

Skat Mandu

Horris Kew might have been a Disney artist's rendering of Ichabod Crane. He was tall and gawky and had the look of a badly assembled puppet. His head was too small, his arms and legs too long, and his ears, nose, Adam's apple, and hair stuck out all over the place. He looked harmless and silly, but he wasn't. He was one of those men who possess a little bit of power and handle it badly. He believed himself clever and wise and was neither. He was the proverbial snowball who always managed to turn himself into an avalanche. As a result, he was a danger to everyone, himself included, and most of the time he wasn't even aware of it.

This morning was no exception.

He came up the garden walk to the swinging gate without slowing, closing the distance in huge, loping strides, slammed the gate back as if annoyed that it had not opened of its own accord, and continued on toward the manor house. He looked neither left nor right at the profusion of summertime flowers that were blooming in their meticulously raked beds, on the carefully pruned bushes, and along the newly painted trellises. He did not bother to breathe in the fragrant smells that filled the warm upstate New York morning air. He failed to give a moment's notice to the pair of robins singing on the low branches of the old shagbark hickory centered on the sweeping lawn leading up to the manor house. Ignoring all,

1

he galloped along with the single-mindedness of a charging rhino.

From the Assembly Hall at the base of the slope below the manor house came the sound of voices rising up like an angry swarm of bees. Horris's thick eyebrows furrowed darkly over his narrow, hooked nose, a pair of fuzzy caterpillars laboriously working their way toward a meeting. Biggar was still trying to reason with the faithful, he supposed. Trying to reason with the *once*-faithful, he amended. It wouldn't work, of course. Nothing would now. That was the trouble with confessions. Once given, you couldn't take them back. Simple logic, the lesson a thousand charlatans had been taught at the cost of their lives, and Biggar had somehow missed it.

Horris gritted his teeth. What had that idiot been thinking?

He closed on the manor house with furious determination, the shouts from the Assembly Hall chasing after him, elevated suddenly to a frightening new pitch. They would be coming soon. The whole bunch of them, the faithful of so many months become a horde of unreasoning ingrates who would rip him limb from limb if they got their hands on him.

Horris stopped abruptly at the foot of the steps leading up to the veranda that ran the entire length of the gleaming home and thought about what he was losing. His narrow shoulders sagged, his disjointed body slumped, and his Adam's apple bobbed like a cork in water as he swallowed his disappointment. Five years of work gone. Gone in an instant's time. Gone like the light of a candle snuffed. He could not believe it. He had worked so hard.

He shook his head and sighed. Well, there were other fish in the ocean, he supposed. And other oceans to fish.

He clumped up the steps, his size-sixteens slapping against the wooden risers like clown shoes. He was looking around now—looking, because this was the last chance he would get. He would never see this house again, this colonial treasure he had come to love so much, this wonderful, old, Revolutionary American mansion, so carefully restored, so lovingly refurbished, just for him. Fallen into ruin on land given over to hunting and snow sports deep in the Finger Lake region of upstate New York, not fifty miles off the toll road linking Utica and Syracuse, it had been all but forgotten until Horris had rediscovered it. Horris had a sense of the importance of history and he admired and coveted things historical—especially when yesterday and today could be tied together for his personal gain. Skat Mandu had allowed him to combine the two, making the history of this house and land a nice, neat package tied up at Horris's feet waiting to be opened.

But now Skat Mandu was history himself.

Horris stopped a second time at the door, seething. All because of Biggar. He was going to lose it all because of Biggar and his big mouth. It was inconceivable. The fifty acres that formed the retreat, the manor house, the guest house, the Assembly Hall, the tennis courts, the stables, horses, attendants, cars, private plane, bank accounts, everything. He wouldn't be able to salvage any of it. It was all in the foundation's name, the tax-sheltered Skat Mandu Foundation, and he couldn't get to any of it in time. The trustees would see to that quick enough once they learned what had happened. Sure, there was the money in the Swiss bank accounts, but that wouldn't make up for the collapse of his empire.

Other fish in the ocean, he repeated silently—but why did he have to go fishing *again*, for pity's sake?

He kicked at the wicker chair next to the door and sent it flying, wishing with all his heart that he could do the same to Biggar.

The shouts rose anew from the Assembly, and there was a very clear and unmistakable cry of "Let's get him!" Horris quit thinking about what might have been and went quickly inside.

He was barely inside the house when he heard the beating of wings behind him. He tried to slam the door, but Biggar was too quick. He streaked through at top speed, wings flapping wildly, a few feathers falling away as he reached the banister of the stairway that curved upward from the foyer to the second floor and settled down with a low whistle.

Horris stared at the bird in bleak appraisal. "What's the trouble, Biggar? Couldn't get them to listen?"

Biggar fluffed his feathers and shook himself. He was coal black except for a crown of white feathers. Quite a handsome bird, actually. A myna of some sort, though Horris had never been able to determine his exact lineage. He regarded Horris now with a wicked, gleaming eye and winked. "Awk! Pretty Horris. Pretty Horris. Biggar is better. Biggar is better."

Horris pressed his fingers to his temples. "Please. Could we forgo the dumb-bird routine?"

Biggar snapped his beak shut. "Horris, this is all your fault."

"My fault?" Horris was aghast. He came forward threateningly. "How could this be my fault, you idiot? I'm not the one who opened his big mouth about Skat Mandu! I'm not the one who decided to tell all!"

Biggar flew up the banister a few steps to keep some distance between them. "Temper, temper. Let us remember something here, shall we? This was all your idea, right? Am I right? Does this ring a bell? You thought up this Skat Mandu business, not me. I went along with the program because you said it would work. I was your pawn, as I have been the pawn of humans and humankind all my life. A poor, simple bird, an outcast . . ."

"An idiot!" Horris edged closer, trying unsuccessfully to stop the clenching of his hands as he imagined them closing about the bird's scruffy neck.

Biggar scooted a bit farther up the railing. "A victim, Horris Kew. I am the product of you and your kind. I did the best I could, but I can hardly be held to account for my actions based on your level of expectations, now can I?"

Horris stopped at the foot of the stairs. "Just tell me why you did it. Just tell me that."

Biggar puffed out his chest. "I had a revelation."

Horris stared. "You had a revelation," he repeated dully. He shook his head. "Do you realize how ridiculous that sounds."

"I see nothing ridiculous about it at all. I am in the business of revelations, am I not?"

Horris threw up his hands and turned away. "I do not believe this!" He turned back again furiously. His scarecrow frame seemed to fly out in half-a-dozen directions at once as he gestured. "You've ruined us, you stupid bird! Five years of work out the window! Five years! Skat Mandu was the foundation of everything we've built! Without him, it's gone, all of it! What were you thinking?"

"Skat Mandu spoke to me," Biggar said, huffy himself now.

"There is no Skat Mandu!" Horris shrieked.

"Yes, there is."

Horris's broad ears flamed and his even broader nostrils dilated. "Think about what you're saying, Biggar," he hissed. "Skat Mandu is a twenty-thousand-year-old wise man that you and I made up in order to convince a bunch of fools to part with their money. Remember? Remember the plan? We thought it up, you and I. Skat Mandu—a twenty-thousand-year-old wise man who had counseled philosophers and leaders throughout time. And now he was back to share his wisdom with us. That was the plan. We bought this land and restored this house and created this retreat for the faithful—the poor, disillusioned faithful—the pathetic, desperate, but well-heeled faithful who just wanted to hear somebody tell them what they already knew! That's what Skat Mandu did! Through you, Biggar. You were the channeler, a simple bird.

I was the handler, the manager of Skat Mandu's holdings in the temporal world."

He caught his breath. "But, Biggar, there is no Skat Mandu! Not really, not now, not ever! There's just you and me!"

"I spoke to him," Biggar insisted.

"You spoke to him?"

Biggar gave him an impatient look. "You are repeating me. Who is the bird here, Horris?"

Horris gritted his teeth. "You spoke to him? You spoke to Skat Mandu? You spoke to someone who doesn't exist? Mind telling me what he had to say? Mind sharing his wisdom with me?"

"Don't be snide." Biggar's claws dug into the banister's polished wood.

"Biggar, just tell me what he had to say." Horris's voice sounded like fingernails scratching on a chalkboard.

"He told me to tell the truth. He told me to admit that you had made it all up about him and me, but that now I really was in contact with him."

Horris's fingers locked in front of him. "Let me get this straight. Skat Mandu told you to confess?"

"He said that the faithful would understand."

"And you believed him?"

"I had to do what Skat Mandu required of me. I don't expect you to understand, Horris. It was a matter of conscience. Sometimes you've simply got to respond on an emotional level."

"You've short-circuited, Biggar," Horris declared. "You've burnt out all your wiring."

"And you simply don't want to face reality," Biggar snapped. "So save your caustic comments, Horris, for those who need them."

"Skat Mandu was the perfect scam!" Horris screamed the words so loudly that Biggar jumped in spite of himself. "Look around you, you idiot! We landed in a world where people are convinced they've lost control of their lives, where there's so much happening that it's overwhelming, where beliefs are the hardest things to come by and money's the easiest! It's a world tailor-made for someone like us, just packed full of opportunities to get rich, to live well, to have everything we ever wanted and a few we didn't! All we had to do was keep the illusion of Skat Mandu alive. And that meant keeping the faithful convinced that the illusion was real! How many followers do we have, Biggar? Excuse me, how many *did* we have? Several hundred thousand, at least? Scattered all over the world, but making regular pilgrimages to visit the retreat, to listen to a few precious words of wisdom, to pay good money for the experience?"

He took a deep breath. "Did you think for one minute that telling these people that we tricked them into giving money to hear what a bird would tell them—never mind who the bird said he was getting the words from—would be something they would be quick to forgive? Did you imagine that they would say, 'Oh, that's all right, Biggar, we understand,' and go back to wherever they came from in the first place? What a joke! Skat Mandu must be laughing pretty hard just about now, don't you think?"

Biggar shook his white-crested head. "He is displeased at the lack of respect he is being accorded, is what he is."

Horris's mouth tightened. "Please tell him for me, Biggar, that I could care less!"

"Why don't you tell him yourself, Horris?"

"What?"

Biggar had a wicked gleam in his eye. "Tell him yourself. He's standing right behind you."

Horris sniggered. "You've lost your mind, Biggar. You really have."

"Is that so? Is that a fact?" Biggar puffed out his chest. "Then have a look, Horris. Go on, have a look."

Horris felt a chill climb up his spine. Biggar sounded awfully sure of himself. The big house suddenly felt much larger than it really was, and the silence that settled into it was immense. The riotous cries of the approaching mob disappeared as if swallowed whole. It seemed to Horris that he could sense a dark presence lifting out of the ether behind him, a shadowy form that coalesced and then whispered with sullen insistence, *Turn around, Horris, turn around!*

Horris took a deep breath in an effort to stop shaking. He had the sinking feeling that somehow, once again, things were getting out of control. He shook his head stubbornly. "I won't look," he snapped—and then added maliciously, "you stupid bird!"

Biggar cocked his head. "He's reeeeeaching for you," the myna hissed.

Something feather-light brushed Horris Kew's shoulder, and he whirled about in terror.

There was nothing there.

Or almost nothing. There was a faint something, a darkening of the light, a small waver of movement, a hint of a stirring in the air.

Horris blinked. No, not even that, he amended with satisfaction. Nothing.

Outside, shouting rose up suddenly from the edge of the gardens. Horris turned. The faithful had caught sight of him through the open door and were trampling through the bedding plants and rosebushes and heading for the gate. They carried sharp objects and were making threatening gestures with them.

Horris walked quickly to the door, closed and locked it, and turned back to Biggar. "That's it for you," he said. "Good-bye and good luck."

He walked quickly through the foyer and down the hall past a parlor and a library sitting room to the kitchen at the back of the house. He could smell fresh wax on the pegged oak floors, and on the kitchen table sat a vase of scarlet roses. He took in the smells and colors as he passed, thinking of better times, regretting how quickly life changed when you least expected it. It was a good thing he was flexible, he decided. It was fortunate that he had foresight.

"Where are we going?" Biggar asked, flying up next to him, curious enough to risk a possible blow. "I assume you have a plan."

Horris gave him a look that would have frosted a small child at play in midsummer. "Of course I have a plan. It does not, however, include you."

"That is mean, Horris. And small-minded as well." Biggar flew ahead and swung back, circling the far end of the kitchen. "Beneath you, really."

"Very little is beneath me at this point," Horris declared. "Especially where you are concerned."

He went to a pantry, pulled open the doors, reached in, triggered the release for the panel behind, and stepped back as the whole assemblage swung open with a ponderous effort. It took a few seconds; the panel was lined with steel.

Biggar swooped down and landed on the top of the open pantry door. "I am your child, Horris," he lamented disingenuously. "I have been like a son to you. You cannot desert me."

Horris glanced up. "I disown you. I disinherit you. I banish you from my sight forever."

From the front of the house came a pounding of fists on the locked door followed rather swiftly by a breaking of glass. Horris tugged nervously on one ear. No, there would be no reasoning with this bunch. The faithful had become a ragged mob of doughheads. Fools discovering their own lack of wit were famous for reverting to form. Would they be sadder but wiser for the experience? he wondered. Or would they simply stay stupid to the end? Not that it mattered.

He had to stoop to pass through the opening behind the panel, which was well under his six-foot-eight height. He had raised all the other doors in the house when he had renovated it. He had told everyone that Skat Mandu needed his space.

Inside was a stairway leading down. He triggered the release once more, and the heavy steel panel swung slowly back into place. Biggar flew through just as the door sealed and sped down the stairwell after Horris.

"He was there behind you, you know," the bird snapped, flying so close he brushed the other's face with his wing tip. Horris lashed out with one hand, but missed. "Just for a minute, he was there."

"Sure he was," Horris muttered, still a little unnerved by the experience, angry all over again for being reminded of it.

Biggar darted past. "Trying to blame me for your mistakes won't save you. Besides, you need me!"

Horris groped for the light switch against the shadowed wall as he reached the bottom of the stairs. "Need you for what?"

"Whatever it is you are planning to do." Biggar flew on into the dark, smug in the knowledge that his eyesight was ten times better than Horris's.

"Rather confident of that, aren't you?" Horris cursed silently as his searching fingers snagged on a splinter of wood.

"If for nothing else, you need me as a cheering section. Face it, Horris. You cannot stand not having an audience. You require someone to admire your cleverness, to applaud your planning." Biggar was a voice in the dark. "What is the purpose of concocting a well-devised scheme if there is no one to appreciate its intrinsic brilliance? How shallow the victory if there is no one to hail its masterful execution!" The bird cleared his throat. "Of course, you need me, too, to help with your new plan. What is it, anyway?"

Horris found the light switch and flicked it on. He was momentarily blinded. "The plan is to get as far away from you as possible."

The basement spread away through a forest of timbered

pillars that held up the flooring of the old manor house and cast their shadows in dark columns through the spray of yellow light. Horris marched ahead resolutely, hearing pounding now on the steel panel above. Well, let's see what they can do with that! he sneered. He wound his way through the timbers to a corridor that tunneled back into shadow. Another light switch triggered a row of overheads, and stooping again to avoid the low ceiling, he started down the passageway.

Again Biggar passed him by, a fleet black shadow. "We belong together, Horris. Birds of a feather and all. Come on. Tell me where we're going."

"No."

"Very well, be mysterious if you must. But you admit we are still a team, don't you?"

"No."

"You and me, Horris. How long have we been together now? Think about all we've been through."

Horris thought, mostly about himself. Hunched down in a crablike stance as he angled through the narrow tunnel, legs bent, arms cranked in, nose plowing through musty air and dusty gloom, ears fanned out like an elephant's, he considered the road he had traveled in life to arrive at this moment. It had been a twisty one, rife with potholes and sudden curves, slicked over with rain and sleet, brightened now and again with brief stretches of sunlight.

Horris had a few things going for him in life, but none of them had served him very well. He was smart enough, but when the chips were down he always seemed to lack some crucial piece of information. He could reason things through, but his conclusions frequently seemed to stop one step short. He possessed an extraordinary memory, but when he called upon it for help he could never seem to remember what counted.

Skill-wise, he was a minor conjurer—not a magician who pulled rabbits out of hats, but one of a very few in the whole world who could do real magic. Which was because he was not from this world in the first place, of course, but he tried not to dwell on that point since his abilities were somewhat marginal when measured against those of his fellow practitioners.

Mostly, Horris was an opportunist. To be an opportunist one needed an appreciation for the possibilities, and Horris knew about possibilities better than he knew about almost anything. He was forever considering how something might be turned to his advantage. He was convinced that the wealth of the world—of any world—had been created for his ultimate benefit. Time and space were irrelevant; in the end, everything belonged to him. His opinion of himself was extreme. He, better than anyone, understood the fine art of exploitation. He alone could analyze the weaknesses that were indigenous to all creatures and determine how they might be mined. He was certain his insight approached prescience, and he took it as his mission in life to improve his lot at the expense of almost everyone. He possessed a relentless passion for using people and circumstance to achieve this end. Horris cared not a whit for the misfortune of others, for moral conventions, for noble causes, the environment, stray cats and dogs, or little children. These were all concerns for lesser beings. He cared only for himself, for his own creature comforts, for twisting things about when it suited him, and for schemes that reinforced his continuing belief that all other life-forms were impossibly stupid and gullible.

Thus the creation of Skat Mandu and his cult of fervid followers, believers in a twenty-thousand-year-old wise man's words as channeled by a myna.

Even now, it made Horris smile.

Horris admitted to only one real character flaw, and that was a nagging inability to keep things under his control once he started them in motion. Somehow even the most carefully considered and well planned of his schemes ended up taking on a life of their own and leaving him stranded somewhere along the way. And even though it was never his fault, it seemed that he was always, inexplicably, being relegated to the role of scapegoat.

He reached the end of the corridor and stepped into a thirty-foot-square room which housed stacks of folding tables and chairs and crates of Skat Mandu pamphlets and reading material. The tools of his trade, enough fodder for a fine bonfire.

He looked beyond the mounds of useless inventory to the single steel-lined door at the far side of the room and sighed wearily. Beyond that door was a tunnel that ran for almost a mile underneath the compound to a garage, a silver and black 4WD Land Cruiser, and safety. A careful planner was never without a bolt hole in case things went haywire, as they had just done here. He had not expected to put this one to use quite so soon, but circumstances had conspired against him once again. He grimaced. He supposed it was a good thing that he was always prepared for the worst, but it was an annoying way to live.

He glared purposefully at Biggar, who was perched on the crates safely out of reach. "How many times have I warned you against giving in to acts of conscience, Biggar?"

"Many," Biggar replied, and rolled his eyes.

"To no purpose, it seems."

"I'm sorry. I am only a simple bird."

Horris considered that mitigating circumstance. "I suppose you expect another chance, don't you?"

Biggar lowered his head to keep from snickering. "I would be most grateful, Horris."

Horris Kew's gangly frame bent forward suddenly in the manner of a crouched wolf. "This is the last time I ever want to hear of Skat Mandu, Biggar. The last. Sever whatever lingering relationship you share with our former friend right now. No more private revelations. No more voices from the distant past. From this moment on, you listen only to me. Got it?"

The myna sniffed. Horris didn't understand anything, but there wasn't any point in telling him so. "I hear and obey."

Horris nodded. "Good. Because if it happens again, I will have you stuffed and mounted."

His wintry gray eyes conveyed the depth of his feelings far more eloquently than his words, and Biggar's beak clacked shut on the snappy retort he was about to make.

From far back in the cellar came a rending sound—the prying of nailed wood away from its seating. Horris stared. The faithful were tearing up the floorboards! The steel door had not deterred them as completely as he had anticipated. He felt a tightening of his breathing passages as he hurried not toward the tunnel door but through the crates and furniture to a series of pictures bolted to the wall. He reached the fake Degas, touched a pair of studs in the gilt frame, and released the casing. It swung away on concealed hinges to reveal a combination safe. Horris worked the dial feverishly, listening to the sounds of the enraged mob as he did so, and when he heard the catch release, he swung open the layered steel door.

He reached inside and withdrew an intricately carved wooden box.

"Hope springs eternal," he heard Biggar snicker.

Well, it did, he supposed—at least in this instance. The box was his greatest treasure—and he had no idea what it was. He had conjured it up quite by accident shortly after coming into this world, one of those fortuitous twists of fate that occur every so often in the weaving of spells. He had recognized the importance of the box right from the first. This was a creation of real magic, the carvings ancient and spell-laden, rife with secret meaning. Something was sealed inside, something of great power. The Tangle Box, he had named it, impressed by the weave of symbols and script that ringed its surface. It was seamless and lidless, and nothing he did would release its secrets. Now and again he thought he could hear something give in its bindings, in the seals that bound it close about, but conjure though he might the box defied his best efforts to uncover what lay within.

Still, it was his best and most important treasure from this world, and he was not about to leave it to those cretins who followed.

He tucked the Tangle Box under his arm and hastened on across the room, weaving through the obstacle course of spare furniture and worthless literature to reach the tunnel door. There he worked with a steady hand a second combination dial set close against a lever that secured the door's heavy locks, heard them release, and shoved down.

The lever did not budge.

Horris Kew frowned, looking a little like a truant caught out of school. He spun the dial angrily and tried the combination again. Still the lever would not budge. Horris was sweating now, hearing shouts to go along with the tearing up of floorboards. He tried the combination again and yet again. Each time, he clearly heard the lock release. Each time, the lever refused to move.

Finally his frustration grew so great that he stepped back and starting kicking at the door. Biggar watched impassively. Horris began swearing, then jumping up and down in fury. Finally, after one last futile try at freeing the inexplicably recalcitrant lever, he sagged back against the door, resigned to his fate.

"I can't understand it," he murmured woodenly. "I test it myself almost every day. Every day. And now it won't work. Why?"

Biggar cleared his throat. "You can't say I didn't warn you."

"Warn me? Warn me about what?"

"At the risk of incurring your further displeasure, Horris—Skat Mandu. I told you he was displeased."

Horris stared up at him. "You are obsessing, Biggar."

Biggar shook his head, ruffled his feathers, and sighed. "Let's cut to the chase, shall we, Horris? Do you want to get out of here or not?"

"I want to get out," Horris Kew admitted bleakly. "But . . ."

Biggar cut him short with an impatient wave of one wing. "Just listen, all right? Don't interrupt, don't say anything. Just listen. Whether you like it or not, I am in fact in touch with the real Skat Mandu. I did have a revelation, just as I told you. I have reached into the beyond and made contact with the spirit of a wise man and warrior of another time, and he is the one we call Skat Mandu."

"Oh, for cripes sake, Biggar!" Horris could not help himself.

"Just listen. He has a purpose in coming to us, a purpose of great importance, though he has not yet revealed to me what that purpose is. What I do know is that if we want out of this basement and away from that mob, we must do as he says. Not much is required. A phrase or two of conjuring, nothing more. But you must say it, Horris. You."

Horris rubbed his temples and thought about the madness that ran deep within the core of all human experience. Surely this was the apex. His voice dripped with venom. "What must I say, O mighty channeler?"

"Skip the sarcasm. It's wasted on me. You must speak these words. 'Rashun, oblight, surena! Larin, kestel, maneta! Ruhn!' "

Horris started to object, then caught himself. One or two of the words he recognized, and they were most definitely words of power. The others he had never heard, but they had the feel of conjuring and the weight of magic. He clutched the Tangle Box against his chest and stared up at Biggar. He listened to the sounds of the mob's pursuit, louder now, the flooring breached and the basement open. Time was running out.

Fear etched deep lines in his narrow face. His resistance gave way. "All right." He rose and straightened. "Why not?" He cleared his throat. "Rashun, oblight, sur—"

"Wait!" Biggar interrupted with a frantic flutter of wings. "Hold out the box!"

"What?"

"The Tangle Box! Hold it out, away from you!"

Horris saw it all now, the truth behind the secret of the box, and he was both astonished and terrified by what it meant. He might have thrown down the box and run for his life if there had been somewhere to run. He might have resisted Biggar's command if there had been another to obey. He might have done almost anything if presented with another set of circumstances, but life seldom gives you a choice in pivotal moments and so it was now.

Horris held out the box before him and began to chant. "Rashun, oblight, surena! Larin, kestel, maneta! Ruhn!"

Something hissed in Horris Kew's ears, a long, slow sigh of satisfaction laced with pent-up rage and fury and the promise of slow revenge. Instantly the room's light went from white-gold to wicked green, a pulsing reflection of some color given off deep within a primeval forest where old growth still holds sway and clawed things yet patrol the final perimeters of their ancient world. Horris would have dropped the Tangle Box if his hands would have obeyed him, but they seemed inexplicably locked in place, his fingers turned to claws about the carved surface, his nerve endings tied to the sudden pulse of life that rose from within. The top of the box simply disappeared and from out of its depths rose a wisp of something Horris Kew had thought he would never see again.

Fairy mists.

They rose in a veil and settled across the steel door that

blocked entry to the tunnel, masking it like paint, then dissolving it until nothing remained but a vague hint of shadows at play against a black-holed nothingness.

"Hurry!" Biggar hissed at his ear, already speeding past. "Go through before it closes!"

The bird was gone in an instant, and his disappearance seemed to propel Horris Kew on as well, flinging himself after, still carrying the once-treasured box. He could have looked into it now to see what was hidden there. It was lidless, and he could have peeked to discover its secret. Once he would have given anything to do so. Now he dared not.

He went through the veil, through the web of fairy mists come somehow out of his past, eyes wide and staring, thinking to find almost anything waiting, to have almost anything happen. There was a sudden vision of vanishing gold coins and fading palatial grounds, the bitter tally of his losses, the sum total of five wasted years. It was there and then gone. He found himself in a corridor that lacked floor or ceiling or walls, a thin light that he swam through like a netted fish seeking to escape its trap. There was no movement around him, no sound, no sense of being or time or place, only the passage and the frightening belief that any deviation would see him lost forever.

What have I done? he asked himself in terror and dismay.

No answer came, and he struggled on like a man coated in hardening mud, the freeze of night working down to the marrow of his bones, the cold of his fate a certainty that whispers wretchedly of lost hope. He thought he could see Biggar, thought he could hear the bird's paralyzed squawk, and took heart from the fervent hope that the miserable creature's suffering was greater than his own.

And then abruptly the mists were gone, and he was free of the paralytic light. It was night, and the night was velvet black, the warm air filled with pleasant smells and reassuring sounds. He stood upon a plain, the grasses thick and soft against his feet and ankles, their wind-swept flow running on like an ocean toward distant mountains. He glanced skyward. Eight moons glowed brightly—mauve, peach, burnt rose, jade, beryl, sea green, turquoise, and white. Their colors mixed and flooded down upon the sleeping land.

It can't be!

Biggar emerged from somewhere behind him, flying rather unsteadily, lighting on the nearest of a cluster of what appeared to be small pin oaks colored bright blue. He shook himself, preened briefly, and glanced around.

When he saw the moons, he jumped a foot. "Awk!" he croaked, forgetting himself momentarily. He spit in distaste and shivered. "Horris?" he whispered. His eyes were as wide as saucers, no small feat for a bird. "Are we where I think we are?"

Horris was unable to answer. He was unable to speak at all. He simply stared skyward, then around at the landscape, then down at his feet, then at the rune-scripted surface of the Tangle Box, lidded once more and closed away.

Landover! This was Landover!

"Welcome home, Horris Kew," a low hiss came from over his shoulder—insidious, pervasive, and as cold as death.

Horris felt his heart drop to his feet. This time when he turned around, there really was something waiting.

Child

Ben Holiday came awake slowly, languidly, and smiled. He could feel Willow's deliberate stillness next to him. He knew without having to look that she was watching him. He knew it as well as he knew that he loved her more than his own life. He was facing away from her in the bed, turned on his side toward the open windows where dawn's faint light crept through to dapple the shadowed bedchamber with patches of silver, but he knew. He reached back for her and felt her fingers close over his hand. He breathed deeply of summer air fresh with the smell of forest trees, grasses, and flowers and thought how lucky he was.

"Good morning," he whispered.

"Good morning," she replied.

He let his eyes open all the way then, rolled over on his other side, and propped himself up on his elbow. She faced him from inches away, her eyes enormous in the pale light, her emerald hair cascading down about her face and over her shoulders, her skin smooth and flawless, as if she were impervious to age and time. He was always stunned by how beautiful she was, a sylph born of a woodland nymph and a water sprite, an impossibility in the world from which he had come, but merely a wondrous truth here in Landover.

"You were watching me," he said.

"I was. I was watching you sleep. I was listening to you breathe."

Her pale green skin seemed dark and exotic in the early half light, and when she stirred beneath the covers she had the look of a cat, sleek and silky. He considered how long they had been together, first as companions, then as husband and wife. How mysterious she still seemed. She embodied all the things he loved about this world—its beauty, mystery, magic, and wonder. She was these and so much more, and when he woke like this and saw her, he thought he might have somehow mixed up dreaming with real life.

It was a little more than two years since he had come to Landover, a journey between worlds, between lives, between fates. He had come in desperation, unhappy with the past, anxious for a different future. He had left his high-rise in Chicago for a castle called Sterling Silver. He had given up his law practice to become a King. He had buried the ghosts of his dead wife and unborn child and found Willow. He had bought a magic kingdom out of a Christmas catalog when he knew full well that such a thing could not possibly exist, taking a chance nevertheless that perhaps it might, and the gamble had paid off. None of it had come easy, of course. A transition of worlds and lives and fates never does. But Ben Holiday had fought the battles his journey required of him and won them all, so now he was entitled to stay, to lay claim to his new life and world and fate, and to be King of a place that he had believed once upon a time to be only a dream.

To be Willow's husband, lover, and best friend, he added, when he had given up on the possibility that he could ever be any of those things to a woman again.

"Ben," she said, drawing his eyes to her own. There was warmth there, but something else, too—something he could not quite define. Expectation? Excitement? He wasn't sure.

He shifted higher on his elbow, feeling her hand tighten about his.

"I am carrying your child," she said.

He stared. He didn't know what he had expected her to say, but it definitely wasn't that.

Her eyes glistened. "I have suspected as much for several days, but it was not until last night that I was able to make certain. I tested myself in the way of the fairy people, kneeling among the garden's columbine at midnight, touching two vines to see if they would respond. When they reached for each other and entwined themselves, I knew. It has happened as the Earth Mother once foretold."

Ben remembered then. They were engaged in the search for the black unicorn and each had, on separate occasions, gone to the Earth Mother for help in the quest. She had told them then that they were important to her and specifically charged Ben with protecting Willow. When the quest was finished and the secret of the unicorn discovered, Willow had revealed to Ben what the Earth Mother had confided in her—that one day they would share a child. Ben had not known what to think then. He was still haunted by the ghost of Annie and not yet certain of his future with Willow. He had forgotten the Earth Mother's prophecy since, preoccupied with the business of being King and lately of dealing with the old King's son, Michel Ard Rhi, who had almost succeeded in stealing away the medallion that gave Ben power over the Paladin, the King's champion. Without the Paladin, Ben could not continue as Landover's King. Without the medallion, Ben would have a tough time just staying alive.

But all that was past now, the threats posed by the appearance of the black unicorn and Michel Ard Rhi ended, and what surfaced from the memories of those events was the Earth Mother's prophecy, a promise of yet another change in an already indelibly changed life.

Ben shook his head. "I don't know what to say." Then he

caught himself, his eyes snapping up. "Yes I do. I know what to say. It's the most wonderful news I can imagine. I thought I would never have a child after Annie died. I had given up on everything. But finding you . . . And now hearing this . . ." His smile broadened and he almost laughed at himself. "Maybe I don't know what to say after all!"

She smiled back, radiant. "I think you do, Ben. The words are mirrored in your eyes."

He reached over and pulled her close to him. "I'm very happy."

He thought momentarily of what it would be like to be a father, to have a child to raise. He had tried to imagine it once, long ago, and had since given up. Now he would begin again. The impact of the responsibilities he faced sent him spinning. It would be hard work, he knew. But it would be wonderful.

"Ben," she said quietly, drawing away so that he could see her face. "Listen to me a moment. There are things you have to understand. You are no longer in your world. Everything is different here. This child's coming to life will be different. The child itself will likely not be what you expect . . ."

"Wait a minute," he interrupted. "What are you saying?"

Her gaze fell, then lifted again, steady but uneasy. "We are from two different worlds, Ben, from two different lives, and this child is a joining of both, something that has never happened before."

"Is the baby in some sort of danger?" he asked hurriedly.
"No."

"Then nothing else matters. It will be ours, whatever the mix of its blood and history. It will be the best of both of us."

Willow shook her head. "But each world remains a mystery in some ways, yours to me, mine to you, and the differences cannot always be easily explained or understood . . ."

He put a finger to her lips. "We'll work it out. All of it." He was firm, insistent. He misread entirely the nature of her concern and brushed her words aside in his haste to experience the euphoria he was feeling. "A baby, Willow! I want to go tell someone about this! I want to tell everyone! C'mon! Let's get up!"

He was out of bed in an instant, springing up and rushing about, pulling on his clothes, charging to the window and yelling wildly with glee, coming back to kiss her over and over. "I love you," he said. "I'll love you for ever and ever."

He was dressed and out the door before she had even left the bed, and the words that perhaps she would have spoken to him were left forever unsaid.

He went down the castle stairs two at a time, bounding as if he were a child himself, humming and talking and whistling, buoyant as a cork. He was a man of average size with a hawk nose and frosty blue eyes. His brownish hair had begun to recede slightly, but his face and hands were smooth and taut. He had been a boxer when he was younger, and he still trained regularly. He was lean and fit and moved easily. He was approaching forty when he first crossed into Landover, but he didn't know how old he was anymore. He sometimes felt as if he had quit aging altogether. This morning he was certain of it. He could feel the pulse of Sterling Silver beneath his feet, the beat of her heart, of her lifeblood, of her soul. He could feel the warmth of her stones and mortar, the whisper of her breath in the fresh morning air. She was alive, the home of Landover's Kings, a thing of such magic that she sustained herself and relied only on the presence of a Master to function. When Ben had first come to her, twenty years of neglect had reduced her to a tarnished wreck. Now she was restored, polished and shining and vibrant, and he could sense her thoughts as clearly as his own when he was safe within her walls.

He could feel her joy for him now as he skipped off the stairs and headed for the dining hall. He could hear her wish for his unborn child's long life and happiness.

A child, he thought over and over. *My child.*

He was getting used to the idea a whole lot more quickly than he would have believed possible.

It occurred to him as he entered the dining hall, with its tapestry-hung walls and its long trestle table already set and occupied, that he should have waited for Willow—that he should still wait, for that matter—before delivering the news. But he didn't think he could do that. He didn't think he could help himself.

Abernathy and Bunion sat at the table. Abernathy, the Court Scribe, was a man who had been turned into a soft-coated Wheaten Terrier by a bit of misguided magic and forced to stay that way. Abernathy was shaggy-faced and splendidly dressed, possessed of human hands and feet and able to talk better than most regular humans. Bunion, the King's messenger, was a kobold who, so far as anyone knew, had never been turned into anything other than what he was. Bunion was monkey-faced and gnarled with sharp teeth and a smile that belonged on an interested shark. The one quality they shared was an unswerving loyalty to Ben and the throne.

They paused in unison with forks raised to mouth as they saw the High Lord's face on entering.

"Good morning, good morning!" he beamed.

The forks stayed poised. A mix of astonishment and suspicion crossed their faces. Two sets of eyes blinked.

Abernathy recovered first. "Good morning, High Lord," he greeted. He paused. "Slept well, I trust?"

Ben came forward, ebullient to his toes. The china and glassware glittered, and the smell of hot food rose from the silver serving trays. Parsnip, the cook and other kobold who served the throne, had outdone himself again. Or at least it seemed that way to Ben in his euphoria. He snatched up a small apple muffin and popped it into his mouth on his way to his seat. He glanced about for Questor Thews, but the wizard was nowhere in sight. Maybe he should wait, he thought. Questor's absence gave him a reason. Wait for Questor and Willow. Call in Parsnip from the kitchen. That way the announcement could be made to everyone at the same time. That seemed like a good idea. Just wait. That's what he would do.

"Guess what?" he said.

Abernathy and Bunion exchanged a hasty glance. "I have to tell you, High Lord, that I am not particularly fond of guessing games," declared his scribe. "And Bunion hates them."

"Oh, come on. Guess!"

"Very well." Abernathy gave a large, put-upon sigh. "What?" he asked compliantly.

Ben took a deep breath. "I can't tell you. Not yet. But it's good news. It's wonderful news!"

Bunion showed a few teeth and muttered something unintelligible. Abernathy went back to eating. "Be sure to let us know when you feel the moment is right."

"As soon as Questor gets here," Ben advised, seating himself. "And Willow. And Parsnip. Everyone. Don't leave until they get here."

Abernathy nodded. "I'm glued to my seat, High Lord. By the way, I hope this announcement will take place before this morning's scheduled land-use planning meeting with the representatives of the Greensward and the River Country?"

Ben slapped his forehead. "I'd forgotten!"

"And the noon lunch with the new district judges you appointed for the northern lands?"

"I'd forgotten that, too!"

"And this afternoon's meeting with the irrigation planning committee to start work on the deserts east of the Greensward?"

"That one I remember."

"Good. Did you also remember the meeting with the

kitchen staff to discuss the ongoing disappearance of food from the larder? It is getting worse, I am afraid."

Ben frowned in annoyance. "Drat it, why did you schedule all this for today?"

"I didn't. You did. It is the beginning of a new week and you always like to start off a new week by cramming in as many projects as you can manage." Abernathy dabbed at his mouth with his napkin. "Overscheduling. I've warned you about this before."

"Thanks for reminding me." Ben reached for a plate and shoveled food onto it from the platters. Bread with jam, eggs, and fruit. "Well, we'll get to it, all of it. There's plenty of time." He put the plate down in front of him, his mind already skipping ahead to the matters Abernathy had listed. Why, in the name of sanity, did anyone feel compelled to steal from the larder? It wasn't as if there was a food shortage. "If Willow isn't down here in a few minutes, I'll go up and get her. And Bunion can find Questor, wherever he's . . ."

At that a door was flung open at the far end of the hall leading up from the lower entry inside the castle gates, and Questor Thews appeared.

"This is the last straw, simply the last!" he declared furiously.

He strode to the table without a pause, muttering with such vehemence that those gathered were left staring. The Court Wizard wore his trademark gray robes decorated with brightly colored patches of cloth and wrapped at the waist with a crimson sash, a ragtag scarecrow figure, tall and thin, all sticks and wisps of flying beard and hair. It was immediately apparent that he might have dressed and groomed himself better—at least to the extent of new robes and a trim about the ears, as Ben had tried to suggest on more than one occasion—but he saw no reason to change what he was comfortable with and so did not. He was mild and gentle and not given over easily to fits of pique, and it was strange to see him so agitated now.

He came to a halt before them and threw back his robes as if to shed himself of whatever it was that so burdened him this beautiful summer morning. "He's back!" he announced.

"Who's back?" Ben asked.

"Back and not a bit repentant for anything he's done! There is not the least shame in him, not the least! He comes up to the gate as bold as you please and announces he's here!" Questor's face was reddening as he spoke, turning dangerously crimson. "I thought we'd seen the last of him twenty some years ago, but like the proverbial bad penny, he's turned up anew!"

"Questor." Ben tried to get a word in edgewise. "Who are you talking about?"

Questor's gaze was fierce. "I'm talking about Horris Kew!"

Now Abernathy was on his feet as well. "That trickster! He wouldn't dare come back! He was exiled! Questor Thews, you've been out in the sun too long!"

"Feel free to walk down and have a look for yourself!" Questor gave him a chilly smile. "He presents himself as a supplicant, come to ask forgiveness from the High Lord. He wants the ban of exile lifted. He wants back into Landover!"

"No!" Abernathy's exhortation came out as something very close to a growl. He wheeled on Ben, bristling. "High Lord, no! Do not see him! Refuse him entrance! Send him away immediately!"

"I wouldn't send him away if I were you!" Questor snapped, crowding forward to stand next to the dog. "I'd have him seized and thrown into the deepest, darkest prison I could find! I'd lock him up and throw away the key!"

Willow had come down the stairs and into the room and was now seating herself next to Ben. She gave him a questioning stare as she listened, but he could only shrug to indicate his own lack of understanding.

"Hold up a minute," he interjected finally. Bunion was the only one who wasn't giving any indication of what he thought, sitting across from Ben with that disconcerting grin on his face. "I'm not following any of this. Who is Horris Kew?"

"Your worst nightmare!" Abernathy sniffed, as if that explained everything.

Questor Thews was only slightly more eloquent. "I'll tell you who he is. Horris Kew is the biggest troublemaker who ever lived! A conjurer of a very minor sort, one with just enough magic to get into mischief. I thought we were rid of him, but I should have known better! Abernathy, remember the cow episode?"

"The cow episode?" Ben asked.

Consumed by his tirade, Questor wasn't listening. "Horris claimed he was trying to establish communication with the cows to permit better control over their milking habits, and things got out of hand. His conjuring efforts drove the poor beasts to a frenzy. They broke loose country-wide and trampled down the entire wheat harvest and several towns in the bargain. It was the same with the chickens. The next thing you know he's subverted the evolutionary process, and they're flying like birds and dropping eggs all over the place."

Ben grinned. "What?"

"And don't forget about the cats!" Abernathy snapped. "He found a way to organize them into hunting packs in some harebrained scheme to rid the country of mice and rats, but it backfired and they ended up hunting dogs!" He shivered.

"That was bad," Questor agreed, nodding emphatically at Ben. "But the worst thing he did, the thing that got him banished, was to conjure up that fast-growing plant that took seed overnight and turned everything within fifty miles of Sterling

Silver into a jungle!" Questor folded his arms defiantly. "It took weeks to cut a way through it! And while it was being cut down, while the King and his court were trapped in the castle, Abaddon's demons took advantage of the Paladin's absence to raid the countryside in earnest. Dozens of towns, farms, and lives were lost. It was a mess."

"I don't get it," Ben admitted. "What was all this supposed to accomplish? It sounds like he might have had good intentions."

"Good intentions?" Questor Thews was livid. "I hardly think so! These were schemes of extortion! The cows and chickens and cats and plants were levers with which to pry loose the purse strings of those with money! Horris Kew never cared a thing about anyone but himself! Ten minutes after one scheme collapsed, he was already hatching a new one! Excuse the choice of words."

"But, Questor, this was more than twenty years ago, you said." Ben was trying hard not to laugh.

"There, you see?" Questor snapped irritably, the other's facial contortions not escaping his notice. "Horris Kew always seems harmless enough, just a bit of an annoyance. No one takes him seriously. Even my brother ignored him until that last bit with the demons, and then Meeks wanted him gone, too. Seems the unexpected appearance of the demons interfered with one of his own schemes, and my brother could tolerate almost anything but that."

Meeks—Questor Thews's brother, the Court Wizard before him, the man who had tricked Ben into coming into Landover and thereafter become his worst enemy. Gone, but hardly forgotten. He would surely not suffer a man like Horris Kew to cross up his plans.

"Anyway," Questor finished, "my brother persuaded the old King to banish Horris, so Horris was banished, and that was that."

"Uh-huh." Ben rubbed his chin. "Banished to where?"

Questor looked decidedly uncomfortable. "To your world, High Lord," he admitted reluctantly.

"To Earth? For the last twenty years?" Ben tried to remember reading anything about someone named Horris Kew.

"A favorite dumping ground for rejects and annoyances, I'm afraid. Not much you can do with magic where there's so little belief in its existence, you know."

Abernathy nodded solemnly. They stood staring at Ben, apparently out of steam, waiting for a response. Ben looked at Willow, who was eating now and refused to look back, and he remembered that he had wanted to tell his friends about the baby. He guessed that would have to wait.

"Well, why don't we hear what he has to say," Ben suggested, rather curious about someone who could upset even the normally unflappable Abernathy. "Maybe he's changed."

Questor went from crimson to flaming scarlet. "Changed? When cows fly!" He stopped, apparently thinking that where Horris was concerned perhaps that wasn't qualification enough. "Never, High Lord!" he amended, just to make things perfectly clear. "Don't see him. Don't let him set one foot into this castle. I would have sent the guard to greet him on the road if I had known he was coming. I still cannot believe he had the gall to return!" He paused, suddenly perplexed. "In fact, how *did* he return?"

"Doesn't matter. He is a supplicant," Ben pointed out patiently. "I can't be sending supplicants away without even speaking to them. What sort of precedent would that set? I have to at least speak to him. What can it hurt?"

"You don't know, High Lord," Abernathy said ominously.

"You really don't," Questor agreed.

"Get rid of him right now."

"Don't let him within a mile of you."

Ben pursed his lips. He had never heard his advisors so

adamant about anything. He did not see how a simple conversation could cause problems for him, but he was not inclined
to dismiss their warning out of hand.

"Do you believe that your magic is a match for his?" he
asked Questor after a moment.

Questor drew himself up. "More than a match. But he is
a very slippery character."

Ben nodded. "Well, I can't just send him away. Why
don't we all see him together. That way you can warn me if
he tries anything. How about it?"

Abernathy sat down without a word. Questor stiffened
even further, but finally nodded his agreement. "Don't say I
didn't warn you," he declared curtly, and signaled to a retainer
standing at the far end of the hall.

They sat in silence then, waiting. Ben reached for Willow's hand and squeezed it gently. She smiled back at him. At
the far end of the room, Parsnip appeared from out of the
kitchen, gave a brief greeting to the silent assemblage, and disappeared back in again. Ben was thinking that he would like
to dispose quickly of Horris Kew and get on with his day. He
was thinking about the meetings he had scheduled and the
work that needed doing. He had believed once that no one
worked harder than a trial lawyer, but he had since discovered
that Kings did. There were constant decisions required, plans
to consider, and problems by the score to resolve. So much depended on him. So many people were affected by his actions.
He liked the challenge, but was continually daunted by the
amount of responsibility. Sometimes he thought about the circumstances that had brought him to this place in his life and
wondered that such a thing could happen. It was proof that
anything was possible. He would measure where he was from
where he had been and be amazed. He would measure, and he
would tell himself once again that however severe the pressures
and demands he would never exchange his present life for his
past.

"You could still change your mind about this, High Lord," Questor advised quietly, not quite ready to let the argument die.

But Ben was still thinking about his life, applied the comment accordingly, and found the wizard's assessment wrong. He was a man who had rediscovered himself by daring to take a chance that others would not have, and changing his mind now was not a reasonable option. He was going to be a *father*, he thought with renewed amazement. What would that be like for a man who had passed his fortieth year with no children? What would it be like for a man who'd had no sense of family for so long? He wanted a child, but he had to admit that he didn't know if he was ready for one.

There was a clomping of boots at the far end of the room, and a man entered. He was tall and gangly and strange-looking. He had arms and legs that were akimbo, and a nose, ears, and Adam's apple that stuck out like they were parts attached to a Mister Potato Head. He was dressed in gray supplicant's robes that looked like they had seen service last as floor mats in a stable. His feet were dusty and bare, his hands were clasped before him beseechingly, and his body was stooped. He came forward at something approaching a weary shuffle, his head bobbing. A bird with black feathers and a white crest sat on his shoulder, bright eyes searching.

"High Lord," Horris Kew greeted, and dropped to his knees. "Thank you for agreeing to see me."

Ben rose, thinking to himself that this fellow was the most harmless-looking threat he had ever seen. "Stand up," he ordered. "Let's hear what you have to say for yourself. Your press has been pretty bad up to now."

Horris rose, a pained look on his field-plow face. He had a rather bad tic in one eye that gave him the look of a man flinching from an imagined blow. "I confess everything, High Lord. I have done all that I am accused of doing. Whatever

Questor Thews and Abernathy have told you, I admit. I don't propose to argue any of it. I just want to ask forgiveness."

Questor snorted. "What are you up to, Horris Kew? You're up to something."

"Awk! Biggar is better!" the bird squawked.

"That bird looks familiar," Abernathy declared, squinting darkly at Biggar.

"Just a common myna, my companion on the road." The tic in Horris Kew's eye twitched double-time.

Abernathy frowned. "I suppose you've trained him to attack dogs?"

"Awwwkk! Fleas! Fleas!" the bird cried.

Ben came around the table to put himself between Abernathy and the bird. "Aren't you supposed to be in exile, Horris? What brings you back?"

"High Lord, I simply want another chance." A truly penitent look settled across Horris Kew's angular face. "I have had twenty years to repent, to consider my mistakes, to think about my misconduct. I was lucky I escaped Landover alive, as Questor Thews can tell you. But now I wish to come back to my home and start over again. Is this possible?"

Ben studied him. "I don't know."

"Don't do it, High Lord," Questor cautioned at once.

"Don't even think about it, High Lord," Abernathy added.

"Awk! Hooray for Horris, Hooray for Horris!" the bird declared.

"Thank you, Biggar." Horris patted the bird affectionately and returned his gaze to Ben. "I have a plan, should you decide to let me return, High Lord. I ask nothing of you or anyone but to be left alone. I shall live out my life as a hermit, a bother to no one. But should the need arise, I stand ready to serve in any capacity required. I have some little knowledge of magic that may someday be of use. I offer it for when you think it appropriate. You can depend on me to come if called."

"I believe that it was your use of magic that got you in trouble the last time," Ben admonished softly.

"Yes, yes, too true. But I will not involve myself in the affairs of the country or her people unless I am asked," Horris said. Tic, tic went the bad eye. "Should I violate this covenant, you may restore the ban immediately."

"No," Questor Thews said.

"No," Abernathy echoed.

Ben tried to keep from smiling. He should probably be taking this more seriously than he was, he thought, but it was hard to get too excited over someone who looked like this fellow and whose worst offense was making chickens fly and cows rebel against farmers.

"Awk! Pretty lady," the bird whistled suddenly.

Willow smiled and glanced at Ben. He remembered the child.

"I will think about it and give you an answer in several days," Ben announced, ignoring the groans from Questor and Abernathy. "You can come back then."

"Happily, High Lord," Horris Kew responded, bowing deeply. "Thank you, thank you. I am indebted."

He backed quickly from the room and was escorted away. Ben wondered what kind of bird Biggar was. He wondered how many words the bird could say.

"Well, that was a monumentally foolish decision!" Questor Thews snapped in disgust. "If I am permitted to say so, High Lord!"

"You are," Ben replied, since it was already said.

"There's something familiar about that bird," Abernathy muttered.

"Just because a man looks harmless doesn't mean he really is," Questor went on. "In Horris Kew's case, appearances are not just deceiving, they are an outright lie!"

Ben was already tired of the subject, and he held up his hands imploringly. "Gentlemen!" he admonished. He was hoping for looks of chagrin but had to settle for hostile silence. He sighed. You couldn't have it your way all the time, he supposed. That was why most matters required compromise. "We'll discuss this later, all right?"

Willow rose to stand beside him, and he smiled as she looped her arm through his. "Parsnip!" he yelled, and when his cook appeared to stand with his wizard, scribe, and messenger, he asked, "How would you feel about our adding another member to our family?"

"As long as it's not Horris Kew," Questor Thews muttered and looked not the least chagrined for saying it.

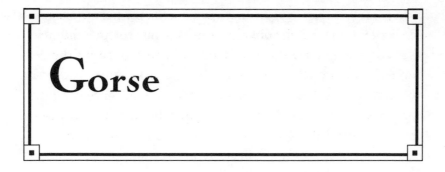

Gorse

Horris Kew departed Sterling Silver like a fugitive in the night, hastening away as swiftly as propriety and pride would allow, casting nervous glances left and right with every step he took. He hunched along with purposeful, ground-eating strides, his tall, gawky frame rolling and swaying with the movement, a strange figure in this strangest of lands. The tic he had mysteriously developed caused the corner of his eye to jump like a trapped cricket. Biggar rode his shoulder, an omen of doom.

"I really dislike that dog," the bird muttered, ruffling his feathers in a show of distaste.

Horris Kew's lips tightened. "Shut up about the dog."

"He almost recognized me. Did you see? He'll remember, sooner or later, mark my words."

"Consider them marked." They passed across the bridge that connected the island to the mainland and set out towards the forests west. "What's the difference if he does? Meeks is dead and gone."

Biggar had belonged to the wizard in the old days. It was Meeks who had performed the magic that enhanced Biggar's intelligence, hopeful of using the bird as a spy against his enemies. But Biggar had been as obnoxious and outspoken then as he was now, and Meeks had quickly grown tired of him.

When Horris Kew had been exiled to earth by the old King, Meeks had sent the troublesome bird along for the ride.

Biggar hunched down into a black featherball. "If the dog connects me with Meeks, Horris, you can kiss our chances of ever getting back inside those castle walls good-bye."

Horris tried to look unconcerned. "You're worrying about nothing."

"I don't care. I don't like the way the dog looked at me. In fact, I don't like any of this."

Horris didn't say so, but he wasn't sure he liked any of it either. Nothing had gone the way he had expected from the moment he had mouthed "rashun, oblight, surena, whatever" and that *thing* had come out of the Tangle Box. He shivered just thinking about it, picturing how it had looked when he had turned around on hearing its greeting, thinking of it waiting for them now. It was loathsome beyond description. It was the foulest being he had ever encountered.

And now it had taken charge of his life, ordering him about like a common servant, telling him where to go and what to do. It was his worst nightmare come to life, and Horris Kew didn't think for a moment that he had better try to cross it.

"Why do you think it sent us to see the King?" Biggar asked suddenly, as if reading his mind. They passed up the hillside and into a meadow fronting the edges of the forest trees.

Horris exhaled wearily. "How would I know? It told me to go make this pitch to Holiday, so I did. It said to do it, so I did it. You think I was going to argue?"

Biggar didn't have anything to say to that, which was just as well since Horris Kew's temper was already on edge from the events of the past twenty-four hours. This was all Biggar's fault anyway, he was thinking. The channeling scheme, the concoction of Skat Mandu (Skat Mandu, what a joke!), the releasing of that thing, and the return to Landover. Horris didn't know what game it was they were playing, but he knew it was a dangerous one, coming back to the very last place in the universe they should have come, a place where they were anything but welcome. Except, of course, that the old King was dead and this new one, Holiday, at least seemed willing to consider his petition. No matter. What were they doing here? Sure, this was his homeland and all, but it was not a place that held fond memories. It was a place in which he had been born (luck of the draw, that), had grown up, had gotten himself in considerable trouble, been declared persona non grata, and left under duress. He had been perfectly happy in his new world, in the land of milk and honey and believers of Skat Mandu ready to pay him money for a wisp of smoke and a shimmer of light. He had been well settled, content with himself, his surroundings, and his prospects.

Now what did he have? Nothing. And it was all Biggar's fault.

Except, of course, it really wasn't. It was as much his fault as Biggar's, and that made him even madder.

What was going to happen to him now? What did good old Skat Mandu have planned?

"I really don't like that dog," Biggar repeated, and finally lapsed into silence.

They journeyed on through the morning, and as midday passed they reached the Heart. The Heart was sacred ground, the wellspring of Landover's magic and the touchstone of her life. It was here that all of Landover's Kings, including Ben Holiday, had been crowned. It appeared as a clearing amid a forest of giant broad-leaved trees, its perimeter encircled by Bonnie Blues, its floor a mix of green, gold, and crimson grasses. A dais stood centermost, formed of gleaming white oak timbers and anchored by polished silver stanchions in which massive white candles had been set. Standards ringed the dais, and from their tips flew the flags of the Kings of Landover in a sea of bright colors. Holiday's was newest, a set of balanced scales held forth against a field of green, a nod back to his years as a lawyer in the old life. All about the dais and across the remainder of the clearing were rows of white velvet kneeling pads and rests.

All of it was clean and perfectly kept, as if in anticipation of the next coronation.

Horris Kew entered the Heart and looked around solemnly. A country's history winked back at him from every polished timber and post. "Take off your hat, Biggar," he intoned. "We're in church."

Biggar looked about doubtfully, sharp eyes gleaming. "Who in the world takes care of this place?"

Horris stared at him and sighed. "What a philistine you are."

Biggar flew off his shoulder and settled down on one of the velvet rests. "So now you're resorting to name calling, are you, Horris? That's really pathetic."

And very deliberately he relieved himself on the white cushion.

Horris went rigid for a moment, and then his lanky frame uncoiled as if part serpent and his long limbs worked this way and that, like sticks pinned to a rag doll. "I've had about all I'm going to take from you, Biggar. How would you like me to wring your worthless neck?"

"How would you like me to peck out your eyes, Horris?"

"You imbecilic jackdaw!"

"You moronic baboon!"

They glared at each other, Horris with his fingers hooked into claws, Biggar with his feathers ruffled and spread. The rage swept through them, then dissipated, evaporating like water on stone in the midday sun. The tension eased from their bodies and was replaced by wonder and a vague sense of uneasiness over the spontaneity of their embarrassing behavior.

"That *thing* is responsible for this foolishness," Horris announced quietly. "Good old Skat Mandu."

"He's not what I expected, I admit," Biggar declared solemnly.

"He's not even a *he*. He's an *it*."

"A maggot."

"A serpent."

Biggar closed his eyes. "Horris," he said, a note of wistfulness creeping into his bird voice. "What are we doing here? Wait, don't say anything until you've heard me out. I know how we got here. I understand the mechanics. We let that thing out of the Tangle Box where it was locked away in that patch of fairy mist, and it used the fairy mist to open a door into Landover. I got that part. But what are we doing here? Really, what? Just think about it a moment. This is a dangerous place for us."

"I know, I know," Horris sighed.

"All right, then. Why don't we go somewhere else? Somewhere less . . . threatening. Why don't we? Maybe it would listen to a suggestion that we go somewhere else. Maybe it would at least consider sending *us* through, even if *it* still wanted to stay. After all, what does it need us for?"

Horris fixed him with a hard stare. "Where would we go, Biggar? Back to where we came from, where the faithful are waiting to tear us apart? You took care of that option quite nicely."

"It wasn't me, Horris. I already told you that. It was Skat Mandu! Or whoever." Biggar hopped one rest closer. "You want to know where we can go? There are lots of choices. I've read about a few. How about that place with the yellow brick road and the emerald city and all those little people running around, the Munchies or whatever?"

Horris looked at him and sighed. "Biggar, that wasn't a real place. That was in a book."

Biggar tried frowning and failed. "No, it wasn't. It was real."

"No, Biggar. You've short-circuited again. That was Oz. Oz isn't a real place. It's a make-believe place."

"With the wizard and all? With the witches and the flying monkeys? That wasn't a story. That was real."

"It was a story, Biggar! A story!"

"All right, Horris, all right! It was a story!" The bird clacked his beak emphatically. He thought a minute. "Okay. How about going to the place with the little people with the furry feet?"

Horris turned red. "What's the use!" he hissed furiously. He strode past Biggar without looking at him, headed for the trees. "Let's just report back and get this over with!"

He moved away again, disappearing back into the forest, leaving the Heart behind. After a moment, Biggar followed. They passed out of the sunlight to where it was dark and cool, even at midday, and shadows draped their intricate patterns like spider's webs across the woodland. They traveled without speaking, Horris striding on determinedly, Biggar hopping from limb to limb, now flying ahead, now winging his way back. Locked in a brown study, Horris pointedly ignored him.

Less than a mile from the Heart, where the light was all but screened away by the interlocking branches of the trees overhead, they descended a steep slope to a dense thicket of brush backed up against a rocky overhang. Easing their way past the brush, they came to a massive flat stone into which symbols had been carved on both sides and across the top. Horris stared at the stone, sighed his weariest sigh, reached up, and touched various symbols in quick succession. He stepped back quickly as the door opened, stone grating on stone. Biggar landed on his shoulder again and together they watched the black opening of the cave beyond come into focus.

Rather reluctantly, they entered. The stone door grated shut behind them.

There was light in the cave to guide them back into its farthest reaches, a sort of dim phosphorescence that seemed wedded to the rock. It gleamed like silver ore in scattered patches and random streaks, breaking up the gloom sufficiently to allow a relatively safe passage through. It was hot within the cave, an unpleasant sort of warmth that suffused the skin and left it damp and itchy. There was a distinctive smell in the air, too. Horris and Biggar recognized it immediately and knew where it came from.

They reached the deepest part of the cave in moments, the part where the light was brightest, the heat hottest, and the stench rawest. The cave widened and rose some twenty feet at this point, and a scattering of stalactites jutted down from the ceiling like a medieval spear trap. The chamber was empty save for a rickety wooden bed set to one side and an equally rickety wooden table on which a metal washbasin sat. The bed was unmade and the basin unemptied.

Next to the wash basin sat the Tangle Box.

From the deepest corner of the cave came a stirring. "Did you do as you were told?" a voice hissed menacingly.

Horris tried to hold his breath as he spoke so as not to inhale any more of the smell than he had to. "Yes. Just as we were told."

"What was the response?"

"He said he would think it over. But the wizard and the scribe are going to try to convince him not to let me stay."

The speaker laughed. It shifted in the gloom, a lifting of its body, a straightening of its limbs. Really, it was hard to tell what was happening, which was very disconcerting. Horris thought back again to when he had laid eyes on it for the first time, realizing suddenly that he was already unsure of what it was he had seen. The thing that was Skat Mandu had a way of showing only part of itself, a flicker of body or limb or head (never face), a hint of color or shape. What you were left with, ultimately, was a sense of something rather than a definite image. What you were left with, inevitably, was unpleasant and harsh and repulsive.

"Do I frighten you?" the voice asked softly. In the smoky gloom something gleamed a wicked green.

Horris suddenly regretted coming back, thinking that perhaps Biggar had been right after all. What sort of madness was this that they had embraced in releasing the monster? It had been imprisoned in the Tangle Box, and it had tricked them into freeing it, using Biggar as channeler, Horris as conjurer, both as instruments for picking the locks that held it chained. Horris Kew understood in the most secret part of his heart that nothing he had done in creating Skat Mandu had ever really been his idea—it had all come from the *thing* in the Tangle Box, the *thing* that had been locked within the fairy mists, dispatched into exile just as they had been, and consigned to oblivion except for a fate that had brought Horris and Biggar to its unwitting rescue.

"What are we doing here?" Biggar piped up suddenly, a frightened stiffness in his reedy voice.

"What I tell you to do," the voice hissed.

Skat Mandu came out of the gloom, rising up like a cloud of smoke that had somehow coalesced into a vaguely familiar but not yet complete form. Its smell drove Horris and Biggar back a step in response, and its laugh was low and satisfied. It rippled like fetid water as it shifted about, and they could hear the hiss of its breathing in the sudden silence. It was huge and fat and dominant, and it had the feel of something ancient and terrible.

"I am called the Gorse," the monster whispered suddenly. "I was of the people who live within the fairy mists, one of their own until I was trapped and confined centuries ago, imprisoned in the Tangle Box for all time. I was a sorcerer of great power, and I will be so again. You will help me."

Horris Kew cleared his throat. "I don't see what we can do."

The Gorse laughed. "I will be your eyes, Horris Kew. I see you better than you see yourself. You are angry at losing what you had in that other world, but what you want most lies here. You arc frightened at what has been done to you, but the courage you lack can be supplied by me. Yes, I manipulated you. Yes, you were my cat's paw. You will be again, you and the bird both. This is the way of things, Horris. The people of the fairy mists bound me within the Tangle Box with spells that could not be undone from within, but only from without. Someone had to speak them, and I chose you. I whispered the incantations in your mind. I guided your conjuring steps. One by one you spoke the spells of Skat Mandu. One by one you turned the keys to the locks that held me bound. When I was ready to come out, I made the bird confess that Skat Mandu was a charade so that you would be forced to flee. But your escape could only be managed by setting me free. But do not despair. It was as it should be, as it was meant to be. Fate has bound us one to the other."

Horris wasn't sure he liked the sound of that, but on the other hand he was intrigued in spite of himself with the possibility that there might be something in this for him. "You have a plan for us?" he asked cautiously.

"A very attractive plan," the Gorse whispered. "I know of your history, the both of you. You, Horris, were exiled for your vision of what conjuring should be. The bird was exiled for being more than his creator had expected."

Oddly enough, Horris and Biggar found themselves in immediate agreement with this assessment (although Biggar didn't much care for constantly being referred to as "the bird").

"You were embarrassments and nuisances to those who pretended friendship towards you but in truth feared you and were jealous of you. Such is the nature of the creatures against whom we stand." The Gorse eased back ponderously into the gloom, smoke, and shadow along the rock. The movement produced a sort of scraping sound, like a knife trimming fish scales. It should not have been possible with something that appeared to be so insubstantial. "Wouldn't you like to gain a measure of revenge on these fools?" the Gorse demanded.

Horris and Biggar would have liked nothing better, of course. But their uneasiness with the Gorse remained undiminished for all the reassuring words. They didn't like this creature, didn't like the sight or smell of it, didn't even like the idea of it, and they were still of a mind that they had been better off back where they had come from. Still, they were not foolish enough to say so. Instead, they simply waited to hear more.

The darkening atmosphere of the cave seemed to tighten down like a coffin lid as the Gorse suddenly expanded into the shadows, stealing the light. "For myself, I will secure dominion over the fairy mists from which I was sent and over those who dwelt free within them while I was imprisoned. I will have them for my slaves until I tire of them, and then I will see them closed away in such blackness that they will scream endlessly for death's release."

Horris Kew swallowed the lump in his throat and forgot about any attempt at backing farther away. On his shoulder, Biggar's claws tightened until they hurt.

"To you," the Gorse hissed softly, "I will give Landover— all of it, the whole of it, the country and her people, to do with as you choose."

The silence that filled the cave was immense. Horris found suddenly that he could not think straight. Landover? What would he do with Landover? He tried to speak and could not. He tried to swallow and could not do that either. He was dry and parched from toes to nose, and all of his conjuring life was a dim recollection that seemed as ephemeral as smoke.

"You want to give us Landover?" Biggar squeaked suddenly, as if he hadn't heard right.

The Gorse's laugh was rough and chilling. "Something

even Skat Mandu could not have done for you in your exiled life, isn't that so? But to earn this gift you must do as I tell you. Exactly as I tell you. Do you understand?"

Horris Kew nodded. Biggar nodded along with him.

"Say it!" the Gorse hissed sharply.

"Yes!" they both gasped, feeling invisible fingers close about their throats. The fingers clenched and held for an impossibly long moment before they released. Horris and Biggar choked and gasped for air in the ensuing silence.

The Gorse drew back, its stench so overpowering that for a moment it seemed there was no air left to breathe. Horris Kew was down on his knees in the cave's near blackness, sick to his stomach, so frightened by the monster that he could think of nothing but doing whatever was required to keep from feeling worse. Biggar's white crest was standing on end, the sharp bird eyes were squeezed shut, and he was shaking all over.

"There are enemies who might threaten us," the Gorse whispered, its voice like the scratching of coarse sandpaper on wood. "We must remove them from our path if we are to proceed. You will help me in this."

Horris nodded without speaking, not trusting what the words might be. He wished he had learned to keep his conjuring mouth shut a whole lot earlier.

"You will write three letters, Horris Kew," the monster hissed. "You will write them now." The gloom it occupied shifted, and its eyes (or so they seemed) found Biggar. "And when he is finished, you will deliver them."

Night descended over Sterling Silver, the sun dropping below the horizon and changing the sky to deep crimson and violet, the colors streaking first the patterned clouds west, then the land itself. The shadows lengthened, darkening ever deeper, reflecting off the polished surface of the castle and the waters that guarded it, disappearing at last into a twilight lit by the eight moons in one of the rare phases of the year in which all were visible at once in the night sky.

With Willow on his arm, Ben Holiday climbed the stairs to their bedchamber, smiling now and again at what he was feeling, still caught up by the news of their baby. A baby! He couldn't seem to say it often enough. It produced a giddy feeling in him, one that made him feel wonderful and foolish both at once. Everyone in the castle knew about the baby by now. Even Abernathy, normally not given to displays of emotion of any kind, had given Willow a huge hug on learning the good news. Questor had immediately begun making plans for the child's upbringing and education that stretched well into the next decade. No one seemed the least bit surprised that there should be a baby, as if having this child here and now was very much in the ordinary course of events.

Ben shook his head. Would there be a boy or a girl? Would there be both? Did Willow know which? Should he ask her? He wished he knew what to do besides tell her over and over again how happy he was.

They reached a landing that opened out onto a rampart, and Willow pulled him out into the starlit night. They walked to the battlement and stared out across the darkened land. They stood there in silence, holding hands, keeping close in the silence.

"I have to go away for a little while," Willow said quietly. It was so unexpected that for a moment he wasn't certain he had heard right. She did not look at him, but her hand tightened in warning over his. "Let me finish before you say anything. I must tell my mother about this child. She must know so that she can dance for me. Remember how I told you once that our life together was foretold in the entwining of the flowers that formed the bed of my conception? It was on the night when I saw you for the first time at the Irrylyn. I knew at once that there would never be anyone else for me. That was the foretelling brought about by my mother's dance."

She looked at him now, her eyes huge and depthless.

"The once-fairy see something of the future in the present, reading what will be in what now is. It is an art peculiar to each of us, Ben, and for my mother the future is often told in her dance. It was so when I went to see her in my search for the black unicorn. It will be so again now."

She seemed to have finished. "Her dance will tell us something about our child's future?" he asked in surprise.

Willow nodded slowly, her gaze fixing him, her flawless features carved in starlight. "Not us, Ben. Me. She will tell only me. She will dance only for me, not for someone who is not of her people. Please don't be angry, but I must go alone."

He smiled awkwardly. "I can come most of the way, though. At least as far as the old pines."

She shook her head. "No. Try to understand. This must be my journey, not yours. It is a journey as much into myself as into the River Country, and it belongs only to me. I make it as mother of our child and as child of the once-fairy. There will be other journeys that belong to both of us, journeys on which you will be able to go. But this one belongs to me."

She saw the doubt in his eyes and hesitated. "I know this is difficult to understand. It touches on what I tried to tell you earlier. Carrying a child to term and giving birth on Landover is not the same as in your world. There are differences that run to the magic that sustains the land, that gives life to us all but particularly to the once-fairy. We commune with Landover as a people who have spent all our lives caring for and healing her. It is our heritage and bond."

Ben nodded, but felt something drop away inside him. "I don't see why I can't go with you."

He saw her throat constrict, and there were tears in her eyes. "I know. I have tried to find a way to tell you, to explain it to you. I think that I will have to ask simply that you trust me."

"I do trust you. Always. But this is hard to understand."

And more. It was worrisome. He had not felt comfortable being separated from her since their journey back to
Earth to recover Abernathy and the missing medallion, when
she had almost died. He had relived all the nightmares of Annie's death, of the death of their unborn child, and of the sev-
ering of some part of himself that had come about as a result
of their dying. Each time there was a separation from Willow,
however necessary, however brief, the fear returned. It was no
different now. If anything, the feeling was stronger because the
reasons for their separation were so difficult to grasp.

"How soon must you go?" he asked, still struggling to
come to grips with the idea. All of his earlier happiness
seemed to have leaked away.

"Tomorrow," she said. "At sunrise."

His desperation doubled. "Well, at least take Bunion with
you. Take someone for protection!"

"Ben." She held both of his hands in her own and moved
so close to him that he could see himself reflected in her eyes.
"No one will go with me. I will go alone. You needn't worry.
I will be safe. I don't need looking after. You know that. The
once-fairy have their own means of protection within Landover, and I will be in the homeland of my people."

He shook his head angrily. "I just don't see how you can
be sure of that! And I still don't see why you have to go
alone!"

In spite of his efforts to keep calm, his voice had risen
and taken on an angry edge. He stepped away from her, trying
to distance himself from what he was feeling. But she would
not release his hands.

"This child is important to us," she said softly.

"I know that!"

"Shhhh. The Earth Mother told us of its importance, do
you remember?"

He took a deep breath. "I do."

"Then accept that our needs must give way to those of

the child," she whispered. "Even though it hurts, even though the reasons are not clear, even though we might wish it otherwise." She paused. "I do not want this any more than you do. Do you believe that?"

He was caught off guard. It had not occurred to him that she was not a willing party to this decision. "Yes, I believe it," he told her finally.

"I would have you come if it were possible. I would never leave your side for a moment if it were possible. But it is not. It is not in the nature of life that we can be together in all things."

She waited for him to speak. He stared at her wordlessly for a long time, thinking. Then he said, "I guess that's true."

"It will be all right," she told him.

She put her arms around him and held him close against her. He lowered his face into her emerald hair and found himself aching already from having her gone. His fear was a black cloud that scudded about in the corners of his heart. He realized anew how different they really were, a human and a sylph, and how much there was about her that he still didn't know.

"It will be all right," she repeated.

He did not argue, because he knew there was no point in doing so. But he could not help wondering if he shouldn't try.

Roots

Willow's journey from Sterling Silver was a relatively uneventful one. She departed under cover of darkness, slipping from the castle unseen and unheard. The guards of the night watch might have sensed her in some dim, quickly forgotten way, but the once-fairy retained enough of the old ways that she could disappear as surely as shadow into light. Willow went down a back staircase, through the castle's deserted halls, along the darkened walls of several inner courts, and out through the central portcullis, which was always kept raised in time of peace to welcome late travelers and supplicants to a sure and friendly shelter. Forgoing use of the lake skimmer, she instead crossed the bridge that spanned the castle moat, a bridge built by Ben when the monarchy was restored and travelers began to come again to the land's seat of power. She waited until the brightest of the moons were shadowed by clouds and the guards were turned away, speaking of things far removed from duties assigned, and in the blink of an eye she was gone.

She did not wake Ben on leaving. She stood looking down at him in the darkness for a time, watching him sleep, thinking how much she loved him. She did not want any more harsh words to pass between them. It was better that she left now. He loved her, but he was the product of a world that did not accept the existence of fairy creatures, and he was still learning to believe in them himself. That was why she had not told him everything. That was why she couldn't.

She walked for the remainder of that night and all through the next day, winding her way along lesser-traveled paths, not hurrying or attempting speed, keeping herself unseen. She passed farmers in the field, plowing and laying in their second-season crop, harvesting the first. She watched peddlers and traders come and go between the communities of man south and east. There were travelers come from the once-fairy country and from the western hills where trappers and hunters roamed. There were families in wagons with possessions stacked high and tied down en route to new homes. Everywhere, there was activity, the bustle and energy of the warm seasons facilitating the plans made when it was cold. It made her smile. She followed the rolling flow of the forested hills, a small bit of movement in a vast sea of green that undulated like waves against the horizon when the breezes blew out of the west as they did at midsummer. She ate and drank from the Bonnie Blues, Landover's most plentiful source of food and drink, and she sang softly to herself when there were only birds and small animals to hear.

She pondered as well. She weighed the wisdom of what she had done, knowing the consternation it would cause Ben, appreciative of the worry it would engender. But hers was a cause born of primal necessity, and there was no room for debate over what was required. She must have this baby in the way that nature dictated, and the patten of birth had been established generations ago in a time when humans did not even exist. The birthing of fairy people was complex beyond that of humans in any case, peculiar in each instance to the physical characteristics of the creature involved, different for each depending on the genetics that had spawned them. She might have discussed it with Ben earlier, when the immediacy of their child's birth was removed and the requisite time for acceptance was still available. But she had not and there was no time now, and she knew him well enough to recognize that his reaction to what she would tell him was as likely to be damaging as helpful. Though Landover's King, he remained a man from another world in many ways still, and he struggled constantly to accept what he viewed as strange and unusual. It was especially hard where she was concerned because he loved her and was committed to her and wanted so to be comfortable with who and what she was. She knew that, and she did what she could to make easier the transition he was still experiencing.

In the end it had been the Earth Mother's dream that had decided her. It had not been so much a dream as a vision and not so much a vision as a sense of being. Fairy creatures spoke to each other in that way, coming often in sleep to give counsel and warning, speaking out of distant places, traveling on the back of swift winds to reach the listener, a whisper in stillness, a brightening in the dark. Willow sometimes spoke with her mother that way, her mother a wood nymph so wild that nothing could reach her if she did not wish it, a creature that not even the once-fairy could trace. Willow had slipped away from her old life as she made her new one with Ben, but now and again the old would intrude in some small fashion, and the Earth Mother's coming had been the latest reoccurrence.

The Earth Mother was an elemental, the most powerful in Landover, a creature of great magic. She was as old as the land itself and embodied its spirit. Some believed that she was the creator of the land, but Willow thought her too fundamental in her ethics and too mired in her work to be anything so lofty. Nevertheless, she was a creature to be harkened to. Ben and Willow had both gone to her during their search for the black unicorn, and she had told them then that they were important to her and would share a child that was special. There had been no explanation then or since, and after a time both had ceased to think on the matter. Willow had heard nothing from the Earth Mother in all this time.

Yet now she was summoned, unexpectedly, abruptly, out of dreams. The Earth Mother had come to her twice, calling her back to the River Country, to Elderew, to the once-fairy country where the elemental most frequently surfaced. The calling was urgent and unarguable and so had decided Willow to leave Ben without attempting a full explanation. More than the words themselves, it was the Earth Mother's tone that had compelled the sylph to put aside deliberation and act at once.

She camped that night on the shores of the Irrylyn, close by the cove where she had first encountered Ben and known in the fairy way that he was for her and she for him. She ate despite having little appetite, for her child required her strength. Then she stripped away her clothing and stepped into the Irrylyn's waters. The lake was warm and soothing and drew her into its embrace. She floated in the silence of the night, the skies overhead clear and filled with the light of colored moons and silver stars, and she let her memories of Ben envelop her. She could still feel the rush of excitement his appearance had triggered within her. She could still feel the certainty of her love. They had been chosen for each other, and until death they would be together. She had caught a glimpse of their future, for the once-fairy were so blessed (or cursed), and she had known then their lives would be changed irrevocably.

It had proven to be so. Ben had given up his old life, compelled to stay within Landover, decided by many things but by none more certain than his love for her. He had stayed as King and become a leader of strength and vision, and while he was tormented at times by what being King required of him, he had carried out his responsibilities faithfully. Most thought him fair and effective. Only a few still harbored doubts, and most of those were potential rivals for the power of the Kingdom's magic. Her father was one, the leader of the once-fairy, and a wielder of considerable magic himself. The River Master would have preferred a Kingdom in which he alone controlled the magic, but he was no fool and he rec-ognized the benefits that Ben Holiday provided as King—a stabilizing force, a well-reasoned juggler of diverse interests, and a decisive leader—and while he mistrusted Ben on occa-sion as an outworlder, he respected him always as a man.

Willow, as the River Master's daughter, had lived an un-settled life in the lake country, the child of a union that had lasted but a single night, a constant reminder to the water sprite of the woman he had loved and been unable to hold. For Willow had been born of a hurried coupling and then left behind by her mother for her father to raise, her mother too wild to stay bound to anyone, even a child. Her father had done what was required and nothing more; he had many chil-dren and liked most better than her. Ben's coming had opened the door to the life she had long known was waiting for her, and she had been quick to step through. He had questioned at first that they were meant to be together or even that he loved her, but Willow had never doubted, the prophecy of their joining immutable and fixed. Eventually what was promised at the moment of her birth had come to pass, and now there was to be a child.

She rose from the waters of the Irrylyn and stood upon its shore, her smooth green skin shedding water and drying in the cooling night air. She had not been entirely honest with Ben. She would let her mother dance for her, but then move quickly on. She would not see her father at all. She did not expect their help in the birth of this child. She might have wished it could be otherwise, but she knew there was little they could offer. She had returned to the lake country to see the Earth Mother. It was the Earth Mother alone who could provide useful insight, she sensed—for that was what the dream had whispered in summoning her. So she would go there and listen, and then she would have her child alone.

She slept long and well that night, her sleep undisturbed

by dreams, and when she woke she found the mud puppy looking at her.

"Hello, little one," she greeted softly, lifting to her knees.

The mud puppy regarded her with great, soulful eyes. It was short and long and with a vaguely beaverlike face, and it had great floppy ears and a lizard's tail. It was splay-footed with broad, webbed feet, and its body was colored in various shades of brown as if streaked by dirt. Mud puppies were rare in Landover, being something of a fairy creature, and they were reputedly imbued with magic of their own, though Willow had never seen evidence of it. She recognized this one from her early years. Its name was Haltwhistle, and it served the Earth Mother.

"Good old Haltwhistle," she murmured, smiling, and the mud puppy swung its tail to and fro.

She would have petted it, but the Earth Mother had warned her long ago that you should never touch a mud puppy. No explanation for this piece of advice had been offered, but Willow had learned to trust the Earth Mother. She had known the elemental since she was a little girl growing up in the lake country. The Earth Mother had come to her first when she was still quite small, rising from the ground one day while she was playing, an unexpected apparition that was more intriguing than frightening. The Earth Mother had come to her, she was told, because she was special. The Earth Mother would teach her things that no one else knew, and they would be friends always. Willow accepted this as a child does, a bit wide-eyed, but not disbelieving because when you are a child all things are possible. She found the Earth Mother strange and wondrous, a spirit creature rather than a human or once-fairy, but their friendship seemed natural and welcome. She was one of many children in the home of the River Master and not one to whom much attention was paid or of whom much was expected. Willow was lonely, and the Earth Mother helped fill the void that the absence of her real mother had created. As she grew, the Earth Mother counseled her, coming to her less often as she became more sure of herself and her time filled with other things. She had seen nothing of the Earth Mother after Ben's coming save when she went in search of the black unicorn.

But now she was summoned, and Haltwhistle had been sent to guide her to where the Earth Mother waited.

She rose, washed, ate a little, and, with the mud puppy leading, set out anew. The day was warm and sun-filled, and the forests of the lake country smelled of grasses and wildflowers. As they walked, lake and river waters sparkled like gemstones through breaks in the trees and cranes and herons swooped across the surfaces in flashes of white. They traveled on through the morning and by midday were nearing Elderew. Haltwhistle turned east then, away from the city of the River Master and his people, and entered a stretch of forest thick with old-growth trees. Vines and mosses clung to the barked surfaces in brilliant green strips and patches. Insects skittered here and there, bright-colored birds darted through the canopies overhead, and small, furry-faced animals appeared like apparitions and were gone in the blink of an eye. Dust moats floated in streamers of sunlight, lazy and inconsequential.

On nearing the Earth Mother's refuge, Willow found herself wondering as she did from time to time at the elemental's interest in her. Happy for the companionship and special attention, she had never thought to ask when she was a child. When she had grown, she had accepted the Earth Mother's assurances that destiny had provided an important fate for her, and she had never pressed the matter further. Elementals frequently possessed the ability to read the future, and so Willow never doubted that the Earth Mother could see things yet to come, things hidden from her. Nevertheless, it was disconcerting to know that someone besides yourself knew what was fated for you and would not reveal the specifics. She had thought to ask of her future on more than one occasion, but she could never quite bring herself to do so. Perhaps it was her awe of the Earth Mother's history as the keeper of the lands. Perhaps there was a small part of her that did not want to know her future in any event.

But now, with the impending birth of her child, she thought that she must know, and she determined that this time her reverence for the Earth Mother would not prevent her asking.

Haltwhistle took her on through the thickening forests, back from the sunlit clearings into the deep shadows, and finally to where the silence was complete and unbroken by the sound of any life. The mud puppy stopped finally at the edge of a broad, empty clearing filmed with pond waters collected from streams all about, a still, black, mirrored surface that reflected the old-growth canopy that sheltered everything.

The mud puppy lingered for a soulful look back and then disappeared into the trees. Willow waited in the silence.

After a moment the pond stirred and the Earth Mother rose from the waters, her form taking shape out of the slick mud, lifting to stand within the shadowed silence.

"Welcome, Willow," she greeted. "Are you well, child?"

"I am fine, Earth Mother," Willow answered. "And you?"

"Unchanging. The land is stable and healed since the coming of Ben Holiday. It makes my work much easier." She gestured vaguely with her hand, and the light flickered dimly from the damp. "Does your life with him go well and the love between you continue?"

"Of course, Earth Mother."

"It gives me great pleasure to hear you say so. Now you will share a child, and it is for that reason that I have summoned you. There are things you must know, and I would not tell them to you through dreams. Have you come alone, then? And without the King?"

"I thought it better." Willow's gaze slid away momentarily. "He does not accept easily what he finds strange."

"You have not told him about your birthing? About the cycles of life and the periods of growth and the ways of the once-fairy?"

Willow sighed. "I cannot seem to find a way to do so. I had planned to tell him, but when your dream came, I thought it best to wait."

The Earth Mother nodded. "Perhaps you are right." Her face was young and vibrant, a constant surprise when one considered that she had been alive since the creation of the land. "You will tell him when you think it best. For now, we must concentrate on the birthing. You know it nears?"

"I can feel it, Earth Mother. The child stirs inside me already, anxious to be born. It will happen soon." She hesitated. "It is not like that with humans. Ben expects our child to grow within me for months in the manner of the women of his world. He has not said so, but I can read it in his looks. He thinks the child, since it is his, will be like him. But it will not. I can sense it already, and I do not know how to tell him." She was surprised to find herself suddenly on the verge of tears. "What if he will not accept this child? What if he finds it loathsome?"

The Earth Mother's smile was filled with kindness. "No, Willow, that will not happen. This child belongs to you both and was conceived of the love you bear for each other. His commitment to you, and now to the child, is complete. He will not find the child loathsome. Nor shall it be so. It shall be beautiful."

Willow's eyes brightened. "Is this promised, Earth Mother? Can you see it in my future?"

The Earth Mother passed her hands before Willow's face,

and the question fell away, forgotten. "We will speak now of what you must do to prepare for your child's birth, Willow. Conditions will not be entirely as you anticipate. Your child will not be born while you are in your human form. It will be born during your cycle of transformation into spirit form."

"As my namesake," Willow said. "I have sensed this might be so. It was one of the reasons for my worry about telling Ben. I did not think he could conceive of such a thing."

"Do not trouble yourself further about Ben Holiday, child. What must concern you now are the conditions required for your birthing. Listen carefully. When you take root to give life to your child, it must be in a mix of soils from three worlds. The soils must come from Landover, from Earth, and from within the fairy mists. The soils reflect the child's heritage, a mix of bloods. This child is a product of each world, born of the union of a human and a once-fairy. It does not happen often. It is a rare and special occurrence."

The Earth Mother paused, and one hand lifted, a strange and compelling gesture. "The soils must be gathered by you, Willow, and by no one else. You must collect them, you must mix them, and you must take root in them when it is time to give birth. The soils must come from special places in each world, for they must reflect the character of that world, combining what is best and worst about the creatures who inhabit each. There is within your child some part of all three worlds, you see—something of Landover, of Earth, and of the fairy mists. If the child is to grow strong and healthy, if it is to secure wisdom and understanding, if it is to sort through and choose from the seeds of good and evil that exist in all living creatures, there must be a balance of possibilities inherent within it. The soils offer that balance. They offer magic that will sustain and secure."

"Fairy magic, Earth Mother?" Willow asked doubtfully.

"As surely as any other. This child's heritage is long and

complex, Willow. Its bloodlines run back to when the people of the River Country were part of the fairy world. You carry both bloods within you; so must your child."

Willow's face was drawn and frightened. "Must I go into these worlds to gain possession of the soils, Earth Mother? I cannot do that. I cannot pass into the fairy mists or even out of Landover to Ben's world if he does not take me there. The medallion he wears as King will be needed. I must take him with me after all."

"No, Willow, he cannot go with you on this journey. Your own words—do you remember?" The elemental's face was kind and sad and hard and certain all at once, such a strange mix of emotions that Willow took a step back. "Listen to me now. Hear everything that I would tell you. This will be difficult, but you will have help. There are things at work here that even I do not yet understand. But one thing is certain. Your child must have the soils I have described. You must gather them, mix them, and take root in them. You alone. You must not be deterred by your fear. You must be brave. You must believe. Your child's life depends on it."

Willow was ashen now, gone cold with the enormity of what she was being asked to do. Ben could hot help her. Who then would?

"You will begin at the old pines where you go to see your mother dance," the Earth Mother whispered in the stillness of the glade, her voice a ripple across the muddied waters on which she stood. "I will see you safely there. The first of the soils shall come from the lake country, where the best and the worst that is Landover can be found in a single grain. Take from the clearing where your mother dances a small bag of the soil you will find there. When you have finished, you will be met by someone who will guide you into Ben's world."

"Who will meet me, Earth Mother?" Willow asked softly. "Who will it be?"

"I am not given to see that yet," came the reply. "I am

given to see only this. Your guide will come from the fairy people, who are equally committed to the safe birth of your child. I have visited them in dreams and found that it is so. This child, this firstborn of human and fairy, of Landover's King and Queen, is special to them as well, and they will do everything they can to keep it protected. Thus they will provide one of their own as guide, one whose magic will allow you safe passage, first into Ben Holiday's world and then into their own. Your guide will know where to take you to find the soils you need.

"But, child, take warning," she added quickly, her voice gone dark with premonition once more. "The fairy people harbor secrets in all that they do, and nothing with them is ever what it appears. They will have reasons beyond what they reveal for giving you aid. Do not accept everything you are told without question. Do not think that you know the whole truth. Be wary always. They will give you the help they have promised; that much is certain. They will see the child safely born; that is certain as well. But all else remains in doubt, so stay cautious in all that you do."

"Can you tell me nothing more?"

"I have told you all."

"There is too much uncertainty in this journey, Earth Mother," the sylph whispered. "I am frightened."

The Earth Mother sighed, the sound of the wind passing through the trees at eventide. "As I am frightened for you, child."

"Must I go, then?"

"If you wish your child safely born, you must."

Willow nodded, resigned. "I do." She looked away into the trees, as if thinking to see something of what was hidden from her. "How much time do I have to make this journey?"

"I do not know."

"The baby, then. How much time until the baby is born?"

"I do not know that either. Only the child knows. The child will decide when it is time. You must be ready when that time comes."

A sudden desperation tightened Willow's throat. "Can you see where the child is to be born? Can you tell me at least that much?"

"Not even that," the Earth Mother replied sadly. "The child will decide the place of its birth as well."

Willow fought back against her despair. "Little is left for me to choose, it seems. All decisions are given to others." She could not keep the bitterness from her voice. "I am the mother of this child. I am the one who carries it within her body. I am the giver of its life. Yet I have almost nothing to say about its coming into the world."

The Earth Mother did not speak. They stood facing each other in the silent clearing, the sunlight filtering down from the south where it eased toward day's end, the waters of the pond between them reflecting their images as if through poorly blown glass. Willow wondered suddenly if her own birth had been so complicated, if the very complexity of it had contributed to her mother's decision to leave her to her father, to abandon any further involvement, to forgo the pain of rais-ing her when the pain of giving her life had been so intense. There was no way to know, of course. Her mother would never tell her the truth. Willow thought then of how she had left Ben, slipping away without saying good-bye, and she wished now that she had woken him.

She straightened. Well, there were few second chances given in life, and it was best not to dwell on their scarcity.

"Good-bye, Earth Mother," she said, for there was noth-ing else to say, no other words to speak. "I will remember what you have said."

"Good-bye, Willow. Keep strong, child. All will be well."

It was almost exactly the same thing she had said to Ben. All will be well. The words reached out to mock her. Willow's smile was bleak and ironic. She turned and walked to the edge of the clearing.

When she looked back again, the Earth Mother had disappeared.

Ensorcelled

When Ben Holiday woke that first morning to find Willow gone, he was not a happy man. She had told him she was leaving, of course, so he was not surprised to discover she wasn't there. He even understood why she had left without waking him to say good-bye; he probably would have reacted every bit as badly as she had imagined. But none of that made him feel any better about the situation. He simply didn't like being separated from her, even for the best of reasons—and he wasn't sure this visit was one. He had listened to her explanation and tried to be fair about what she was doing, but in the end he still didn't understand any of it. Why did she have to go alone? Why did she have to go now?

Why did the feeling persist, despite his efforts to suppress it, that she was keeping something from him?

He might have sat about stewing for the entire day or even the rest of the week if it hadn't been for the fact that once again he had scheduled a full day of meetings in his continuing effort to find a way to be a good King. It wasn't as easy as people might suppose. In the first place, there was a decided clash of cultures at work in his stewardship of Landover. This was a place in which the feudal system had been at work for hundreds of years (according to Abernathy's carefully maintained histories), while Ben Holiday was a product of what passed in his world for a democracy. Instinctively almost, he found himself from day one looking for ways to implement the kind of government he knew and believed in. The lawyer in him wanted law and order to be the cornerstone of his government and to guarantee justice of, for, and by the people. But you didn't come into a strange country and simply throw out the system already in place. That was a swift and certain path to anarchy. As they were fond of saying where he came from, you had to work within the system.

So Ben settled early on for working toward the establishment of a benevolent dictatorship (still didn't sound too good when he said it, but it remained the best description he could come up with). The emphasis, of course, was supposed to be on the word *benevolent* and not on the other. The trick in all this was to introduce the changes he wanted without making it too obvious. People always accepted change more readily when they didn't realize it was happening. Thus the need for Ben Holiday as King to constantly walk a tightrope. Of course, after two years he was getting pretty good at it.

The process was convoluted, and only Questor and Abernathy really knew what was going on. As the King's closest advisors (not counting Willow), they were pretty much privy to everything that happened. In most instances, they supported Ben's ideas, arguing mostly on the side of caution and restraint in the introduction of his somewhat-revolutionary ideas. Once Ben had established himself as an acceptable and resilient King, one not likely to be dislodged, the next step was to bring the Kingdom's warring factions into some kind of accord. That meant getting at least a semblance of cooperation from such diverse peoples as the once-fairy, the humans, the kobolds, and the rock trolls—not to mention various smaller groups—none of whom wanted much to do with the other. Ben had succeeded in that endeavor through a combination of threats, promises, and bribes. A King had to be something of a magician—apologies to Questor Thews—and there was a great deal of on-the-job training. Thus a hard stand here led to a compromise there. You had to know when to bend and when to hold fast.

Starting out as a lawyer was good training, as Ben was fond of saying, for becoming a King.

So here was how matters stood at present in the reign of Ben Holiday, latest King of Landover, a place every reasonable person who hadn't been there knew couldn't possibly exist. The King still had the final say in all matters, particularly in disputes between lesser rulers and leaders of the various peoples of the Kingdom. Because Ben had finally garnered a solid base of support throughout the whole of the land and because he was backed by the armored might of the Paladin, almost no one ever considered using force against him. Ben, on the other hand, had to be careful not to give any of those lesser rulers and leaders reason to feel that their own stature was in any way being diminished. Thus they had to be left to govern where it was reasonable and sensible to allow them to do so. Where the King's own special brand of magic came into play was in getting them to govern the way he wanted.

Ben established early on a series of advisory committees (his designation) to oversee such matters as resource management (land, water, air, and magic—well, of course, in a magic kingdom!), commerce and travel (trading of goods between peoples and the transportation of same), currency exchange (frequently bartering), public works (road building and repair and management of the King's lands), and judicial review (resolution of civil disputes and criminal violations). He set up administrative officials in each part of the Kingdom to oversee the workings of all this, and periodically he brought them to Sterling Silver for a review of how the process was working and what could be done to make it stronger. It wasn't a perfect system by any means, but it had the added benefit of teaching Landover's many and diverse citizens—whether they realized it or not—how to participate in a government system. It was a learning process that took time, but Ben thought that he could see it building on itself. Where once the peoples of the lake country and the Greensward wouldn't have given each other the time of day, now they were working together to solve such common problems as how to conserve and protect water resources and how most effectively to use crop lands for growing. He had them sharing their knowledge and reconsidering their prejudices. He had them behaving better than they had behaved in centuries.

In some ways it was all very primitive compared to where he had come from. But in other ways it was like being able to start over before so much was poisoned. Ben was careful about choosing what knowledge he introduced from his old world. He kept it pretty basic. Good health habits and improved farming techniques, for example. He stayed away from things that would result in drastic change and possible harm— Industrial Revolution inventions and gunpowder. Some things he didn't know enough about to introduce, and that limited what he could choose from. He was at heart a lawyer in any event—not an engineer or a chemist or a doctor or a manufacturer. Maybe, he reflected now and again, it was just as well.

Besides, Landover had something going for it that his old world didn't, and it was important to remember to add it into the equation. Landover had magic. Real magic, the kind that changed things just as surely as electricity. Landover was infused with it, and many of her citizens practiced it in one form or another, and what they did with it obviated the need for many of the things that science had introduced once upon a time in Ben's old world. So it wasn't as simple as it first seemed, this business of categorizing and defining the pluses and minuses, pros and cons, and good and bad of the Kingdom of Landover.

In any case, Ben Holiday's schedule that first day of Willow's absence kept him from dwelling on his dissatisfaction with the matter of her going in the first place, and it wasn't until he retired after a rather late dinner, alone in their bedchamber, that he found himself confronted by his personal demons once again. He stood on the balcony that opened off the room, staring out across the starlit land for a long time, trying to decide how he should handle the situation. He could go after her, of course. Bunion could probably track her down in nothing flat. But he knew even as he considered the idea that he would never do anything so contrary to what she expected of him. He considered using the Landsview, the strange instrument that allowed him to go out into the land and find anyone or anything to be found there, all without ever leaving the castle. He had used it more than once to see what was happening in a faraway place. That was a tempting alternative, but in the end he discarded it as well. It was too much like spying. What if he were to see something that he wasn't supposed to see, something that she preferred to keep hidden from him? When you loved someone as much as he loved her, you didn't resort to spying on them.

He settled finally for going to bed and lying awake most of the night thinking about her.

The second day passed very much like the first except that he was required to spend an extraordinarily long time with a delegation of Rock Trolls, convincing them of the wisdom of carting a portion of their raw ores down out of the Melchor for sale to others rather than insisting that the forging be done entirely in their furnaces and according to what they decided was needed. This in turn resulted in dinner coming even later, which of course delayed bedtime until well after midnight, so that when he finally crawled beneath the covers he was so tired that he was almost asleep before he happened to turn over one final time on the pillow and so bring his hand in contact with the piece of paper tucked under it.

He sat up at once. He didn't know why, but he was instantly certain of the importance of this paper. He brought light to one of the bedside lamps with a touch of his hand, the castle awake even when he slept and responsive to his wishes.

He angled the paper into the circle of the lamp's faint glow. The paper was folded in quarters, and he opened it carefully and read:

> Holiday,
> If you would know of an invasive magic that threatens Landover in a way even I cannot tolerate then meet me two nights hence on the eve of the new moon at the Heart. Come alone. I will do so as well. I pledge you no harm and safe passage.
>
> Strabo.

Ben stared. His mind raced. Strabo the dragon can write? How did this get here? The dragon couldn't manage to fit through the bedchamber window, could he?

He stopped himself and reconsidered. The dragon wouldn't have written this. Or delivered it. He would have had someone else do both. Somehow. If the letter really was from him. If this wasn't some sort of trick. Which it likely was. Strabo had never written him before—or even contacted him. Strabo, Landover's last dragon, a reclusive, melancholy curmudgeon of a creature who resided far east in the wasteland of the Fire Springs, didn't even *like* Ben Holiday and had made it abundantly clear on more than one occasion that he would be ecstatic if he never saw the King again in his entire life.

So what was this letter all about?

Ben read it twice more, trying to picture the dragon speaking the words. It wasn't hard. The letter sounded like him. But the sending of it was odd. If the dragon was indeed seeking a meeting, this threat of which he warned must be a serious one. Ben discounted the danger of a personal attack. Strabo wasn't interested in harming him, and even if he was he wouldn't bother sending a note to lure him out—he would just take wing and come after him. Asking Ben to come alone was in keeping with the dragon's personality. Strabo didn't care for humans in general and would want any meeting kept private and personal. He also was quite honorable in his own peculiar way, and if he promised safe passage he would keep his word.

Still, the whole business made Ben uneasy.

Come alone?

Come at midnight?

He read the letter again and learned nothing new. He sat propped up against the massive iron headboard, pillows at his back, thinking the matter through. He knew what Questor and Abernathy would say. He knew what reason dictated. But there was something compelling about this letter, something that refused to let him simply discard it and go on about his life. It kept him reconsidering the matter, insisting that it was imprudent to ignore the warning. A sixth sense whispered that there was indeed something to heed here, something of which to be wary. Strabo did not act without reason, and if he felt there was a danger facing Landover then he was probably right. If he felt Ben should know about it, then Ben probably should.

So what should he do?

He went to sleep finally without having made a decision. He thought about the letter all the next day, mulling it over between meetings and conferences, during meals and while reading documents, and as he ran the perimeter of the castle in the late afternoon hours before dinner, keeping up his training habits even now, Bunion as always his silent, invisible protector.

He retired to bed that third night following Willow's departure with the matter still unresolved.

But by morning he had made his decision. He knew he must go. He must take whatever risk was involved on the chance that the letter and warning were real. Besides, he convinced himself, the risk wasn't all that great. The Heart was only several hours away on horseback. He would take a mounted patrol of King's Guards for protection. He would not tell anyone until just before he was ready to leave. That would keep Questor and Abernathy and the kobolds out of the matter. He would leave the Guards safely back from the Heart, go in alone to check things out, meet with Strabo if the dragon was there, and still be back before dawn. Easy enough, and it would satisfy his need to do something besides stand around wondering what he should do!

There was a deciding factor in all this, although he would not let himself dwell on it. No matter the danger he might actually face in any situation, he was protected always by the Paladin. The King's Champion was the single most powerful being in the realm, and it existed for the sole purpose of seeing that the King was kept safe. It could be summoned at a moment's notice, its appearance requiring nothing more than Ben's grasping the medallion he wore always about his neck, the medallion with the graven image of a knight riding out of Sterling Silver at sunrise. Grasp that medallion, call for the Paladin, and the knight of ghosts and shadows would be there instantly.

The problem with the Paladin, of course, was that the King's armored champion was in truth the King himself. Or another side of the King. Or, more accurately, another side of *whoever* was King at any given moment. In this case it meant that the Paladin was really another side of Ben, a dark, destructive side born out of some well of being that he would rather not acknowledge even existed. But it did, and it hovered somewhere at the edges of his consciousness, waiting. Ben had struggled with the knowledge of what this meant ever since he had discovered the truth about the Paladin. The Paladin was a killing machine that had served in the ranks of the Kings of Landover since the beginning, a creation of the fairy folk to give protection to the ruler they had installed to keep the gates to the fairy world safe. The Paladin had fought in every battle visited on Landover's many and diverse rulers, championing all causes, standing fast against all enemies. It had been challenged time and again. It had never lost. It died only when the King died. It was reborn when a new King was crowned. It was a timeless, eternal being that lived only to fight and fought only to kill.

And it was a part of Ben Holiday, an integral part of who and what he was, not merely by virtue of the office he held and the responsibility he had accepted, but because there existed in every living creature the potential for deliberate, controlled destruction. Ben had discovered early on that the Paladin's infusion into his being, their joining as one, was due as much to the darkness of his human side as to any conjuring of fairy magic. He was the Paladin in great part because the Paladin was in truth another side of him, a side that until he had become King of Landover he had kept carefully closed away.

So he could rely on the Paladin to come to his rescue if required, though he was loath to call the dark warrior out again unless the need was great indeed. Summoning it was a last resort, he constantly told himself, but it was something he could do if he must. It was something he no longer believed, as once he had, that he would never do again.

He went through the fourth day in deliberate fashion, standing just outside himself most of the time, watching as Ben Holiday went through the motions of being King. He felt so peculiar about what he was doing, keeping the knowledge of the coming night's plans carefully tucked away, that he was surprised no one noticed. Questor Thews and Abernathy seemed to find him normal and did not question if something was wrong. No one did. He fulfilled his day's duties, ate his dinner, retired to his room, and sat down to wait.

When it was nearly dark, the twilight easing quickly toward night, he went downstairs to the stables, ordered Jurisdiction, his favorite mount, a big bay gelding, saddled, called for a guard of six men, and rode out. He did so quietly and with-

out advising anyone, and he was able to slip away without being noticed. Patrols came and went from Sterling Silver all the
time; one more riding out at dusk attracted no particular attention. Even Bunion would probably be resting by now, anticipating a sunrise run with Ben. It was a typical summer
night, lazy and warm, and there was that sense of all being
right with the world and sleep being just a yawn and a deep,
slow breath away. As Ben and his guard rode over the causeway, Sterling Silver was a shimmer of polished starlight against
the hazy darkness, a reflection that lingered as they climbed
into the forested hills west, then faded as the trees closed
about.

They traveled swiftly, Ben pushing the pace, anxious to
reach the Heart before midnight, navigating by the stars and
his own sense of time's passage. He had learned to live without
clocks and watches since coming into Landover, and he could
now tell time in the old way—by a reading of the heavens, by
the length and position of shadows on the ground, and by the
feel of the air and the condensation that gathered on the
grasses. His senses were stronger in this world, he discovered,
perhaps because he was forced to rely on them more. He wore
black clothing and boots and black chain mail devised by
Questor Thews out of magic and iron to be lightweight but
very strong. He wore the precious medallion of the Kings of
Landover and a long knife. A broadsword was strapped to his
back because the King was expected to travel armed on night
sorties and patrols. Riding gloves protected his hands, and a
dark scarf was wrapped about his throat to ward off the dust.

There was no wind as yet, no air movement of any sort,
and the night was thick and sultry. Insects buzzed about his
head when he slowed, so he kept the pace at a quick trot or
canter when the way was clear enough to do so. The new
moon left the land bereft of much of its nighttime light—in
Landover, the new moon was a combination of some of its
eight moons dropping below the horizon and some entering

their dark phases (Ben never had figured out exactly how it worked, only when it occurred, which was about every other month). What light there was came from the stars which gleamed all across the cloudless sky, a maze of brilliant pinpricks that seemed to have been placed there for no better reason than to inspire dreaming in those who gazed up at them. Ben did so when the trees cleared enough to allow, but his thoughts this night were occupied mostly with the meeting that lay ahead.

Time passed swiftly, and it was still almost an hour short of midnight when the riders closed on the Heart. Ben brought the patrol up while they were still some distance away, had the Guards stand down, and ordered them to wait for him there. He rode on until he was within several hundred yards of his destination, then dismounted from Jurisdiction, left the horse to graze unfettered, and walked on alone.

The woods were dark and empty-feeling as he passed through them, and although he listened for familiar sounds in the blanketing silence he heard nothing. The smells of the forest were pungent and intoxicating, causing his thoughts to drift to other times and places, to events that had once seemed momentous and now were only memories of building blocks used in the construction of his life. He walked easily and without concern for his safety; oddly enough, he did not feel threatened. Perhaps it was the sense of peacefulness that the summer night instilled within him. Perhaps it was the presence of the medallion, a constant reminder of the power bequeathed him as King. Perhaps it was simply that nothing actually did threaten. Whatever the case, he traveled on toward the Heart as if undertaking no more than a nighttime stroll in his gardens, one that would end with sleep and a waking into the new day.

He reached the Heart shortly before midnight, entering from the trees and standing momentarily at the edge of the rows of white velvet rests and kneeling pads, facing toward the white oak dais with its polished silver stanchions and limp pennants. The clearing was silent and seemingly empty. Nothing moved; there was not the whisper of a wind in the stillness. Memories of all that had transpired here came and went. Ben looked about a moment longer, then walked down an aisle between the benches and rests toward the dais.

A breath of wind brushed his cheek and was gone. *Careful.*

He was almost to the stage when the dark figure materialized from out of nowhere to his right, lifting, it seemed, from the very earth. He stopped, a chill racing down his spine, a lurch in the pit of his stomach. The dark figure was robed and bathed in shadow, the light behind it unrevealing.

"Play-King," a familiar voice greeted.

Nightshade!

Ben froze, on guard now for the first time. Why was Nightshade here? The Witch of the Deep Fell was no friend of his, and if she was present there was reason to believe that the meeting was a trap after all.

She came forward a few steps, tall and imperious, the light catching her features now, etching out the lean, cold, flawless face, the raven black hair with its single streak of white, the narrow shoulders and long, thin arms. "Why did you send for me?" she hissed at him, her voice cold and angry. "What is all this about a threat of magic to my home?"

Ben stared, speechless. Send for her? What was she talking about? He was here because Strabo had sent for him! What sort of game was she playing?

"I didn't . . ." he began.

"You annoy . . ." she started.

And then a shadow fell over them both, and the sky was filled with Strabo's dark bulk as the dragon settled gingerly down at the edge of the dais, serpent body coiling up, wings folding in. Steam rose from his black-as-pitch, fire-slicked, scaled body, and the stench of him filled the air. Even Night-

shade drew back in repulsion as he swung his horned and fear-
some head from one of them to the other.

"What is this?" he growled, the sound a deep, unpleasant
rumble, the grating of stone against the earth. His huge, implacable bulk was outlined against the forest. "Why is Holiday
here, Witch?" he demanded ominously. "What does he have
to do with your note?"

"My note?" Nightshade's voice was a rasp of disbelief. "I
sent you no note! I came in answer to the play-King's mis-
sive!"

"Foolish old crone," the dragon purred, a big cat contemplating dinner. "You waste my time with your idiotic denials.
The note was yours, the words all too clearly your own. If you
have some treasure you wish to trade, then offer it up and be
done with it."

Nightshade's face was livid with fury. "Treasure?"

Ben saw what was happening then, recognized the truth
of what had been done to them, and knew instinctively that it
was already too late to escape. Separate notes sent to each,
seemingly from one another, actually from someone else entirely, meant to lure them to this spot—the bait for a trap.
Why? The word screamed at him as he started forward, catching sight suddenly of someone who had appeared just long
enough to set something down, a tall, gawky figure, vaguely
familiar, backing away from a box that sat open at the edge of
the dais, smoke or mist or whatever already lifting from its interior, the box unfamiliar but the figure someone he knew . . .

Horris Kew!

What in the name of sanity was going on?

"Wait!" he managed to yell, pointing at the scarecrow figure. Strabo's scaled head whipped around, the fire leaking from
his maw as he hissed in warning. Nightshade's arms came up
threateningly, the magic forming streaks of wicked green light
on her fingertips. There was a sudden crackling in the air.

Ben's hand went instinctively to the medallion, and he called forth the Paladin to his rescue.

All too late. Light flared suddenly from all about, thrusting from the blackness on every side, born of some origin earlier fixed and triggered now as the jaws of the trap set to ensnare them closed tightly about. They were hammered forward toward each other and the box, all three of them, King, witch, and dragon, and there was not a moment's time to react. The light caught and carried them across the velvet benches and rests, across the distance separating them from one another, and locked them in a knot of magic that bound them up with ferocious purpose. Then mist and gloom closed about, rising to receive them as if they were an expected offering. Abruptly they began to fall into a deep, impenetrable void. The void opened beneath them, growing in size as they neared it (or were they shrinking?), a vast, empty sinkhole that sucked them inexorably downward.

But there was something more. All were experiencing an odd sense of loss, as if some essential part of who and what they were was being stripped away in layers. And there surfaced within each a demon, a nameless, formless, terrible beast they had kept sealed away, but was now suddenly, inexplicably set free. All three howled in fury and despair.

Where did Horris Kew get such power? was Ben's last, desperate thought.

Then down he tumbled with the dragon and the witch, voiceless and powerless, to disappear into the interior of the Tangle Box.

When they were gone, the Gorse lifted out of the gloom at the edge of the trees behind the dais and hissed coldly at Horris Kew, "Pick up the box."

Horris was shaking so badly he could not make himself move. He stood with his hands clenched tightly and his size-

sixteens rooted in place. He was stunned by the magnitude of
what he had just witnessed—Holiday, Nightshade, and Strabo
picked up like rag dolls by the magic and hurtled down into
the murky depths of the Tangle Box. Such power! Yes, the
Gorse had taken great pains to set the underpinnings of its implementation, to cast the nets of sorcery, to speak the spells
that would lie waiting for the three. Or rather, to have Horris
do all this, for the Gorse still seemed unable to act on its own.
Horris had glimpsed the depth of the creature's power even
then, sharp twinges and stabs that pricked his psyche, but even
so he could not have imagined that all these little conjurings
could be brought together to form such a singularly devastat-
ing magic.

To one side, the Gorse hissed purposefully.

"The box, Horris!" Biggar whispered in his ear, an urgent plea from his perch on the conjurer's shoulder.

Horris started out of his shock, then hurriedly stumbled
forward onto the dais. He stared down at the swirling, misty
surface of the Tangle Box. There was nothing to be seen. The
box was closed once more.

Horris stepped back, sweating, breathing hard. He exhaled slowly. It had worked just as the Gorse had promised.
The Gorse told them the notes would attract the three, their
greatest potential enemies, the only ones in Landover who
could offer any real threat. It told them the notes were spell-
bound so that their readers would find them impossible to
resist, even should their reason and good sense caution otherwise. It told them the conjurings and magics and symbols of
power cast and set about the Heart would ensnare the unsus-
pecting trio so swiftly that none would escape. It told them finally that the Tangle Box was a prison from which they would
never escape.

But Horris couldn't help asking again anyway. "What if
they get out?"

The Gorse laughed, a low, humorless sound in the darkness. "They will never get out. They won't even know enough to want to get out. I've taken steps to see to that. By now, they are hopeless prisoners. They don't know who they are. They don't know where they are. They are lost to the mists."

Biggar ruffled his feathers. "Serves them right," he croaked dismissively.

"Pick up the box," the Gorse ordered once more.

Horris was quicker to respond this time. He snatched up the carved wooden container obediently, being careful nevertheless to hold it away from him. "What do we do now?"

The Gorse was already moving. "We take the box back to the cave, and we wait." The voice was smooth and self-satisfied. "After the King's absence has caused sufficient panic, you and the bird will pay another visit to your friends at Sterling Silver."

The Gorse eased through the gloom like smoke. "Only this time you will take them a little surprise."

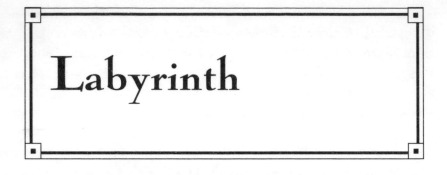

Labyrinth

The Knight woke startled and alert, lifting off the ground as if jerked erect by invisible wires. He had been dreaming, and while the dream itself was already forgotten, the impression it had made on him lingered. His breathing was quick and his heartbeat rapid, and it seemed as if he had run a long way in his sleep. He felt a damp heat on his body beneath his clothing and along his hairline. He felt poised on the edge of something about to happen.

His eyes shifted anxiously through the gloom. He was in a forest of huge, dark trees that rose like columns to hold up the sky. Except there was no sky to be seen, only the mist that roiled overhead, blotting out everything, even the highest branches. The darkness of the forest was a twilight that was as much a part of day as night, as much of morning as evening. It was not real, and yet the Knight recognized instinctively that it was the only reality of this place in which he found himself.

Where was he?

He did not know. He could not remember.

There were others. Where were they?

He came to his feet swiftly, aware of the weight of the broadsword slung across his back, of the knife at his waist, of the chain mail that warded his chest and back. He was dressed all in black, his clothing loose-fitting and leather-bound, with boots, belt, and gloves. His armor was somewhere close, though he couldn't see it. It was close, he knew, because he could sense its presence, and his armor always came to him when he needed it.

Although he didn't know why.

A medallion hung against his chest beneath his tunic. He lifted it free and stared at it. It was an image of himself riding out of a castle at sunrise. It was familiar to him, and yet it was as if he were seeing it for the first time. What did it mean?

He brushed his confusion aside, and cast about in the gloom. Something stirred at the clearing's far edge, and he moved toward it swiftly. A figure who lay curled upon the ground straightened as he neared and pushed itself up with both arms extended. Long black hair with a single streak of white through its center hung down across face and shoulders, and robes trailed on the earth like liquid shadows.

It was the Lady. She was still with him. She had not run away while he slept (for she would run if the chance presented itself, he knew). Her head lifted at his approach, and one slim hand brushed back the raven hair. Her pale, beautiful features tightened as she saw him, and she hissed at him in anger and dismay.

"You," was all she said, that single word conveying the depth of her dislike for him and for what he had done to her.

He did not try to go closer. The Knight knew how she felt about him, knew that she blamed him for what had been done to her. It could not be helped. He turned away and scanned the rest of the clearing in which they had slept. It was small and close, and there was nothing about it to suggest why they were there. They had come to this place earlier, he knew. They had come here in flight, pursued by . . . something. He had brought the Lady with him—and one other—fleeing the beast that would devour them all.

He shook his head, an ache developing behind his eyes as he tried to see into the past. It was as misty and gloom-filled as his present, as this forest in which he found himself.

"Take me home!" the Lady whispered suddenly. "You have no right!"

He turned to find her standing with her hands clenched into fists at her sides. Her strange red eyes burned with rage, and her lips were skinned back from her teeth like an animal's. It was said that she could do magic, that she possessed incredible power. You did not want to make an enemy of her, it was said. But the Knight had done so. He was not sure how it had happened, but there was no getting away from it now. He had taken the Lady from her home, from the haven of her life, carrying her off to this forest. He was the King's Champion, and he existed only to do the King's bidding. The King must have sent him to bring the Lady, although he could not remember that either.

"Knight of black thoughts and deeds!" she scorned. "Coward behind your armor and your weapons! Take me home!"

She might have been threatening him now, preparing to use her magic against him. But he did not think so. What magic she possessed seemed lost to her. He had come this far, and she had not attacked him with it. If she had been able to do so, she would have tried long ago. Not that it would have mattered. He was a weapon built of iron. He was less man than machine. Magic had no more effect on him than dust thrown in his eyes; it had no place in his life. His was a world of simple rules and tight boundaries. He was not frightened of anything. A Knight could not allow fear. His was an occupation where death was always as close as life. Fighting was all he knew, and the battles he fought could end in only two ways—either he would kill his enemy or his enemy would kill him. A thousand battles later, he was still alive. He did not believe he would ever be killed. He believed he would live forever.

He brushed the musing aside, the thoughts that came unbidden and were unwelcome. "You are traveling to a new home," he told her, letting her anger fall away from him like leaves thrown against stone.

She shook with her rage, balled fists lifting before her breast, the tendons of her neck as tight as cords. "I will not go with you further," she whispered, and shook her head back and forth. "Not one step!"

He nodded noncommittally, not wishing to spar with her verbally, feeling inadequate to the task. He turned away again, walked to the far side of the clearing, and peered out into the gloom beyond. The trees were packed together like bundles of giant sticks, shutting out the light and the view, closing everything off. Which way to go? Which way had he been headed? The King would be waiting for him, he knew. It was always thus. But which way led home again?

He turned as the Lady came at him with the knife she had somehow kept hidden, the blade black and slick with poison. She shrieked as he seized her wrist and forced the knife away, then twisted it from her grasp. She beat at him and kicked wildly, trying to break free, but he was far stronger and immune to her fury, and he subdued her easily. She collapsed to the ground, breathing hard, on the verge of tears perhaps but refusing to cry. He picked up the blade and cast it far out into the gloom.

"Be careful what you throw about, Knight," a new voice warned, deep and guttural.

He saw the Gargoyle then, resting on its haunches close by, come from the woods as silent as a shadow at midnight. The creature's eyes were yellow and hooded as they studied him, and there was nothing in their reptilian depths to offer even the slightest hint of what the mind behind them might be thinking.

"You've chosen to stay," the Knight said quietly.

The Gargoyle laughed. "Chosen? A strange word in these circumstances, don't you think? I am here because there is nowhere else to go."

The Gargoyle was loathsome to look upon. Its body was gnarled and misshapen, with its arms and legs bandy and crooked, its body all sinew and corded muscle, and its head sunk down between its powerful shoulders. Its hands and feet were webbed and clawed, and the whole of it was covered in bristly dark hair. Its face was wrinkled like a piece of dried fruit, and its features were jammed together like a child's clay model of something only vaguely human. Fangs peeked out from beneath its thick lips, and its nose was wet and dirty.

From atop its hunched shoulders, wings fluttered weakly, leathery flaps too tiny to be of any use, appendages that seemed strangely out of place. It was as if its forebearers might have flown once but had long ago forgotten how.

The Knight was repulsed, but he did not look away. Ugliness was a part of his life as well. "Where are we?" he asked the Gargoyle. "Have you looked about?"

"We are in the Labyrinth," it replied, as if that answered everything.

The Gargoyle glanced at the Lady, who had looked up again on hearing him speak. "Don't look at me!" she hissed at once, and turned away.

"In what part of our country is the Labyrinth?" the Knight persisted, confused.

The Gargoyle laughed anew. "In every part." He showed his yellowed teeth and black tongue. "In all parts of every part of everything. It lies north and south and east and west and even in the center. It is where we are and where we would go and where we will always be."

"He is mad," the Lady whispered quickly. "Make him keep still."

The Knight shifted the heavy broadsword on his back and glanced around. "There is a way out of every maze," he declared. "We will find the way out of this one."

The Gargoyle rubbed his hands as if seeking warmth. "How will you do that, Sir Knight?" His voice was disdainful.

"Not by staying here," the Knight said. "Do you come with us or not?"

"Leave him!" the Lady hissed, rising suddenly to her feet and drawing her dark robes close. "He does not belong with us! He was never meant to be with us!"

"Us?" the Gargoyle repeated slyly. "Are you bound together now, Lady? Are you joined to this Knight as mate and companion? How unexpected."

The Lady curled her lip at the creature and turned away. "I am joined to neither of you. I would rather be killed now and have it done."

"I would rather you were killed as well," the Gargoyle agreed.

The Lady whirled back upon him once again. "You are an ugly beast, Gargoyle. If I had a mirror, I would hold it up to your face so that you could see how ugly!"

The Gargoyle flinched at the words, and then hissed back at her, "And you would need a mirror inside yourself to see the ugliness that possesses you!"

"Do not fight!" the Knight thundered, and stepped between them. He looked changed suddenly, the man in dark clothing and chain mail suddenly gone even darker. It was as if the light about him had been sucked away. It was as if he had been plated in shadows.

"Do not," he repeated, more softly now, and then the dark cast that had enveloped him disappeared, and he was himself again.

There was a long moment of silence as the three faced one another. Then the Lady said to the Knight, "I am not afraid of you."

The Knight looked off into the gloom as if he had not heard, and in his eyes there was a lost, faraway look that reflected memories of missed chances and lost possibilities.

"We will walk this way," the Knight said, and started out.

They traveled through the remainder of the day, and the forest that was the Labyrinth did not change. The gloom persisted, the mist clung tenaciously, the trees did not thin save at scattered clearings, and the cast and shape of the world did not alter. The Knight led them afoot (where was his mount?), trying to travel in a straight line, hoping that at some point the forest would end and the grasslands or hill country that surely lay beyond would appear and suggest to him where they must go next. He pondered with every step the inconsistencies of his memory. He tried to reason out what he was dong there, what had brought him to this abysmal place. He tried to remember how the Lady and the Gargoyle had come to be with him. He tried to think through the fog that enveloped almost the whole of his past. He was a Knight in service to the King, a champion of countless battles, and that was virtually all he knew.

He clung to that, and it kept him just ahead of the madness that too much thinking would bring.

They found streams from which to drink and did so, but they found nothing to eat. Yet they experienced no hunger. It was not as if they were full, but as if hunger's presence had left them entirely. The Knight was puzzled by this, but did not speak of it. They walked through the day, through the twilight that changed only marginally, and when darkness finally came, they stopped again.

They were in another clearing, a clearing that looked much like the first. The forest about them had not changed. They sat down together in the deepening gloom and stared out at the darkness. The Knight did not think to build a fire. They were not cold, or hungry, or in need of light. They could see quite well in the darkness; they could hear sounds they should not have been able to. The Gargoyle sat a little way off from the other two, not wishing to endure the scorn of the Lady again so soon, not feeling a part of them in any case. The Knight could sense the other's distancing, even when traveling together, as if the Gargoyle understood that there would always be a wall between them. The creature hunkered down in the shadows, then stretched his misshapen body and seemed to melt into the ground.

The Lady sat facing the Knight. "I do not like you," she told him. "I wish to see you dead."

He nodded impassively. "I know."

She had been silent and introspective all day, journeying obediently but without interest. He had glanced at her now and again, and sometimes found her openly hostile and sometimes as lost and searching as himself. She held herself as if armored, tall and straight and unafraid, but there was a vulnerability to her that she could not disguise and did not quite seem to understand, as if it was newly come to her and unexpected.

"Why don't you just take me back?" she pressed, a sudden urgency in her voice. "What difference can any of this make to you? There is no enemy for you to fight. There is no battle to be won. Why are you doing this? Am I your enemy?"

"You have said so."

"Only because you steal me from my home!" she exclaimed desperately. "Only because of that!" She inched forward across the grassy earth until she was quite close. "Why have you taken me?"

He could not answer. He did not know why.

"Your King has ordered you to do so? Why?"

He could not remember.

"What does he want with me? I will never be any good for him, no matter what he thinks! I will be neither wife nor consort! I will be his worst enemy until I am dead!"

The Knight inhaled the forest air, smelling the green freshness of the leaves and grass, the musky damp of the soil, and the pungent dryness of bark and old wood. What were the answers to her questions? Why could he not remember them? He withdrew into himself, thinking to find peace. He took comfort in knowing who he was and what he did. He found reassurance in his strength and skill, in the press of his weapons against his body, in the smooth fit of his battle dress.

Yet his armor was still missing. He had felt its presence when he had been forced to step between the Lady and the Gargoyle, but it had not shown itself. Why was that? It reached out to him, yet stayed hidden, as if playing cat and mouse. His armor—it was lifeless and yet seemingly possessed of life, a paradox. Like the medallion he wore about his neck, it was a part of who and what he was. Why then could he not remember its source?

The Lady was a silent ivory carving before him, watching intently, wanting to come forth from within herself he sensed, but unable to do so. What was she hiding from him? Something frightening. Some deep, secretive admission.

She folded her slim hands within her lap, and the disdainful look crept back upon her face. "You are powerless," she declared bitterly. "You have no self-will, no independent spirit with which to act. You are a tool to be wielded by whoever wears the crown. How sad."

"I am a *servant* of that crown."

"You are a slave to it." She cocked her head slightly, the raven hair shifting in a glimmer of black light. Her eyes fixed him. "You can make no decision that conflicts with your master's orders. You can make no judgment on your own. You took me without asking why. You keep me without wondering why. You do what you are bidden, and you are careless of the reasons for your actions."

He did not like to argue with her. It gained nothing for either of them. He was not good with words; she was not possessed of his sense of honor and obedience. They came from different lives.

"Who is this King who would have me for his own?" she asked pointedly. "Speak his name."

Again, he could not. He stared at her, trapped.

"Are you so ignorant as to not know it?" she pressed, irony sharpening the edges of her anger. "Or are you afraid to give it to me? Which is it?"

He kept silent. But he could not look away.

She shook her head slowly. She was hard-faced and cold-looking with her dark hair and white skin, with the set of her jaw and the glint in her eyes. But she was beautiful, too. She was as perfect as a fond memory lovingly worked over the passing of time, all the roughness rubbed away, all the flaws removed. She enchanted him without trying, without meaning to do so, drawing him past her anger and despair, carrying him out of what was into what should never be.

"Whatever I would tell you," he forced himself to say, "would mean nothing."

"Try, at least!" she whispered at him, and there was a sudden softness in her voice. "Give me something!"

But he could not. He had nothing to give. He had only himself, and she wanted no part of that. She wanted reasons and understanding, and he had neither. He was as adrift as she was, thrown into a place he did not know, into circumstances he did not understand. The Labyrinth was a mystery he could not fathom. To do so, he must first escape it. That, he understood intuitively, would not be easy.

"Have you no feelings at all for me?" she asked plaintively, but this time the falseness in her voice betrayed her immediately.

"My feelings have no place in what I am about. I do what is required of me."

"What is required of you!" she shrieked, angry and bitter all over again, casting off any pretension of weakness. "You do what you are sent to do, you pathetic creature! You bend and scrape because it is what you know! What is required of you? I would rather be cast into the darkest pit in all the land than spend one moment of my life giving heed to what another would demand of me!"

He smiled in spite of himself. "And so you have been," he told her. "For where else are we if not there?"

She shrank back from him, downcast, in silence. They sat like that for a long time. The Gargoyle was sleeping, his breathing nasal and rough, his crooked limbs twitching as if his palms and soles were prodded by hot iron. The Lady glanced at him once and then glanced away. She did not look back. She did not look at the Knight. She stared at a space upon the earth some six feet to her right where the grass had withered away in shadow and the soil had cracked and turned to dust. She sat that way a long time. The Knight watched her without seeming to, without really wanting to, unable to help himself. She was in genuine misery, but the source of her anguish went beyond what she had told him. It was huge and carefully warded, and it transcended his meager understanding of its source.

He felt a strange stirring inside. He should say something to ease her pain. He should do something to lift her burden. But he did not know what. He wondered then at the words she had spoken to him, at the accusations she had cast. There was truth in them. He was given over to another's service, charged with another's wishes, bound to another's cause. It was the essence of his life as King's champion. A Knight in armor whose weapons and strength settled all causes—that was his identity. On reflection, it seemed too small a possession. He was defined by it, yet it was given out in a single phrase. Was that the sum of his parts? Was there nothing more to him?

Who was he?

"Do you know what you have done to me?" he heard the Lady ask suddenly. He looked over at once. She was not looking back. She was still staring at that same patch of earth. Lines of wetness streaked her cheeks, trailing from her cold, empty eyes.

"Do you know?" she whispered in despair.

Night's shadows cloaked Landover as well. All eight moons were down, and clouds layered the sky and masked away the stars. The blackness was intense. The day's heat had left the air windless and damp, and the whole of the land lay hushed and sweltering.

The Gorse felt no discomfort as it moved out of the concealment of its cavern lair and into the forest beyond. It was a fairy creature and at one with nature whatever her disposition. It came forth as a cloud of dark mist, the state to which its long captivity in the Tangle Box had reduced it. But already that substanceless form was beginning to coalesce and take shape anew, freedom returning to it the face and body it had once owned. Quite soon now both would be restored. It would be ready then to exact from those who had wronged it the revenge it so desperately craved.

It had thought about nothing else for centuries. Once it had been a fairy creature of great power, a being whose magic was formidable and feared. It had used that magic in ways that so enraged and disgusted its kin within the fairy mists, the world to which all fairy creatures belonged, that they banded together, seized it when it thought itself invulnerable, and imprisoned it. They cast it down into the mists of the Tangle Box, a device they had constructed from their own magic and from which nothing could escape. Locks were placed upon the box from without where the Gorse could not reach them.

Entombing it thus was meant to wear it down, to destroy its will, to make it forget everything it had known before its confinement and in the end to reduce it to dust. The effort had failed. It had remained trapped a very long time but it had not forgotten and its hatred of those responsible had grown.

It had grown very large indeed.

The Gorse moved easily through the night. It required little time to reach its destination and was in no hurry. It had waited until Horris Kew and the bird were sleeping, not wanting them to discover what it was about, needing them to continue to believe it was their friend. It was not, of course. The man and the bird were pawns, and the Gorse was using them accordingly. If they wanted to believe otherwise, if they chose to do so because they were greedy and foolish, that was as it should be. It was the natural order of things. They were mortal creatures and, so, much less than the Gorse. They were expendable.

It crested a rise and found itself at the edge of the Heart. It paused to send out feelers of sight and sound, taste and smell, and discovered nothing amiss, nothing threatening. It looked out across the rows of white velvet seats and rests, past the burnished dais and its standards, past the encirclement of Bonnie Blues. It savored the presence of the magic that rose out of the earth, here at the wellspring of all the land's life. The power of that magic was enormous, but the Gorse was not yet ready to tamper with it. It would serve a different purpose this night. A greater magic could be used to mask the conjuring of a lesser. It would do so now.

The Gorse gathered itself and sent forth the summons it had prepared. Lines of fire that neither burned nor smoked lanced down into the earth and disappeared. The response was immediate, a harsh, grating rumble, the groan of a great stone wall giving way. After a moment, the rumble faded, and the silence returned.

The Gorse waited.

Then the air before it ripped apart as if formed of fabric, first tearing and then splitting wide. Thunder boomed from within the rent, deep and ominous. A hole opened in the night, and out of that hole rose the clang and scrape of armored riders and the hiss and shriek of their mounts. The sounds heightened to a frightening pitch as the riders gathered speed. A fierce wind whipped across the Heart, tearing at the flags atop their standards and screaming into the trees beyond.

The Gorse held its ground.

With a rush of wind and sound, those it had summoned materialized from out of the warp in time and space. They were formed of armored plates and spikes, bristling with weapons, riding on nightmare creatures that had no recognizable name. There were five of them, massive dark creatures that steamed despite the humid night air and whose breath hissed and rasped through the visors of their helmets. They were lean and shadowy, like dark-hued ghosts, and the reek of their bodies was terrible.

The demons of Abaddon had arrived.

Foremost was the one who was designated as the Mark, their chosen leader, a huge, angular monster with serpents carved into its armor and the severed heads of its enemies hung about its neck. It beckoned to the others, and they fanned out to either side, weapons held ready. As one, they advanced on the Gorse.

The Gorse let them come. When they were close enough to spit on, it disappeared before their eyes in a flash of green light, reappeared as one of them, disappeared a second time, and reappeared finally as a pair of snake's eyes. It stole into their armor and licked at them lovingly, showing them they were kindred spirits. It conjured images of the horrors it had once performed on its own people and let the demons savor its evil.

When they were satisfied that it was one of them, that it was as powerful as they, and that it had summoned them for a reason, the Gorse hissed softly to prick their ears for his words and said, "What if I were to prepare a way for you to come into Landover safely?"

He paused, hearing them growl expectantly. This was too easy. "What if Landover and her people were to be given over to you for good?"

Too easy indeed.

Vision

After parting from the Earth Mother, Willow walked on through the forest for a time toward Elderew, lost in thought. The day was bright and sunny, filled with the smell of summer wildflowers and green grasses, and the forest was noisy and crowded with birdsong. It was beautiful and warm and comforting beneath the canopy of the great hardwoods, but Willow was oblivious to all of it. She walked through unaware, lost somewhere deep within herself, pondering over and over again the Earth Mother's message about her baby.

The words haunted her. She must gather soils from this world, from Ben's world, and from the fairy mists. She must mix them together and take root in them in order for her child to be safely born. She did not know how long she had to do this. She did not know when the child would be born. She did not know where. She could not ask another to gather the soils for her; she must do so herself. Ben could not go with her. He could not help her. No one could.

Well, almost no one. There would be the guide chosen by the fairies to direct her on the last two legs of her journey. But who would they send?

She felt cold inside despite the day's warmth. She had almost died in Ben's world on her one and only visit, so her memories were not fond ones. The fairy mists were even worse for being an unknown; she was terrified of what might happen to her there. A once-fairy was even more vulnerable to their treachery than a human. The mists could so bewilder you, so erode your reason and strength, and so change you from who and what you were that you would end up completely lost to yourself. The mists brought out the dark fears you kept hidden deep inside yourself, giving them substance, giving them sufficient power to destroy you. Life within the mists was ethereal, a creation of the mind and the imagination. It was magical and ever-changing. Reality was what you created it to be, a bog that could swallow you up without a trace.

Willow's fear of the fairy world was the heritage bequeathed to her by her ancestors, those who had been fairies once, those who had come out of the mists. Not all of her ancestors had left, of course; some had remained behind, content with their immortality. Some yet lived and were fairies still. At times she could hear their voices in her sleep, in her dreams, calling out to her, urging her to come back to their way of life. It had been hundreds of years since the once-fairy had departed the mists, but the whispered call to return never ceased.

It was a fact of life for her as it was for all of the once-fairy. Except that now she would be going back in spite of the warnings against doing so, the cautions that were carefully handed down from parents to children by all of the once-fairy. You can never go back. You can never return. But she would be doing so. She would be risking her sanity and her life for the sake of her child. Her needs versus the needs of her baby—it was a conflict that threatened to tear her apart.

She walked on, debating, arguing with herself. The forest began to change perceptibly, the trees rising higher, the look of the land altering subtly, and she saw that she was drawing near to Elderew. She did not intend to enter the city. Her father was there, and she did not want to see him. He was the River Master, leader of the once-fairy and Lord of the lake country. They had never shared a close relationship and had grown further apart when she had defied his wishes and gone to Ben Holiday when Ben had first come into Landover. She had known she was meant for Ben and he for her, that they would share a life, and she had decided that whatever the consequences she would find a way to be with him. It had not helped that he had succeeded as King when others who craved power over Landover, her father included, had hoped he would not. It had not helped that she had made her life with him, a human, and left her own people. The relationship was further strained by the closeness she shared with her mother. The River Master was still in love with Willow's mother, the only woman he had coveted and been unable to possess. He had fathered Willow on the single night they lay together, and then Willow's mother, a wood nymph so wild that she could not live anywhere but in the deepest forest, had returned to her old life. The River Master had searched her out repeatedly and had even tried to trap her on one or two occasions, but all his efforts had failed. Willow's mother would not come back to him. That she appeared now and again to Willow and danced for her in the fairy way, sharing emotions and dreams that transcended words, was almost more than the River Master could bear. He had many wives and many more children. He should have been content. He was not. Willow thought that without her mother beside him he never would be.

She eased down a corridor of great white oak and shag-bark hickory leading to the silver ribbon of a tributary that fed into the Irrylin, making her way toward the old pines where her mother would come to her at nightfall. She thought of her old life, her life before Ben, here in the lake country, as a child of the River Master. She had been alone most of the time and had never felt loved. She had kept herself strong with her unshakable belief of what would one day be, the prospect of Ben and her life with him, the promise made to her by the Earth Mother when she was still a small child, the dream that nurtured and sustained her. The realization of that dream had been a long time coming, she thought, but any amount of time would have been worth the wait.

She reached the stream, followed it to a shallows, and crossed. She felt the eyes on her for the first time then and stopped. They were bold and steady. She turned toward them, and they were gone. A once-fairy, like herself, probably in service to her father. She should have known she could not come into the lake country unseen. She should have known that her father would not allow it.

She sighed. Now that he knew she was there, he would insist on speaking with her. She might as well wait where she was.

She turned back to the stream and stooped to drink from a rapids. The water was clean and tasted good. She looked at herself in the ripple of brightness as it passed, a small and slender woman who looked to be barely more than a girl, eyes large and expressive, hair thick and flowing from her head but as thin and fine as gossamer where it ran down the backs of her forearms and calves, all of her colored in various shades of green. She was this image reflected by the waters of the stream, but she was also at regular intervals transformed into the tree for which she was named, a consequence of her genetic makeup and now the cause for this journey she had been sent upon. She thought for a moment about how different things would have been if she had been given other blood, if she had been born of other parents. But a moment of such thinking was enough. She might as well ponder what would have happened if she had been born human.

She rose, and the River Master stood before her. He was tall and lean, his skin an almost silver cast, grainy and shimmering, his hair black and thick about the nape of his neck and forearms. His forest clothing was loose-fitting, nondescript, and belted at the waist. He wore a slim silver diadem on his head, the mark of his office. The features of his face were sharp and small, his nose almost nonexistent, his mouth a tight line that allowed no expression.

"Even for you, that was quick," she greeted him.

"I had to be quick," he replied, "since my daughter apparently did not intend to visit me."

His voice was deep and even. He was alone, but she knew his retainers were close by, concealed back in the trees, staying just within hearing so that they could respond quickly if called.

"You are correct," she said. "I did not."

Her honesty gave him pause. "Bold words for a child to speak to her father. Are you too good for me now that you are the wife of the High Lord?" A hint of anger crept into his voice. "Have you forgotten who you were and where you came from? Have you forgotten your roots, Willow?"

She did not miss the snide reference. "I have forgotten nothing. Rather, I have remembered all too well. I do not feel welcome here, Father. I think that seeing me is not altogether pleasant for you."

He stared at her momentarily and then nodded. "Because of your mother, you believe? Because of how I feel about her? Perhaps so, Willow. But I have learned to put those feelings aside. I find I must. Have you come to see her, then?"

"Yes."

"About the child you are expecting?"

She smiled in spite of herself. She should have known. The River Master had spies everywhere, and there had been no attempt to keep the news of her baby a secret. "Yes," she answered.

"Your child by Holiday, an heir to the throne." Her father's stone face was expressionless, but his voice gave something of what he was feeling away. "You must be pleased, Willow."

"And you are not," she declared softly.

"The child is not once-fairy and therefore not one of us. The child is half-human. I would wish it otherwise."

She shook her head. "You see everything in terms of your own interests, Father. The child is Ben Holiday's and therefore another obstacle in your efforts to gain control of the throne of Landover. You can't just outwait him now. You must deal with his child as well. Isn't that what you mean?"

The River Master came forward to stand directly before her. "I will not argue with you. I am disappointed that you did not intend to tell me of the birth of my grandchild. You would tell your mother, but you would let me find out another way."

"It wasn't so difficult for you, was it?" she asked. "Not with all your spies to tell you."

There was a hard silence as they faced each other, sylph and sprite, daughter and father, separated by distances that could never be measured.

The River Master looked away. The sun glinted off his silver skin as he stared out into the shadows of the great forest trees. "This is my homeland. These are my people. It is important for me to remember them first in all things. You have forgotten what that means. We do not see things the same way, Willow. We never have. I was never close enough to you to find a way to do so. Some of that is my fault. You were ruined for me by your mother's refusal to live with me. I could not look at you without seeing her."

He shrugged, a slow, deliberate movement, a relegation to the past of what was now beyond his grasp. "Yet I loved you, child. I love you still." He looked back at her. "You do not believe that, do you? You do not accept it."

She felt something stir weakly inside, a memory of when she had wanted nothing more. "If you love me," she said carefully, "then give me your word that you will protect my child always."

He looked long and hard at her, as if seeing someone else. Then he placed one hand on his breast. She was surprised to see how gnarled it had become. The River Master was aging. "Given," he said. "To the extent that I can do so, my grandchild shall be kept safe." He paused. "But it was not necessary to ask for my word on that."

Willow held his gaze. "I think perhaps it was."

The River Master's hand dropped away. "You are too harsh towards me. But I understand." He glanced skyward. "Do you go now to your mother or will you come with me into the city, to my home? Your mother," he hurried on, "will not come until night."

Willow hesitated, and for a moment thought she might accept his invitation, for she sensed it was extended in kindness and not duplicitously. Then she shook her head. "No, I will go on," she said. "I have . . . a need to be alone before I see her."

Her father nodded, as if he had expected her answer. "Do you think she . . . ?" he began, and then stopped, unable to continue. Willow waited. He looked away and then back again. "Do you think she would dance for me as well?"

Willow experienced a sudden sadness for her father. It had been difficult for him to ask that. "No, I do not think so. She will not even appear if you come with me."

He nodded again, expecting this answer as well. She reached out then and took hold of his hand. "But I will ask her if she will dance for you another time."

His hand tightened around hers. They stood joined that way for a moment longer, and then the River Master spoke again. "I will tell you something, Willow. Whether you believe me or not is your choice. But my dreams are certain and my vision is true, and of all the once-fairy I am the most powerful and the closest to the old ways. So heed me. Even before I was informed of the birth, I knew of the child. I have dreamed of it before. The dreams show me this. The path of your life is marked by the coming of this child. You must find ways to be strong in the face of the changes it will bring—you and the High Lord both."

Willow swallowed her sudden fear. "Have you seen my child's face? Have you seen anything that you can tell me?"

The River Master shook his head slowly. "No, Willow. My dreams of the child are too large for the specifics you would know. My dreams are shadows and light upon a life path and nothing more. If you would know specifics, speak with the Earth Mother. Perhaps her vision is clearer than mine."

Willow nodded. He would not have known she had already spoken to the elemental. The Earth Mother would not have allowed it. "I will do as you suggest. Thank you."

She released his hand and stepped back. Then she started off into the forest. "You will not try to follow me?" She looked back guardedly.

Her father shook his head once more. "No. If you will remember to ask of the dance."

She turned away. "I will."

She continued on then and did not look back again.

The remainder of the day passed away in a ripple of slow breezes and lengthening shadows, the sun easing west across the cloudless sky and disappearing finally beneath the horizon in a broad sweep of crimson. Willow sat at the edge of the clearing in the middle of the old pines waiting for nightfall and her mother's coming. She had arrived early and spent her time considering the direction of her life. She found she had a need to do so.

When she was still small, she came often to the old pines in search of her mother. She came out of a need to know what her mother was like and a sense that by doing so she would better understand herself. The Earth Mother warned her that her mother might not come for a long time, that she would be reticent and perhaps even fearful of facing the daughter she had abandoned. But Willow was determined, more tough-minded, even then, than anyone expected.

But then Willow had never been what anyone expected. She began life as a small, shy, introspective child, not very pretty, lacking the benefit of a mother's guidance or even a father's interest, and there was no reason to think she would ever be any different. But she surprised everyone. The Earth Mother helped by encouraging and teaching, but mostly it was Willow who managed the transformation, and mostly she did it by being determined. She was quiet about it at first. Because she was left to be on her own a lot of the time, she discovered early on that if she really wanted something she would have to go out and get it on her own. She learned to dig in her heels, roll up her sleeves, work hard, and be patient. She learned that if you wanted something bad enough, you could always find a way to get it. The mental toughness was always there; the rest came later. She became beautiful, though she never thought of herself that way. Others found her striking; she viewed herself as too exotic. Because she had to do so much for herself, she learned confidence and directness. She learned not to be afraid of anyone or anything. She developed her skills and her knowledge with the same fierce determination she brought to everything. She was not that way because she was afraid of failing; it never occurred to her that she might fail. She was that way because it was the only way she knew.

In the end, she waited almost three years for her mother to come. She went to the old pines as least once a week. She waited through the days and sometimes the nights as well. The waiting was hard, but not unbearable. Although she never saw her mother, she sometimes felt her presence. The feeling came in a rustle of leaves, a small animal sound, a whisper of wind, or a scent of new flowers. It was never the same, but always recognizable. She would tell the Earth Mother afterward, encouraged, and the Earth Mother would nod and say, yes, that was your mother. She's watching you. She's judging. Perhaps she will show herself one day.

And one day she did. At midnight, at midsummer, she appeared in a glimmer of moonlight, spinning and leaping from the forest trees into the clearing to dance for the child who had waited so long to see her. There was magic in the dance, and Willow knew then and forever after that her life would be special and wondrous.

Now, after the passing of many years and many visits to the old pines, she had come once again. She had come to tell her mother of the child she was carrying, of the journey she was undertaking, and of the warnings she had received. Her emotions were sharply in conflict. On the one hand she was elated by the anticipated birth of her child with Ben; on the other, she was daunted by the prospect of her journey and frightened by the warnings given to her by the Earth Mother and her father. The latter bothered her most, cautions from two of the most powerful and magical creatures in Landover, both telling her that she must be wary, both warning that this child she so wanted would change everything about her life.

She tried to sort through her emotions as she waited for darkness. She pondered the warnings she had been given. There were no new insights to be gained by doing either. The exercise was merely a means for coming to terms with what she was thinking and feeling. If Ben had been there, she would have talked it through with him. Since he wasn't, she was forced to use what had worked for her when she was small and growing up alone.

Mostly, she was hopeful that her mother would be able to help. They would communicate as they always did through the wood nymph's dance. The dance would provide a vision, and the vision would give insight. It had done so on many occasions. Willow hoped it would do so now.

Twilight deepened and the stars appeared. Two moons were visible in the northern sky, not far above the horizon,

one pale mauve, one peach. The night air was fragrant with
the scent of pine needles and wildflowers, and the clearing was
hushed. Willow sat thinking of Ben. She wished he was with
her. It would have made things much easier having him there.
She did not like being away from him. She did not feel complete when she was.

It was nearing midnight when her mother came. She
leaped out of the trees in a series of flitting movements that
took her from one patch of shadows to the next. She was a
tiny, ephemeral creature, with long silver hair, pale green skin
like Willow's own, and a child's body. She wore no clothing.
She darted along the edges of the clearing as if testing the waters of a moonlit lake, and then disappeared into the trees to
hide.

Willow waited expectantly.

Her mother returned in a flash of silver skin, spinning
swiftly past her, fingers brushing at her cheek, a light ripple of
velvet, and then she was gone once more.

"Mother?" Willow called softly to her.

A moment later her mother danced out from the trees
into the very center of the starlight that cascaded down
through the heavy boughs. She spun and twisted and leapt in
the radiant glow, her arms moving fluidly, reaching out for
her daughter. Willow lifted her own arms in response. They
did not touch each other, but the words began to flow between them, heard only in the mind, visions born out of
thought.

Willow remembered her promise to her father and spoke
first of his desire to see Willow's mother dance. Her mother
drew back immediately, and she let the matter drop. She spoke
of Ben and her life at Sterling Silver. There was happiness in
her mother's response this time, though it was small and measured, for her mother could not understand life beyond the
forest and the dance, life of any kind beyond her own. In a detached way she was happy for Willow; she was not capable of

anything more. Willow had learned to take what her mother offered and make the most of it.

She let her mother speak to her then through the dance, let her share in turn the joy she was feeling. Once Willow had found that joy exhilarating. Now she found it lacking, an oddly empty, circumscribed happiness bound up in self-indulgence and personal gratification, bereft of interest in or concern for others, ultimately puzzling and somehow sad. Neither could ever really understand the other, Willow knew. Still they shared what they could, giving back reassurance and gratitude, reaffirming the bond that existed between them.

Then Willow told her mother of the baby and of the quest that would take her from Landover to Earth to the fairy mists and back again.

Her mother's response was immediate. The dance grew wilder and more frenzied. The silence of the night deepened and the world beyond that starlit clearing slipped further away into the darkness. There were only mother and daughter and the dance they shared. Willow watched, awestruck by her mother's grace, her beauty, her strong presence, and her instinctive response to her daughter's special needs.

And so out of the strange, impossible spinnings and turnings of the dance appeared the vision Willow had anticipated, rising up into the light to fill the space between them.

But the vision was not of her child, but of Ben. He was lost, she sensed—lost in a way that he could not understand. He was himself, but at the same time he was someone else. He was not alone. Two others were with him, and she started as she recognized who they were. Nightshade the witch and Strabo the dragon. All three floundered in a morass of mist and gray light that emanated as much from within as from without. They journeyed onward hopelessly, searching for something that was hidden from her, casting desperately about in a futile effort to find it.

Then she saw herself, consumed by an identical patch of

mist and grayness, as lost as they, searching for something as well. She was near them and yet far away, close enough to touch them and yet nowhere she could be seen. She was dancing, spinning through a prism of light. She could not stop.

There was something more. In a subtle shift of sound and light, the vision revealed one final horror. In its telling of what would be, she could see that Ben was forgetting her and that she was forgetting Ben. She could see it happening in the gloom and shadows; they were turning away from each other. They would never find each other again.

Ben, she heard herself call out in despair. *Ben!*

When the vision faded, she found herself alone. The clearing stood empty, and her mother had gone. She sat staring at the space through which her mother had danced and tried to comprehend what she had been shown. There had been nothing of her baby; everything had been of Ben. Why? Ben was safely back at Sterling Silver, not lost in misty darkness. And what set of circumstances could possibly bring him together with Nightshade and Strabo, his sworn enemies?

None of it made any sense. Which made it all the more maddening.

Her dilemma now was acute. She wanted to turn around and go back to Sterling Silver at once to make certain that Ben was safe. The urge was so strong that she came close to setting out without another thought for the matter.

But she knew she couldn't do that. Her commitment now was to her baby and to the quest that would ensure its safe birth. She could not afford to burden herself with other concerns, no matter who was involved, no matter how compelling, until she had fulfilled the Earth Mother's quest. Ben would agree with that. In fact, he would insist on it. She would have to ignore the vision for now. She would have to let events take their course until she could afford to do something to affect them directly.

She rose then, more tired than she had expected, drained by the events of the day, and moved to the center of the starlit clearing. She bent to where her mother had danced and began to dig with her hands. It was not difficult; the soil was loose and easily gathered. She scooped up several handfuls and placed them in a pouch she had brought to carry extra foodstuffs—one portion of the magic her baby required. She laced the pouch tight, hefted it in her hands, and tied it again to her waist.

She looked off to the east. The sky was beginning to lighten. The dance had lasted through most of the night.

She looked about the clearing one final time. It sat empty and silent, the ancient pines solemn witnesses that would never tell what they had seen. So much had taken place here over the years, so much that remained an indelible part of her life. Now this.

"Good-bye, Mother," she said softly, speaking mostly to herself. "I wish you could come with me."

She stood there alone, thinking again of the vision, and she closed her eyes against what she was feeling. What of Ben? What if the vision were true? She squeezed her eyes tighter to make the questions go away.

When she opened them again, she was thinking of what lay ahead. Earth, Ben's world, somewhere through the fairy mists, where the second soil collection must take place. But where in his world? To what place must she go? What kind of soil was required to fulfill her obligation? What form of magic?

And her guide . . . ?

She saw the cat then, sitting on a log to one side, licking its front paw. It was colored silver with black paws, face, and tail. It was slender and well-groomed and did not appear feral. It paused in its licking and regarded her with emerald eyes as brilliant as her own. She had the strangest feeling that it had been waiting for her.

I know this cat, she realized suddenly.

"Yes, indeed you do," the cat said.

Willow nodded wordlessly. She should have guessed. The fairies had sent her Edgewood Dirk.

Mind's Eye Crystals

Horris Kew trudged along the road to Sterling Silver whistling nervously in the midday sun. Another few miles, two or three at most, and then they would see. Anticipation mingled with trepidation and caused a serious burning sensation in the pit of his stomach. He was sweating profusely, and it was from more than the heat. The tic in his eye jumped wildly. He looked like he was juggling invisible balls.

He gave an anxious glance over his shoulder. No problem, everything was in place. The pack mule was still tethered to the other end of the rope he held, plodding obediently after. The twin chests were still roped tightly in place on the carry rack. Biggar was still perched atop them.

"Keep your eyes on the road, Horris," the myna said.

"I was just checking," he replied irritably.

"Don't bother. That's why I'm back here. You just keep walking. Just keep putting one foot in front of the other. Try not to fall on your face."

Horris Kew turned crimson. *Try not to fall on your face! Ha, ha! Big joke!*

Still looking over his shoulder, he opened his mouth to tell the bird to shut up, tripped, and promptly fell on his face. The road was dusty and dry, and he plowed a fair-size furrow in it with his nose and came up with a mouthful of grit. He heaved himself back to his feet and spit angrily.

"Don't say anything, Biggar!" he snapped, and began brushing himself off. His scarecrow body performed a series of violent contortions as he worked to get clean. "There was a rut! A rut! If you hadn't distracted me, I would have seen it and been all right!"

Biggar sighed wearily. "Why don't you just conjure us up a carriage and we could ride to the castle, Horris? Or maybe a horse. A horse would do."

"A horse! Great idea, a horse!" Horris clenched his hands angrily. "We're supposed to be supplicants, you idiot! Poor, penniless supplicants! Remember the plan?"

The mule yawned and brayed loudly. "Shut up!" Horris screamed furiously.

Biggar blinked and cocked his head thoughtfully. "Let me see. The plan. Ah, yes. The plan. I remember it now. The one that isn't going to work."

"Don't say that!"

"Don't say what? That the plan isn't going to work?"

"Shhhh!" a frantic Horris cautioned, tucking his head down between his shoulders for protection, glancing hurriedly about. His eye jumped. "It could be listening!"

"Who, the Gorse? Out here, in the midday sun, in the middle of nowhere?" Biggar sniffed. "I hardly think so. It's a night creature and not given to prolonged exposure to sunlight. Vampiric, I think they call it."

Horris glowered at him. "You're mighty brave when it isn't around, aren't you?"

"I'm merely making a point."

"I didn't notice you making it last night. I didn't notice you saying anything about the plan not working when it was explained to us."

"So you believe the plan is a good one, do you, Horris? Is that right? You think it will work?"

Horris tightened his jaw defiantly, standing in the middle

of the road facing mule and bird, fists on hips. He was a boxer leading with his chin. "Of course it will work!" he declared.

Biggar sniffed in obvious disdain. "Well, there you are. I rest my case. What is the purpose of my arguing with this creature, this Gorse, if you're going to stand around nodding in agreement with every cockeyed idea it comes up with? What am I supposed to do, Horris? I can't protect you from yourself. You won't listen to anyone when you're like this. Certainly not me. After all, I'm just your pet bird."

Horris gritted his teeth. "Pets are supposed to revere their masters, Biggar. When do you think you might start doing that?"

"Probably when I get a master who's worth the effort!"

Horris let his breath out with a hiss. "This isn't my fault! None of this is my fault! The Gorse is here because of you! You were the one who summoned it up in the first place!"

Biggar clacked his beak. "You were the one who did the conjuring, if I recall!"

"You told me what to say!"

"Well, you didn't have to say it!"

Horris threw down the rope to the mule. He was trembling all over. It was hot standing around in the midday summer sun, out of the shade of the forest trees, on a dry and dusty road. The robes he wore—a supplicant's robes—were coarse and sweat-stained and they stank. He had been walking since sometime after midnight because the Gorse wanted him at the gates of Sterling Silver just before sundown of today so that they would have to admit him into the castle for the night. He was tired and hungry (no food if you were a supplicant either, unless you could stand eating those detestable Bonnie Blues), and his patience was exhausted.

"Look, Biggar." He addressed the bird as calmly as he could. "I'm all done arguing with you. You had your chance to say something before this and you didn't. So you listen up.

The plan will work, got it? It will work! You might not think so and maybe I don't either, but if the Gorse says it will work, it will!"

He bent forward like a reedy tree in a high wind. "Did you see how easily it got rid of Holiday? And Strabo and Nightshade? Like that, Biggar!" He snapped his fingers dramatically. "It has a lot of power, in case you hadn't noticed. With King, witch, and dragon gone, who's going to challenge it? That's why the plan will work. And that's why I don't intend to ask any foolish questions!"

The bird faced him down. "You ought to listen to yourself, Horris. You really should. Got rid of Holiday and the witch and the dragon like that, did it?" He clacked his beak to mimic the other's emphasis. "Did it ever occur to you that it could get rid of us just as easily? I mean, what does it need with us anyway? Have you asked yourself that? We're errand boys, Horris. That's all we are. We're running around doing things it can't do for itself, but once we've done them, what then? If this so-called plan works, what does it need with us afterwards?"

Horris Kew felt a sudden lurch in the pit of his stomach. Maybe Biggar was right. He could still see Holiday and the witch and the dragon being sucked down into the Tangle Box. He could still see them fighting to get free before disappearing into the mists. When he had picked up the box, it seemed as if he could feel them batting around inside like trapped moths. He wondered what the Gorse had done with the Tangle Box after Horris had carried it back to the cave. He wondered if there was room inside for any more prisoners.

Horris swallowed hard. "Don't worry, the Gorse needs us all right," he insisted, but he didn't sound so sure now.

"Why?" Biggar snapped.

"Why?"

"Don't repeat me, Horris. I've warned you about that. Yes, why? Better ask yourself another question while you're at it. If it plans to give us all of Landover, what does it plan to give itself? And don't tell me it's doing this as a philanthropical undertaking. Don't tell me it doesn't want anything for itself. This plan is leading up to something, and so far it's not telling us what!"

"Okay! Okay!" Horris was on the defensive now. "Maybe there is something more than what we're being told. Sure, why not? Say, I've got an idea! Why don't you ask it, Biggar? If you're so worried, why don't you just ask it?"

"For the same reason you don't, Horris! I don't fancy getting dispatched like Holiday and the others!"

"But it's okay for me to chance it, is that it?"

"While it needs you, it is! Think with your brain, Horris! It won't do anything to you while it needs you! It's afterwards that you have to start worrying!"

Horris stamped furiously. Dusty streaks of sweat ran down his narrow, pointed face. "That hardly helps us now, out here on the road, almost to the gates of the King's castle, does it?" he yelled angrily. "Got any other useful suggestions?"

Biggar ruffled his feathers anew, his dark eyes flat and hard. "Matter of fact, I do. This whole plan depends on whether or not the magic it gave us works. If it doesn't, the wizard and the dog are going to have us thrown into the darkest dungeon they can find. Holiday was our only ally when we were here before, and he's long gone. No one is going to be in a very good mood with him missing. So what if the magic doesn't work, Horris?"

Horris Kew glowered menacingly. "I'm getting tired of this, Biggar. In fact, I'm getting tired of you."

Biggar looked unimpressed. "I say we try one out and see if it works before we walk into the lion's den."

The glower deepened. "The Gorse told us not to do that, remember? It warned us explicitly."

"So what?" the bird pressed. "The Gorse isn't the one taking all the risks."

"It said that whatever we did, we were not to use them!

It was pretty emphatic, as I recall!" Horris was shouting. "Suppose it isn't kidding, Biggar? Suppose—just suppose now—that it knows what it's talking about! After all, whose magic is it, you idiot?"

Biggar spit—not easy for a bird. "You are foolish beyond anything I could have imagined, Horris Kew. You are incredibly stupid. And myopic to boot. And, even for a human, exceedingly gutless!"

Horris charged him then, his temper frayed past its limits, his anger exploding through him. Roaring like an enraged lion, he came at Biggar with every intent of tearing him wing from wing. But Biggar was a bird, and birds can escape humans every time simply by flying off, which is what Biggar did now, a casual, lazy lifting into the air so that he circled just out of reach of the leaping, grasping, would-be conjurer. What Horris did succeed in doing was frightening the pack mule within an inch of its life so that it bolted back into the forest to disappear in a cloud of dust with a mighty, terrified bray.

"Oh, drat it, drat it, drat, drat, drat!" Horris mumbled, among other less printable things, when he finally calmed down enough to realize what he had done.

It took him, even with Biggar's help, an hour to round up the mule and the precious chests it carried. Exhausted, sullen, and bereft for the moment of any other plan, the conjurer and the bird continued their journey.

It was nearing sunset when they finally arrived at the gates of Sterling Silver.

Questor Thews was at his wit's end. Three days had passed since Ben Holiday had disappeared and there was still no sign of him. The escort that had accompanied the High Lord to the Heart had ridden directly back to the castle after losing him, and Questor had been able to dispatch a search party immediately. Those sent had scoured the area surrounding the Heart and then the whole of the countryside beyond.

There wasn't a trace of the High Lord. Jurisdiction was found grazing where Holiday had apparently left him and that was it. There was evidence of a disturbance at the Heart—some frayed banners, some scorched seats and rests, a little dirt kicked up—but nothing that you could put a name to and nothing that could help explain what had happened to Holiday. Questor had gone out himself to take a look. He could feel the presence of used magic in the air, but there was so much magic concentrated there anyway that it was impossible to decipher what these odd traces meant.

In any case, Ben Holiday was nowhere to be found. Questor Thews had moved quickly to keep that fact a secret, ordering the guards of the escort and the search party not to speak of the matter to anyone. That was like sticking your finger in a leaking dike, however, as Abernathy was quick to point out. News of this sort could not be kept secret for long. Someone was bound to talk, and once word got out that the High Lord was really and truly gone, there would be trouble for sure. If the River Master didn't start it, the Lords of the Greensward surely would—especially Kallendbor of Rhyndweir, the most powerful of the Lords and an implacable enemy of Ben Holiday's. Kallendbor, more than any of Landover's nobles and leaders, had resented the loss of power that Holiday's coronation had cost him. On the surface, he acknowledged Holiday's sovereignty and obeyed his commands. Inside, he simmered like something kept cooking too long. There were others as well who would welcome news of Ben Holiday's removal, whatever the circumstances, and Questor knew he had to do something to put the rumors to rest at once.

He came up with a rather ingenious plan, one he shared only with Abernathy and the kobolds, keeping the number who knew the truth to a manageable four. What he did was to have Abernathy call off the search and announce that the High Lord had returned safely. To convince those quartered at the castle that the announcement was valid and not a further

rumor, he used magic to create an image of Ben Holiday passing along the castle ramparts at midday where he could be
clearly seen by those below. He even had him wave. He repeated his creation several times, making sure that there were
plenty of witnesses. Sure enough, the word got passed along
gossip-quick.

In the meantime, Questor used every spare minute available (which wasn't nearly enough) employing the quick travel
magic of the Landsview to scour the countryside in search of
Holiday. His efforts yielded nothing. There was no sign of the
High Lord.

Of course, life at Sterling Silver went on, Holiday or no,
and it was important that what needed to be done got done,
and that it got done as if Holiday were doing it. This was a
whole lot tougher to accomplish than the conjuring up of an
image or two. Since Holiday wasn't there to see any of a large
number of representatives and officials who had come from
every quarter of Landover, Questor Thews and Abernathy
were forced to see them for him and to pretend that they had
been requested to do so. Some of those visiting had traveled
great distances to see the High Lord. Some had been summoned. None among them was much pleased at being put off.
Questor resorted to increasingly desperate efforts to quell any
suspicions. He forged the High Lord's name on orders. He
passed out gifts. He issued awards and citations of merit. He
even tried using his magic to throw the High Lord's voice
from behind a curtain. This effort produced a woman's voice
and caused those listening to stare at each other incredu-
lously—who was this woman back there with the High
Lord?—and Questor was forced to salvage the situation by
claiming it was a serving girl who had mistaken Holiday for an
intruder. Some of his magic still needed work.

There was also the matter of Willow's absence, which the
High Lord had failed to explain before disappearing himself,
so that now not just one person was missing, but two. But

since Holiday hadn't seemed unduly concerned about Willow going off, Questor decided he needn't worry either, at least not just now. Really, the only reason for finding her—since he had no particular reason to worry if she was safe—was to tell her about the High Lord's disappearance. Questor decided he didn't need that additional complication in his life. If Holiday hadn't been found by the time the sylph returned, Questor would break the news to her then. There was, after all, only so much he could do.

Which, at the moment, wasn't nearly enough. Trying to split his time between the requirements of his duties and the demands of his machinations was beginning to take its toll. He was hardly in the mood then to hear the news that Abernathy carried on appearing at the door to his work chamber just before sunset of that third day.

"Horris Kew and his bird are back," the Court Scribe announced with something less than enthusiasm.

Questor looked up from the stack of paperwork visited on him in the High Lord's absence and groaned. "Again? What does that wastrel want now?"

Abernathy stepped into the room and closed the door behind him. Even for a dog, he looked put upon. "He wishes to speak with the High Lord—what else? Isn't that everyone's reason for being alive these days? And do not bother telling me to send him away. Although I would love to do so, I cannot. He is cloaked in supplicant's robes; I have to admit him."

Questor pressed his fingers to his forehead, massaging the temples. "Did he say what he wants, by any chance?"

"He said it was important, nothing more. He did not mention his exile, if that is what you are asking."

"To tell you the truth, I don't know what I'm asking! I barely know what I'm doing!" The wizard looked as if he were trying to tear at his beard. "You know, Abernathy, I am very fond of the High Lord. Very. I recruited him myself, if you recall. I saw something special in him, and I was not mistaken. He was the King we had all been looking for, the King Landover needed to become whole again."

He came to his feet. "But, really, I wish he would stop disappearing so often! How many times has he done this now? I don't know how he can be so inconsiderate of us. Going off in the middle of the night, just riding out without a word, leaving us to try to cover for him until he comes back. I must tell you, I find it exceedingly aggravating!"

Abernathy looked away and cleared his throat. "Well, in all fairness, Questor Thews, some of those disappearances were not the High Lord's fault. I am quite certain he would have preferred that they had never happened."

"Yes, yes, I know. My brother and all. The black unicorn." Questor brushed the explanation aside. "Still, a King has responsibilities, and they should not be taken lightly. A King should consult with his advisors on these things. That's what advisors are . . ."

He stopped abruptly. "You don't think he's been kidnapped, do you? Wouldn't there have been a ransom demand by now? Unless Nightshade has him. She wouldn't bother with a ransom demand. She would simply eliminate him! But why wouldn't the Paladin protect him against her? Why wouldn't the Paladin come to his rescue—"

"Questor Thews." Abernathy tried to interrupt.

"—whatever sort of danger he was in? What sort of protector leaves his master—"

"Wizard!" the dog snapped irritably.

Questor jumped. "What? What is it?"

"Stop carrying on so, for goodness' sake! What is the point of it? We have no idea what has become of the High Lord, but it certainly does not help him if we lose our heads. We have to remain calm. We have to carry on as if he were still here and in the meantime hope he shows up." Abernathy took a deep breath. "Have you found anything in the Landsview?"

Questor, duly chastened, shook his head. "No, nothing."

"Perhaps you should send Bunion to look about. A kobold can cover more ground than any twenty search parties
and make no disturbance doing it. Bunion can track anyone.
Perhaps you should let him try to track Holiday."

"Yes." Questor nodded thoughtfully. "Yes, perhaps so."

"In the meantime," Abernathy continued, resisting the
urge to scratch at something low down on his body with his
hind leg, "what about Horris Kew?"

Questor pressed at his temples again, as if reminded of a
headache he had momentarily forgotten. "Oh, dear. Him.
Well, he can't see the High Lord, of course. Confound it, why
does he have to see anyone?"

"He doesn't," Abernathy answered, "but if I read the
depth of his determination correctly, he will keep trying until
he does. I do not think he will simply go away."

Questor sighed. "No, I don't suppose he will." He paused
thoughtfully. "Abernathy, do you think I look anything like
that man?"

Abernathy stared. "What an odd question."

"Well, it bothers me that I might. I mean, we are both in
the conjuring business, aren't we? And sometimes they say that
all conjurers look alike. You've heard that, haven't you? Besides, we're both rather tall and slight of build and at times
awkward, and we both have rather prominent noses and . . .
well, sharp features . . ."

Abernathy held up one paw deliberately. "You look as
much like Horris Kew as I look like his bird. Please, no more
of this. Just decide if we see them tonight or not. I suggest we
do not put it off."

Questor nodded. "No, I agree. Let's get it over with."

They went out of the room, down the hall, and descended two flights of stairs to where visitors were kept waiting until they could be received. They made a strange pair, the
white-haired, gangly wizard with his colorful patched robes

and the dog with his shaggy coat and fastidious dress. Questor grumbled the whole way, griping about this, bemoaning that, keeping such an edge on things that at last Abernathy was forced to ask him in rather rude fashion to be quiet. Two old friends whose shared history made them inseparable in spite of themselves, they could track each other's life steps as if the paths were already laid out before them.

"You know, Abernathy," the wizard confided, as they reached the ground floor of the castle and prepared to turn into the front hall. "If I didn't know better, I'd think Horris Kew had something to do with Holiday's disappearance. It's just the sort of thing he would precipitate with his unbalanced magic, conjuring up trouble here and there, all willy-nilly. But he doesn't have that kind of power!" He thought it over. "He doesn't have enough brains either."

Abernathy sniffed. "It doesn't take brains to be danger-ous."

They walked down the front hall to the anteroom where Horris Kew and his bird would be waiting and stepped inside.

Horris rose from the bench on which he had been sit-ting. The bird was perched on the back of the bench, sharp-eyed and sleek. Next to them on the floor rested two iron-bound wooden trunks.

"Questor Thews and Abernathy!" Horris Kew exclaimed with what seemed excessive delight. "Good evening to you! Thank you for coming to see me so quickly. I am deeply ap-preciative."

"Horris, let's skip past the pleasantries, shall we? What are you doing back here? As I recall, you were told to come back when the High Lord sent for you. Has he done so without my knowledge?"

The conjurer smiled sheepishly. "No, regrettably, he has not. I continue to live in hope and expectation." He bright-ened. "That is not why I have come, Questor. I am here for another reason entirely. I have some very exciting news to share." He paused and glanced past them hopefully. "I don't suppose that the High Lord is about?"

Questor grimaced. "Not at the moment. What is this news you bring, Horris? Nothing dealing with farm animals, I trust."

"No, no," the other answered quickly. "I remember my promise and I will not break it. No conjuring. No, this is something else entirely." Again he paused. "May I confide it to you, to the two of you, as Court Wizard and Scribe, since the High Lord is otherwise occupied?"

Questor said something in response, but Abernathy was looking at the bird. Was he losing his mind or had he heard the bird snicker? He glared at the myna, but the myna simply ruffled its feathers indifferently and looked away.

"Well, then," Horris Kew declared, and cleared his throat officiously. "There are times, more than a few I might add, when stress from work and the burden of our obligations wears us down and we find we need some sort of amusement or diversion to relax us. I am sure you will agree that this is true. I speak now not just of the high-born, but of the common man, the workers in the fields and factories, in the markets and shops of our farms and cities. I speak of every man and woman, of every boy and girl all struggling to make their lives a better and more productive—"

"Get to the point, Horris," Questor interrupted wearily. "It has been a long day."

Horris paused, smiled, and shrugged. "Indeed. A diversion, then. A way of removing stress from our lives for a few hours. I believe I have found something that will provide that relief."

"Very commendable," Abernathy snapped. "But someone already made that discovery quite a long time ago. They are called games. Sometimes they are played in groups, sometimes by a single individual. There are all forms of them. Have you discovered a new game? Is that what you are here about?"

Horris Kew laughed politely, though he seemed to be doing so through clenched teeth. "Oh, no, this is not about games. This is something else entirely." He paused, then leaned forward conspiratorially. "A mind's eye crystal!" he whispered hoarsely.

"A what?" Questor Thews demanded, his brow furrowing.

"A mind's eye crystal," the other repeated carefully. "Do you know of it?"

Questor did not, but he did not want to admit to being ignorant of anything to Horris Kew. "A little something, perhaps." He pursed his lips. "But tell me about it anyway."

"A crystal," Horris said, holding up a single finger. "A crystal that you look into as you would a mirror. And when you do, it shows you images of the past and of the future, images of yourself and those you love. The images are pleasant and welcome, and they take you away from your troubles for a time. The perfect diversion from your cares." He rubbed his hands. "Here, let me show you."

He reached into his supplicant's robes and pulled forth a crystal to hold up before them. It was about the width and length of an average thumb, five-sided, pointed at one end, flat at the other, and clear enough to see through.

"Would you like to try it?" he asked Questor Thews, and held out the crystal for the wizard to take.

"Wait a minute." Abernathy was between them instantly. "This thing is magic, is it?"

Horris nodded calmly. "It is."

"I thought you said you would give up conjuring unless asked. You swore to the High Lord that you would give it up, in fact. What happened to your vow, Horris? Where did this crystal come from if you did not conjure it up?"

Horris Kew held up his hands in a placating manner. "I have not broken my vow, Abernathy. This"—he held forth the crystal a second time—"was shown to me in a dream. I was asleep in the deep woods . . . uh," he hesitated, "north. I was asleep, having fasted and contemplated the misdealings and mistakes of my life all day after returning from my visit here, and I dreamed. In my dream I was shown this mind's eye crystal. It was a vision of great power. It told me of the crystal and where it might be found. It told me to seek it out. When I woke, I was compelled to do so. I did and I found it as promised. Knowing that I have not as yet had my exile lifted, I felt compelled to bring it to you." He paused, looking down at his feet. "I admit I hoped that it might in some small way influence you to take me back."

Abernathy was not impressed. He stood his ground, dog face fixed and dog eyes searching. There was a lie in here somewhere, he was sure of it. "You have never, in your entire life, employed a magic that did not end badly for anyone who came into contact with it. I cannot believe that this mind's eye crystal will be any different."

"But I am not the same man!" Horris Kew protested with a dramatic gesture. "I have changed, Abernathy. I have repented my former life and resolved to follow a different path. This crystal is my first step down that path." He drew himself up. "Tell you what. Why don't you try it out first, instead of Questor Thews? That way if there is a problem, Questor can use his formidable magic to do with me as he will. Surely you agree he is more than a match for me in case this is some sort of trick. And anyway, why would I chance anything so foolish this close to the dungeons into which you have already indicated you would like to see me thrown?"

He had a point. Abernathy hesitated. "I would not put anything past you, Horris," he muttered.

"Hooray for Horris, hooray for Horris!" the bird cawed suddenly, and clacked its beak.

Abernathy glared at the bird. "What do you think, Questor Thews?" he asked, and glanced back at the other.

The wizard's mouth was a tight line. "There are guards all

about. If this goes awry, Horris goes into the keep and stays there. I stand ready if there is magic to be combated." He shook his head. "It's up to you, Abernathy."

"You will not be sorry," Horris offered, advancing the crystal another few inches toward the scribe. "I promise."

Abernathy sighed. "Very well. Anything to put this matter to bed. What do I do?"

Horris was beaming. "Just take the crystal, hold it in your hand, look into it, and think happy thoughts."

Abernathy grimaced. "Good grief. All right, give it to me."

He reached out, took the crystal from the other's hands, held it up before him, and stared into it. Nothing happened. Sure enough, Abernathy thought disdainfully. No surprise here. He was supposed to think happy thoughts, though, so he tried to picture something that would make him feel good and came up with an image of Horris and his bird in a dungeon cell. That made him feel better right away, he decided, and started to smile in spite of himself.

In the next instant the crystal brightened and locked him into it, drawing his gaze into its multi-faceted depths, pulling him out of himself and down into its suddenly brilliant light. He gasped. What was he seeing? There was something there, something wondrous, something familiar . . .

Abernathy saw it clearly then. There was a man in the light, striding out to greet the day from his home, waving hello to friends, calling out to passersby. The man was carrying books in his arms and was on his way to his day's work. He wore glasses and was dressed in the ceremonial clothing of a Court Scribe.

No!

The man was Abernathy as he used to be. Abernathy as a human being. Abernathy before he had been turned into a dog. Himself, once more.

Sudden joy surged through the dog as he watched, a happiness he had not felt for years. He was himself again in the crystal's image! He was restored! It was his greatest wish in life, to become the man he had been—a wish he had not dared even contemplate upon discovering that Questor Thews, having turned him into a dog, could not turn him back into a man. Countless attempts to remedy the situation had failed, and Abernathy had given up all hope. But now, here, in this crystal's image, was a chance to feel again what it was like to be a man! He could sense the other's body—as if it were his own. He could experience anew what it was to be human.

The emotions the magic generated were too powerful to bear all at once. He closed his hand quickly about the crystal and snatched the vision away. He could barely breathe. "How did you do that?" he whispered in disbelief.

"I did nothing," Horris Kew responded promptly. "And we could not see what you saw. Only the holder of the crystal sees the vision. It is his own, personal revelation, private and inviolate. Do you understand now the uses for such a magic?"

Abernathy nodded, thinking of how wonderful it would be to call up that image of himself anytime he wanted to remember what his life had once been like. "Yes, I do," he replied softly.

Now it was Questor who pushed forward. "This thing works?" he asked, turning his old friend about, seeing the look in his eyes. "Well, indeed, I guess it does. Are you all right?"

Abernathy nodded, unable to speak, thinking again of what the image had shown him, of himself restored to who and what he had been. He was fighting hard to stay calm, to keep what he was feeling inside.

Neither saw the brief glance exchanged by Horris Kew and Biggar. *Well, well,* the glance said.

"You can appreciate the enormous potential for this magic," Horris said quickly. "Escape from the drudgery and stress of everyday life is only a moment away if you possess a mind's eye crystal. No group participation required, no equipment needed, no time necessary. Use the crystal on a break from your work and return refreshed!" He smiled benevolently. "Don't you feel happy and rested, Abernathy?" he pressed.

Abernathy swallowed. "Yes," he agreed. "I do."

"There you are, then!" Horris beamed. "Abernathy, this crystal is yours. I want you to have it. A gift, for giving me a chance to fulfill my hopes."

"Thank you, Horris," Abernathy replied, genuinely pleased, already envisioning his next look into the light. All suspicions of the conjurer's motives were forgotten. "Thank you very much."

"You see," Horris continued, anticipating Questor Thews, who was about to offer a further objection, "I have a few more of these to give out. Quite a few more, in fact."

He turned to one of the iron-bound trunks, released the catch, and threw open the lid. The trunk was filled to the brim with mind's eye crystals.

"Thousands of them," he offered, making a sweeping gesture. "The vision showed me one, but when I followed the pathway to where it was hidden, I discovered all these. Two trunkfuls, Questor. I have brought them both. I want you to have them. A little penance, perhaps, for my past misdeeds. I cannot comprehend why I was chosen to find them, but I am grateful that I was and I have decided to accept responsibility for their proper use. So I entrust them now to you. My gift to Landover. Pass them out to her people and let them enjoy the images they find therein. A little happiness to dull the edges of their more stressful moments."

Questor Thews and Abernathy stared at the trunkful of crystals, openmouthed. "Perhaps with the crystals to occupy people's time there will be less violence," Horris Kew went on thoughtfully, looking off somewhere into the room's rafters as if seeking a higher truth. "Perhaps there will be fewer wars and killings over meaningless things when there are so many more pleasant and harmless ways to gain diversion. Perhaps there will be less time spent fomenting rumors that lead to mischief." He gave the wizard and the dog a surreptitious glance. As he said that, he did not miss the look that passed between them. "Fewer loose tongues wagging on about whether Landover's matters are being handled as they should and whether her leaders are leading as they ought to."

"Hmmm." Questor rubbed his beard thoughtfully. "Yes, perhaps. This really works?" he asked again, looking Abernathy directly in the eye, taking hold of the hand that held the crystal.

Abernathy moved the crystal away, tightening his grip on it.

"Of course, I have one for you, too, Questor," Horris Kew advised quickly. He reached back and closed the lid to the trunk. "These are all yours now." He yawned widely. "Well, enough talk. You should both be in bed, resting for tomorrow's challenges. I have tired you out with all this, I am sure. If you could spare a pallet, I would be most grateful. In the morning I will be off again, waiting to hear . . ."

He stopped. "Unless," he went on, as if he had just thought of it, "unless you would consider letting me help in some small way with the distribution of the crystals?"

He smiled at them hopefully and waited for an answer.

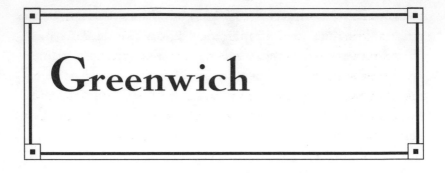

Greenwich

For two days Willow traveled due west through the lake country with Edgewood Dirk, heading for the fairy mists and the invisible path that would take them out of Landover and into Ben's world. Dirk led the way, mostly without seeming to do so, content to keep pace or even follow, moving to the fore only when her path varied from the one he had chosen. He proceeded in leisurely fashion, dictating the pace by his refusal to be hurried, behaving as if time were inconsequential and their journey no more than a stroll through the park on a sunny afternoon.

Willow had encountered Edgewood Dirk only once before, and almost everything she knew about him she had learned from Ben. Dirk had been Ben's constant companion during the search for the black unicorn after Meeks, older brother of Questor Thews and the former Court Wizard of Landover, had tricked Ben into believing he had lost the medallion that gave him the power and authority to be King. Bereft of his identity, spurned by his friends as an impostor, and replaced on the throne by Meeks, Ben had been turned out into the wilderness and left to die. But the fairies, for reasons known only to them, had sent Edgewood Dirk to help him discover the truth about what had been done. Dirk had accompanied him in his wanderings, offering enigmatic cat advice and a sort of vaguely defined direction for the once-King to follow. Ben was tracking Willow, who in turn was tracking the black unicorn, and matters had climaxed in a violent confrontation between Dirk and Meeks that had proved the catalyst to Ben's recovery.

That had been almost two years ago. No one had seen or heard from Edgewood Dirk since. But now, here he was suddenly, and again he had been sent by the fairies, and again no one but the fairies really knew why.

Edgewood Dirk was a fairy being himself, though one of the more independent ones, as much cat as anything, and therefore likely to do exactly as he pleased despite anyone else's wishes, which made it very hard to determine his purpose in events. He had proved that beyond anyone's doubt during his time with Ben. Dirk was a prism cat, a creature possessed of a very rare sort of magic. He could transform himself from flesh and blood to a crystalline as hard as iron that allowed him to capture light and transform it into a deadly fire. Dirk used this power sparingly, but with great confidence. However distant and aloof Dirk appeared, however removed from what was happening around him, he was no one to fool around with.

So Willow accompanied him with some sense of assurance that if trouble threatened, Dirk was probably its equal. She would have preferred to have Ben with her, but that option had already been eliminated by the Earth Mother. Sometimes you took what you could get. Willow was experiencing enough uncertainty about her quest that she was grateful for any sort of company.

Dirk, of course, seemed indifferent to the entire matter.

"Were you sent because of Ben?" she asked him their first night out. They sat together before a small fire that Dirk had insisted be built to ward off some imaginary chill. She had arranged the deadwood, and he had set it afire. The beginnings of a working partnership, she had thought.

Dirk was licking one paw diligently. "I wasn't sent. I am never sent. I go where I choose."

"Excuse me," she apologized. "Why did you choose to come, then?"

Lick, lick, lick. "I can't remember, really. It seemed like a good idea, I guess." Lick, lick.

"Can you tell me where we are going?"

"West," the cat said. Lick, lick.

"Yes, but . . ."

Dirk stopped preening and gave her his cat look, the one that suggested sly amusement, deep understanding, grave concern, and total amazement all at the same time. "Just one moment, please. You are losing me. Don't *you* know where we're going?"

She shook her head in confusion. "No, not really."

He stared at her thoughtfully. "Oh, dear," he said. "Oh, well. I guess we will just have to find our way as best we can." And he went back to licking himself.

A little while later she grew brave enough to ask him again, taking a slightly different approach.

"We should reach the fairy mists by the day after tomorrow," she advised cautiously. "Once there, what do we do?"

Dirk had finished his bath by now and was seated on a patch of grass close by the fire, paws tucked under himself, eyes closed.

The eyes opened to slits. "We pass through the mists into Holiday's world." The eyes closed.

"How do we do that?"

The eyes came open again, a bit wider. "What kind of question is that? I must say I will never understand humans."

"I am a sylph."

"Or sylphs."

Willow's lips tightened. "It is just that I am concerned for my baby. I am required to do these things to protect its birthing, but I do not know how I am to do them."

Dirk regarded her with genuine interest. "Cats learn early on that very little is accomplished by worrying. Cats also know that things have a way of working out, even when the means are kept hidden from us. Best to deal with things as they arise, and let the future take care of itself."

"That seems very shortsighted," she ventured.

Dirk might have shrugged; it was hard to tell. "I am a cat," he offered, as if that explained everything.

She didn't talk to him about the matter again that night or all the next day, and so by nightfall when they had crossed out of the lake country and passed up into the foothills that bordered the fairy mists, she was surprised when he brought it up again of his own accord.

"Tomorrow morning, I will take you through the mists," he advised as she worked on building the requisite evening fire. She had spread her cloak on the ground close by, and Dirk had taken a comfortable seat on it.

She looked over at him. "You can do that?" she asked.

"Of course I can do that," he replied, sounding a bit put-upon. "I live there, remember? I know all the paths and passageways."

"I suppose I just wasn't sure what you could or couldn't do." She rocked back on her heels. "I didn't know if fairy creatures could pass out of the mists anywhere or into any land. I thought it might be limited somehow."

Dirk yawned. "You thought wrong. Cats can go anywhere. Nothing new in that."

"Do you know where we will come out?" she pressed.

He thought it over a moment. "A city, I think. Does it matter?"

She felt her exasperation with him getting away from her. "Yes, it does. I am going back to a world in which I once almost died. I am doing so against my will and for the sake of my child. I want to go there, do what I was sent to do, and leave again immediately. What are the chances of that happening?"

Dirk rose, stretched, and sat. "I haven't the faintest idea." He regarded her solemnly. "It all depends on you, I suppose."

"Yes, but I don't know where we are going," she insisted. "I know I am supposed to gather soil from Ben's world, but I don't know where that soil is supposed to be found. It is a rather big world to be looking through, you know."

"Well, I don't know," the cat said. "I have never been there. But everywhere is pretty much the same to a cat. I am quite certain we will find what we need without having to look too hard. I have a gift for uncovering secrets."

She went back to building the fire, finished the job, stepped back, and looked over at him. "How many secrets do you know, Dirk?" she asked quietly. "Do you know secrets about me?"

The cat blinked. "Of course."

"And about Ben?"

"Holiday? Yes, a few."

"Can you tell them to me?"

"If I choose." Dirk began washing himself. "But cats are secretive by nature and tell little of what they know. It is because no one listens to us, mostly. I spoke of that often to Holiday when I traveled with him last. He was like everyone else. I would tell him things, but he wouldn't listen. I warned him that he was making a mistake, that cats know many things, but no one ever seems to pay attention. It was a mistake he should avoid, I cautioned."

"I will listen, if you will tell me something," Willow offered. "Tell me anything, Dirk. Any of your secrets. I know so little of what is happening, and I am hungry for even a small bit of knowledge. Can you tell me something?"

Dirk looked at her, then began to wash. He licked himself fluffy and then licked himself smooth, stopping every now and then to see if she was still paying attention. He took his time with the job, but Willow waited patiently, refusing to become perturbed. Finally Dirk was finished, and turned his emerald gaze upon her.

"You are going to have a child," he declared. "But matters will not work out as either you or Holiday expect them to. Expectations are dangerous things for parents to have, you know. Cats have none and are the better for it."

She nodded. "We can't help ourselves. Like not listening to cats."

"I suppose that is true," Dirk agreed. "A shame."

"Tell me something more."

Dirk narrowed his gaze. "Are you sure you want to hear what I have to say? I mean, that is part of the reason no one listens to cats."

She hesitated. "Yes, I want to hear."

"Very well." He considered. "You and Holiday will be lost to each other for a time. In fact, you are lost to each other already. Didn't you know?"

"The vision," she said softly. "My mother's vision."

Dirk looked off into the growing dark. "You spend so much time wondering who you are, don't you think? You flounder about, searching for your identity, when most of the time it is as plain as the nose on your face. You struggle with questions of purpose and need, and forget that the answers are found mostly inside yourselves." He paused anew. "Cats are not included in that analysis. Cats don't waste time wondering about such things. Cats just get on with the business of living."

"Is the vision true, then?" she asked, trying to mask the growing sense of desperation she felt that something terrible was happening to Ben, something beyond her control.

Dirk blinked. "What vision?"

"Is Ben in danger?" she pressed.

"How would I know?" Dirk growled, stretching once more. "Better step back from that deadwood."

She did so, and Dirk shimmered and turned to crystalline in the fading twilight, gone from flesh and blood to liquid glass, drew in the glow of sunset, two early moons, and a scattering of stars, and sent fire lancing from his emerald eyes into the wood. The blaze burned hotly, and the prism cat transformed back again, settled himself down anew on Willow's cloak, closed his eyes, and was instantly asleep.

Willow watched him for a time, then fell asleep as well.

She slept poorly, haunted by dreams of Ben and their child, of each being drawn away from her, stolen by invisible hands that wrapped about and pulled them from her side until nothing remained but the echo of her voice calling after them. There was an unspoken suggestion in her dream that somehow she was to blame for what had happened to them, that somehow she had failed them when they needed her most.

She had no appetite for breakfast, and since Dirk never showed any interest in food, they washed and were on their way up to the beginnings of the fairy mists shortly after sunrise.

The day dawned hot and still, the summer air a suffocating blanket that clung to the land even in the high country. Dew formed a slick upon the ground, and its dampness glimmered in the hazy first light. They climbed the rest of the way into the hills, found a narrows that led into a pass, and walked back toward the gray gloom of the mists.

They reached their destination in less than an hour and started in. No words passed between them as they did. Dirk had taken the lead now, no longer content to leave matters to chance. He walked directly in front of the sylph, picking his way carefully over ruts, around stones, and across bare ground where lack of sunlight prevented any grasses from growing. They moved into the haze, following the trail until there ceased to be a trail and all the light from the rising sun had disappeared behind them and there was nothing but mist, swirling about them with relentless purpose, twisting first this way and then that, drawing the eyes to one side and then to the other, obscuring any sense of direction, any chance of keeping track of where they were going or from where they had come. Willow ignored the distracting movement, focusing her attention on Dirk, who sauntered along with his usual indifference, seeming to find his way as much by chance as by plan. He glanced neither left nor right and did not turn to see if she was following. He sniffed the air now and again, but otherwise showed no interest in their surroundings.

The minutes slipped away, but it was not clear to Willow how many of them passed. Time and place lost meaning, and everything took on a disturbing sameness. There was silence at first, deep and numbing, and then a series of small sounds, like the scuffling of forest animals in scrub or birds among leaves. After a time, the noises took on definition and began to suggest the presence of something else. Faces began to appear, just at the corners of her vision, just where they could be glimpsed but nothing more. The faces were sharp-featured and lean, with pointed ears and brows, and hair like trailing moss and spiky straw. Eyes as penetrating as an owl's watched her pass. The fairy folk had come out to see her, to consider her, and perhaps to let her pass. She did not look at them, keeping her eyes fixed on the movement of her feet and on Edgewood Dirk. She did not look at them because she was frightened that if she did, she would be instantly lost.

Something brushed at her cheek, and tears filled her eyes. Something rubbed against her hand, and she felt a sudden heat rush through her. Her skin crawled and her mouth went dry. *Don't look,* she told herself. *Don't turn to see what it is.* She pressed on, following diligently after Dirk, thinking of the baby inside her, thinking of Ben waiting somewhere behind, hardening herself against her fear . . .

Until finally the mists began to drop away, and she could see something solid ahead through the haze. A shadowed darkness cloaked a wall of mortared stone, and rain drizzled down out of leaden skies. There were strange mechanical sounds and muffled shouts, and the wall rose high overhead and was lost in gloom. The mists receded behind her, and she found herself standing in the rain in an alleyway that ran like a deep crevice between two towering buildings. Clouds masked the skies and scraped against the tops of the buildings. Shadows cascaded down off the walls to pool underfoot. Smells rose up from the cracked stone surface on which they stood, pungent and rank.

"Where are we?" she whispered in horror.

Something moved to one side. It was a man in ragged clothing, sprawled in the lee of a doorway, curled up and sleeping. He was wrapped in pieces of cardboard to shield himself from the weather. An empty bottle was clutched in one hand.

Dirk sniffed in the direction of the man and turned away. He looked up and down the alley. One end went nowhere. The other led to a noisy street. Turning toward the latter, he stepped daintily over pieces of garbage strewn from an over-turned container, flinching with displeasure at what he felt, and started in the direction of the noise. Willow followed.

They walked toward the end of the alley, watching the street beyond come into focus through the rain, seeing move-ment begin, hearing the sounds grow louder. There were cars and buses streaming past, moving in fits and starts, horns blar-ing, brakes squealing. Willow knew about these things from her last visit. She had no idea what Dirk knew. What she re-membered was not pleasant. She was already cringing from the impact of the sounds and smells. With the dirt and grit it gath-ered, the rain smeared on the stone beneath her boots and pooled in gutters and low spots amid the garbage. Broken glass glinted everywhere.

They reached the end of the alley and looked out onto the street. The cars and buses were locked close together in the gloom and drizzle, crawling in one direction toward an-other line of vehicles traveling crosswise. Red and green lights blinked down from lines overhead. Yellow lights shone from street lamps and through the windows of buildings with peeling paint and cracked mortar.

And there were people everywhere, most in long coats, some in boots. They walked with their heads bent and carried strange implements—Willow didn't know the proper name—to shield them from the rain. They shuffled along with a sense of urgency and resignation that was palpable. A few glanced in her direction, but looked quickly away again. They climbed in and out of the buses and cars, and they moved in and out of doorways. A few spoke, but most of what they said was shouted in anger at one another.

Dirk sniffed the air and looked about, seemingly unfazed. Then he moved out from the alley and started left down the walkway. Willow followed. A crush of people caught them up and swept them along. Willow pulled her cloak tightly about her shoulders, hating the closeness of the people and the smell they gave off. She thought of Ben living in such a world and found she could not imagine it.

They reached a corner and stopped because everyone else was stopped as well. A few bold looks were directed at her, but she ignored them. She stared about at the buildings, some of them monstrous stone and glass monoliths that soared into the clouds, featureless and impregnable looking. Did people live in those? she wondered. What purpose did they serve?

To her surprise she found she could understand what the people about her were saying. She should not have been able to do that unless they were speaking in the languages of Landover, but she could. She looked up at a sign on the street corner beside her. She could read it. It said Greenwich Avenue.

Above her the light changed, and people began to cross the street. She followed with Dirk.

On the other side, about a block away, a woman with a ring through her nose tried to kick Dirk when he walked in front of her. The kick should have connected, but somehow it missed and struck an iron railing in front of a low window and caused the woman to lose her balance and fall down. The woman shrieked in fury and swore violently at Dirk, but the cat went past the woman without a glance. Willow did the same.

"Hey, lady, spare some change?" a sallow-faced man with long hair and a beard asked. She shook her head and walked on. "It's a little late for St. Patrick's, isn't it?" he called after her, and laughed.

She bent down to Dirk. "Do we understand their language?" she asked curiously.

"We do," Dirk replied. "A little fairy magic lets us do that."

They walked for some time through the crowds. The rains diminished and the skies cleared. The cars and buses began to pick up speed. It grew more dangerous at the crossings. The crowds thinned somewhat, changing character as they moved down the street. The men and women in tailored clothing gave way to a more casual and eclectic group. There were people in leather and chains and metal-tipped boots who slouched along with exaggerated movements or leaned against building walls; people in long, peach-colored robes with shaved heads and earnest looks passing out papers; ragged people with dogs and cats and babies carrying small handmade signs that said things like PLEASE HELP and NO FOOD; people with shopping bags and handbags clutched tightly against their chests as they walked; people of all sorts, all possessed of the same uneasy, guarded look, all with eyes that shifted and searched, all with a posture that either challenged or bordered on flight.

Comments were directed openly at Willow from those they passed, some brazen and insulting, some joking and curious. A few people tried to stop her, but she simply moved past them, following Dirk along the walk.

They reached a particularly busy cross street and Dirk

stopped. A street sign read Avenue of the Americas. Dirk glanced at Willow as if to say, *See there?* Willow did not see. She did not understand where they were or why. She mostly wanted to get to wherever it was they were going and then get out. Everything about this place was unpleasant and un-welcoming. She wanted to ask Dirk if he had any idea at all where he was going, but she did not think he wanted her to speak to him with all these people about. Besides, he must have some idea; he was certainly moving down the street as if he did.

"Are you lost?" a young woman standing next to her asked. The woman was dark-skinned. She was holding a small child in her arms.

"No," Willow said without thinking, but realized as she did that she could speak the language of Ben's world as well as read and understand it. Dirk must be at work with his fairy magic.

"Are you sure? You look confused." She smiled. "You can get lost in this city pretty easy."

"Thank you, I'm fine," Willow said.

The light changed, and the woman walked away. Dirk and Willow crossed to a new street that read West 8th. There were people everywhere. Storefronts opened onto the walk-way, small markets of fruit and vegetables, craft shops with jewelry and bright clothing, doorways leading to food and drink and wares of all sorts. Stands were set up along the street with books and more jewelry. Vendors called to her. Want to buy this, take a look at that? They smiled, some of them, and she smiled back, shaking her head no.

"What a great look!" someone said, and she turned. A young man with a long dark coat, boots, a light beard, and a leather folder stood looking at her. "You aren't an actress, are you?"

"No." She shook her head. Dirk was still moving down the street. "I have to go."

"Wait!" He began walking with her. "Uh, look, I thought that . . . well, because you're colored green, I thought that . . . that because you were dressed up, you might be an actress or something. Like in *Cats*. Sorry, I didn't mean to be rude."

She smiled. "You weren't."

"My name is Tony. Tony Paolo. I live a few blocks away. I'm studying to be an actor. I'm in my second year at American Academy. You been there? Dustin Hoffman went there. Danny DeVito. Lots of people. I just finished a reading for a part on Broadway. A comedy, Neil Simon. This is my portfolio, you know, my pictures and stuff." He indicated the folder. "It's just a small part, just a few lines. But it's a start."

She nodded and kept walking. She didn't have any idea at all what he was talking about.

"Look, can I buy you a cup of coffee or something? If you have some time?"

Ahead of her, Dirk had turned around and come back. Now he moved between her legs and looked up at Tony. "That your cat?" Tony asked. "Hey, kitty, kitty."

"Keep your hands to yourself," Dirk snapped as Tony started to reach down to pet him.

Tony straightened instantly. He stared at Willow. "Hey, that's pretty good! How did you do that?" He grinned. "That's the best I've ever heard that done. Do some more."

"We could use something to eat," Dirk said.

"Man, I couldn't even see your lips move!" Tony declared in amazement. "That's some talent! A bite to eat, huh? Okay, why not? There's a little coffeehouse just around the corner. You know the Village? You from around here?"

He led the way through the crowds to a small shop with round tables covered with checkered oilcloth and straight-backed iron chairs with matching checkered cushions. Tony waved to someone working behind the counter and took a table near the entry. Willow and Dirk both sat down with him.

"So what do you want?" Tony asked. He had lank brown hair, dark eyes, and a quick, unassuming smile.

"You decide," Dirk said.

Tony did, ordering food for himself and Willow and a saucer of milk for Dirk. When the food arrived, Willow found herself hungrier than she thought, and she ate everything without bothering to decide whether she liked it. Tony ate with her, talking about how good she was at throwing her voice and about his life as an actor-in-training. Dirk sat in front of the milk and ignored it.

"You know, I forgot to ask your name," Tony said in midbite.

"Willow," she answered.

"Really? What a great name. So, are you a ventriloquist all the time or do you have a job doing something else?"

She hesitated. What was she supposed to say?

"That's okay, you don't have to tell me. But you're not an actress, I guess, right?"

"No, not an actress."

When they were finished, Tony asked her again, "Do you live around here somewhere?"

She glanced at Dirk, who was staring out the door, ready to be off. "No, just visiting."

"From where?"

"Landover." She said it before she could catch herself.

"Sure, Maryland, right? I know Landover. Who are you staying with here? Do you have friends or something?"

She shook her head. "I have to go now, Tony. Thank you for the meal. I hope you become a good actor."

She stood up and started for the door. Dirk was already outside on the walkway. "Hey, wait!" Tony called, throwing some money on the table and charging after her. He caught up with her outside. "Can I see you again, maybe?"

She shook her head and walked on, wondering how to get out of this. Tony walked with her. "I know this is kind of sudden, but . . . well, I really would like to take you to dinner or a play or something. Even if I have to come down to Landover . . ."

"She's married," Dirk announced. "Happily."

Tony stopped in his tracks. "Oh. Sorry, I didn't realize . . ."

They crossed the street in a clutch of traffic and left him groping for something else to say. He carefully watched their progress.

Nightfall set in shortly after, a sudden darkening of the skies as the sun set and the clouds returned, a fading of the light that brought up the city's lamps. Willow and Dirk were seated on a bench in a park with a large marble arch. It was called Washington Square. It had been filled with people until just a few minutes ago, people with newspapers and babies, people with dogs and toys, but now with the sun gone and with the day ending it was emptying out. There were only a few old men left sitting on other benches and a handful of young boys huddled under a tree at the far end. A ragged man with a dog was holding out a metal cup by the street corner.

Only a few hours had passed since Dirk and Willow had arrived from Landover where it had been early morning, and that meant time did not pass at the same speed in the two worlds. How did that effect aging when you crossed from one world into the other? Willow wondered. Was she aging differently than Ben? She stared out into the gloom, watching the city lights beyond the park brighten. Dirk was hunched down beside her with his paws tucked underneath his body and his eyes closed. He had told her when they were alone that they must wait for night when the park was clear so that they would not be disturbed. It appeared that it was here that she was supposed to gather the soil she needed, but Dirk hadn't volunteered anything specific. Dirk rarely did.

The darkness deepened and the hours passed, and still

they sat on the bench and waited. Willow was patient, and the wait did not disturb her. She understood now why Dirk had wanted her to have something to eat. She might have gone this long without food, but her child needed nourishment even if she did not. The cat understood this. She glanced down at him and wondered how much of his indifference was pretense.

Soon they were alone except for the odd passerby. Midnight came and went, and the city showed no sign of shutting down for the night. The wares shops had closed, but the places where food and drink were served remained open. There were still people on the streets, crowds of them, passing this way and that, calling out, laughing and shouting, on their way to or from somewhere. No one seemed interested in sleeping. No one seemed anxious to go home.

Willow watched the people and the lights in the distance, trying to imagine what it must be like to live here. Stone and mortar and glass everywhere you looked, the buildings long lines of soldiers set at march, the roadways flat and endless, the visible earth reduced to small squares of worn green like this park—it was nightmarish. Nothing was real; everything was manufactured. The smell, taste, look, and feel of it assailed her at every turn and threatened to swallow her up like a tiny bit of light in a massive dark.

Someone left the sidewalk across the way and approached—a familiar figure with long coat, boots, lank hair, and a ready smile. Willow stiffened.

"Still here, I see," Tony declared as he came up and stopped in front of her. "Tell me the truth, Willow. Do you have a place to sleep? I've been following you, and you don't seem to be going anywhere."

She fixed him with her emerald eyes. "Go home, Tony."

"You don't, do you?" he pressed. "I've come by a couple times now to see if you were still here, and sure enough, you were. You wouldn't be out in the park this late if you had somewhere to go. Look, I'm worried about you. Would you like a place to crash?"

She stared. "What?"

"To sleep, for the night." He held out his palms. "This isn't some sort of come-on, I promise."

"Come-on?"

"You told me you were married, right? So where's your ring? I think you made all that up, but that's okay. I just want you to know I'm not after your bod or anything. I like you, that's all. I don't want anything to happen to you. This is a dangerous city."

Dirk rose, stretched, and yawned. Without a word, he climbed down off the bench and began walking across the park. Willow glanced quickly at Tony, then got up and followed. Dirk crossed the park north to south, ambling contentedly, sniffing at this and that, seeming in no hurry, appearing to have no purpose in mind.

"It can be dangerous out here," Tony repeated, walking next to her, looking over. "Especially at night. You don't know."

She shook her head. "I'll be fine."

"I can't just leave you out here like this," he declared. "Look, I'll keep you company, okay? And don't tell me to go home. I won't do it."

Dirk had moved to a spot at the far end of the park beneath an old shade tree tucked within a gathering of small vine maples where the earth was worn and so wrapped in shadows that almost no grass was growing. It was here that a mother had read on a blanket with her baby beside her until it was almost dark. Dirk sniffed about a bit, then sat back on his haunches and waited for Willow to come up.

"Here," was all he said.

Willow nodded. She knelt and touched the earth, then drew her hand back quickly, her fairy senses pricked by what she found.

"Much has happened in this place," Edgewood Dirk said quietly. "Great ideas have been conceived and terrible plans laid out. Hopes and aspirations have been shared. Killings and maimings have been perpetrated on innocent and guilty alike. A baby was born here once. Animals have hidden here. Whispered promises have been given and love consummated." He looked at her. "The soil is rich with memories. It is the wellspring and the epiphany of many lives."

Tony crowded close. "What are you talking about? Was that the cat who said all that? Well, of course it wasn't the cat—I mean, how could it be, right? But it sure sounded like it was. What's going on?"

Willow ignored him and began to dig. She used the hunting knife she carried beneath her cloak, stirring up the earth, bringing buried soil to light so that she could have a thorough sampling. The lifeblood and memories of others to sustain her baby—were they intended as a balm, a preventative, or something else entirely? Would they heal or sear? She did not know. She knew only that they would make her child strong, that they would protect, that they would instill something of life's truths as embodied in humankind.

She finished digging and began scooping the soil into the same leather pouch that held the earth from the old pines. Tony was still talking, but she wasn't paying attention to what he said. Dirk had wandered off in the direction of another cat.

She filled the pouch halfway and laced it tightly closed again. She stood up then and faced Tony.

"This is really weird," he was saying. "Creeping about the park in the middle of the night and digging up bags of dirt? I mean, what's the point? Look, are you a witch or something? Are you involved in some sort of . . ."

He stopped abruptly and looked past her, alarm spreading over his face. She turned. A gang of boys stood behind her, watching. They seemed to have materialized out of nowhere, so quietly had they gathered. They were of varying ages and sizes, all dressed in black T-shirts and blue jeans. Some wore boots, some leather jackets. There was writing on the shirts and jackets, but she didn't understand the words. One carried a baseball bat, one an iron bar. Several sported tattoos. They had hard, old faces, and their eyes were flat and mean.

She looked instantly for Dirk, but the prism cat was nowhere to be seen.

"What's in the bag, Witch Hazel?" one said, smirking.

"Hey, look, we don't want any trouble . . ." Tony started to say, and the speaker stepped forward and hit him in the face. Tony dropped to his knees, his nose and mouth bloody.

"I said, what's in the bag?" the speaker asked again, and reached for Willow.

She eluded his grasp effortlessly and moved over to stand in front of Tony. "Get away from me," she warned.

Several laughed. One of them said something about teaching her a lesson. There was muttered approval.

Edgewood Dirk moved out from the shadows to one side. "I don't think you should say anything else. I think you should leave."

The boys stared in disbelief. There was a raucous exchange and more laughter. A talking cat! They spread out guardedly, trapping Willow and Dirk against the trees. The one with the baseball bat started forward. "Hey, cat?" he called. "How about lunch?"

In the next instant Dirk began to glow. The gang members hesitated, shielding their eyes. The glow brightened, and Dirk began to change form. His cat self disappeared and was replaced by something so terrifying that even Willow was repulsed. He became monstrous and huge, rising up like an apparition out of Abaddon, all teeth and claws. The circle of attackers collapsed. Most broke and ran, screaming at their fellows, cursing at Dirk. A handful froze, undecided, and lived to regret their indecision. Dirk hissed at them with such force that he knocked them off their feet and sent them tumbling back twenty feet to land bruised and dazed. When they were able to scramble up, they fled after the others.

In seconds, the park was empty again.

Dirk stopped shimmering and turned into a cat again. He gazed after the boys for a minute, then yawned. He began to wash himself.

Willow helped Tony back to his feet. "Are you all right?" she asked him.

He nodded, but there was blood smeared all across his face. "How did the cat . . . ?" He couldn't finish.

"Go home, Tony," she told him, brushing him off, straightening his coat about his shoulders. "Go on."

Tony stared at her. She did not like what she saw in his eyes. Then he turned and stumbled away into the darkness. She watched after him until he reached the street and disappeared around the corner of a building. He did not look back. She did not think she would see him again.

She turned wearily to Dirk. She felt sick, as if the terrible harshness of Ben's world had found a way to burrow down inside her soul. "I don't want to stay here any longer. Can we go now?"

Dirk blinked, emerald eyes glinting. "It was necessary that you come," he said to her.

"Yes, but are we finished?"

Dirk stood abruptly and moved off. "Such impatience. Very well. The fairy mists are this way."

She felt a chill pass up her spine. The fairy mists. But she would do what she must. For herself, for Ben, for their child. One last leg to her journey and she would be home again.

Resolved, she set off into the night.

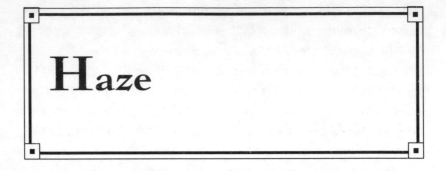

Haze

Three days into their journey through the Labyrinth, the Knight, the Lady, and the Gargoyle came upon a town.

It was late afternoon, the light's wane barely perceptible, a darkening of a gloom that they now knew never brightened beyond twilight. They had walked steadily through a changeless forest world until suddenly, unexpectedly, the town came into view as they crested a small rise. A cluster of ramshackle wooden buildings and worn dirty streets, it hunkered down in a hollow where the trees had been cleared away so that it looked as if the forest had swept around it like the waters of a river around an island. No roads led into it and none away. There were people; the Knight could see them moving on the streets. There were animals, though they were a shabby lot and had the look of creatures beaten down by life. Lights burned in a few of the windows, and as the three stared down more were lit. They gave off a weak and singularly desperate glow, as if they had fought their battle against the coming night too many times and were tired of the struggle.

Overhead, where the trees opened to the skies, there was nothing to be seen of moon or stars, only an endless layer of impenetrable mist.

"People," the Gargoyle said, and there was both surprise and distaste in his voice.

The Knight said nothing. He was thinking that he was

weary of his trek through this dismal world where everything
looked the same and nothing ever changed. The past three
days had dragged away in a mind-numbing crawl, filled with
silence and darkness and an implacable sense of hopelessness.
Twice the Lady had tried to kill him, once with poison in his
drink, once with a sharpened stick when she thought he was
sleeping. Her efforts had been wasted, for he sensed everything
she was about. She seemed to accept this. She went through
the motions as if already resigned to her failure, as if the attempt must be made even when the conclusion was foregone.
Yet he was damaged nevertheless. It was what he saw in her
eyes that wore at him. He was a warrior and could withstand
her physical attacks. But the looks of rage and loathing and
sadness were less easily dealt with, and he was made sick at
heart by their constancy.

Of course, she hated the Gargoyle as well, but her hatred of him was inbred and impersonal and somehow more
acceptable.

"Why is there a town here?" he asked them quietly.

For a moment, no one answered. Why, indeed? A town,
come out of nowhere, materialized as if from a vision, having
no purpose or excuse, existing in a vacuum. Where was the
trade that would support it, since there were no roads? Where
were the crops that would feed it, since there were no fields?
Was this a town of hunters and trappers? If so, to where did
they carry their goods and from where did their supplies
come? The Knight in three days had seen almost no forest
creatures, and what few he had seen had been small and furtive
and somehow natural to the gloom, existing because and not
in spite of it.

"What difference why it is here?" the Lady demanded irritably. "It is here, and that is all that matters. We have a
chance to find our way again. What purpose is there in questioning that?"

The Gargoyle edged forward a step, stooped and hunched

within his dark cloak, keeping as always to shadow. "I mistrust this," he said. "There is something wrong here."

The Knight nodded. He felt it, too. Something was not right. Still, the town was here, and they could not simply pass it by. Someone living there must know of a way to leave the Labyrinth; someone must know of a way back out into the real world.

"We will go down to see what we can learn. We will not stay beyond that." The Knight looked over at the other two.

"If they discover me, they will kill me," the Gargoyle said.

"Remain behind, then," the Lady snapped, unmoved.

"Ah, but I hunger for their words," the Gargoyle murmured, as if ashamed. "That is the puzzle of me. I am loathed by those I would come to know."

"You would be them, you pathetic creature," she sneered. "Admit it."

But the Gargoyle shook his head. "I would not be them. Oh, no, Lady—not for all the gold and silver in the world. They are such uncertain, indecisive beings, all wrapped up in the small measure of their lives. I, on the other hand, am certain, and have the gift of immortality. I am not burdened by the smallness of their existence."

"Nor do you have their beauty. Easy to belittle those whose lives are finite when death for you is so distant you barely need consider what it means." The Lady fixed him with her cold eyes. "I have life beyond that of humans, Gargoyle, but I treasure beauty as well. I would not be ugly like you even if I could live forever."

"Your ugliness is within," the Gargoyle whispered.

"And yours, always and forever, is plainly stamped so that no one can mistake what you are!"

The Knight moved to stand before the Lady, to draw her hard gaze away from the Gargoyle to himself. He shuddered as those cold eyes found his own and he saw the measure of himself mirrored there.

"We will keep to ourselves and not speak if we do not have to. You and I, Lady, will seek the answers we need. He"—he nodded back toward the slouched, cloaked figure behind him—"will remain silent. But be forewarned that if you attempt trickery or betrayal, you will be silenced. Give me your word."

"I will give you nothing!" She sneered openly at him, drawing herself up haughtily.

"I will leave you here with him then," the Knight said softly. "I will be safer on my own down there."

The Lady paled at the suggestion, and the rage that emanated from her was palpable. "You cannot do that!" she hissed.

"Then give me your word."

She trembled with frustration and despair. "Very well. You have it, Sir Knight. May it rise up within you and devour your soul!"

The Knight turned away. He cautioned the Gargoyle to keep hidden within his cloak and stay back from the light. "Do not be drawn into conversation," he warned. "Do not stray from my side."

They descended rapidly in the failing light, the town beginning to vanish already into the growing darkness, the buildings reduced to glimmers of light framed in windows like pictures hung against a black velvet curtain. They slipped through the cloaking gloom like wraiths come from the trees of the forest, following the line of the cradling slope downward. In minutes they had reached the hollow floor and the beginnings of the town. Their eyes adjusted to the shift in light, and they followed one of the short roadways that ran through the town's center, a rutted, worn stretch of earth that began on one side of the clustered buildings and ended on the

other. Men and women passed them in the gloom, but none
spoke. The doors and windows of the houses and shops on either side were closed. Dogs and cats prowled the length of the
building walls and scooted beneath the walkways where they
had been elevated above the earth. Voices were muted and indistinguishable. The Knight listened with his heart as much as
his ears, and he found no hint of solace, no measure of comfort. The town was a coffin waiting to be nailed shut.

At the town's center there was a tavern. Here the doors
were blocked open, and the people came and went freely.
There was the smell of smoke and freshly drawn ale, the clink
of glasses and the scrape of booted feet, and the raw heartiness
of laughter born of momentary escape from the dreariness of
life's toil. The Knight moved toward the doorway, the Lady
and the Gargoyle following. He took note of the cloudiness of
the interior, a mix of smoke and poor lighting. Faces would
not be easily distinguished here; privacy would be valued. He
stepped up onto the porch that fronted the building and saw
that while the tavern was crowded there were tables empty and
seats to be had. They would be recognized as strangers, of
course; it was unavoidable in a town so small. The trick would
be to draw attention to himself and away from his charges.

They entered amidst a swell of raucous laughter that appeared to have its origins at the serving bar where half-a-dozen
workingmen were crowded elbow to elbow over their glasses
facing in toward the counterman. The Knight moved through
the tables to the very back of the room, drawing the other two
with him, and they seated themselves wordlessly. The Gargoyle
turned toward the shadows, circumspect and wary, but the
Lady faced directly into the room, as bold as a spoken threat
with her cloak flung open and her hood lowered. Eyes shifted
toward her at once. Some were filled with hunger.

The Knight seated himself, partially blocking her. It was
too late to tell her to cover herself now. He must assume his
stance as her protector and hope that was enough.

There was a sudden lowering of voices as the room became aware of them, and all present paused to take their measure. The Lady's strange eyes swept the room without settling anywhere, without acknowledging that there was anything worth seeing. The Knight was already regretting his decision to let her come with him; he would have been better off if she had stayed behind. But he had not wanted to let her out of his sight either; he could not chance losing her.

He fixed the counterman with his gaze and signaled for three mugs. The counterman nodded and hastened away to the casks.

The moment passed, eyes shifted away again, and conversation resumed. The room was filled with a mix of men and women, all poorly dressed, all with the harsh, worn look of people who scraped out an existence without luck or skill or the help of others. They might have been anything from farmers to trappers to miners; the Knight could not tell. That they worked with their hands was certain; that they plied some specific trade less so. They were of varying ages, and they sat together in such a fashion that it was impossible to judge who was with whom. Relationships seemed not to matter, as if perhaps they were still forming, as if they were not yet even considered. Now and again people rose and changed tables, but never as couples or in groups. It was as if each man and woman lived a solitary existence and identified only as a singular part of the whole community.

There were no children. There were no signs of any children, no babies, no hint that anyone not grown lived within the town. Not even a sweeping boy worked the floors or mopped the counter.

The counterman crossed the room with the mugs of ale and set them down before the Knight. He glanced at the Knight's weapons and rubbed his hands nervously. "Where do you come from?" he asked as the Knight fished in his pocket for coins he was not even sure he possessed. The Knight finally produced a single piece of gold.

The Knight passed the gold piece over. "We are lost," he answered. "Where are we?"

The counterman tested the gold piece with his teeth. "In the Labyrinth, of course. Right at its heart, in fact."

The counterman was looking at the Lady now, interested. The Lady looked back and right through him.

"Does this town have a name?" the Knight pressed.

The counterman shrugged. "No name. We have no need for one. Did you come from the north?"

The Knight hesitated. "I'm not sure."

The counterman lowered his voice conspiratorially and leaned down a bit, his attention on the Knight now. "Did you see anything strange in the woods?"

"Strange?"

"Yes." The man wet his lips. He seemed reluctant to use a name, as if speaking it might somehow bring what he inquired after through the tavern door.

"We saw nothing," the Knight said.

The counterman studied him a moment as if to make certain he was not lying, then nodded, relief in his face, and walked away.

The Lady leaned forward, and her voice was cool and measured. "What is he talking about?"

The Knight shook his head. He did not know. They sat in silence and drank the ale from the glasses, listening to the conversations around them. There was talk of work, but in a general way. There was mention of the weather and the seasons and the absence of this and that, but it was all vague and indistinguishable. No one spoke of anything specific or made mention of the particulars of their lives. There was something odd about the conversations, about their tone, about the inflection of the voices speaking. It was quite some time before the Knight was able to figure out that woven into the exchanges was a sense of anticipation, of uneasy expectation, of waiting for something unspoken to happen.

An old man edged by the table and stopped. "Come a long ways, have you?" He slurred his words, his speech thick from the ale he had consumed.

"Yes," the Knight replied, looking up. "And you?"

"Oh, no, I don't go nowhere. This is my home, this town. Always and forever. I been here, oh, years and years." He grinned, toothless. "Can't go nowhere else, once you're here."

The Knight felt something turn cold in the pit of his stomach. "What do you mean? You can leave if you choose, can't you?"

The old man cackled. "That what you think? That you can leave? You must be new, son. This is the Labyrinth. You can't leave here. Can't no one leave here ever!"

"If you can come in, you can go out!" the Lady snapped suddenly, anger flaring in her voice.

"You just try it!" the old man replied, still laughing. "Been lots who have before, but they always come back. This is where they have to stay once they're here. You, too. You, too."

He tottered away, mumbling to himself. The Knight signaled the counterman for three fresh mugs, trying to think his way clear of the tangle of the old man's words. No way out, the Labyrinth a trap that no one could escape—he listened to the whisper of the words in his mind.

"Anything to eat?" the counterman asked, coming up with the glasses of ale. "You got some credit yet from that gold piece."

"Can you draw us a map?" the Knight asked perfunctorily.

The counterman gave them his patented shrug. "A map to where? Maps all lead to the same place, eventually. Right back here."

"I need a map that will show us a way out of the Labyrinth."

The counterman smiled. "So does everyone else here. Trouble is, no one can find it. Some—like that old fellow—been trying for years. He can't get out, though. None of us can. We try, but we always end up coming back here."

The Knight stared at him in stunned silence.

"It's all right, really," the other continued quickly, worried by the look that appeared on the Knight's face. "You get used to it. We don't have too many worries. Just the . . ." He shook his head.

"The what? What are you talking about?" the Lady demanded.

The counterman took a slow breath. When he spoke again, the words were barely a whisper. "The Haze."

The Knight glanced quickly at his companions. Neither spoke. He turned back to the counterman. "We don't know what that is."

The counterman was suddenly sweating, as if the temperature in the room had just risen to a midday heat. "Best if you never do!" he hissed. "There's stories. It lives in the woods. It comes out when you least expect it and devours everything! Eats it right up, and when it's done there's nothing left!" His mouth tightened. "I've never seen it myself. No one here has. But we hear it sometimes. More so recently, like maybe it's looking us over. They say a monster always precedes its coming—a thing out of myth and legend, a beast out of the old world."

He shook his head. "I've said enough. It's bad luck to even talk about it. It doesn't come often. But when it does . . ."

He shook his head again, then wheeled about and walked hurriedly away. The Knight stared after him, then turned back to his companions. "Do you know of this?" he asked quietly.

"I have heard rumors," the Gargoyle offered, his voice a

disembodied growl from within the shadows of his hooded cloak. "An ancient legend, thousands of years old. Men see the Haze as divine retribution for their sins."

"What rubbish!" the Lady sneered. "Would you give credence to the superstitions of these common people? Is this how you would identify with them?"

The Gargoyle said nothing, keeping his gaze fixed on the Knight. The Knight drank his ale and tried to think. No one knew of a way out of the Labyrinth. Whatever direction you went, they claimed, you ended up back at this nameless town. Was this belief commonly accepted by these people or was there at least one among them who knew differently? The Knight had not spoken with anyone beyond the counterman and the oldster. Perhaps he should try.

"Stay here," he ordered.

He rose, glass in hand, and walked to the counter. He was aware for the first time of the notice being taken of his weapons and light armor, for none of the townsfolk wore either. He began asking questions of those men gathered at the bar. Had any of them ever been outside the Labyrinth? Did any of them know of a way out? Was there anyone who might know? The men shook their heads and looked away.

"River Gypsies might," one said. "They been everywhere there is to be. 'Course, you got to find them first."

There was a burst of shared laughter, a private joke. The Knight glanced back at the table where he had left the Lady and the Gargoyle and froze. Two men had moved over and were taking seats, one on either side of the Lady. She had pulled her cloak tight around her body and was staring straight ahead while they talked and smiled at her. The Gargoyle was shrinking farther back into the shadows.

The Knight moved away from the counter and began to cross the room. He was too slow. One of the men touched the Lady, and she wheeled on him, nails raking at his face. He surged to his feet with a yowl and stumbled back into the Gargoyle. The concealing cloak fell away, revealing the Gargoyle, and the other man lurched to his feet screaming. Instantly, the room was bedlam. Men and women shrieked in terror and loathing as the Gargoyle tried to cover himself. Weapons flashed into view, long-handled hunting knives and daggers of varying shapes. Fighting to keep his balance in the surging melee, the Knight bulled his way past those separating him from his charges. Mugs crashed to the floor and lamps went out. Men rushed for the doors.

"Look what you've done!" the counterman shouted wildly, pointing at the Knight. "You've brought a monster into our town! You've doomed us! Damn you forever!"

The Knight reached the table, snatched up the Lady, and threw her over his shoulder. He had his broadsword free, and he swung about to level it between himself and those threatening. The Gargoyle crouched behind him, his ineffectual wings beating frantically, his breath hissing through his sharp teeth. The Knight swung the broadsword downward with all his might and splintered the table before him. Men fell back quickly as he made his way toward the door, the Lady kicking and screaming over his shoulder, the Gargoyle hunching close against his back for protection. One man tried to rush him from behind, but the Gargoyle's claws laid his arm open to the bone.

Then they were through the door and back out into the night. The screams and shouts followed after them, but the street had cleared as the people fled to the protection of their homes. The Knight moved quickly through the town, his eyes readjusting to the gloom. Nothing to do but to try to find the way on their own. He cursed their misfortune and the ignorance of the townsfolk.

At the base of the hollow's slope, he set the Lady on her feet, keeping hold of her wrist to make certain she did not try to flee.

"Let me go!" she snarled, pulling back against him.

"How dare you touch me!" She spit at him. "I hate you! I will see you cut apart while you are still alive for this!"

He ignored her, heading for the darkness of the trees, ascending the slope toward the concealment of the forest beyond. Behind, the lights of the town burned weakly from the windows of the buildings, and the shadows of the people milled about in their glow. The Knight spared them only a glance, his attention focused on the line of the trees ahead. Pursuit was not improbable.

They had reached the edge of the forest when the Gargoyle wheeled about and went into a guarded crouch. "Something comes!" he warned, his voice thin and breathless.

In the same instant, new screams of terror rose from the townsfolk. The Knight and the Lady turned to look. A towering wall of wicked green light had appeared within the trees on the far side of the hollow. It flickered like fire and hissed like acid, eating away at the silent dark. It moved steadily forward, and as it came it seemed to change appearance, taking on the look of a heavy rain, a rush of shadows and light that tore mercilessly at everything in its path.

The screams of the people below heightened. *"The Haze! The Haze! It's here! Run! Oh, run!"*

But there appeared to be nowhere to run and no time left in which to do it. The greenish rain came out of the trees and descended the slope toward the town. The world disappeared in its wake. Not a tree, not a shrub, not a hint of life remained. All were consumed. The Haze reached the town and began to tear at the buildings. One by one, they were drawn into its strange curtain. The townsfolk went too, shrieking in frenzy, unable to escape. The Haze claimed them as they fled, and they did not come out. Even their screams were swallowed.

On the ridge of the hollow, the Knight tensed as the last building and inhabitant of the nameless town disappeared and the Haze came on. But suddenly, without reason, the Haze began to draw back. In a matter of seconds, it had reversed itself—a storm front that had suddenly shifted, its thunder-heads turned by an unexpected head wind. Slowly, deliberately, it climbed back up the slope of the hollow, melted into the trees, and vanished.

The Knight, the Lady, and the Gargoyle stared down into the empty hollow. The town they had fled was gone—every building, every person, every beast, every trace that any of it had ever been. Bare earth alone remained, steaming like scalded flesh. The Haze had burned it bare.

The Knight looked over at the Gargoyle. The Haze was more than legend, it seemed. But what had brought it from the woods this night? Was it in fact preceded by a monster as the counterman had warned? Was that monster the Gargoyle? Was there some link between the two, a terrible pact to devour life and ravage the earth that lived upon it? The Gargoyle was, after all, a monster come out of the most ancient of times. The Knight pondered the possibilities. The Lady was looking at the beast as well, and there was a hint of fear in her cold eyes. Staring off into the dark, the Gargoyle did not return their looks.

The Knight turned away. All those people gone, he thought. All. He could see them vanish anew in his mind. He could hear them screaming still. The sound was horrific, but familiar. He had heard such screams before. He had heard them all his life. They were the screams of the men he had fought and killed in battle. They were the screams of his victims. The screams were captured in his memory like trapped souls in a net, and he would carry them with him forever.

He wondered then, in the terrible aftermath of the destruction he had witnessed, if the burden of these newest screams was his to bear as well.

River Gypsies

They walked all that night, too nervous to sleep. They did not speak of what had happened, but each knew that the others were thinking of it. The endless forest closed about them again, a vast impenetrable canopy of leafy boughs and misty skies. The Labyrinth stretched on once more, and after a time it seemed as if the town and her people might never have been at all.

When it was morning and the darkness lightened to gray, they found a clearing and slept for a time. The Knight rested in the half doze that he had long since mastered for when there was need, a sort of trance in which some small part of him, some singular instinct, remained awake and alert against danger. He might have dreamed, but he was haunted by the screams of all those he had seen die and by his inability to rid himself of them. They were the shades of the dead, all that remained of what had once been human. They lived on in him, as if they had attached themselves and would not release until death came to him as well.

When he did not doze, he lay thinking on the Gargoyle, wondering still what part the creature had played in what had happened to the town. He was bothered anew by the fact that he could not remember how the Gargoyle had come to be with him, why it was that they were traveling together. He could remember nothing of the beast beyond knowing that he should be there. Where had the Gargoyle come from? What reason had he to be with the Knight and the Lady in the Labyrinth? The Gargoyle might belong here, the Knight kept thinking. He had known first of the common belief that the Labyrinth was a maze without an exit. He had said first what the townsfolk had said later. The Gargoyle had known of the Haze. There was so much that the Knight did not know that the Gargoyle did. It was troublesome. The Knight did not fear the creature, but was wary of his purpose. There seemed a fundamental honor and fairness to the beast, but try as he might the Knight could not bring himself to trust him.

On waking, they went on. They traveled now because they had little choice. If they did not go on, they would be admitting defeat. The Knight would not allow that. He could sense his control of things slipping away, his self-assurance and certainty of purpose slowly eroding. Little by little he was coming to see how fragile was his place in the scheme of things. Here, he was a pawn of circumstances he could not fathom or control. There was nothing recognizable in the Labyrinth, and what he remembered of life before was a shadowy play of figures against a too-vague and distant backdrop. Try as he might to concentrate and remember, nothing of his former life would come into focus for him. It was as if he had been born here, and only the presence of the Lady—and perhaps the Gargoyle—reassured him that there was something that had gone before.

The Lady talked to him this day, almost as if she were compelled. She did not converse as a friend or intimate, merely as his charge and companion on the road. She questioned him repeatedly about who he was and why he was there. She questioned him about what he remembered of his life before. She wanted to know why he had taken her and for whom. He avoided her questions, turning each aside as deftly as he could manage. He avoided them because he could not

answer them. He had no answers to give. She pressed him until she grew weary, and then she fell silent once more.

"You toy with me," she said, the sadness and despair
come back into her voice, replacing the otherwise-always-
present anger. "You play games with me because I am your
prisoner."

He shook his head, gazing off into the mist. "I would not
do that to you."

"Then tell me something of yourself," she begged, just
managing to keep her voice level and controlled. "Give me
something as reassurance that you do not lie."

He walked without speaking for a moment, then lowered
his head. "I do not like it that things must be this way. I wish
they could be otherwise. I am sorry for taking you, whatever
the purpose, whatever the cause. If there is a way to do so
later, I will make it up to you."

He thought she would laugh outright at the suggestion.
He thought she would simply scorn him. She surprised him
by doing neither. Instead, she simply nodded without speaking
and walked on.

It was midafternoon when they reached the river. It appeared as the town had appeared, coming into view as they
crested a rise and the trees broke apart. The river was broad
and slow, and it ran in either direction across their path for as
far as the eye could see. On the far bank, the forests of the
Labyrinth resumed, stretching away forever. Overhead, the
skies remained shrouded and empty.

They walked down to the river's edge and stopped, looking first across, then upstream, then downstream. There was
no sign of life. The water was cloudy and smooth where rapids
and rifts did not churn it to foam amid rocky outcroppings.
No debris floated in it, nor did fish jump to mar the glassy
surface.

"If there is a river, there must be a town somewhere
along it," the Lady said hopefully.

"But does the town lie within the Labyrinth or beyond?" the Knight queried. He looked at her. "We shall follow it and see. Which way shall we go?"

Again, she surprised him. "You decide. You are the one who leads us."

He took them downstream. The riverbank was broad and grassy and easily traversed. The trees of the forest ended some hundred yards back at most points, and the way was clear and open for travelers. As gray daylight waned toward nightfall, the mist moved out of the trees and settled down across the river and its banks. It crept to their boot tops and then to their knees. By darkness, it was waist-high and they could no longer see where the bank ended and the river began.

The Knight had just decided to move back into the trees for the night when they heard the singing. They stopped as one, listening. The sound came from just a little farther ahead, around a bend not two hundred yards away. The Knight took them back to the fringe of the trees so that they would escape a fall into the river, and they continued from there. When they reached the bend and rounded it, they saw light from several fires. The singing came from there. They moved toward the fires, peering intently through the gloom. As they neared, a handful of painted wagons came into view. There were mules tethered nearby, and tents of bright cloth that had been tied to poles and the ends of the wagons and made fast by rope stays. The singers were more than a dozen in number, men and women both, all dressed in colorful garb with many sashes, cloaks, and headbands, all gathered about the fires as they sang.

The Knight and his companions approached and were seen, but the singing continued as if their appearance did not matter. The Gargoyle was hanging back, wrapped in his cloak for concealment, but one of the singers rose and beckoned them all forward, making certain that the beast was included. They came up slowly, cautious by nature and circumstance, even in these seemingly friendly surroundings.

"Welcome to our camp," the one who had encouraged them to join in greeted. "Will you sing with us? Sing for your supper, perhaps?"

The man was heavy and round and had great, gnarled hands. His hair and beard were thick and black. He wore several gold earrings and a chain with a locket. A brace of daggers were tucked in a sash at his ample waist, and another protruded from the top of his boot.

"Who are you?" the Knight asked.

"Ah, ah—no names, my friend," the other said. "Names are for enemies we would avoid, not for friends we would make. Will you sit with us?"

"River Gypsies," the Gargoyle said, come to a full stop, and the Knight looked quickly at him.

The big man laughed. "That's us! Well, look at you, my friend. A Gargoyle! Not many of your kind left in the world, and none have been seen in my lifetime, I think, within the Labyrinth. So, now. Don't be shy, don't lurk about at the edges of the light. You are all welcome. Come sit with us and sing. Come share the fire."

He shepherded them forward to join the others. Space was made, drinks were brought, and the singing went on. Smiles passed from face to face as songs were begun and finished. One man played a stringed instrument of some sort. One played a flute. The Knight and his companions listened to the songs, but did not join in. They drank the wine they were offered, but only a little at first. They looked about at the assemblage and wondered how they had gotten there.

"Have you come far?" the big man asked of the Knight after a time, leaning close to be heard.

"Five days' walk," the Knight answered. "We cannot seem to find our way out."

"A common enough problem here," the other replied, nodding.

"Do you know a way?" the Knight pressed.

The other began to clap along with a song. "Perhaps. Perhaps."

The singing went on for a long time. The Knight began to grow sleepy. The Lady had drunk more than he had and was already stretched out upon the grass, eyes closed. The Gargoyle sat hunched down within his cloak, featureless in his hood's shadows. Some of the Gypsies had begun to dance, leaping and spinning in the firelight. The women had fixed bells to their fingers, and the silvery tinkle lifted above the singing. The men trailed scarves that were crimson and gold. Wine was drunk freely. There had been mention of food earlier, the Knight thought, but none had appeared.

"Is this not the way life should be lived?" the big man asked suddenly, leaning over once more. He was flushed and smiling. "Give no thought to tomorrow until it comes. Do not worry about that over which you have no control. Sing and dance. Drink and laugh. Leave your troubles for another time."

The Knight shook his head. "Troubles have a way of catching up with you."

The other laughed. "Such a pessimist! Look at you! You neither sing nor dance! You drink so little! How can you enjoy yourself? You must give life a chance!"

"Is there a way out of the Labyrinth?" the Knight asked again.

The Gypsy shook his head merrily, climbed to his feet, and shrugged. "Not this night, I think. Tomorrow, maybe." And off he went, dancing lightly for all his size across the firelight.

The Knight drained away the last of his wine and looked over for his companions. The Lady was still sleeping soundly. The Gargoyle had disappeared. The Knight cast about for him in vain, even beyond the firelight. He was gone.

The Knight tried to rise and found he could not. His legs would not work, and his body felt encased in iron. He struggled against a weight that seemed to chain him down, managing to come almost all the way up before falling back. The River Gypsies danced and sang about him, oblivious. Colors and shapes spun past him as he turned toward the darkness. Something was wrong. Some trick had been played.

He was still wondering what was amiss as he toppled over into blackness.

When he came awake, he was alone. The River Gypsies were gone—the men, the women, the wagons, the mules, everything. All that remained were the ashes of the fires, still smoldering faintly in the hazy dawn. The Knight was stretched full length upon the grassy earth. He rolled over weakly and came to his knees. His head throbbed from the wine, and his muscles were cramped from his sleep. To his left, the river flowed past, smooth, soundless, and undisturbed. To his right, the forest was a dark curtain filled with mist.

The Knight rose to his feet and waited for the dizziness to pass.

The Lady was gone as well.

He felt his breath quicken and his chest constrict with anger and disbelief. Where had she gone? He cast about through the early morning gloom for some sign of her, but there was none. She had disappeared.

He was still in the process of regaining his bearings when the Gargoyle emerged from the trees and came toward him. The Knight realized suddenly that his weapons were missing as well, all of them. He was defenseless.

"Sleep well?" the Gargoyle queried as he reached the Knight, the sarcasm in his voice unmistakable.

"Where are my weapons?" the Knight demanded angrily. "What has become of the Lady?"

The Gargoyle hunched down before him, dark-featured. "The River Gypsies have them both. They took them while you were sleeping."

"Took them?" The Knight was stunned. "You mean they stole them?"

The Gargoyle laughed softly. "The Gypsies do not look at it like that. To them, the weapons and the woman are our payment for last night's pleasures. Fair is fair, they think. They relieved you of what you do not need."

The Knight glowered. "And you did nothing to stop them?"

The Gargoyle shrugged. "Why should I? What difference does it make to me what happens to the Lady or your weapons? I care for neither. In truth, you are better off without them. There is no need for weapons within the Labyrinth— only wits and patience. The Lady was a millstone about both our necks, an annoyance that no sane man should have to bear."

"That was not your decision to make!"

"Nor did I make it." The Gargoyle was unruffled, his ugly face lifting slightly into the light, his yellow eyes calm. "I let events take their own course and nothing more."

"You could have warned me!"

"You could have warned yourself if you had been think-ing straight. There is no mystery to Gypsies of any kind—they are the same the world over and always have been. They live by their own rules, and if you choose to drink and sing with them you accept that this is so. Consider it a lesson, Sir Knight, and let it pass."

The Knight forced down his rage. Fear lurked just be-neath, the feeling that he was losing control and could do nothing to stop it. The Lady and his weapons were gone, and he had been powerless to prevent it. Why hadn't he seen better what might happen? Why hadn't he taken the precautions he knew were necessary?

He breathed in deeply and looked up and down the river. "Which way did they go?" The Gargoyle did not respond, and the Knight turned on him quickly. "Do not give me reason to mistrust you further!" he snapped.

The Gargoyle held his angry gaze. "I have given you no reason ever."

"Haven't you?" The Knight squared himself. "When I woke in the Labyrinth, you were already there. You knew where we were; you called the Labyrinth by name. You said that there was no way out, before anyone else had even mentioned it. When we reached that town and we were told of the Haze, you knew the story. The counterman identified you as a monster that preceded its coming. Last night, when we came upon the River Gypsies, you knew who they were when the Lady and I did not. You seem to know a great deal about a place which you do not claim to come from. I cannot help but wonder what cause you serve in all of this."

The Gargoyle stared at the Knight, and for a long moment he said nothing. "You have cause to be suspicious, I suppose," he replied finally, reluctantly. "I would be suspicious as well, were I you. It must seem as if I am duplicitous. But I am not. What I know comes from living for a very long time and having been to a great many places. I have acquired knowledge for which I can no longer name the source. I remember things that I heard about or discovered centuries ago. I am very old. Once, as the River Gypsy said, there were many of my kind. Now there is only me in all the world."

He paused, as if reflecting. "This place and those who live here and the things that happen within are familiar to me, known from another time, one for which my memory has long since been erased. I sense, as well, some of what will be. I know this place; I recognize it. I anticipate some events. But I am not from here, and I am not sure I have ever visited before." The Gargoyle scowled. "It bothers me that this is so. My memory is quite fragmented, and I confess that nothing of my previous life is clear to me anymore. Save," he added darkly, "that I am no longer who or what I was."

The Knight nodded slowly. He sensed truth in the Gargoyle's words. "Nor am I. The past seems long ago and far away."

"But there are associations that trigger memories, as with the River Gypsies last night," the Gargoyle said. "I knew them without ever having met them. I knew what they were about. I could have told you, it is true. I did not. I wanted them to take the Lady. I wanted her gone." His gaze was direct. "I am not ashamed."

"I must get her back from them," the Knight said.

"Why? What reason is there to do so?" The Gargoyle seemed genuinely interested.

The Knight was silent. His hands clenched as he struggled to speak. "Because it is what I was given to do before I came here. It is the only certainty I possess. Without her, I am lost. She is all that keeps me going. She is the reason for my being. I exist because of her. Do you see?"

The Gargoyle thought for a moment and then nodded. "I think I do. You have no cause beyond taking her to your master, no cause that you can remember. But do you remember anything even of that, Sir Knight?"

The Knight shook his head. "This place seems to have stolen my past."

"And mine." The Gargoyle's voice was bitter. "I wish my life back again. I wish my memories restored."

"Did you see which way they went?" the Knight repeated.

"You are better off without her," the Gargoyle replied. There was no response from the Knight, no change in his expression. The Gargoyle sighed. "Upstream, back the way we came." He shook his head wearily. "I will go with you."

They set out at once, moving through the long grasses of the riverbank, following the earth-colored ribbon into the misty gray. They found tracks almost immediately, and it wouldn't have been hard for the Knight to have discovered for himself which way the River Gypsies had gone. It made him suspicious anew of the Gargoyle's place in the scheme of things; after all, the Gargoyle might have told him simply to serve his own purpose. But that was harsh thinking, and the Knight was not comfortable with it. He believed the Gargoyle to be a fundamentally honorable creature. He did not sense lies in what he had been told. They had both come into this world from some other, and their destiny here, along with that of the Lady, was of a single piece.

They pushed on through the day, moving steadily ahead in the wake of the wagon tracks, pausing infrequently to rest themselves, intent on completing their chase by sunset. The river broadened after a time, growing so large that the far bank was little more than a dark line against the clouded skies. The Knight was growing depressed by the constant grayness, by the absence of any sunlight, by the oppressive lowering of the sky toward the earth. He missed people and animals and the presence of other life. He had enjoyed those once, he knew. Mostly, he felt the loss of his identity beyond the vagueness of his present existence. It was not enough to sense who and what you were; memories were needed as well, clear pictures of the life you had lived and the things you had done while you lived it. He had almost none of those—fewer, it seemed, than the Gargoyle. He was cast adrift in a limbo, and the emptiness he felt was beginning to breed madness.

It was after sunset when they came upon the River Gypsies again. They were fortunate to see the firelight well before they were close enough to be seen themselves. The Gypsies were encamped on the riverbank once more, and the sound of their singing rose into the twilight stillness with careless disregard. The Knight and the Gargoyle moved back within the trees and edged along within the protective fringe until they were close enough to see what was happening. There were no surprises. The River Gypsies sat about their fires drinking wine, letting the night close in about them. The Lady sat with them. She did not appear to be restrained in any way. She held a cup in one hand and sipped at it. Her face was cold and empty, but she did not appear afraid.

"Perhaps she wants to be with them," the Gargoyle whispered. "Perhaps she is freer with them than she was with you."

The Knight ignored him. "I need my sword back."

The Gargoyle shook his head reprovingly. "You are of a single mind, aren't you? No deviation in your life." His laugh was deep and soft. "We are both cast in a mold that can never be changed."

He rose abruptly. "Wait here for me."

He disappeared into the trees. The Knight waited, watching the camp. Darkness deepened until everything beyond the glow of the firelight disappeared. The drinking and singing went on, uninterrupted, unabated. All other sounds and movements disappeared behind the gaiety, submerged as deadwood in a river's flow. Time passed, and the Knight grew anxious.

Then the Gargoyle was there beside him again, holding out the broadsword, sharpened teeth gleaming along the edges of a smile. The Knight accepted the sword, balanced it in his hand to study its condition, then slipped it back into the sheath he wore across his back.

"Now we will ask them to give the Lady back," he said, rising.

"Wait." The Gargoyle's clawed hand restrained him. "Why ask when there is no need? Wait until early morning, then slip down and take her while they sleep. It might be the easier way."

The Knight thought it over a minute and nodded. "We will wait."

They sat together in silence within the concealment of the forest trees. The River Gypsies began to dance, and the merriment went on. It did not end until the night was mostly gone and the fires burned away. Then the men and women rolled themselves into their blankets and were still. The Lady slept with them. She had not moved from the place she had been sitting; she had merely eased herself down onto the grass. Mist edged in about the wagons and animals, no longer kept at bay by the heat of the flames, and soon it covered the sleepers.

The Knight and the Gargoyle rose then and slipped from the trees. They made their way in silence through the long grasses toward the camp. They searched for a sentry and found none. When they reached the wagons, they paused again, listening. There was only the sound of the Gypsies sleeping and the distant rustle of the river against her banks. They edged along the wagons until they were close to where the Lady lay. Then the Knight went forward alone.

He found her, knelt close, and placed his hand over her mouth. She came awake at once, looking up at him with cool, appraising eyes that were free of any fear. He started to help her up, then saw the chain that ran from a clamp fastened about her ankle to a wagon wheel.

The Knight stood, fury racing through him. He'd had enough. He walked through the sleepers heedlessly until he found the one who had spoken so enticingly to him of leaving one's cares for another day. He reached down, fastened his fingers in the man's tunic, and hauled him to his feet.

"I will cut you end to end if she is not freed at once," he hissed.

The man looked him in the eye and nodded wordlessly. The Knight steered him back across the camp to where the

Lady waited. The bearded Gypsy reached into his pocket, produced a key, released the lock, and stood back.

"You should not be angry at us," he said quietly.

The Knight pulled free the clamp from the Lady's leg and brought her to her feet. She reached down to rub her ankle, then turned and strode out of the camp for the trees.

"Wine and entertainment come at a price," the Gypsy declared. "You owe us."

The Knight turned. "Be grateful I do not kill you."

The Gypsy put his fingers to his lips and whistled, a shrill, piercing sound. Instantly the camp was awake, and there were armed men all about. They held daggers and short swords and axes, the metal blades gleaming wetly in the damp air. They took in the situation at a single glance and edged toward the Knight.

"Do not be foolish," the Knight warned, placing his back to the nearest wagon.

"It is you who have been foolish, I think," the bearded Gypsy replied.

They came at the Knight in a swarm, but he scattered the rush with a huge sweep of his blade. His chain mail protected him from the dirks thrown at his chest, and he turned and moved swiftly past the wagons for the woods. Where was his heavy armor? he wondered suddenly. Where were his plates and greaves and helmet? He sensed them somewhere close at hand once more, but still they would not come to him. This was twice now that he had been forced to stand and fight without them. He had never had to do so before. His armor had always been there when he needed it. Why didn't he have it now?

Again the Gypsies rushed him, and this time he was forced to defend himself. He cut two of them down and wounded a third, taking no injury himself. He could hear the Gargoyle calling. When he glanced back, he saw the Lady standing at the edge of the trees, watching him.

Rage at the stupidity of the River Gypsies washed through him. He braced himself for another rush.

It never came. A familiar, wicked green light lifted off the river in a towering curtain and began to advance on the camp. The Gypsies turned at its coming and screamed in recognition. The Haze swept out of the mist and dark, a terrible hissing rain that ate away the landscape. The Knight turned and ran for the woods, taking advantage of the Gypsies' terror and confusion. He gained the trees as the Haze reached the camp. It ate its way through the wagons and animals and people so quickly that they disappeared in seconds. Even the screams lingered only an instant. No one seemed able to escape.

It was over in moments. The Haze advanced until the camp was devoured and then it drew back. As with the town, it retreated across the scorched, barren earth and disappeared from view. As with the town, nothing of the River Gypsies remained behind.

The ravaged ground steamed in the early dawn light. The Knight stared out from the trees in shock. The Lady stood at one elbow, the Gargoyle at the other. No one spoke. The Knight was wondering how this had happened, how it was that the Haze had come again, how it could be that it took only the camp and left them alone. What had brought it? What had kept it from destroying them as well? Something in all of this was not right. There was a surreal aspect to everything that had happened—in their discovery of that nameless town, in their encounter with the River Gypsies, in the coming of the Haze. There was an unmistakable skewing of reality that lacked identity, but not form. Ignorant of its source, he was nevertheless aware that it existed.

An unpleasant suspicion began to form at the back of his mind, one so terrible that he could not give it voice. He buried it away deep inside himself in despair and disbelief.

"What monstrous thing is this," the Lady whispered,

stepping forward to stare out across the river. "Does it track us like dogs at hunt?"

"It does," the Gargoyle growled softly. "I can sense its hunger."

The Knight could sense it, too. And while he would not say so, while he could not bring himself to speak the words, he thought that its hunger had not yet been sated.

Costs You Nothing

They must have seemed an odd sight, Abernathy thought as they approached the gates of Rhyndweir, castle fortress of Kallendbor, the most powerful of the Lords of the Greensward. A tall, scrawny, gangly man with a bird on his shoulder, a smallish, wiry beast that looked a little like a crazed monkey, and a dog with human hands and wearing reading glasses— Horris Kew, Biggar, Bunion, and himself. Up the roadway through the town surrounding the fortress they trudged, carrying before them (well, Bunion carrying, actually) the banner of the current and still absent King of Landover. Their horses trailed on a line behind them, grateful no doubt to be rid of riders who didn't much care for the beasts anyway. The mule with the chests of mind's eye crystals plodded along with them. The day was hot and humid, the air still, and the prospect of a bath and a cold drink was foremost in everyone's mind.

Townspeople gathered to watch them come, standing in the shade of doorways and awnings, nudging one another and whispering. Perhaps they knew, Abernathy thought. Perhaps by now, everybody knew.

They had departed Sterling Silver three days earlier, a delegation of King's emissaries dispatched for the particular purpose of distributing mind's eye crystals to the people of the Greensward, both high-born and low. The decision to allow the crystals to be shared had been reached with some reservations, but reached nevertheless. Questor Thews was growing desperate in his efforts to cover for the missing King. It was getting harder and harder to invent excuses to explain why the King refused to see anyone personally, delegating all meetings to his chief advisor. A diversion of some sort was needed to keep the more persistent questioners at bay. If nothing else, perhaps the crystals could provide this. Take them out, spread them around, let them amuse for a time, and hope the novelty wouldn't wear off too fast.

Questor, of course, could not go himself. So Abernathy, despite his objection to the idea, was the logical choice to go in his place. Someone had to represent the King besides Horris Kew and his bird. Someone had to keep an eye on Horris and maybe the bird as well. So Abernathy was pressed into service, and Bunion was sent along for protection and support. An escort of soldiers was offered as well, but no one wanted them, including Abernathy, who preferred to keep matters simple and straightforward. Visit the Lords of the Greensward with an escort and you called immediate attention to yourself. That was a bad idea, Abernathy had decided, and therefore the escort was unnecessary.

Besides, this was a time of peace. What sort of trouble would they run into with the King's banner paraded before them?

So off they had gone, marching out of the castle gates and heading northeast through the forests and across the hills to the grasslands of the Greensward. Everyone they met along the way was offered one of the crystals. Most accepted them gladly, entranced by what they could do. One or two, more curmudgeonly than their fellows, wouldn't even consider such nonsense. There were a great many farms and small communities between Sterling Silver and the castles of the Lords of the Greensward, so hundreds of crystals were distributed. Word began to spread, and before long there were people waiting for them on the road. More crystals were passed out, and more people went away happy. So far, so good.

Abernathy had to give credit to Horris Kew. The conjurer made certain that each person given a crystal knew that it was a gift from the King and that he was acting solely as the King's representative. There was no attempt to take credit for anything, no hint of self-promotion. It was very unlike the Horris Kew Abernathy remembered, and it made him suspicious all over again.

But the faithful Court Scribe was compromised on the matter. As much as he distrusted Horris Kew and his schemes, including this one, he was desperately attached to his own, personal crystal. When he could admit it to himself, which was less and less often, he worried that his attraction bordered on addiction. He seemed to have been snared from the first moment he had looked into the crystal's wonderous depths. What had he been shown, not once, but each time he looked? Himself, restored to who and what he had once been, a man with a man's features, the dog body in which he was trapped forever gone. It was his deepest, fondest wish in life, the dream he lived to fulfill, and when he gazed into the faceted light of his mind's eye crystal, it all came to pass. He could stay there and watch himself for as long as he chose—an increasingly longer period of time each day. He could not only see but feel himself as a man; he could remember what it had been like before Questor Thews invoked his unfortunate incantation and consigned him to his present fate.

It was a wickedly pleasurable pastime, and Abernathy could not get enough of it. It was not as good as being himself again, as looking as he once had, but it was as close as he was likely to get. It was immensely satisfying. And he owed it all to Horris Kew.

Even now, as he approached the towering gates of Rhyndweir and thought gratefully of the bath and cold ale that would be waiting, he was thinking as well of his crystal and the prospect of time alone in his room to look into its depths once more.

The gates opened to receive them, and they marched through and past the handful of guards standing watch. A single minor court official waited to receive them and guide them on. No trumpeted greeting, no turning out of the garrison, no personal attendance by Kallendbor as there would have been for the King, Abernathy thought. Minimal respect was accorded to envoys, and less-than-minimal interest. Kallendbor had never liked Holiday, but he was growing more open in his disdain. Memories of Holiday's triumphs and accomplishments were growing dim, it seemed. Holiday had faced down Kallendbor on several occasions and done what the Lords of the Greensward had been unable to do—defeat the Iron Mark, disperse the demons back to Abaddon, and unite the kingdom under a single rule. He had defeated every opponent sent against him and overcome every obstacle. All this had been accepted by Kallendbor, if never appreciated. Now, perhaps, even acceptance was in question.

Kallendbor met them at the palace doors, resplendent in crimson robes and jewels, accompanied by his advisors and current favorites. He was a tall, well-built man with hair and beard so red they shown almost gold in the sunlight. His hands and forearms were callused and marked with battle scars. He stood waiting for them to approach, arrogant head held erect, giving the impression that he was looking down on them, that he was lending them his time and attention out of the generosity of his heart. His attitude did not bother Abernathy; the scribe was well used to it. Nevertheless, he did not appreciate the deliberate insolence.

"Lord Kallendbor," Abernathy greeted, foremost of the three as they came up to him, and inclined his head slightly.

"Scribe," the other replied with an even slighter bow.

"Awk! Mighty Lord! Mighty Lord!" Biggar squawked.

Kallendbor blinked. "What's this we have here? A trained bird? Well, now. Is this gift for me, perhaps?" He was suddenly beaming. "Of course it is! Very well chosen, Abernathy."

Now here was an opportunity that Abernathy would have given almost anything for—a chance to get rid of Biggar. Abernathy had not liked the bird from day one and the bird had not liked him—and each knew how the other felt. There was something about Biggar that bothered Abernathy more than he could say. He couldn't define what it was exactly, but it was most certainly there. He had not wanted the bird on this trip; he had argued against it vehemently. But Horris Kew insisted that the bird must accompany them, and in the end—in large part because the mind's eye crystals were the conjurer's offering and the entire reason for the journey—the bird went.

Abernathy opened his mouth to speak, to tell Kallendbor that, yes, indeed, the bird was all his. He was too slow.

"My Lord, forgive me for letting this poor creature distract you from our purpose in coming to see you," Horris Kew interjected quickly. "The bird, alas, is not a gift. He is my companion, my sole treasure in this world from my old life and the people who meant so much to me, who gave me all that I have and made me what I am. You understand, I am sure." He was speaking very quickly. "The bird, truth be told, is an unpleasant sort, given to fits of temper and biting. You would not be happy with him."

As if to emphasize the point, Biggar reached over and pecked hard at Horris Kew's ear. "Ow! There, you see!" Horris took a swipe at Biggar, who flew off a few yards before settling back down on the other's shoulder, alert for further attempts.

"Why am I not offered this bird if I wish it?" Kallendbor demanded, his face darkening. "Are you saying I cannot have this bird if it pleases me?"

Abernathy was thinking that this was the end of the crystal distribution program, that they might all just as well turn around and go home right now—except for Biggar, who, it appeared, was destined to stay.

"My Lord, the bird is yours if you wish him," Horris Kew declared at once. Biggar squawked anew. "But you should know that he speaks very little, and what he said just now—'Mighty Lord'—is a phrase he learned from the King. In other words, the King taught him to say that about himself."

Abernathy stared. There was a very long silence. Kallendbor flushed and straightened further, looking as if he might explode. Then slowly the dangerous color drained away.

"Never mind, I don't wish him after all," he said disdainfully. "If he is mine to take, that is enough. Let Holiday keep him." He took a steadying breath. "Now, then. Since we have dispensed with the matter of this bird, what is it you wish?"

"My Lord," Horris Kew said, jumping in again before Abernathy could speak, "you were right in your assumption. We do bring you a gift, something far more intriguing and useful than a bird. It is called a mind's eye crystal."

Kallendbor was interested once more. "Let me see it."

This time Abernathy was quicker. "We would be happy to show it to you, my Lord, perhaps inside where it is cooler and we can be shown to the quarters that I am sure you have arranged for us as envoys of the King."

Kallendbor smiled, not a pleasant sight. "Of course, you must be exhausted. Riding is hard for you, I expect. Come this way."

Abernathy did not miss the intended snub, but he ignored it and the little company followed Kallendbor and his retinue inside to the great hall. Glasses of ale drawn from casks kept cooled in the deep waters of the Bairn and the Cosselburn, the rivers bracketing Rhyndweir, were brought and arrangements were begun for rooms and baths. Kallendbor took them over to an area before a series of doors that opened onto a training field and seated them in a circle of chairs. Most of his retinue was left standing, gathered at their master's shoulder.

"Now, then, what of this gift?" Kallendbor asked anew.

"It is this, my Lord," Horris Kew declared, and produced from his clothing one of the mind's eye crystals.

Kallendbor accepted the crystal and studied it with a frown. "It doesn't look to be precious. What is its worth. Wait!" He leaned forward, looking now at Abernathy. He pointed at Horris Kew. "Who is this?"

"His name is Horris Kew," the scribe answered, resisting the urge to add more. "He is at present in service to the King. He is the discoverer of these crystals."

"*These* crystals?" Kallendbor turned back to Horris Kew. "There are more than one? How many are there?"

"Thousands," the conjurer replied, smiling. "But each is special. Hold it before you, my Lord, so that it catches the light and then look into it."

Kallendbor studied him suspiciously for a moment, then did as he was bidden. He held the crystal out to catch a streamer of sunlight, then bent down to peer into its depths. He remained that way until the crystal seemed to ignite with white fire, then gasped and jerked back sharply, but kept his eyes fixed. Suddenly he was open mouthed, bending close once more, a bright gleam in his eyes. "No, is it so?" he muttered. "Is it possible?"

Then he snatched the crystal from view, shutting off its light and whatever the light had shown him. "All of you, out!" he demanded to those peering over his shoulder expectantly. "Now!"

They disappeared with surprising quickness, and when they were gone Kallendbor looked again at Horris Kew. "What are these?" he hissed. "What power do they command?"

Horris seemed confused. "Why, they . . . they offer visions of many things, my Lord—visions peculiar to each holder. They are a diversion, nothing more."

Kallendbor shook his head. "Yes, but . . . do they show the future, perhaps? Tell me that."

"Well, yes, perhaps," Horris Kew went along, no fool he. "To some, of course, not to everyone."

And suddenly Abernathy found himself wondering if perhaps it was so. Horris himself did not seem to know the truth of the matter, but what if Kallendbor's guess was right? Did that mean that the visions shown might come to pass? Did it mean that Abernathy might be seeing himself not as he had been but as he would be again?

"The future," Kallendbor whispered, lost in thought. "Yes, it might be so."

Whatever he had seen had certainly pleased him, Abernathy thought, barely interested in what that might be, too caught up in considering his own use of the crystal. His chest constricted with the emotions that gathered at the prospect that he might become a man again. If it could only be true!

"How many of these do you have?" Kallendbor demanded suddenly.

Horris Kew swallowed, not sure where this was leading. "As I said, thousands, my Lord."

"Thousands. How much do they cost?"

"Nothing, my Lord. They are free."

Kallendbor seemed to choke on something. "Have you given many out yet?"

"Yes, my Lord, many. It is our purpose in coming to the Greensward—to give these crystals to the people so that they may be amused by what they see in them when their daily work is done. Of course, for you, my Lord," he added quickly, not missing an opportunity when he saw one, "they perhaps offer something more."

"Yes, something more." Kallendbor thought. "I have an idea. Allow me to distribute those crystals intended for the other Lords of the Greensward. I shall pass them about in the King's name, of course. That would save you visiting each stronghold and leave you free to visit the common people."

It was not a request. Horris Kew looked at Abernathy for help. Abernathy surmised what Kallendbor intended. He would not give the mind's eye crystals to the other Lords for nothing; he would charge dearly. Probably he would tell them that these crystals, unlike those given for free to the working people, foretold the future. But Abernathy frankly didn't care one way or the other. News would travel fast enough. Let Kallendbor deal with his neighbors as he chose.

Abernathy shrugged. "Of course, my Lord," he replied. "Whatever you wish."

Kallendbor stood up abruptly. "Your rooms are ready. Wash and rest until dinner. We will speak more of this then." He turned from them, and it was apparent that he could barely restrain himself from peering once more at his crystal. "Oh, yes. Ask my servants if you require anything."

He went out the door as if catapulted, and was gone.

Alone in his room, Abernathy bathed, dressed, drank another glass of the fine, cold ale, and settled back in his bed, stretched full-length across its covering. He took his crystal from where he kept it hidden, held it up to the light, and stared into it. He was practiced in its use by now, to the extent such practice was needed, and the light and images came at once. He watched himself appear in his old form, a young man with a bright, happy smile and an expectant look, rather handsome for his bookish appearance, rather appealing. He was playing with children and there was a woman watching, pretty and shy. Abernathy felt his breath catch in his throat. There had never been a woman in his life before, no wife, no lover, and yet here one was now. The future, perhaps? Was it possible he was seeing what would be?

He closed his hand over the crystal abruptly and focused everything on the idea. The future. Anything was possible, wasn't it? What would he give if it were so? He knew the answer without asking. He stared up at the ceiling, at the cracks in the old mortarwork, at the faded paint that had once clearly detailed a pageant of some sort. Like his past, time had faded the event. So much of what once was had been lost in the passing of the years and in the changes wrought. He would not wish to recapture much, he told himself. Just the essence of who he was. Just the whole of who he had been.

He thought suddenly of Ben Holiday, who had been so anxious to leave his past behind. The King had few memories to sustain him, and the changes he had sought had been not of lifestyle but of life. It was not so with Abernathy, but there were parallels to be drawn. He wondered where Holiday was, what had become of him. There remained no trace of the King, no sign of him anywhere, though the search had been long and thorough and was continuing still. It was disturbing that he should vanish so utterly; it did not bode well for any of them if he was gone for good. Another King could bring changes that were not necessarily welcome. Another King would not possess Holiday's strength of character and determination. For another King, the magic might not work.

He drank the last of his ale, sitting on the edge of his bed, dejected. Nothing seemed right with Holiday gone. Everything seemed disrupted and out of joint. He wished that there were something he could do to change things.

Bunion had gone out to scout the surrounding countryside, to see if there was anything to be learned of the missing King. Perhaps he would find something in his quest. Perhaps something good would come of this trek through the Greensward. Perhaps.

Abernathy lay back upon his bed once more and held his crystal out to catch the light.

Kallendbor did not appear for dinner. Neither did Bunion. Horris Kew and Abernathy ate dinner alone with Biggar looking on from the back of the conjurer's chair like some foul omen of doom. Abernathy tried to ignore him, but it was difficult since the bird was sitting directly across the table, staring down malevolently from his perch. Abernathy couldn't help himself. At one point, when Horris wasn't looking, he bared his teeth at the bird.

Biggar told Horris about it later, but Horris wasn't interested. They were back in their room, sitting in near darkness with but a single candle burning on the bedside table. Horris was seated on the bed, and Biggar was hunched down on the deep window ledge.

"He growled at me, I tell you!" the bird was insisting. "He practically snapped at me!"

Horris was looking about the room nervously. The tic was working furiously at the corner of his eye. "Growled at you? I didn't hear anything."

"Well, all right, maybe he didn't actually growl." Biggar was not up to hair-splitting. "But he showed all of his considerable teeth, and there was no mistaking his intent! Horris, pay attention, will you? Quit looking all over the place!"

Horris Kew was indeed scanning the room end to end. He stopped long enough to stare at Biggar in a rather harried, suspicious manner. Tic, tic went the eye. The bird cocked his head. "Are you all right, Horris?"

Horris nodded doubtfully. "I keep seeing something . . ." He gestured vaguely. "Our there." He shrugged. "Sometimes in the shadows of trees and buildings, and sometimes at night in dark corners I think I see it. I feel like I'm being watched." He took a deep breath. "I think *it* might be here."

"The Gorse?" Biggar sighed. "Don't be ridiculous. How could it be here? It never leaves the cave. You're imagining things."

Horris hugged his lanky frame as if cold. His plow-blade nose thrust forward. "I keep thinking about Holiday and the witch and the dragon and what it did to them. I keep worrying that you were right, that it might do the same to us."

"Well, you can't say I didn't warn you." Biggar felt an immense satisfaction at the admission. "On the other hand, we've gone a bit far with this crystal business to be worried about that now."

Horris rose and walked about the room uneasily, checking into corners and behind furniture. Biggar cocked his white-crested head. A waste of time, he was thinking. If the Gorse doesn't want to be seen, it won't be. Not a creature like that.

"Will you sit down and relax?" he said irritably. Horris was making him nervous.

Horris moved back to the bed and seated himself once more. "Do you know what the Gorse said when I asked what would become of Holiday and the others in the Tangle Box?"

Biggar couldn't remember and didn't care. But he said, "What, Horris, tell me."

"It said they would become entangled in the fairy mists. It said that the spell of forgetfulness would start them down a road that had no end. They would not know who they were. They would not remember from where they had come. They would be sealed away in the mists, and the mists would play with them and eventually drive them mad." Horris shuddered. "The Gorse said it would take a very long time to happen."

"None of this is our concern," Biggar sniffed. "We have enough to worry about as it is."

"I know, I know." Horris fidgeted and looked off into the shadows as if he had heard something. "I just can't stop thinking about it."

Biggar was disgusted. "Well, you better find a way to stop thinking about it. We have a lot to lose if this crystal-giving program doesn't work out the way the Gorse expects. On the other hand, we have a lot to gain if it does. For the Gorse, Landover is a stepping-stone to other things, but for us it's the pot of gold at the end of the rainbow. If we stick to business, we can do a lot better than we did with Skat Mandu."

"I know, I know."

"Stop saying that—I hate it when you're condescending!"

Horris came to his feet, shaking with anger. "Shut up, Biggar! I'll be condescending if I choose!" He wrung his hands and swept the room with his eyes. "I know what to do, and I'll do it! I've been doing it right along, haven't I? But I don't like being watched! I don't like the idea of someone being there when I can't see them!"

Biggar spit. "Horris, for the last time, the Gorse isn't here!"

Horris clenched his fists in frustration. "But what if it is?"

"Yes, what if I am," the Gorse said from the shadowy depths of the clothes cabinet, and Horris fainted dead away.

When it was done with them, when it had frightened them both so thoroughly that it was satisfied they would do exactly as it wanted them to and not step one inch outside the lines it had directed them to follow, the Gorse went down the outside wall of the castle like a spider. Once on the ground, it changed to a man and went out through the gates to the town beyond. It was getting easier to move about, its magic growing stronger the longer it was free of the fairy mists and the Tangle Box. It was now able to assume different forms. It could be anything or anyone it wished.

It smiled inside to think of the possibilities.

Horris and the bird were idiots, but useful idiots, and the Gorse intended to keep them just long enough to complete its plan for Landover's destruction. After that, it would dispense with them.

They had not expected it to come with them on their journey. They could not fathom how it had managed to do so. Well, a few more surprises awaited them on this trip. It was best to keep them just a little off balance, a little uncertain. They could say what they wished about it as long as they worried when they did. A little fear was a useful thing.

Once outside the castle and the town, the Gorse shape-changed once more and moved off toward a darkened stretch of woods in the countryside beyond, become barely more than a shadow skimming over the land. Worried for Holiday, the witch, and the dragon, were they? Well, they should worry. It could happen to them just as easily. It could be as terrible as they imagined. Surely his three captives in the Tangle Box must be wishing they could escape their nightmare existence just about now. They must wonder what it would take. Too bad they would never know.

It reached the woods and gathered its magic to summon up the demons of Abaddon. Time for another conference. Their entry into Landover was not far off. The Gorse wanted them ready and waiting. Lines of fire speared downward from its hands into the earth.

The answering rumble of discontent came almost immediately.

Gristlies

The Knight, the Lady, and the Gargoyle followed the river downstream through the Labyrinth for the remainder of that day and all the next. It broadened at times so that the far bank disappeared entirely in the mist, and the flat, gray surface stretched away like smooth stone. No fish jumped from its depths; no birds flew over its surface. Bends and twists came and went, but the river flowed on unchanged and unending.

They encountered no other people, River Gypsies or otherwise. They saw no animals, and the small movements that caught their attention came from the deep shadows of the forest and were gone in the blink of an eye.

The Knight searched often for the Haze, but there was no sign of it. He thought long and hard on its origins, compelled to do so by his certainty that it was somehow tied to them. There was, as the Gargoyle had said, a hunger in the way it came after them. It tracked them for a reason, and the reason was somehow connected to why they were trapped in the Labyrinth. He could not see or hear the Haze, but he could sense its presence. It was always there, just out of sight, waiting.

But what was it waiting for?

On the evening following her rescue from the Gypsies, the Lady asked the Knight why he had come after her. They were seated in the gloom as the last of the day's faint light filtered away into darkness, staring out at the mist as it crawled out of the trees toward the river. They were alone; the Gargoyle had gone off by himself, as he frequently did at night.

"You could have left me and gone on," she observed, her voice cool and questioning. "I thought you had done so."

"I would not have done that," he replied, not looking at her.

"Why? Why bother with me? Am I really so important to your master that you would risk your life for me? Am I such a rare treasure that you would die before losing me?"

He stared off into the dark without answering.

She brushed at her long black hair. "I am your possession, and you would not let anyone take your possessions from you. That is why you came for me, isn't it?"

"You do not belong to me," he said.

"Your master's possession, then. A chattel you dare not lose for fear of offending him. Is that it?"

He looked at her and found derision and bitterness in her eyes. "Tell me something, my Lady. What do you remember of your life before waking in the Labyrinth?"

Her lips tightened. "Why should I tell you?"

He held her gaze, not looking away this time when the anger sparked and burned at him. "I remember almost nothing of my own life. I know I was a Knight in service to a King. I know I have fought hundreds of battles on his behalf and won them all. I know we are tied together somehow, you and I and, I think, the Gargoyle as well. Something happened to me to bring me to this place and time, but I cannot recall what it was. It is as if my whole life has been stolen away."

He paused. "I am tired of not answering your questions because I have no answers to give. I do not know the name of the master I serve. I do not even know my own name. I do not know where I came from or where I was going to. I came for you not out of loyalty to a master I do not remember or to fulfill an obligation that I cannot recall, but because you are all I have left to hold onto of my life before coming here. If I lose you, if I give you up, nothing would remain."

She stared at him, and the anger and bitterness dimmed. In their place there showed understanding and a hint of fear. "I cannot remember anything either," she said softly, speaking the words as if it caused her pain to do so. "I was important and strong, and I knew what I was about. I had magic once."

Her voice caught in her throat, and he thought she might cry. She did not. She regained control of herself and continued. "I think that magic sent me here. I think you are right, that we were together before and sent here for the same reason. But I think, too, that it was your fault that it happened, not mine."

He nodded. "That may be."

"I blame you for this."

He nodded again. "I am not offended."

"But I am glad that you are here and that you came for me, too."

He was too astonished to reply.

On the second night, when the Gargoyle had disappeared into the growing darkness and they were hunkered down by the riverbank, she spoke to him again. She was wrapped in her cloak as if cold, although the air was warm and humid, and there was no wind.

"Do you think we shall escape this place?" she asked in a very small voice.

"We shall escape," he replied, for he still believed they would.

"The forest and this river go on and do not show any sign of ending. They show no change. The mists still wrap us about and close us away. There are no people or animals. There are no birds." She shook her head slowly. "There is magic everywhere; it controls everything in the Labyrinth. You may not be able to feel it, but I do. It is a place of magic, and without magic to aid us we shall not escape."

"There will be a town or a pass through mountains or—"

"No," she interrupted, her slim white hand coming up quickly to stop him. "No. There will be nothing but the river and the forest and the mists forever. Nothing."

He woke early the following morning, having spent an uneasy, mostly sleepless night. The Lady's words haunted him, a grim prophesy he could not forget. She was sleeping still, curled into her cloak in the tall grass, her face serene and smooth, no trace of anger or despair, no hint of bitterness or fear. She was very beautiful lying there, all pale skin and dark hair, flawless and perfect, the coldness that sometimes marked her when she was awake replaced in sleep by softness.

He looked down at her, and he wondered what they had been to each other before coming into the Labyrinth.

After a moment, he rose and went down to the river's edge. He splashed water on his face and wiped himself dry. When he rose, the Gargoyle was standing next to him. The beast had cast off his cloak. Dew glistened on the bare patches of his bristly hide, like water on a reptile newly risen from the river's depths. His wings hung ribbed and listless against his hunched back. His face, so ugly and misshapen, seemed contemplative as he looked out over the river. He did not speak at first, but simply stood there.

"Where do you go at night?" the Knight asked him.

The Gargoyle smiled, showing his yellow teeth. "Into the woods where the shadows are thickest. I sleep better there than in the open." He looked at the Knight. "Did you think I was off hunting down and eating small creatures too slow and soft to escape me? Or that I was performing some diabolical blood rite?"

The Knight shook his head. "I did not think anything. I simply wondered."

The Gargoyle sighed. "The truth is, I am a creature of habit. We spoke of what we remembered—or did not remember? I remember my habits best. I am ugly and despised by most; it is a fact of my life. Since I am loathsome to others, I take comfort in keeping to myself. I search out the places others would not go. I conceal myself in darkness and shadows and the privacy of my own company. It works best for me when I do."

He looked away again. "I did eat other creatures once. I ate whatever I chose and traveled wherever I wished. I could fly. I soared the skies unfettered, and there was nothing that could hold me." The yellow eyes shifted back. "But something changed that, and I think it is tied somehow to you."

The Knight blinked. "To me? But I do not even remember you."

"Odd, isn't it? I heard what the Lady said to you, about how she believes the Labyrinth is magic. I was listening from the trees. I think she is right. I think we were somehow transported by magic, and that magic keeps us prisoners. Do you feel it as well?"

The Knight shook his head. "I don't know."

"The Labyrinth does not feel like any real place," the Gargoyle said. "It lacks the small things that would make it so. It feels artificial, as if it were created by dreams, where everything happens a short step out of time from how we know things to be. Did you not sense it to be so with that town and after the Gypsies? Magic would do that, and I think it has done so here."

"If so," the Knight said quietly, "then the Lady is also right when she says we shall not escape."

But the Gargoyle shook his head. "It only means that since magic brought us in, magic must take us out. It means we must look for our escape in a different way."

The Knight stared off again. What other way was there? he wondered. He could not think of any. They lacked magic themselves; to sustain them they had only the weapons he carried and their wits. That didn't seem enough.

They followed the river again that day, and nothing

changed. The river rolled on, the forest stretched away, and the mist and gray permeated everything. The Labyrinth's sameness was growing almost unbearable. The Knight found himself imagining that the ground they were covering now was the same ground they had covered before. He found himself catching sight of landmarks he recognized and geography he knew. It was impossible, of course. They had gone on the same way without once turning back, so there was no chance that they could be repeating their steps. Still, the feeling persisted, and it began to wear at the Knight's resolve.

They camped at a bend in the river where the forest came almost to the water's edge and they could settle themselves back within its shelter. They did so because the Knight wanted the Gargoyle to be able to sleep with them and not have to go off by himself. The creature was scarred already by his hideous appearance, and it seemed cruel that he should be compelled to hide himself away from them each night. They were companions on this journey and had only themselves for support. They must do what they could to keep the bond between them strong. Even the Lady had quit baiting the Gargoyle, had ceased referring to him in derogatory terms, and had begun to speak to him in a civil tone now and again. It was a start, the Knight believed.

His thoughtfulness was rewarded when the Gargoyle did not go off into the dark, but curled up only a few feet off, in the shadow of an old shade tree. For this night, at least, he would sleep with them.

Rough hands brought them awake, pulling them from their sleep as if they were logs from a woodpile. The Knight came to his feet with a bound, staring about wildly. How had they managed to get so close without his hearing them? The Lady was pressed against him, and he could hear the harsh sound of her breathing. The Gargoyle was hunched down a few feet off, yellow eyes gleaming in the faint new light.

There were monsters all about them, ringing their camp and closing off any avenue of escape. There were at least a dozen huge, gnarly brutes, standing upright on two legs, but bent over in a half crouch as if they might be just as comfortable going down on all fours. They were vaguely manlike in appearance—two legs, two arms, a torso, hands and feet, and a head—but their bodies were knotted and muscled grotesquely and covered with some sort of rough hide. Their faces were almost featureless, but their eyes and snouts gleamed wetly as they peered at their three captives.

One of them spoke, his mouth splitting wide to reveal huge fangs. He gibbered at them, a mixture of snorts and grunts. He gestured vaguely, first at them, then at the river, and finally at the forest.

"They want to know where we come from," the Lady said.

The Knight stared at her in surprise. "Do you understand them?"

She nodded. "I do. I can't explain it. I've never seen them before. I don't speak their language. I am not even able to put words to all of the sounds. But the meaning is clear. I can decipher it. Here, let me see if I can make them understand me."

She made a few deft motions with her fingers and hands. The creature who had spoken grunted some more. Then he looked about at his fellows and shook his head.

"They want to know what we are doing here. They say we don't belong, that we are intruders." The Lady had stepped away again from the Knight, her composure recovered. "They don't like the look of us."

"What sort of things are they?" the Gargoyle growled, his own teeth showing.

There was another exchange. "They call themselves Gristlies," the Lady reported. Her face tightened. "They say that they are going to eat us."

"Eat us?" The Knight could not believe he had heard right.

"They say we are humans and humans are to be eaten. I can't make all of it out. It has something to do with custom."

"They had better keep away from me," the Gargoyle hissed. His muscles bunched into iron cords, and his claws came out. He was on the verge of doing something that would doom them all.

The Gristlies had engaged in a new discussion, all of them grunting loudly and gesturing. There was apparently some sort of disagreement. The Knight made a quick appraisal of the beasts. All of them were huge, and any two more than a match for him in a contest of strength. He felt the weight of his broadsword on his back. The sword would give them a better chance, but still there were too many to stand against. He had to find a way to even the odds.

The Gargoyle had been thinking the same thing. "We will have to make a run for it," he rasped.

"Stay where you are." The Lady's voice was cool and calm. "They are arguing over what is to be done with us. They are very primitive and superstitious. Something about us bothers several among them. Let me try to determine what it is."

The argument continued, sharper now. Fangs bared, claws unsheathed, two of the Gristlies began growling at each other. They were ferocious-looking creatures, and the Knight began to suspect that they were much quicker and stronger than he had first believed.

"We have to get out of this circle," he said quietly, and his hand stole back toward the handle of his sword.

In that instant, the two combative Gristlies attacked each other, tearing and ripping and shrieking horribly. Their fellows fell back before the onslaught, and the circle about the Knight and his companions collapsed. Instantly the Gargoyle bolted for the river. The Knight followed, pulling the Lady after him. To their surprise, the Gristlies did not give chase. The Knight looked back over his shoulder as he ran, but no one was there. From the shadow of the trees came the sounds of the battle between the two who had argued. Improbable as it seemed, the captives no longer appeared to matter.

They had reached the river's edge and were looking for a way to cross over when the Gristlies reappeared. It was immediately apparent why they had been in no hurry. They bounded from the trees like cats, covering ground so fast that they were upon the three in seconds. There were only seven now, but they looked formidable in the dim light, massive bodies uncoiling, claws and teeth gleaming like knives.

"Draw your sword!" the Lady cried in warning, and, when he was too slow to act, seized the weapon in her own hands and tried to draw it free.

"Don't!" he snapped, breaking her grip and thrusting her away.

She held her ground furiously. The Gristlies slowed and began circling. "Listen to me!" she snapped. "Your sword does more than you think! Remember the townsfolk? Remember the Gypsies? It was when you drew your sword and did battle that the Haze appeared!"

He stared at her in disbelief. "No! There is no connection!"

"There must be!" she hissed. "We have seen the Haze no other time. And when it comes, it never comes for us, only for those who threaten us! The two must be joined in some way! The Sword and the Haze, both weapons that eliminate our enemies! Think!"

She was breathing hard, and her pale face was bright with perspiration. The Gargoyle had moved close to them, keeping his sharp eyes fixed on the circling Gristlies.

"She may be right," he said quietly. "Take heed of her."

The Knight shook his head stubbornly. "No!" he said again, thinking, *How could that be, how could it possibly . . . ?*

And suddenly he knew. The truth appeared like a beast come out of hiding, monstrous and terrible. He should have recognized it earlier; he should have seen it for what it was. He had suspected a link between the Haze and themselves, known there was a tie he could not fathom. He had thought all this time that the Haze hunted after them, a stalker awaiting its chance to strike. He had been wrong.

The Haze did not track after them; it traveled with them.

Because it belonged to *him*.

The Haze was his missing armor.

He went cold to the bone. His armor had not been there when he awoke in the Labyrinth, and yet he had sensed it close at hand. His armor had always been like that, hidden, awaiting its summons. It came on command and wrapped itself about him so that he could do battle against his enemies. That was how it worked.

But here, in the mists of the Labyrinth, its form had been altered. Magic had subverted it, had poisoned it, had made it over into a thing that was unrecognizable. His armor had become the Haze. It must be so. Why else would the Haze come to their rescue each time they were threatened and then retreat back into the mists? What other explanation was there?

He could not breathe, the cold so deep inside him that he was paralyzed. It was true, as he had feared, that he was responsible for the deaths of all those people, that he had destroyed the townsfolk and the River Gypsies, that he had killed them all in his warrior's guise without even realizing what he was doing.

He stood there, stunned by the impact of his recognition. "No," he whispered in despair.

He felt the Lady's hands on his shoulders, bracing him, trying to give him strength. The Gristlies were edging closer, emboldened by his indecision, by his inability to act.

"Do something!" the Lady cried.

The Gargoyle made a quick feint at the Gristlies, but the foremost only snarled in challenge and held its ground.

"I have no magic!" the Lady wailed in despair, shaking the Knight violently.

He shook her off then, come back to himself, recognizing their danger. The Lady was powerless. The Gargoyle was overmatched. They needed him if they were to survive. But if he drew his broadsword the Haze would come, destroying these creatures as it had destroyed the townsfolk and the River Gypsies—and he could not bear that.

But what other weapon did he possess?

In desperation, almost without thinking about what he was doing, he reached into his tunic and pulled out the medallion with its graven image of a knight riding out of a castle at sunrise. He yanked it free and held it forth before him, as if it were a talisman. What he hoped it would do, he did not know. He knew only that it was all he possessed from his former life, and that it had the same feel of strangeness and remoteness as his armor.

The effect of its appearance on the Gristlies was astonishing. They cringed away from it instantly, some dropping to their knees, some shielding their eyes, all shrinking from it as if it were anathema to them. Whining, weeping, shivering with fear and awe, they began to withdraw. The Knight lifted the medallion higher and took a step toward them. They broke and ran then, bolting for the trees as if pursued by demons, all the fight taken out of them, anxious only to put as much distance between themselves and the medallion as they could manage. They bounded away on all fours and were gone.

Why? the Knight wondered in amazement.

In the silence that followed, his breathing was audible. His hands lowered to his sides, and he lifted his face to the mists.

The lady went to the Knight and stood so that her face was directly before his. He did not see her; he was staring straight ahead at nothing, his eyes dangerously fixed and empty.

"What did you do?" she asked quietly.

He did not answer.

"You saved us. Nothing else matters."

He made no response.

"Listen to me," she told him. "Forget about the people of that town, and forget the Gypsies. What happened to them was not your fault. You could not have known. You did what you had to do. If you had acted otherwise, we would be dead or imprisoned."

The Gargoyle hunched down at her elbow, his cloak pulled about him, his face hidden away. "He does not hear you."

The Lady nodded. Her voice hardened. "Would you abandon us now? Would you give up on yourself because of this? You have killed men all your life as a King's Champion. It is the essence of who you are. Can you deny this? Look at me."

His eyes did not move. There were tears in them.

She reached out and slapped him hard three times, each slap a sharp crack in the silence. "Look at me!" she hissed.

He did then, the life coming back into his eyes as they turned to meet hers. She waited until she was certain he saw her. "You did what you should have done. Accept that sometimes the consequences are harsh and unforeseen. Accept that you cannot always allow for every result. There is nothing wrong in this."

"Everything," he whispered.

"They threatened us!" she snapped. "They might have killed us! Is it wrong that we killed them first? Is your guilt such that you would give them their lives at the cost of ours?

Have you lost all reason? Where is your great strength? I would not have you for my keeper if it is gone! I would not be taken by such a man! Give me my freedom if you are so compromised!"

He shook his head. "I acted out of instinct, but I should have used judgment. There is no excuse."

"You are pathetic!" she sneered. "Why do I waste my time with you? I owe you nothing! I am trapped in this world because of you, and I don't even know why that is so! You have stolen away my life; you have stripped me of my magic! Now you would deny us the protection of your own small measure as well! Don't use it, you would say, because it might cause harm! You would pity those who try to destroy us because we must destroy them first!"

His lips tightened. "I pity anything that must die at my hands."

"Then you are nothing! You are less than nothing! Look about you and tell me what you see! This is a world of mist and madness, Sir Knight! Could it be that you have failed to notice? It will destroy us quickly enough if we underestimate its dangers or show weakness in the face of its considerable strengths! Stand on your hind legs, or you are just another dog!"

"You know nothing of me!"

"I know enough! I know you have lost your nerve! I know you are no longer able to lead us!" Her face was as cold and hard as ice. "I am stronger now than you. I can make my own way! Stay on your knees, if you must! Stay here and wallow in your pity! I want nothing more to do with you!"

She started to rise, shoving past the Gargoyle. The Knight reached out, grasped her arm, and pulled her back down before him. "No!" he shouted. "You will not leave!"

The Lady swung at him with her fist, but he blocked the blow. She swung again, but he caught her wrist. She looked into his face and found it hard-edged and taut. The weakness was gone from his eyes.

"When you leave," he hissed at her, "you will leave with me!"

She stared at him without speaking. Then her free hand came up slowly and touched his cheek. She felt him flinch, and she smiled. She let her fingers trail down to his neck and drop away.

Then she leaned forward and kissed him on the mouth.

Handful of Dust

Abernathy stopped halfway down the stairs leading from his bedroom to the great hall of Rhyndweir and listened in dismay. At the foot of the stairs, Kallendbor was screaming at Horris Kew. At the gates of the fortress, the people of the Greensward were trying to break through. Across the countryside, there was chaos.

It was not a happy time.

From the start Abernathy had known that something would go wrong with Horris Kew and the great mind's eye crystal giveaway. He had known it as surely as he had known his own name. It was so predictable that it could have been written in stone. Horris Kew had been involved in a lot of schemes over the years, had come up with a whole bushel full of ideas for quick fixes and cure-alls, and not a one of them had ever worked. It was the same story every time. Things would start out in promising fashion and then somewhere along the way go haywire. No matter what the circumstances, the result was always the same. Somehow, some way, Horris Kew invariably lost control of the events he had set in motion.

In this instance, however, knowing it was so was not enough to save Abernathy. Knowing didn't do you any good if you didn't also believe. In truth, Abernathy needed to believe the exact opposite, because once he accepted that nothing had changed with Horris Kew and his schemes, even twenty years later, he had to acknowledge that the mind's eye crystals weren't what they seemed, and he couldn't possibly bring himself to do that. Abernathy was in the throes of serious denial. His own wondrous crystal had captivated him totally. Its visions had enslaved him. He was a prisoner of the prospect of being forever able to recapture glimpses of his former self and to live with the hope that what he was seeing might be a promise of what one day would be again. The visions were his private ecstasy, his own secret personal escape from the hard truths of life. Abernathy had always been a pragmatic sort, but he was helpless before this particular lure. The more he called the visions up, the more entranced he became by them. His addiction progressed from mild to severe. It wasn't just that he found pleasure in the visions; it was that they offered him the only escape that meant anything.

So he ignored his suspicions, his innate distrust, and his common sense, and he accompanied Horris Kew and his hateful bird down the path to chaos.

Hard evidence of where things were going surfaced quickly enough. The little company had progressed from Kallendbor and Rhyndweir to the other parts of the Greensward and to other people who had learned of the mind's eye crystals and were waiting to see if what they had heard was true. Crowds gathered at every crossroads and hamlet, and crystals were passed out by the handfuls. When Horris Kew failed to visit the remaining Lords—in deference to Kallendbor's false promise to deliver their crystals himself—the Lords quickly came to him. Where were their crystals? Was there to be none for them? Were they to be deprived of a treasure given so freely to common folk? Fearing personal harm and silently cursing Kallendbor for his duplicitous nature, the conjurer quickly gave them what they wanted. It became clear to Abernathy that Kallendbor hadn't taken those extra crystals to sell them. He had taken them to be certain that if his own was lost or stolen or broken, he would still have others. His greed was pointless, though. There were more than enough crystals to go around. The supply appeared inexhaustible. No matter how many were given out, the number remaining never seemed to diminish. Abernathy noted this phenomenon, but as with everything else connected with the great crystal give-away, he blithely ignored it.

Then the rumors started. There were only a few at first, but the number quickly grew. People were starting to balk at doing their work. Farmers were letting their lands lie fallow and their stock go untended in the fields. Fences broke and barns collapsed, and repairs went unmade. Shopkeepers and merchants were opening and closing when they felt like it and showing little interest in selling their goods. Some were simply letting their wares be stolen, some were giving their merchandise away. Road and construction crews were failing to show up for their jobs. Building had come to a halt. The courts were down to half-day sessions and sometimes less than that. Justice was being dispensed in a cavalier and disinterested manner. Couriers with important dispatches were arriving days late. The dispatches themselves were being written in haphazard fashion by scribes. Home life was no better than the workplace. Husbands and wives were ignoring each other and their children. Housecleaning was being left for someone else, and unwashed dishes and cookware were piling up. No one had clean clothes. Dogs and cats were going hungry.

The cause of this mass neglect was no secret. Everyone was spending every free moment gazing into their newly ac-quired mind's eye crystals.

It was astonishing how quickly things began to fall apart once the obsession with the crystals set in. One failure led to another, one moment of disregard to the next, and pretty soon it was like toppling a line of dominoes. Work could wait, the reasoning went; after all, there was always tomorrow. Besides, work was boring. Work was hard. Gazing into the crystals was infinitely more interesting and enjoyable. It was amazing how quickly time passed when you peered into their depths. Why, entire days seemed to disappear in the blink of an eye!

So it went. And the loss of one day led to the loss of the next. Everyone quit doing everything, and soon no one was doing anything except sitting around staring into the crystals. Abernathy knew, somewhere in the back of his mind, where the truth of things still flickered with a candle's dim glow, that what was happening to the people of Landover was also happening to him. But he could not accept it. He could not give up his use of the crystal, not even for a single second. Not today—maybe tomorrow. Anyway, things weren't really so bad, were they?

They were, of course. And they quickly got worse. Abernathy was the first to discover how bad they would get. One morning, two weeks out of Rhyndweir, he awakened, reached into his pocket, pulled out his crystal, summoned up his favorite vision, and watched the gem turn to dust in the palm of his hand. He stared at it in disbelief, then in shock, and finally in despair. He waited for it to come back together again, but it stayed a pile of dust. He carried it to Horris Kew, desperate to have it restored. But Horris didn't have a clue about what was happening. Maybe it was a bad crystal, he suggested. He would give Abernathy another.

But when he opened the chests to get one, they found both empty. Not a crystal remained, although Abernathy was certain there had been crystals the day before or at least the day before that—no one was quite sure. Had they somehow given them all away without realizing it? Where had all the crystals gone?

They were far out on the eastern border of the Greensward by now, having visited most of that land and some parts of the Melchor, and they quickly turned for home. Maybe more crystals could be found on their return, Abernathy suggested hopefully, trying the very best he could not to sound too anxious, conscious of Horris and that stupid bird hanging on his every word. Maybe so, Horris agreed. Yes, quite possibly so. But he didn't sound like he believed it.

As Abernathy, Bunion, Horris, and the bird journeyed back, new rumors began to crop up. Crystals everywhere were turning to dust. People were furious. What was happening? What were they supposed to do without their visions? Lethargy gave way to violence. Neighbors turned on one another, looking to beg, borrow, or steal crystals to replace the ones they had lost. But no one had any to give. Everyone was in the same terrible position, deprived of what had been seen initially as a diversion but had evolved all too rapidly into a necessity of life. The people milled about and bumped up against each other for a few days in anger and despair, searching for crystals. Then they did what people always do when they get frustrated enough—they turned on the government. In this case, they turned on the Lords of the Greensward. Hadn't they authorized and facilitated the dispensing of the crystals in the first place? Surely they must be able to get more.

With single-minded resolve, the people marched on the castle fortresses of their Lords, determined to seek redress for their perceived wrongs.

Abernathy should have seen then where things were headed, but he was still so traumatized over the loss of his own crystal that he could not think of anything else. He trudged along despondently, trying to imagine what life would be like if there were no more crystals and the visions were really gone for good. It was a prospect too awful to contemplate. He was barely aware of the others and what they were doing. When Horris and his bird began whispering anxiously at each other and casting uneasy glances over their shoulders, he failed to pay attention. When the black-cloaked stranger joined them— absent one moment, there the next—he didn't see. Even when Bunion reappeared from one of his frequent scouting patrols and hissed in warning that there was something wrong with the stranger, Abernathy only just heard him. He was beyond such concerns, consumed by private grief, on the edge of slipping away completely.

They arrived at Rhyndweir and found matters in such turmoil that they almost bypassed the castle completely. But they were without supplies by now and anxious to discover if Kallendbor still had his own crystal supply intact. They had heard nothing to suggest otherwise, and indeed by the time they worked their way past the crowds jammed up against the gates and gained the interior of the fortress they discovered that, yes, things were apparently just fine. Kallendbor met them with self-absorbed indifference, provided a brief greeting, and then immediately disappeared again. His crystals were fine, it seemed. Why they remained unaffected when all the others were turning to dust was a mystery, but it was a mystery they thought it wise not to pursue. The plan was to spend the night, replenish supplies, and leave at first light for Sterling Silver. No lingering about, they decided. None of them wanted to be there if anything went wrong with Kallendbor's crystals.

Abernathy retired to his room and stayed there. He wasn't hungry, so he didn't go down for dinner. He wanted to spend as little time with Kallendbor as he had to. Bunion disappeared almost immediately after they arrived, and Abernathy neither knew nor cared where the kobold had gone. Bunion had escaped the trap of the crystals and their visions. Like most kobolds, he was disinterested in and mistrustful of magic and had refused the offer of one early on. Leaving Horris and Abernathy to manage the great crystal giveaway, Bunion had spent his time scouring the countryside in search of the missing Ben Holiday. He had found nothing so far, but he refused to give up looking. Sooner or later, he was convinced, he would find some trace of the missing King.

So Abernathy was alone when night set in and the mob at the gates began to light huge watch fires before the castle, fueling them with the thatched roofs and wooden walls of the

closest of the city's shops and market stalls. As the fires rose and
the heat built, the mood of the people began to grow uglier
and uglier. Soon they were throwing things against the gates
and over the parapets. Shouts turned mean and threatening.
Something had to be done, they cried, and it had to be done
right now! Where were their crystals? They wanted their crystals back! The castle guards hunkered down and waited out the
storm, their own mood a bit uncertain. Many among them
had lost crystals as well and were sympathetic to the crowd's
demands. Many had friends and relatives out there yelling up
at them. There were some who were leaning toward opening
the gates. The only thing that kept them from doing so was a
threadbare sense of duty, an ingrained force of habit, and a
healthy fear of Kallendbor. It was not clear how long such bar-
riers would keep them in check.

Kallendbor seemed oblivious to the problem. There had
been no sign of him since they arrived, and Abernathy had
been just as grateful. But when the sound of the mob without
began to undergo an ominous change, he found himself wondering what the Lord of the manor house was planning on
doing about it. Boiling oil would be a likely choice, if temper-
ament dictated Kallendbor's reaction. But maybe Kallendbor
was ensconced in his private chambers, curled up alone with
his wondrous crystal, gazing into its depths, absorbed in what
he found there, in the kind of visions that Abernathy himself
had once enjoyed . . .

Abernathy squeezed his eyes shut and gritted his teeth. It
was too much, really. He was suddenly furious at the prospect
of Kallendbor and his mind's eye crystals. It wasn't enough that
he enjoyed the use of one; he was hoarding several dozen!
Shouldn't he be willing to share one or two with his guests,
especially emissaries from the King himself? Shouldn't custom
and good manners dictate it? Shouldn't a complaint be lodged
and a demand be made?

Abernathy went out of his room in a huff, driven by

an itch in his soul, compelled by a need he could barely comprehend.

So it was that he was halfway down the stairs when he heard the sound of Kallendbor and Horris Kew arguing over the din of the crowds outside the castle walls.

"They're gone, charlatan!" Kallendbor was screaming in fury, his voice echoing up the stairwell from the great hall below. "Every last one of them, gone! Turned to dust! What do you know of this?"

"My Lord, I don't—"

"You listen to me, you idiot!" Kallendbor wasn't interested in explanations. "You are responsible for this! I hold you responsible! You had better find a way to restore them right now, right this instant, or I will inflict such pain on your body that you will beg me to put you out of your misery! You and your bird both!"

Abernathy caught his breath. So Kallendbor's crystals had turned to dust as well! He felt both satisfaction and disappointment. Steeling himself, he crept slowly down the stairs, one cautious step at a time.

"Well?" Kallendbor's patience had the life span of a moth caught in a candle's flame.

"My Lord, please, I shall do what I can . . ."

"You shall do what I tell you!" Kallendbor screamed, and there was the sound of shaking, of teeth rattling together, and of Biggar squawking and flying off in a rush.

Abernathy gained a bend in the stairs that allowed him to look down on what was happening below. Kallendbor was holding Horris Kew off the floor by his supplicant's robes and shaking him as hard as he could. The unfortunate conjurer was whipping back and forth in the big man's grasp like a rag doll, his feet kicking wildly, his head snapping on his skinny neck. Biggar circled overhead, crying out in dismay, swooping here and there, looking decidedly undecided about what to do.

"Give—me—back—my—crystals!" Kallendbor spit out the demand like a curse, giving Horris Kew a punctuating shake with each word uttered.

"Put him down," a voice said from the shadows.

Kallendbor turned, startled. "What? Who speaks?"

"Put him down," the voice repeated. "He isn't to blame for any of this."

Kallendbor threw Horris Kew to the floor, where the conjurer lay twitching and gasping for breath. The Lord of the Greensward wheeled toward the voice. His hand dropped to his broadsword, the weapon he always carried. "Who's there? Show yourself!"

A black-cloaked figure detached from the wall to one side, materializing out of nowhere. It glided into view rather than walked, all darkness and smooth motion. Abernathy shrank back instinctively. It was the stranger who had joined them on the road. How did he come to be here? Had he entered the fortress with them? Abernathy could not remember him doing so.

"Who are you?" Kallendbor asked sharply, but the edge had disappeared from his voice and been replaced by a hint of uncertainty.

"A friend," the stranger answered. He stopped moving a dozen feet away. Although Abernathy tried, he could not see the man's face. "You can shake Horris Kew until his bones come out of his skin, but that won't get your crystals back. Horris Kew doesn't have them to give."

Kallendbor stiffened. "How do you know this?"

"I know a good many things," the stranger said. His voice had an odd hissing quality to it, as if the vocal cords had once suffered some severe injury. "I know that Horris Kew and his companions are dupes in this matter, that they do only what they were instructed to do, and that they have no more crystals to give you. I know as well that they did not realize that the crystals they were giving you would turn to dust after only a short period of use. You have been cheated, my Lord. You have been tricked."

Kallendbor's hand tightened on his sword. "Who is responsible for this? If you know so much, tell me that!"

The stranger was motionless, enigmatic, impenetrable in the face of the other's rage. "Take your hand away from your weapon. You cannot hurt me."

There was a long moment of silence. Horris Kew inched carefully away from Kallendbor, crawling on his hands and knees. Biggar sat on the edge of the stair banister as if carved from stone. Abernathy held his breath.

Kallendbor's big hand dropped away. "Who are you?" he repeated once more, confused.

The stranger ignored the question. "Think a moment," he said softly. "Who sent you these crystals? Who sent the conjurer and his bird? Who sent the scribe and the runner? Who do they serve?"

Kallendbor went rigid. "Holiday!" he hissed.

Oh, oh, Abernathy thought.

The stranger laughed, a curiously grating sound. "Do you see now? How better to weaken your position, my Lord, than to make you seem a fool? You have been a thorn in the King's side from the beginning, and he would have you removed for good. When the crystals turn to dust, the people turn on you. You are their Lord and therefore must answer for their misery. The plan works well, don't you think?"

Kallendbor could not seem to manage an answer. He was choking on whatever he was trying to say.

"There are more crystals to be had," the stranger was saying, his voice gone smooth and persuasive. Abernathy was leaning forward to hear every word now. Who was this lying troublemaker? "There is an entire chamber full of them at Sterling Silver, hidden away for a time when they are needed. I have seen these crystals myself; there are thousands and thousands of them. Shouldn't they be yours?"

For just a moment Abernathy was persuaded. All he could see was a shimmering pile of the precious crystals, hoarded away like gold, selfishly kept from those who needed them. But in the next instant he saw the argument for the lie it was, knowing that Ben Holiday would never do anything like that, remembering in fact that the crystals had come from Horris Kew and not until after the King had disappeared.

He wondered suddenly and for the first time if the two events were connected somehow.

"There is a simple solution for your problem," the stranger was saying. He had walked over to Horris Kew and pulled him to his feet again, seemingly without effort. "Tell your people the truth of the matter. Tell them that the crystals are being kept secretly at Sterling Silver by the King. Tell them to march on his castle and demand that he give them up! Call together all the Lords of the Greensward. Have them gather their armies and their subjects and march them down to the King's doorstep. He cannot refuse all of you. He cannot withstand you even if he tries."

Kallendbor was nodding, persuaded. "I have had enough of Holiday—enough of his interference!"

"Perhaps," the stranger whispered thoughtfully, "it is time for a new King. Perhaps it is time for a man who would be more responsive to those like yourself, a man who would not behave so intractably towards his betters."

Abernathy almost barked. He was not proud of the reaction, but it was an honest one. He swallowed the sound in a muffled gasp.

"There are those who appreciate the proper uses of power." The stranger's voice was low and compelling. He made a brief, encompassing gesture toward Horris Kew. "There are those who understand the nature of loyalty, who comprehend the realities of its implementation. In other words, Lord Kallendbor, there are those who would serve any master who paid the right price."

Horris Kew was staring at the stranger, openmouthed. There was another long moment of silence.

Then Kallendbor nodded thoughtfully. "Perhaps so. Yes, why not? If he would agree to certain terms, of course. Yes. Why not make another King?" Then he shook his head abruptly. "But there is still Holiday to contend with. It is one thing to demand the release of the crystals and another altogether to remove him from the throne. He commands the services of the Paladin, and none can stand against him."

"Ah, but what if Holiday were to simply vanish?" the stranger asked in response. He paused meaningfully. "What if he already has?"

Abernathy felt his heart drop. So there it was—the truth at last. Ben Holiday's disappearance was indeed tied to Horris Kew and his mind's eye crystals, and all of it was tied to this mysterious stranger. Something terrible was going on, something that Abernathy still didn't fully comprehend, but the stranger was most definitely behind it.

What was he going to do?

He exhaled softly. He didn't know, but whatever it was he would have to get out of here to do it.

He began to back carefully up the stairs.

Not carefully enough, however. His boot scraped on the stone as he turned. It was a small noise, but one pair of ears was sharp enough to hear it.

"Awk! Someone's there!" Biggar rasped out in warning.

They all wheeled toward the stairs. "Find him!" the stranger hissed at once.

Abernathy bolted, deciding that it would not be a good idea for him to be captured at this juncture. He remained upright on two legs for the first couple of steps, then gave it up and went down on all fours. Speed took precedence over dignity, and after all a considerable part of him was dog. He raced up the stairs and down the hall for his room, not knowing where else to go. He could hear the flapping of wings behind him and the pounding of boots further back. All chance of slipping away quietly in the dead of night was gone. What was he going to do? If they found him they would throw him into the darkest hole in the castle keep. If he was lucky, that was. Otherwise, they would just eliminate him on the spot.

He reached his room and raced inside, slamming the door shut behind him and throwing the bolt. The room was shadowed and dark, the candles not yet lit. He stood gasping for breath with his back to the door and listened to the beating of wings as Biggar flew past, shrieking, "Up here! He's hiding here!"

Stupid bird talks a lot better than he lets on, Abernathy thought darkly, and found himself staring through the gloom at a pair of yellow eyes that stared back.

"Arf!" he barked, unable to stop himself this time. He flattened back against the door, frozen in place. He was trapped now on both sides. He groped through his clothing for a weapon, but he didn't have one, so he bared his teeth instead. The yellow eyes blinked curiously, and a familiar face came into view.

"Bunion!" Abernathy gasped in relief, for it was indeed the kobold. "Am I glad to see you!"

Bunion chittered something in response, but Abernathy wasn't listening. "We have to get out of here, Bunion. Kallendbor and Horris Kew and that stranger caught me listening in on them. They want Holiday off the throne! They have done something to him already, I think. I will tell you all about it later if you can just get us out!"

Bunion jumped down off the window ledge where he had been perched, sped across the room to the door, threw it open, and made a diving grab for Biggar, who was trying to fly inside. Biggar shrieked and swooped aside, but Bunion came away with a handful of black feathers. The bird flew off, crying out in pain and indignation. Bunion beckoned hurriedly to Abernathy, and the scribe followed him out the door.

Kallendbor and Horris Kew were just rounding the head of the stairs. There was no sign of the stranger.

Bunion and Abernathy fled in the opposite direction, both of them down on all fours. Like whipped curs, Abernathy thought as he ran.

They went down a back stairs and along a lower hall and into a small storage room. There was a hidden passageway behind a section of the wall, and in seconds they were groping their way through the dark—or at least Abernathy was, since he lacked Bunion's extraordinary eyes. It took them a long time, but when the passageway ended they were outside the castle walls once more.

From there, they made their way back through the mostly sleeping town and out into the countryside. As they traveled, Abernathy remembered anew the loss of his crystal. It made him cry, and he hid his tears from Bunion. But the pain faded after a while, lessened considerably by the knowledge that the recapturing of his past had been the gift of a false prophet. Horris Kew had used him, and that hurt far more than the loss of his visions. As unpleasant as it was to admit, his self-indulgence had allowed a travesty to take place, and now perhaps Ben Holiday was paying the price for it. Certainly he must do what he could to salvage the situation, and that meant getting word to Questor Thews as quickly as possible. It would be hard to face the wizard after what had happened. It would be hard to tell him the truth. Questor had not taken one of the crystals, after all. He was too stubborn and proud to accept anything from Horris Kew, Abernathy guessed—and right in being so, as it turned out. Yes, facing him would be terribly hard. But it was necessary. Perhaps there was still a way to put things right.

They slept that night in an old barn some miles south and west of Rhyndweir. The straw they used for bedding was rife with fleas and smelled of manure, but Abernathy reasoned that it was minimal penance to pay for his gross stupidity and a small price for his freedom. As he lay squirming and shifting in the dark, listening to Bunion breathe easily next to him, Landover's Court Scribe promised himself that one day soon there would be a reckoning for all this, and that when that day came he would make certain that Horris Kew, his bird, and that black-cloaked stranger got what was coming to them.

Dream Dance

Night waned toward morning, a slow, dull ebbing of sound and motion, and the streets of Greenwich Village grew empty and still. A few cars and trucks crawled by, aimless and solitary, and people still meandered the walks, but that was all. The traffic lights blinked through their sequence of green, yellow, and red with steady precision, and their colors glared off the concrete where a light rain had left its gritty sheen. In the doorways and alleys there were homeless sleeping, ragged lumps of clothing, shadows hunched down against the gloom. The rank smell of garbage wafted on the air, mingling with the steam and mist that rose out of the sewer and subway grates and off the newly washed streets. Somewhere out in the harbor, a fog horn blew.

Willow walked in silence with Edgewood Dirk, feeling trapped and alone. She should not have felt that way. Her confidence should have been higher, her expectations greater. Two-thirds of her journey to gather the soils of three worlds for the birth of her child was complete. Only one leg remained. But it was the one she dreaded most. For as much as she disliked and abhorred Ben's world with its sprawling cities that ate away at the land and its almost compulsive disregard for the sanctity of life, it was the fairy mists that frightened her most.

It was a difficult fear to reconcile. It grew out of the history of her people and their deliberate distancing from the

222

mists, their choice to accept the burdens and responsibilities of reality over fantasy, their decision to embrace mortality. It grew out of the stories of what happened to mortals who ventured into the fairy mists, of the madness that claimed them because they could not adjust to the dictates of a world where everything was imagined and nothing fixed. It grew as well out of the Earth Mother's warning to beware the motives of the fairy people in offering their help, for in all things they kept their real purposes hidden, secret from those like her.

She glanced at Edgewood Dirk and wondered what secrets the prism cat kept from her. How much of what he did was for reasons known only to him? Was there duplicity in his accompanying her to this world and the next? She could ask him, but she knew he would not answer. Neither the part of him that was fairy nor the part that was cat would let him tell. He was an enigma by nature, and he would not give up his identity as such.

So she walked and tried not to think too hard about what would happen next. They left the main streets and maneuvered their way down alleys clogged with garbage bins, debris, and rusting vehicles. They passed out of street light into misty gloom, the way forward marked faintly by faraway lamps, a dimly reflected glow on the building walls. Mist and steam mingled in the close corridor, shrouding the passageway, cloaking the night. Willow shivered with its touch and wished she could see the sun again.

Then they were at a gap in the buildings where the haze was so thick she could see nothing of what lay beyond. Dirk slowed and turned, and she knew instantly that all her choices were gone.

"Are you ready, my lady?" he asked deferentially, unusual for Dirk, and she was instantly afraid all over again.

"Yes," she replied, and could not tell afterward if she had spoken the word.

"Stay close to me," he advised, and started to turn.

"Dirk," she called quickly. He glanced back, hesitating. "Is this a trap?"

The prism cat blinked. "Not of my making," he said. "I cannot speak for what you might intend. Humans are known well for stumbling into traps of their own making. Perhaps this will happen to you."

She nodded, folding her arms about herself for warmth. "I am trusting you in this. I am afraid for myself and my child."

"Trust not the cat," Dirk philosophized, "without a glove."

"I trust you because I must, glove or no. If you deceive me, I am lost."

"You are lost only if you allow it to happen. You are lost only if you quit thinking." The cat regarded her steadily. "You are stronger than you think, Willow. Do you believe that?"

She shook her head. "I don't know."

A veil of mist blew between them, and for a moment the cat disappeared. When he was back again, his eyes were still fixed on her. "I told Holiday once that people should listen more closely to what cats would tell them, that they have many useful lessons to teach. I told him it was a failing common to most humans—that they did not listen as closely as they should. I tell you the same thing now."

"I have listened well," she said. "But I am not sure I have understood."

Dirk cocked his head. "Sometimes understanding has to wait a bit on events. So. Are you ready?"

She came forward a step. "Do not leave me, Dirk. Whatever happens, do not. Will you promise me that?"

Edgewood Dirk shook his head. "Cats do not make promises. Are you ready or not?"

Willow straightened. "I depend on you." The cat stayed silent. "Yes," she said then. "I am ready."

They moved into the narrow passageway and the mists

that clogged it and were immediately swallowed up. Willow kept her eyes lowered to where Dirk walked before her, vaguely visible in the haze. The mists were dark at first, and then lightened perceptibly. The walls of the buildings fell away, and the smells of the city disappeared. In the blink of an eye, everything about them changed. They were in a forest now, a world of great old trees with canopied limbs that hid the skies, of thick brush and tall ferns, and of smells of an ancient, forgotten time. The air was thick with must and rot and with a misty gloom that shrouded everything, turning the forest to shadows and half light. There was a suggestion of movement, but nothing could be certain where everything was so dim.

Dirk walked steadily on, and Willow followed. She glanced back once, but there was nothing left of the city. She had come out of that world and into this. She was within the fairy mists, and it would all be new again.

She heard the voices first, vague whisperings and mutterings in the gloom. She strained to understand the words and could not. The voices rose and fell, but remained indistinct. Dirk walked on.

She saw their faces next, strange and curious features lifting from the shadows, sharp-featured and angular with hair of moss and corn-silk brows, eyes as penetrating as knife blades when they fixed on her, and bodies so thin and light-seeming as to be all but ethereal. The fairy folk darted and slowed, came and went, flashes of life in the shifting gloom. Dirk walked on.

They arrived at a clearing ringed by trees, fog, and deeper gloom, and Dirk walked to its center and stopped. Willow followed, turning as she did to find the fairy people all about, faces and bodies pressed up against the haze as if against glass.

The voices whispered to her, anxious, persuasive.

Welcome, Queen of Landover

Welcome, once-fairy, to the land of your ancestors

Be at peace and stay with us awhile
See what you might have here with the child you bear . . .

And she was walking suddenly in a field of bright red flowers, the like of which she had never seen. She carried a baby in her arms, the child wrapped carefully in a white blanket, protected from the bright light. The smells of the field were wondrous and rich, and the sunlight warm and reassuring. She felt impossibly light and happy and filled with hope, and below where she walked the entire world spread away before her, all of its cities and towns and hamlets, all of its people, the whole of its life. The child moved in her arms. She reached down to pull back the blanket so that she could peek at its face. The baby peeked back. It looked just like her. It was perfect.

"Oh!" she gasped, and she began to cry with joy.

She was back in the clearing then, back within the fairy mists, staring out into the gloom.

The voices whispered once more.

It will be so, if you wish it

Make your happiness what you would, Queen of Landover. You have the right. You have the means

Keep safe within the mists, safe with your child, safe with us, and it shall be as you were shown

She shook her head, confused. "Safe?"

Stay with us, once-fairy

Be again as your kind once were

Stay, if you would have your vision come true . . .

She understood then, saw the price that she was being asked to pay for the assurance that her child would be as the vision had shown. But it was not really so, for they would both end up living in an imaginary world and the vision would be nothing more than what they created in their minds. And she would lose Ben. There had been no mention of Ben, of course, because he was not to be included in this promised land, an outsider, an other-worlder who could never belong to the fairy life.

She looked down at Dirk, but the prism cat was paying no attention to her. It sat turned slightly away, washing its face carefully, lick, lick, scrub, scrub. The indifference it showed was studied and deliberate.

She looked back at the sea of faces in the mist. "I cannot stay here. My place is in Landover. You must know that. The choice was made for me a long time ago. I cannot come back here. I do not wish to."

A grave error, Queen of Landover.

Your choice affects the child as well. What of the child?

The voices had changed in tone, turning edgy. She swallowed back her fear of what that might mean. "When my child is old enough to decide, it shall make its own decision."

There was a general murmuring, and it did not sound supportive. It whispered of dissatisfaction and thinly veiled anger. It whispered of bad intent.

She held herself stiffly. "Will you give me the soil my child needs?" she asked.

The whispers died into stillness. Then a voice answered.

Of course. You were promised this soil in coming. It is yours to take. But to take it, it must first be made your own

Fairy earth cannot pass out of the mists until it has been celebrated and embraced by its taker

Willow glanced again at Dirk. No response. The cat was still washing as if nothing else in all the world could be quite so important.

"What must I do?" she asked of the faces.

What is in your blood, sylph child. Dance as your wood nymph mother has taught you to dance. Dance across the earth on which you stand. When you have done so, it will be your own, and you may take it with you and depart these mists

Willow stood transfixed. Dance? There was something

hidden here. She could feel it; she was certain of it. But she could not fathom what it was.

Dance, Queen of Landover, if you would have the soil for your child

Dance, if you would complete your journey and give birth

Dance, Willow of the once-fairy

Dance . . .

So she did. She began slowly, a few cautious steps to see what would happen, a few small movements to test if all was well. Her clothes felt heavy and cumbersome, but she was not persuaded to take them off as she might have done otherwise, anxious to stay ready to flee if something should go wrong. Nothing did. She danced a bit further, increased the number of her steps, the complexity of her movements. Her fear and caution eased a bit in the face of her joy at doing something she loved so much. The faces of the fairies seemed to recede into the mist, sharp eyes and thin noses, stringy hair and stick-like limbs, bits of light and movement gone back into the gloom. One minute they were there, and the next they were gone. She was alone.

Except for Dirk, who had moved away from her and was watching carefully. He sat as if carved from stone.

She danced faster, caught up suddenly in the flow of the steps, in the rhythm of the movements, in the joy that swelled and surged inside. It seemed to her as if she could dance more quickly, more lightly, more precisely here in the fairy mists than in the real world. All of her efforts were rewarded with success beyond anything she had ever known. Her joy increased as she performed ever more complicated movements, spinning and twirling, leaping and twisting, as light as air, as swift as the wind. She danced, and she could tell that she was suddenly far better than her mother had ever been, that she had mastered in seconds that which her mother had worked for all her life.

She shed her clothes now, her inhibitions forgotten, her

promise of caution and restraint abandoned. In seconds, she was naked.

Across the clearing she flew, alone in her flight through mist and half light, oblivious to all else. Yes, the dance was everything she had ever wanted it to be! Yes, it would give her things she had never thought possible! She rose and fell, rose again, and sped on. Colors appeared before her eyes, rainbow-bright and as fresh as flowers in a vast, limitless garden, all carefully arranged and fragrant beyond belief. She was flying over them, soaring in the manner of a bird, as free as air. There were other birds with her, all brightly colored and singing wonderfully, sweeping about her, showing her the way. She lifted from the garden into the sky, rising toward the sun, toward the heavens. Her dance carried her, bore her on, gave her wings.

She was dreaming anything she wished, any possibility, any hope. It was all there, and it all belonged to her. She danced, and all else was forgotten. She no longer remembered where she was or why she had come. She no longer remembered Ben or her child. The dance was everything. The dance was all.

From the mists surrounding the clearing, the fairies watched and smiled among themselves, unseen.

Willow might have been lost then, caught up forever in her dance, had Dirk not sneezed. There seemed to be no reason for it; it just happened. It was a small sound, but it was enough to draw her back from the precipice. For just a second she caught a glimpse of the prism cat somewhere at the corner of her vision and remembered. She saw him looking at her, his steady, impenetrable gaze an open accusation. What was it he had told her? She had asked him of traps, and he had warned her that humans mostly stumbled into those of their own making. Yes, like this one. This dance.

But she could not stop. She was too deep in the throes of its pleasure, of its wonder, to cease moving. The dreams it in-

duced were too compelling to give up. She had done what he
had warned her against and trapped herself, and now she could
not get free. It was the fairies' plan for her, she saw—that she
should dance and keep dancing and never leave. Here is where
her child would be born, here in the fairy mists, and when it
was born it would belong to them. They would both belong
to the fairies for all time.

Why? Why did they wish it so? She had no answer.

Her thoughts scattered, and for a moment she was in
danger of slipping back into her dreams. But she kept her eyes
on Dirk as she spun across the clearing, watching him watching her, desperately trying to think what to do. Dance forever.
She would never stop. But she must. She must! She would not
let this happen to her, she told herself. She would find a way
to break free.

Ben. If Ben were there, he would help her. Ben, who she
could always rely upon to stand with her, who had pledged
himself to her forever. Ben, the strength that sustained her
when all else failed. He would always come. Always.

But how could he come this time?

Ben!

Had she called out loud to him? She couldn't be sure.
She felt Dirk beginning to slip away. She could barely see him
through the haze of her dance, through the magic that en-
snared her.

Ben!

And for just an instant, he was there—a glimpse of his
face, of his eyes come out of time and distance. He was there,
still a long way off, but within reach.

Suddenly she saw a chance for escape. She would use the
fairy magic to her own advantage, turn it to her own use. It
had been set to trap her and she had allowed it to do so, but
there was still a way out. The dance was a dream, and the
dream could be altered if she was strong enough. She was not

completely lost, not yet. Not if she didn't wish it. Not if she didn't forget.

She closed her eyes and in the sweep of her dance called out to Ben Holiday. She could imagine him as she could imagine everything else. That was the magic of the fairy world. Banish her fear, and she would be able to control her vision, to make it her own, to affect its direction. That was the lesson Ben had once learned. It was the one Dirk had cautioned her to. Use the magic to free yourself. Use the dance to escape.

Ben! She called to him, her voice strong and steady.

And then something wondrous and completely unexpected happened.

The Knight lay sleeping in the Labyrinth, stretched full-length upon the ground within the cover of a grove of hardwood that canopied overhead like a tent. The Lady lay pressed against him, curled to his body, her head resting on his shoulder, her arm draped across his chest. She was smiling, the hardness that so often marked her features absent this night. Mist and gloom hung all about, shrouding the world and those who stalked it, but for the moment at least the Knight and the Lady had left it behind.

The Gargoyle sat hunched down within his cloak a few feet away and watched them uneasily. It did not feel right to him. He could not explain it, but there was a lie in what was happening. That was unmistakable. These two were enemies and this new alliance lacked wisdom and reason. Their impetuousness would catch up to them, he believed. Perhaps it would destroy them.

His misshapen features wrinkled in distaste, and he looked purposefully away.

As he slept, the Knight began to dream. At first the dream lacked focus, a blurring of sound and movement as he was carried across time and space toward some unknown destination. He was at peace, and so he did not resist the pulling that bore him on. Then he began to hear voices—no, a single voice—calling out a name. He could hear it repeating, over and over. He recognized the voice, but could not place it. The name seemed familiar, too.

Ben.

He listened to the sounds as he traveled, knowing he was closing on them, that he was being drawn, that he was called deliberately.

Ben.

Then he was jolted as if by a massive hand and found himself earthbound once more and upright. The voice was distinct now and quite close. It was a woman, and she called with need. She was someone he knew, someone to whom he was bound, and she called for his protection.

The Knight went to her at once, drawing forth the great broadsword as he pushed through the trees of a forest that loomed about him. It was the Labyrinth and yet it was not. He could not explain it, but while the two were separate they were also somehow joined. All of the elements were the same. He brought the broadsword before him, prepared to do battle. He lacked his heavy armor still, cloaked only in chain mail, in his leather clothing, in his belt and boots and gloves. He gave it less than a passing thought. He felt no fear of what waited for him. The certainty he felt for his cause overwhelmed any doubts. He was meant to give aid to those to whom he was pledged, and the woman who called was foremost of these.

He reached a clearing, the light where it widened to the skies a vague brightness in the smoky haze. Figures scattered at his coming, small creatures that were thin and angular, all sharp edges and bits of moss and stick. They fell back from him as if he bore a plague, hissing and muttering like cornered rats. He went through them without slowing to the clearing's center and stopped.

The woman who danced through the shadows and half light spun into his arms and held him as if he were a line to safety from a raging sea. Naked, she shivered as if chilled to the bone, and her face and body pressed up against him.

"Ben," she whispered. "You came."

The Knight held her close in an effort to still her shaking, and as he did so recognition flooded through him.

"Willow!" he whispered back fiercely.

He knew then. The deception that had shackled him fell away at her touch, at the sound of her voice, at the sight of her face. Though he dreamed, in some way the dream was real. He had been called to her in sleep, but they were joined as surely as if awake and together in the flesh. She clung to him, whispering his name, telling him things he could not understand. They were within the fairy mists. She was imprisoned by the fairies in a dance and could not break free. Their child was to be kept from them, kept here forever. But all was reality if you could imagine it, and so she had imagined him coming to save her in a desperate effort to break free. And come he had, but not as she had believed he would. He was really there. How had this happened? How had he breached the fairy mists?

All about the fairies swarmed like maddened bees, hissing and darting through the gloom, enraged. He saw Edgewood Dirk sitting close by, watching in his cat way. Edgewood Dirk? What was he doing here?

Ah, but more important, what had been done to the Knight of the Labyrinth, who knew himself now to be Ben Holiday? Memories flooded through him, the spell of forgetfulness broken. He had been snatched away from the Heart by magic and imprisoned in a rune-carved box. It was the last thing he remembered had happened before his waking in the Labyrinth. Except that Horris Kew had been standing there, had set the box down, had stepped away just before Ben fell into it, tumbling down with . . .

His heart stopped.

With Nightshade and Strabo.

With the Lady and the Gargoyle.

The truth stunned him so that for a moment he could not breathe or move. He held onto Willow as if their positions had been reversed and now she was the lifeline that kept him from being swept away. She sensed his shock and looked up at him quickly, and her hands came up to hold his face.

"Ben," she whispered anew. "Please. It's all right."

With a massive effort he shrugged off his immobility. There was a tearing at the corners of his vision. The dream that bound them was fragmenting, coming to a close, the magic expending itself. Willow could feel it as well. With the ending of the dance, the dream could not sustain itself. She moved to dress, ignoring the small sounds of fury that emanated from the mists, come back to herself once more and determined that she would not be tricked again. Clothed, she bent to the earth across which she had danced and scooped a handful of the soil into the pouch she carried.

Ben watched her without understanding. He started toward her, then found he could not move. He looked down at himself and saw to his horror that he was fading away.

"Willow!" he cried out in warning.

She rose at once and hurried toward him. But he was already losing shape and definition, returning to his dream, to his sleep, to the prison that still held him. He heard her call out to him, saw her reach for him, watched her try to hold him back. But she could not. The magic that had joined them from the fairy mists of two worlds was breaking up.

"Willow!" he cried out again, desperate now, unable to slow his going. "I'll find you somehow! I promise! I'll come for you!"

"Ben!" he heard her call to him one final time, and then he was lifting away, transparent in the mists, a bit of air and wind borne back across the gap that separated them in waking, back into the sleep from which he had come.

Alone once more in the silent clearing, Willow stared skyward at the roiling gloom. Ben was gone. The magic of her vision had been strong enough to bring him, but not to hold him. He had set her free of the dance, but could not stay to help her further. She felt a renewed desperation settle through her and fought back against her tears. But there was no time for grief, for anything but her child, and she used her anger as armor and wheeled on Edgewood Dirk.

"I want to go home," she said quietly, deliberately. "Right now."

The prism cat blinked. "Then go, Queen of Landover."

"You will not stop me?"

"Not I."

"Nor the fairies that ring this clearing?"

Dirk yawned. "They have lost interest in playing this particular game. Interesting, don't you think, how they failed to challenge Holiday?"

She considered. It was interesting. Why had they let him go? And her. What was it that stopped them from interfering?

"What path do I take, Dirk?" she asked him.

Edgewood Dirk rose and stretched. "Any path will do. All lead to where you are meant to go. Your instincts will guide you. As I said earlier, you are stronger than you think."

She did not respond to him, too angry with what had been done to her to accept compliments. He had helped her in his own peculiar way, whether by accident or on purpose she still wasn't certain, but the prism cat was no friend in either case. The fairy mists and the creatures who lived within them, Dirk included, were anathema. She wanted gone from them all.

"You are not coming with me?" she questioned.

"No," he answered. "You have no further need of me. Your quest is finished."

So it was. She had the soils she had been sent to gather, the soils of the three worlds to which her child's blood could be traced. If the Earth Mother spoke the truth, the birth of her child could take place now. There was nothing more for her to do, nothing else required. She could go home.

Folding her cloak about her, clutching her pouch of soils close against her body, she turned and began to walk. She did as she was told and followed her instincts. Surprisingly, they seemed quite clear. They took her in a straight line through the trees.

They took her deep into the mists until she disappeared.

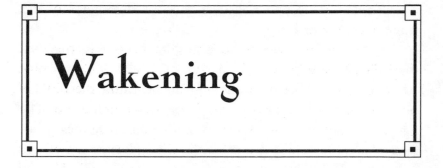

Wakening

Ben Holiday awoke with a start. His eyes snapped open, and he stared straight ahead through the predawn gloom into the trees of the Labyrinth. He did not move; he could not make himself. He was frozen in place as surely as if he had been encased in ice. Questions raced through his mind, one after the other, whispers and dark teasing. Had he dreamed of his meeting with Willow or had it actually taken place? Was it truth or a wild concoction of his imagination? How much of anything that had happened to him that he could remember was real?

The Lady lay pressed up against him, still sleeping. The Gargoyle sat hunched down at the edge of the trees several yards away, head bowed. Ben blinked. Nightshade? Strabo?

He closed his eyes and kept them shut for a moment, thinking. Something had happened to reveal the truth—that much was certain. He was not the Knight; he was Ben Holiday. The Knight was some personification of his real identity. It was so with the Lady and the Gargoyle as well. They had been changed by the Labyrinth and its magic, or by the magic that had sent them here, or by some foul deception they did not yet understand. They had been given identities that mirrored some part of who they were but concealed the rest. They appeared significantly different than they were. Strabo had been changed most; he was not even a dragon anymore.

Nightshade was recognizable, yet she was different too in a way he could not quite explain. Neither had the use of their magic. Neither possessed the strength and power that was theirs in Landover.

He opened his eyes again. Mist hung amid the trunks and limbs of the trees. It carpeted the grasses on which he lay. The Labyrinth was a vast, endless mirage their vision could not see through.

What had been done to them?

Horris Kew. The conjurer had something to do with this, though in truth it was hard to believe he possessed power enough to imprison them in this otherworld. But he had been there watching. He had provided the box into which they had been lured, in which they were now trapped. Ben repeated the words. Trapped in a box. How, he wondered abruptly, had that been done? Horris Kew. He breathed slowly, carefully, trying to think. Did knowing Horris Kew was involved help in any way? Where were they? Oh, yes, the Labyrinth, but where was that?

His mind sideslipped. Willow. He had gone to her. He had not dreamed it—or if he had, there had been a large piece of reality in the dream. All was possible if you went into the fairy mists, where reality was fluid and anything could be brought to pass. Magic had brought him to her, magic born of her dance and of her imaginings. She had called him to her because she could not break free. Was she free now? Had he helped her escape before the dream had ended? What was she doing in the fairy mists in the first place?

There were no answers for his questions, only more questions. He could not allow too many. Too many would strangle him. Only one thing mattered now—that he break free of the Labyrinth and find her. There must be a way. Magic had been used to conceal the truth about who he was, and there was a reason for that. Somewhere in that concealing there was something that would help him, that would help them all.

He looked back at them again, at their silent, sleeping forms.

Once they knew, of course. Once they were told.

He eased himself away from Nightshade, thinking of what had passed between them as the Knight and the Lady, recognizing the damage they had inadvertently done to themselves. He remembered how she had kissed him. He remembered her touch. His eyes closed in dismay. How could he tell her that it was all a lie? How could he tell her that she was not his charge as he had believed, that the magic of their prison had misled them, had tricked them into thinking that their relationship was something other than what it really was and caused them to . . .

He could not finish the thought. Only one thing mattered. There was now and had always been only Willow.

He climbed to his feet, not yet ready to do so. He walked away from her, moving toward the trees, trying to assemble the fragments of what he knew into some recognizable whole. He thought of how he had been made to appear, a Knight with no past and no future, a nameless warrior, a champion for a master with no name and of a cause without identity. His worst nightmare. His worst . . .

Fear.

He saw it then, the truth that had been hidden from them all this time. They were in the fairy mists, too!

The Gargoyle was next to him suddenly, a dark shadow moving out of the haze. Gnarled hands balanced his disjointed body as he leaned forward. "What is it?" he asked, seeing Ben's face.

Ben looked at him, trying to see past the ugliness, past the mask the magic had created. He could not. "I know what has been done to us," he said. "I know where we came from. I know who we are."

The Gargoyle's face twisted and froze, his eyes glittering like candles. "Tell me."

Ben shook his head. He motioned to the Lady. "We must wake her, too."

They walked to her, and Ben reached down and touched her arm. She awoke at once, flawless, cold features softened by sleep, a smile upon her face. "I dreamed of you," she began.

He placed a warning finger to her lips. "No, say nothing. Don't speak. Sit up and listen to me. I have something to tell you." He moved back from her, letting her rise. "Listen carefully. I know who we are."

She stared at him for a moment, then shook her head quickly. "I don't want to know." There was fear in her voice, recognition that something was about to be stolen away. "What difference does it make to us here?"

He kept his voice calm, even. "By knowing who we are and where we come from, we give ourselves a chance to escape. Our only chance, I think."

"How is it that you know and we do not?" she snapped at him, angry now, defensive.

"I was given a dream," he told her. "In the dream I discovered what had happened to us. We have been trapped in this place by magic. We were sent here from another world, our world. Magic was used to make us forget who we are, to make us seem different. We were sent here to wander about forever, I think—to spend what was left of our lives futilely attempting to find a way out. But there is no way out of here except by using magic. You were right—magic alone can save us. But first we have to understand how that magic works. To do that, we have to understand ourselves, who we are, where we came from, what it is we do."

"No," she said quietly and shook her head back and forth. "Don't say anything else."

"I am not the Knight," he said, pressing quickly ahead, anxious to get this over with. "I am Ben Holiday, King of Landover."

Her hands flew to her mouth, shaking. She made a noise deep in her throat.

Unable to bear her look, Ben turned to the Gargoyle. The monster was staring at him, expressionless. "You are called Strabo. You are a dragon, not a Gargoyle."

He turned back to the Lady, determined. "And you are . . ."

"Nightshade!" she hissed in fury. She shrank from him, and her smooth face contorted with despair and recognition. "Holiday, what have you done to us? What have you done to *me?*"

Ben shook his head. "We have done it to ourselves, each of us in turn. This place has made it possible. Magic stole our memories when we were sent here from the Heart. Do you remember? There was a man with a box. There were notes purportedly sent by each of us to the other, bait for the trap that was used to ensnare us. Some sort of spell wrapped us about and sent us here, into the box . . ."

"Yes, I remember now!" Strabo growled, who in spite of having his identity uncovered still did not look like the dragon. "I remember the man and his box and the magic netting us like fish! Such power! But why was it done? Look at me! How could I have been changed so?"

Ben knelt before him. The clearing was hushed and closed about. It was as if their world had stopped moving.

"We are in the fairy mists," he said quietly. "Think about how we appear. We have become the things we most fear we might really be. You are a monster, loathed and despised, an outcast that no one wishes to look upon, hunted by all, blamed for everything that cannot otherwise be explained. And you cannot fly, can you? Your wings have been stripped away. Haven't you always feared being earthbound? Flying has always provided you with a form of escape, no matter how terrible things were. Here, you have been cheated even of that."

He paused. "And look at me. I am what I feared most to become. I am the King's Champion, his hand-picked destroyer, his butcher of enemies, nameless and empty of everything but my fighting skills and my desire to use them. Even my armor has become a weapon, a monstrous apparition called the Haze that eliminates any enemy who threatens. I fear killing more than anything, and so for me it comes to pass."

He stopped himself, unwilling to say more. They did not know he was the Paladin, only that the Paladin served the King. He would not have them know more.

"Nightshade," he said softly, turning back to her again. She crouched down like a cornered beast. "What is it you fear most? What frightens you? Loss of your magic, certainly. You have said as much. But something more . . ."

"Silence!" she screamed.

"Being human," Strabo snapped. "She loses power when she acknowledges her humanness. Her emotions make her weak; they steal away her strength. She must not let herself feel. She must not be tender or soft or give love . . ."

Nightshade flew at him, nails raking at his face, but Ben pushed her aside, bore her to the ground, and pinned her there while she spit and screamed like a madwoman. Nightshade had been changed in more ways than one, he thought as he held her. He would never have been able to do this in Landover, for Nightshade had ten times his strength. She was indeed without her power.

She went quiet finally and turned her head aside from him, tears coursing down her pale face. "I will hate you forever," she whispered, the words barely audible. "For what you have done to me, for what you have made me feel—all of it a lie, a monstrous deceit! That I could care for you, could love you, could have you as a woman would a man—how could I have been so stupid? I will hate you forever, Holiday. I will never forget."

He stood up and left her lying there, still turned away.

There was nothing he could say to her that would help. That she had been made to feel something for him was unpardonable; that she had been deceived into thinking him her lover unforgivable. It did not matter what she had felt before. The chasm that had opened between them would never be bridged now.

"The Labyrinth is a part of the fairy mists." He straightened his cloak, knocked askew in his struggle. "It was Willow who called to me in my dream. She called from another part of the mists. When I went to her, I could sense that where she was and where I was were joined. I was reminded how the mists work on those who are human or have left that world. They use fear against us, to change who we are, to make us over, to confront us with that which will drive us mad. Where there is no reality but that which we create, imagination plays havoc with our emotions. Particularly fear. We are lost when that happens. We cannot control it as the fairy people do. They told me so once. They warned me against it."

He took a deep breath. "What we have done in our travels, where we have gone, who we have encountered, is not real. Or not real beyond the Labyrinth. Do you see? We made it up, all of it! Together or separately, I don't know which. The townsfolk, the River Gypsies, the Gristlies—they were all representations of creatures from Landover. The people of the Greensward, the once-fairy, Rock Trolls, G'home Gnomes, or whatever. They don't exist outside our minds or these mists or this prison in which we are confined."

Strabo shook his head. "The fairy mists would not affect me or the witch as they would you. We are fairy creatures ourselves. Yet look at me. I am more changed than you! And no less riddled with the fear you describe. And I did not sense it! I should have been able to do so, having access to the mists in my passage from world to world. Nightshade might be banned from the mists, but I am not. No, Holiday. There is more to this."

"There is the box!" Ben snapped. "The box is something more than a container for the mists. It is a trap strong enough to hold such as we. Another magic works within it."

"It is possible," the other agreed thoughtfully. "But if so, then what magic can free us?"

"I've been thinking about that," Ben said. "When I remembered who I was, I remembered something else, too. I think that our identities were stripped from us to wipe out any chance that we might remember anything that would help us escape. This trap was set up to work two ways. First, to make us forget who we are. Second, to steal away any magic we commanded, to render us impotent. Well, we've overcome the first, so that leaves the second. No magic. And we can't escape this trap without magic."

He glanced from one to the other. Nightshade was back on her feet, ramrod straight, her expression flat and set. "But I think that Horris Kew or whoever it was who put us here might have made a mistake. The magic intended to be stolen from us was innate. That's why we were changed in different ways. You were changed most of all, Strabo. Your magic is inherent in what you are—a dragon—so you were changed to something else entirely. Otherwise, you could use your fire to escape this trap, because your fire is your greatest power and among other things it lets you cross between worlds."

He turned to Nightshade. "And you were stripped of your magic for the same reason, although it was not necessary to change your appearance because how you looked made no difference to whether your magic worked. But the result was the same. Like Strabo, you were trapped without a means of escape because the magic you relied on most, the magic inside yourself, was gone."

He paused. "But it is different with me. I have no innate magic. I came to Landover without any and still possess none. So I was not affected. My memory was stolen, and that was enough. As long as I didn't remember who I was, what danger did I pose?"

"Get to the point," Nightshade snapped coldly.

"This is the point," Ben replied. He reached into his tunic and pulled forth the medallion with the graven image of the Paladin riding out of Sterling Silver at sunrise. "The medallion of the Kings of Landover, given to me when I was brought over from my own world. It invests me with the right to rule, it gives me command over the Paladin, and it does one thing more. It lets me pass through the fairy mists."

There was a protracted silence. "Then you think . . ." Strabo began and stopped.

"It is possible that the magic of the talisman was not leached away in the same manner as your own, that our prison is designed to render the magic of living creatures useless, but not the magic of inanimate things." Ben paused. "Beyond Landover, the medallion lends no authority to rule and will not summon the Paladin. But it will allow passage through the fairy mists. Perhaps it can do so here. It has retained its link to the armor of the Paladin, even though that armor comes in the form of the Haze. It was recognized by the Gristlies and warded us from them. Perhaps it can set us free as well."

"If we are indeed imprisoned in some part of the mists," Strabo pointed out dourly.

"If," Ben agreed.

"This is a very slim chance you offer us," the other mused.

"But the only one we have."

Strabo nodded, his ugly face almost serene. "The only one."

Nightshade came forward then, all black anger and hard edges, and stopped before Ben. "Will this really work?" she demanded, her voice dangerously quiet.

He met her gaze and held it. "I think so. We will have to

take the medallion into the mists and test it. If it does what it
should, we will emerge from the mists where we entered
them."

"Restored to ourselves?" Her eyes glittered.

"I don't know. Once we are beyond the prison and its
magic, we should be."

She nodded. Her face was white marble, her eyes gone
almost red. There was such fury mirrored there that he shrank
inwardly from it.

"You had better hope so, play-King," she said softly. "Because if we do not escape this madness and I am not made
whole again, every part of me, every piece of who and what
I am, I will spend the rest of my days waiting for a chance to
destroy you."

She drew her long cloak close about her, a dark ghost in
the misty dawn. "You have my word on that. Now get us out
of here."

Time seemed stopped.

Willow walked slowly, steadily through the mists, placing
her feet carefully with each step. She could not tell where she
was going. She could barely see the ground she trod. If this
was a trap, she was finished. The haze was so dense that she
would be on top of whatever snare might be waiting long before she could identify it. She was proceeding on trust, and
where the fairies were concerned this was not particularly reassuring.

But after a while, the air began to clear. It thinned gradually, like dawn coming out of night, a slow giving way of
greater shadows to lesser. The light strengthened from black to
gray, but still there was no sun. Gradually the mist receded until it was entwined within a wall of trees and scrub. Willow
looked about. She was in a jungle of tangled trees and vines,
damp and fetid earth, and silence. There was no sound about
her, no movement, as if all life had been destroyed.

She moved forward a few tentative steps and stopped. She looked about again. A sinking feeling unsettled her stomach. She knew where she was. She was in the Deep Fell, the home of Nightshade.

For an instant she thought she must be mistaken. How could she possibly have come here, of all places? She moved forward again, searching the jungle about her, trying to peer through the thick canopy of the trees, to see beyond the shadows, to convince herself she was wrong. She could not. Her instincts and memory were quite clear on the matter. She was in the Deep Fell.

She took a slow breath to steady herself. This might be another fairy trick, she thought. It might be their revenge on her, letting her wander into Nightshade's lair. Trust your instincts, Edgewood Dirk had advised. Trust not the cat. She exhaled. Whatever the case, she must escape quickly or she would be discovered.

She moved swiftly through the thick, green tangle of the Fell, anxious now to gain the rim of the Hollows while it was still light. Though morning was not yet here, it was quite conceivable that she could wander the Fell until nightfall without getting free. Many had. Many had never come out. She kept silent in her passage, using her skills as once-fairy, taking heart in the fact that at least she was back in Landover. She wondered how her instincts could have misled her so. She had to have been deceived by fairy magic. How cruel and spiteful of them, she thought angrily.

Then sudden pain shot through her stomach and limbs, and she doubled over. She dropped to one knee, gasping. The pain lasted only a moment and was gone. She came back to her feet and hurried on. Within minutes, it returned. It was stronger this time and lasted twice as long. She knelt in the tall grass and clutched at herself. What was happening to her?

A jolt of recognition snapped her head up.

It was the baby! It was time!

She closed her eyes in frustration and disbelief. But not here! Please, not here!

She struggled to her feet and continued on, but in seconds the pain returned, dropping her back to her knees, so strong she could barely breathe. Her teeth clenched, she tried to rise one final time and then gave it up. The baby would decide, the Earth Mother had said. Apparently the baby was doing so now. Willow knelt on the floor of the Deep Fell and cried. Her child should not be born in this foul place! It should not be born in shadows and darkness, born out of the sunlight! Did the fairies have anything to do with this? Had they planned it this way, their spite so great at losing the child that they now wished it harmed?

Tears continued to leak from Willow's clenched eyes as she groped at her waist for the pouch containing the precious soils. She found it and pulled it free. She loosened the drawstrings. The pain was coming in sudden spurts that wracked her body. No preparation for this birth, no time to adjust. It was happening quickly, coming so fast that there was no time left for thinking.

She crawled a few feet further to a patch of bare ground and clawed at the soil with her fingers to loosen it. It was not difficult to do; the Deep Fell's earth was damp and soft. When she had cultivated a small patch, she opened the pouch and spread the soils she had gathered in a wide swath about her, reaching down to mix them in. The pain was continuous now, rising and falling in steady waves. She wished she knew more about what to expect, wished she had asked the Earth Mother. Giving birth for the once-fairy was an inconstant and differing experience with each child conceived, and she knew so little of how it worked. She gritted her teeth harder, mixing the soils together, those of the old pines in the lake country, of the place called Greenwich in Ben's world, and of the fairy mists, working them into the soil of the Deep Fell.

Please, she thought. Please don't let this harm my child.

Then she cast down the empty pouch and with an effort came to her feet. Wracked with pain, feeling the child stirring anxiously now within her womb, she prepared to give herself over to the change. The child would come when she was in tree form. She had not been able to tell Ben that. She did not know that she ever could.

She shed her clothing and was naked. Then she placed herself at the very center of the soils she had mixed and dug her toes into the earth.

At the moment of her transformation, she was at peace. It was out of her hands now. She had done all she could do to assure her child's safe birthing. She had kept the trust of the Earth Mother; she had brought back the soils that were required. There was nothing left for her to do but to let her child be born. She wished suddenly for Ben. She wanted to feel his presence, to have him touch her, to hear some small words of reassurance. She did not like being alone now.

Her eyes closed.

Slowly she transformed, fingers and toes lengthening to twigs and roots, arms splitting into branches, legs fusing to a trunk, the whole of her body changing shape and color and look. Her hair disappeared. Her face vanished. She twisted sinuously as bark covered her over. She sighed once, and then she was still.

Hours passed and nothing moved within the Deep Fell where the willow tree rooted. No wind rustled its leaves. No birds flew onto its branches. No small creatures climbed its smooth trunk. The air brightened to a dull, hazy gray, and the summer heat intensified, trapped within the jungle's dank tangle. A rain passed through and faded. Water dripped from the supple limbs onto the ground.

Noon approached.

Then the tree seemed to shiver with some inner turmoil. Slowly, agonizingly, where the trunk began to branch skyward, the skin split apart and a broad shoot pushed out into the light. It appeared quickly, as if its growth were accelerated, thrusting and twining upward. It broadened as it grew and changed shape.

In moments, it had become a pod.

Within the pod, there was movement.

Stash

Questor Thews and Abernathy stood together on the parapets of Sterling Silver and looked out across the lake that surrounded the castle island to the throngs of people streaming onto the grasslands. They had been coming all day, tens growing to hundreds, hundreds to thousands. Most had come from the Greensward, though there was a scattering of Trolls from the Melchor, wights from the barren wastelands east, and villagers and farmers from some dozen or so small communities directly north and south. They came as if vagabonds, bearing no food or blankets or even the most rudimentary implements for firemaking. They seemed not to care. Men, women, and children, some with old plow horses and mules, some with a ragtag following of dogs and cats, they had trekked their way here from wherever, as diverse a gathering as ever there was. Now they milled about across the lake from the castle and stared over at it as if hoping someone might invite them in for a good meal.

It was not food they sought, however. What each of them craved, what every single one of them had come to obtain, what all of them were determined to have at any cost, was a mind's eye crystal.

"Look at them," Abernathy muttered, then shook his head so that his dog ears flapped gently. "This is truly dreadful."

251

"Worse than what we had anticipated, I'm afraid," Questor Thews agreed solemnly.

They had been anticipating some sort of trouble ever since Abernathy and Bunion had returned from Rhyndweir with the story of the black-cloaked stranger and Horris Kew. A vast stash of mind's eye crystals awaited them at Sterling Silver, the stranger had insisted. It was there for the taking. Abernathy had dutifully reported every last word to Questor Thews, and so they had braced themselves. But it was Kallendbor and the other Lords of the Greensward they had expected to face, appearing with their armies to exact an accounting, marching up to the gates to force an entry. Instead they found themselves confronted by thousands of farmers and tradesmen and their families, simple people who bore no weapons and wore no armor, all of them hungry and tired and misguided, all of them standing about like cattle waiting for someone to lead them to the barn.

Well, the barn was back the way they had come, of course, but none of them wanted to hear that. They didn't want to hear anything that didn't involve the words "mind's eye crystals" and that was the sad but inescapable fact of the matter.

They certainly weren't listening to anything Questor Thews or Abernathy had to tell them. When the first of them had arrived, quite early that morning, they had come onto the bridge that linked the island with the mainland. The portcullis had been lowered during the night, so they halted at the gates and shouted up for Ben Holiday to come down. Questor Thews had appeared on the ramparts and shouted back that the King was absent at the moment—what did they want? Mind's eye crystals, they declared vehemently, one for each of them. Well, there weren't any to be had, Questor had replied. They called him a liar and a few other names, and started making disparaging remarks about his lineage. Abernathy had appeared beside his friend, still feeling very responsible for the whole mess, and assured the people massed on the bridge—the number growing even as they argued—that Questor Thews was telling the truth, that there were no mind's eye crystals inside the castle. That didn't fly with anyone. The threats and name-calling continued. The mob grew larger.

Finally Questor sent a squad of King's soldiers out to move the people back off the bridge and to set up a picket line on the far side of the lake. Amid much pushing and shoving, the soldiers cleared the bridge, but no one turned about and started for home as the Court Wizard had hoped. Instead they held their ground just beyond the picket line and waited for something to happen. Nothing did, of course. Questor wasn't entirely sure what they thought might. In any event, the number of people swelled into the thousands by midday, all crammed down off the high plains and surrounding hills onto the lower grasslands fronting the castle. The summer heat worsened on a day that was gloriously clear and cloudless, and tempers grew short.

Then someone on one side of the picket line said something and someone on the other side said something else, and as quick as that the mob rushed the line, overpowered the soldiers, and threw them into the lake. Then they charged across the bridge for the castle gates.

This might have been the start of real trouble except that Questor was still standing out on the battlements with Abernathy trying to decide what else he could do. When he saw the mob rush the castle, he pushed up the sleeves of his old gray robe and called on his magic. This was a precipitous act if ever there was one, since Questor's conjuring never worked well when rushed (or even when it wasn't, for that matter), but no one was really thinking too clearly by now. He meant to send a bolt of lightning flashing down into their midst, something to scatter them or to fling them into the waters of the lake. Instead, he sent down the equivalent of several gallons of oil—not the flaming kind, the plain old greasy kind—right into the foremost of those leading the charge. The oil splashed down across the wooden surface of the bridge and the entire leading edge of the mob went down in an oily tangle of arms and legs. Those following stumbled over their fellows while trying to slow themselves or break past, and they went down, too. In seconds, the entire bridge was awash in oil-slicked bodies.

Questor Thews ordered the gates closed, and the castle was summarily sealed up. The mob dragged its collective self back off the bridge, cursing and threatening with every step. *This isn't finished by any means! You watch and see if it is, Questor Thews! Just wait until the Lords of the Greensward arrive! You'll see what real trouble is then, all of you!*

True enough, Questor Thews had agreed silently, but there wasn't much he could do about it. So here they were, some long hours later, the day edging toward night, waiting to see which would arrive first, Kallendbor or sunset.

Sunset seemed a pretty good bet. The skies east were already darkening and the skies west turning gold. Several of the moons were out to the north, hanging low in the horizon, lifting gradually toward the stars. There was no sign of Kallendbor and the Lords of the Greensward—no shouts announcing their imminent arrival, no dust upon the approaching plains, no thud of horses' hooves or clank of armor. It looked as if any further trouble was going to be delayed until morning.

Abernathy hoped so. It had been difficult telling Questor Thews how he had been tricked by Horris Kew. It had been like pulling teeth to admit that he had been duped so thoroughly that he had aided and abetted the dissemination of the wretched mind's eye crystals to the people of Landover, thereby permitting the present situation to come to pass. He was still struggling with the loss of his own crystal and the visions it had presented, and in the end he told that to Questor

Thews as well. Might as well admit everything, he decided. What difference could it make now?

As it happened, Questor had been extraordinarily understanding and supportive. Quite all right, he had said. Who could blame you? I would have done the same if it were me. He actually thanked Abernathy for putting aside personal feelings in favor of the greater well-being of the Kingdom of Landover and of the missing Ben Holiday in particular.

"I was as much a fool as you," he said solemnly, his wispy hair stuck out as if he were a porcupine taking a defensive stance. "I accepted Horris Kew's word as gullibly as you. I did not question the worth of these crystals he presented to us. They seemed the perfect answer to our dilemma. To tell you the truth, I was on the verge of asking for one myself."

"But you did not," Abernathy observed sadly. "I have no such excuse."

"Nonsense!" Questor shook his head vehemently. "I practically forced one on you when he asked for a trial. I could have tried it out myself, but I let you take the chance. Anyway, it was not too long ago that I stood in your shoes, old friend. I was the one who conjured the magic that sent you and the King's medallion back to his old world. No, I can't allow you a bit of the blame in this."

All of which made Abernathy feel not a minute's worth better about what he had done. Still, Questor was trying to make him feel less guilty, and Abernathy appreciated it. What would make him feel a whole lot cheerier was finding out what had become of Ben Holiday. Questor had used the Landsview anew just that morning, Bunion had scoured the countryside close at hand once more, and neither had a thing to show for their efforts. Wherever Ben Holiday was, he was well hidden. Abernathy wanted to get his teeth on that black-cloaked stranger and bite down real hard on his ear or some such. He was ashamed that his animal side was coming to the fore in this matter, but he was desperate to redeem himself for the harm he had caused.

"Uh-oh," Questor Thews said suddenly, and put an end to the scribe's contemplation. "Look over there."

Abernathy looked. A gang of men had emerged from the trees of the forest west bearing a huge log that had been fashioned into a battering ram. They lugged the log down the hillside and onto the grasslands. They bore it across the flats toward the lake. They were chanting and huffing as they came, and those thousands of their fellows gathered about cheered them on lustily.

"They can't be serious," the wizard gasped.

But they were, of course. They were dead serious. There were thirty or more, evenly split to either side of their makeshift ram, trotting slowly across the grasslands and up to the bridge. All about them, people had come to their feet and were thrusting their fists into the air.

"You, there!" Questor Thews shouted, white hair flying. "Turn back right now! Drop that log!"

No one could hear him; they were shouting too loud. They were practically screaming in anticipation. The gang of men and their ram turned onto the bridge and started across, picking up speed. A howl of determination burst from their lips.

Questor Thews rolled up his sleeves once more atop the parapets. "We'll see about this!" he muttered furiously.

Abernathy stood frozen in place. What should he do? His ears twitched, and he let out a growl.

The men on the bridge crossed in a final rush and slammed their battering ram into the castle gates. There was a monstrous thud and a splintering of wood. The ram and the men carrying it bounced back a few feet and collapsed on the causeway. It seemed to Abernathy as if he could feel the force of the blow on the gates all the way atop the wall where he stood in his half crouch, hands clamped over his muzzle.

"All right for you!" Questor Thews cried out, arms and
robes flying. He looked ready to do something. He looked
poised to strike. White light gathered at ends of his fingertips.
Abernathy clenched his teeth. Something bad was about to
happen.

The men with the ram picked themselves up and charged
once more, undaunted.

Questor's arms windmilled wildly. Too wildly. He was
working so hard at whatever spell he was conjuring that he
lost his balance. When he tried to regain it, he tripped on his
robes. He stumbled forward dangerously close to the edge of
the ramparts. Abernathy reached out hurriedly and grabbed
him. As he did so, Questor's magic released from his fingers
and flew down into the mob. From the sound that emanated
from the wizard's lips, Abernathy could tell that something unexpected was about to happen.

He was not wrong. The magic fell onto the bridge like
silver rain, soft and gentle. Perhaps it was meant to be a bolt
of lightning that would scatter the men with the ram. Perhaps
it was supposed to be another dousing of oil. Neither happened. Instead the magic fell upon the causeway and disappeared into its wooden surface as if water into sand, and a
moment later the bridge shuddered and arched as if a sleeping
snake awakened. Down went the men with the ram a second
time, only yards from their objective, cursing and screaming.
The bridge heaved, throwing the men about like rag dolls.
The ram flew up into the air and rolled off the bridge and
into the moat. The men screamed and cursed some more.
Questor and Abernathy hung onto each other and stared
downward in disbelief. The bridge was writhing now. It detached from the castle and the far shore and began to twist
back on itself. The few men still clinging to its surface abandoned their perch and dived for safety. Boards cracked and
snapped apart. Iron nails popped. Bindings frayed and gave
way. Up rose the bridge one final time, a serpent breaching

from the deep, then it broke into a million pieces and collapsed into the lake and was gone.

There was a long moment of stunned silence. The men who had carried the battering ram were pulling themselves back ashore with the help of friends and relatives. The rest of the ragtag mob was gathered on the shoreline, staring. The waters churned and roiled like a kettle set to boil.

Questor looked at Abernathy and blinked. "Well, what do you know about that!" he said.

Sunset arrived and there were no further incidents. The mob had apparently had enough for one day and now turned its attention to building cooking fires and scrounging for food. With the causeway destroyed, the last open link with the mainland was severed, and Sterling Silver was truly an island in the middle of a lake. No way to reach her now, it was clear, unless you wanted to swim. Most of those gathered couldn't swim and in many cases distrusted water in general. Questor was inclined to congratulate himself on a well-executed bit of magic, but he refrained from doing so since the whole business had gone completely awry and Abernathy knew it.

Abernathy, for his part, had gone back to wondering how ever in the world they were going to get out of this mess without Holiday.

It was still light when, despite Questor's and Abernathy's fondest hopes and unspoken predictions, Kallendbor and a substantial army arrived to take up a position directly across from the castle gates. Peasants and common folk were shoved aside and room was made for the fighting men and their leader. Close by Kallendbor's side was Horris Kew and his bird, the former shuffling about distractedly, the latter riding his shoulder like the proverbial omen of doom. Abernathy watched them bleakly. The cause of all of this, he thought darkly. Horris Kew and his bird. If he could just reach them.

If he could just get his hands on them for five seconds. The image lingered.

There was no sign of the black-cloaked stranger. Questor and Abernathy both searched for him without success. Maybe he had stayed behind, but neither of them believed so.

Darkness fell, the sun disappeared, and the fires brightened against the night. Sentries took up positions on the banks of the lake, visibly placed so that those in the castle could see that a siege had been laid. Questor and Abernathy remained on the ramparts where they had stood all day and brooded.

"Whatever are we going to do?" Abernathy muttered disconsolately.

The camp milled about below, people jostling for room in the crowded meadow. The smell of meat cooking wafted up. Cups of ale were being passed about, and laughter grew loud and raucous.

"A regular picnic, isn't it?" Questor replied irritably. Then he started. "Abernathy, look there!"

Abernathy looked. Kallendbor was standing at the edge of the lake with Horris Kew and the bird. Right next to him was the black-cloaked stranger, bold as you please. They stood apart from everyone else, staring out across the water at Sterling Silver.

"Making plans for tomorrow, I'll warrant," the wizard said. He shook his head wearily. "Well, I've had enough of this. I'm going up to the Landsview to see if there is anything new to be learned of the King. I shall scour the countryside once more, and maybe this time something will reveal itself." He made a dismissive gesture with his hands and started away. "Anything is better than watching those idiots."

He departed in a sweep of gray robes, leaving Abernathy to keep watch alone. Contemplating the unfairness of life and the stupidity of men become dogs and wondering anew what he could do to redeem himself, Abernathy continued standing there despite Questor's assessment of the act as a waste of time. There seemed little he could accomplish so long as he was penned up in the castle. He thought vaguely about swimming the lake and sneaking up on Horris Kew and his bird, but that would only get him taken prisoner or worse.

On the far bank, Kallendbor, Horris Kew, Biggar, and the stranger continued to huddle in the near dark, co-conspirators of the night.

Abernathy was trying quite unsuccessfully to read their lips when a commotion from behind brought him sharply about. Two of the castle guards had appeared from out of the stairwell holding in their burly hands two small, grimy, struggling figures.

"Great High Lord!" one moaned pitifully.

"Mighty High Lord!" the other wailed.

Well, there you are, Abernathy thought as the two were brought forward. Just when you think things can't get any worse, somehow they always do. There was no mistaking these two—the stout, hairy, dirt-encrusted bodies; the bearded, ferretlike faces with pointed ears and wet noses; the peasant-reject clothes topped off with ridiculous leather skullcaps and tiny red feathers. They were as familiar and unwelcome as deep winter cold and sweltering summer heat, unavoidable visitations that came and went more frequently than the weather. They were G'home Gnomes, the most despised people in the entire kingdom of Landover, the lowest of the low, the final step down the evolutionary ladder. They were thieves and pilferers who lived hand-to-mouth and by the deliberate misfortune they brought to others. They were that variety of creature that scavenges what it consumes and thus cleans up what all others leave behind—except, of course, that G'home Gnomes also cleaned up much of that which was not intended to be left behind in the first place. They were particularly fond of pet cats, which was all right with Abernathy, and pet dogs, which was decidedly not.

These two Gnomes, in particular, were a source of unending distress to the members of the court of Ben Holiday. Ever since they had appeared unexpectedly to pledge their fealty to the throne some three years earlier—a decidedly mixed blessing if ever there was one—they had been underfoot. Now here they were again, the same two troublemakers, back for another shot at making Abernathy's life miserable.

Fillip and Sot cringed when they saw him. They were still whining for Holiday, who at least would tolerate them. Abernathy had no such compunction.

"Where is the High Lord?" Fillip asked immediately.

"Yes, where is the King?" Sot echoed.

"Found them messing about in the King's bedchamber," one of the guards advised, giving Fillip a good shake in an effort to still his struggling. The Gnome whimpered. "Thieving, I expect."

"Never, no never!" Fillip cried.

"Never from the High Lord!" Sot cried.

Abernathy felt a headache coming on. "Set them down," he ordered with a sigh.

The guards dropped them in a heap. The Gnomes fell to their knees, groveling pitifully.

"Great Court Scribe!"

"Mighty Court Scribe!"

Abernathy rubbed his temples. "Oh, stop it!" He dismissed the guards and motioned the Gnomes to their feet. They rose hesitantly, glancing about with worried looks, thinking perhaps that some terrible fate was about to befall them, thinking perhaps of trying to escape.

Abernathy studied them wearily. "What is it that you want?" he snapped.

The G'home Gnomes exchanged a hurried glance.

"To see the High Lord," Fillip answered hesitantly.

"To speak with the High Lord," Sot agreed.

They were terrible at lying, and Abernathy saw at once

that they were being evasive. It had been a very long, disappointing day, and he had no time for this.

"Eaten any stray animals lately?" he asked softly, leaning forward so that they could see the faint gleam of his teeth.

"Oh, no, we would never . . ."

"Only vegetables, I promise . . ."

"Because every so often I have this craving for roast Gnome," Abernathy interrupted pointedly. They went as still as stone. "Now give me the truth, or I shall not be responsible for what happens next!"

Fillip swallowed hard. "We want a mind's eye crystal," he answered miserably.

Sot nodded. "Everyone has one but us."

"We just want one."

"Yes, just one."

"That is not asking too much."

"No, not too much."

Abernathy wanted to throttle them. Was there no end to this nonsense? "Look at me," he said, a very real edge to his voice. They met his gaze reluctantly. "There are no mind's eye crystals here. None. Not a one. There never were. If I have anything to say about it, there never will be!" He almost checked himself on that last statement, but then decided he really meant it. He reached out and caught them by their skinny, gnarly arms. "Come here."

He dragged them over to the parapets, ignoring their moans and cries about being thrown to their doom. "Look out there!" he snapped irritably. "Go on, look!" They looked. "See that man with the bird? Next to Lord Kallendbor? Next to the man in the black cloak?"

They hesitated, then nodded as one.

"That," Abernathy declared triumphantly, "is the one who has the mind's eye crystals! So go talk to him!"

He let go of them and stepped away, hands on dog hips.

The G'home Gnomes looked at each other uncertainly, then back at Horris Kew, then back at Abernathy.

"There are no crystals here?" Fillip asked, sounding hurt.

"None?" Sot asked.

Abernathy shook his head. "You have my solemn word as Court Scribe and servant to the King. If there are any crystals to be found, that is the man who can find them."

Fillip and Sot wiped dirt-encrusted fingers across damp snouts and teary eyes and stared down at the conjurer with increasing interest. They sniffled rather anxiously, and their jaws worked to no discernible purpose. They stepped back.

"We shall speak with him, then," Fillip announced, taking the lead as always.

"Yes, we shall," Sot reinforced.

They started to turn away and move back toward the stairwell. In spite of himself, Abernathy called them back. "Wait!" he hailed. "Hold on a moment." He walked over to them. He didn't owe them this, but he couldn't let them go unwarned either. "Listen to me. These men, the one in black particularly, are very dangerous. You cannot just walk up to them and ask for crystals. They are likely to cut you into tiny pieces for your trouble."

Fillip and Sot looked at each other.

"We will be very careful," Fillip advised.

"Very," Sot agreed.

They started away again.

"Wait!" Abernathy called a second time. Something had just occurred to him, something he had missed before. The G'home Gnomes turned. "How did you get in here?" he asked suspiciously. "You did not come over the bridge. And you do not look like you swam the lake. So how exactly did you get in?"

They exchanged another in that endless series of furtive looks. Neither spoke.

Abernathy came right up to them then and bent down. "You tunneled in, didn't you?" Fillip bit his lip. Sot clenched his jaw. "Didn't you?"

They nodded. Reluctantly.

"All the way from the far bank?" Abernathy was incredulous.

Fillip sulked. "The forest, actually."

Sot sulked harder. "Back in the trees."

Abernathy stared. "No, how could you? That would take days, weeks." He stopped himself. "Wait a minute. How long has this tunnel of yours been in place?"

"Awhile," Fillip muttered, and scuffed the stone rampart with the claws of his feet.

"And where does this tunnel come out?"

Another pause, this one longer. "The kitchen larder," Sot admitted finally.

Abernathy straightened once more. Memories of food mysteriously disappearing from the larder surfaced like dead fish at moonrise. Cooks' helpers had been blamed. Accusations had been made. No resolution had ever been reached.

"So," he said softly, drawing the word out like a hangman's noose. "The kitchen larder."

Fillip and Sot cringed and waited for the blow to fall. But Abernathy wasn't even looking at them. He was looking away, toward the ramparts and beyond. He was not considering retribution against the G'home Gnomes; he was weighing instead the prospect of getting even with Horris Kew. With the glow of the watch fires dancing off the shadowed stone of Sterling Silver, he stood poised on the brink of a decision that would either redeem him or cost him his life.

It took him only a moment to make up his mind.

He bent down again and asked pointedly, "Is this tunnel of yours big enough for me?"

Gnome Time

Abernathy was not by nature compulsive in his behavior or even remotely venturesome, so it was with some surprise that he found himself contemplating squeezing into the narrow tunnel hollowed out by Fillip and Sot far back in a corner of the kitchen larder, intent on crawling its length to the woods behind the siege lines ringing Sterling Silver, there to undertake some precarious and probably foolhardy effort to capture and squeeze information out of Horris Kew. It wasn't that he didn't realize what it was he was doing or appreciate the danger involved that disturbed him; it was that he would even consider such madness in the first place.

He consoled himself by determining it was his dog side taking over and therefore entirely the fault of Questor Thews.

The wizard had no idea what Abernathy was about. If he had known, he would have put a stop to it at once or insisted on going himself, neither of which the Court Scribe could permit. After all, this was Abernathy's mess to clean up, his pride to redeem, his self-esteem to regain. Besides, Questor was needed where he was, within the walls of the castle where he could present at least a semblance of a defense against the inevitable assault Kallendbor and his army would mount. Questor's magic might be erratic, but it was a force to be reckoned with nevertheless and would give the castle's assailants at least some pause in their efforts.

Meanwhile, he hoped, he would be able to find out what had become of Ben Holiday.

He was forced to strip off his clothes to get into the tunnel; it was that tight. Nudity was an indignity he was prepared to endure. The G'home Gnomes had made the tunnel for themselves, after all, and not for him. In the shadows of the larder, the kitchen staff dismissed summarily and without explanation to other parts of the castle, Abernathy pulled off his clothing and thought for a moment about what he was doing. He did not think about Horris Kew or his bird or Kallendbor or the black-cloaked stranger this time. The danger from that quarter was known. He thought instead about placing himself in the hands—and, possibly teeth—of Fillip and Sot: They were dubious allies at best, given their history as scavengers and consumers of cats and dogs. He was quite certain that if the opportunity presented itself they would not hesitate to eat him. Why not? It was in their nature, wasn't it? Since that was so, however, it was incumbent on Abernathy, given his present precarious circumstances, to give them a very good reason not to make a meal of him.

He decided to appeal to the one character virtue he was able to accord them.

"Listen carefully to me," he told them, crouching naked at the tunnel entry, trying hard not to feel foolish. "There is something I have not told you. What we are doing is very important to the well-being of the High Lord. We have not given out the news, but something bad has happened to him. He has disappeared. Those men out there, the one with the mind's eye crystals and the black-cloaked one, are responsible. I have a plan to save Holiday, but you will have to help me. You want to save the High Lord, don't you?"

"Oh, yes!" Fillip declared.

"Yes, indeed!" Sot insisted.

They nodded so hard he thought their heads might shake loose from their shoulders. He was stretching the truth here concerning Holiday and any plan for his rescue, but in a good cause. The one thing he could count on where the G'home Gnomes were concerned was their unswerving loyalty to the High Lord. It had been set in concrete from the time of their first meeting, when Ben Holiday had done what no one else would have even considered doing—he had gone to their rescue in a cause that was recognizably questionable, determined that a King must serve all of his subjects equally. He had saved their lives, and they had never forgotten. They continued to be thieves and scavengers and acted in misguided ways more often than not, but as they had shown already on more than one occasion, they would do anything for the High Lord.

Abernathy was counting on that now. He was counting on it quite heavily.

"Once we are through the tunnel, I will tell you my plan," he continued. "But we must work together on this. Holiday's life is at risk."

"You can depend on us," Fillip advised eagerly.

"You can," Sot agreed.

Abernathy hoped so. His life was at risk as well.

They went down into the tunnel, Fillip first, Abernathy second, Sot trailing. They crawled in headfirst, stretching out full-length along an earthen passageway that twisted and burrowed down into blackness. Abernathy found that he could not see a thing. He could hear Fillip moving ahead of him and followed the sound of his squirming. From behind, Sot nudged his feet to prod him along. Roots scraped his belly and back. Insects skittered past him in a flurry of legs. In places, patches of damp soaked into him and matted his fur. Everything smelled pungent and close. Abernathy hated tunnels. He hated anything that confined him (another dog trait, he assumed). He wanted out of there very badly, but he forced himself to go on. He had initiated this venture and he was determined to see it through.

The Gnomes must have tunneled all the way under the

lake, a feat that Abernathy could not comprehend, given its well-known depth. He envisioned the earth collapsing on top of him; he imagined the lake waters pouring in. The crawl went on endlessly, and at more than one point he thought that he had reached the limit of his endurance. But he refused to quit.

When he emerged once more into the light of moons and stars within a clump of bushes behind the siege lines, there to brush dirt and insects away and to breathe anew and with much gratitude a cool night air which smelled and tasted sweeter than anything in recent memory, he vowed that whatever happened from here on out, he was not under any circumstances going back into that tunnel.

His composure regained, he followed the G'home Gnomes out of the bushes and through the trees to the rise that looked down on the meadow and the makeshift army besieging Sterling Silver. Cooking fires were dying out, and people were stretched out on the grass sleeping. Sentries from Kallendbor's war party still patrolled the shores of the lake, keeping close watch over the island castle, and small knots of men still drank and joked restlessly, but for the most part everyone had settled in for the night. Abernathy searched the meadow, particularly along the shoreline, for some sign of Horris Kew or the black-cloaked stranger. There was none to be found. Not even Kallendbor was visible.

"What do we do now?" Fillip asked anxiously.

"Yes, what?" Sot echoed.

Abernathy wasn't sure. He licked his nose worriedly. Somehow he had to find Horris Kew. But how was he supposed to do that given his present circumstances? To begin with, he looked like a dog, and without any clothes he had little hope of disguising the fact. If he went down into the camp like this, he would be spotted in a moment.

Reluctantly, he turned to the Gnomes. "Do you think

you could sneak down there and find the man I showed you from the castle, the one with the bird?"

"The man with the mind's eye crystals," Fillip announced brightly.

"That one," Sot declared.

Abernathy had hoped they might focus on something besides the crystals. It was Ben Holiday he was after, and G'home Gnomes were easily distracted from what mattered in favor of what interested. It was Abernathy's biggest fear that they would get sidetracked. They just couldn't seem to help themselves.

"We can find him," Fillip said.

"Easily," Sot said.

Abernathy sighed. "All right, give it a try. But just find him, then come right back and tell me where he is. So I can tell you my plan. Do not do anything else. Do not let him know you are there. Can you remember that?"

"Yes, we can remember," Fillip said, nodding.

"Easily," Sot repeated.

They slipped away into the darkness and disappeared from view. We can remember, they had promised. Abernathy wished he could be sure.

Not too far away, back somewhat from the rabble that crowded the meadow, Horris Kew and Biggar sat conversing quietly in the dark. Horris was crouched within the shadows of an old spreading maple that edged out from the forest behind, coming halfway down the slope like a scout. Biggar was perched on the trunk of a tree that had once been the maple's companion but had fallen victim to lightning. Horris sat with his back against the maple, the trunk of the other tree close by his legs where they stretched out before him like tent poles.

"You are a coward, Horris," the bird sneered. "A pathetic, craven coward. I would never have thought it of you."

"I am a realist, Biggar." Horris was having none of this coward business. "I know when I am in over my head, and this is definitely one of those times."

It was a bitter admission, but not an unfamiliar one. Sooner or later Horris Kew always found himself in over his head in his machinations. Why these things never worked out as he intended, why they always went wrong somewhere along the way, was a mystery that continued to baffle him. But it was clear that this time, just as all the other times before, things had gone dangerously haywire.

He had been convinced of it since the Gorse had showed itself to Kallendbor and instigated the march on Sterling Silver. *At least* that long, he corrected. Perhaps he had been convinced of it before, given the nature of the being with which he had become entangled. The Gorse was just what Biggar had warned it was—an incredibly powerful monster that could turn on them in a moment. That it would do so sooner or later was no longer in doubt. Since the march from Rhyndweir, Horris could see his usefulness to the creature coming to an end. For one thing, the Gorse had regained its human form and could walk among men, night or day. That meant it no longer relied on Horris to run its errands. Worse, it was beginning to disregard the fact that Horris was even there. When siege was laid to Sterling Silver, it addressed Kallendbor as an equal and barely deigned to notice Horris. Forgotten were all the promises of the role Horris would play in the new order. There was no longer any mention, veiled or otherwise, of Horris becoming King in Holiday's place. Horris was being shoved aside, no mistake about it.

"So you simply plan to give it all up once again?" the bird snapped, bringing him out of his reverie. "Just walk away from the chance of a lifetime? What's the matter with you? I thought you had some backbone about you!"

Horris glowered. "Just exactly what is it that you expect me to do, Biggar? Tell that monster I don't like how I'm being treated and I want what's fair? That should prove interesting. Given what we now know, I should say we will be lucky to get out of this alive even if we keep our mouths shut!"

Biggar spit, an ugly sound. "You can tell it you want to be King, Horris! You can tell it that! The Gorse suggested it, after all! It's a good plan. You be King for a day, we get our hands on as much wealth as we can, then we get out of here. But we don't cut and run with nothing!"

Horris folded his arms across his bony chest and huffed. "Tell it I want to be King, you think? Haven't you been paying attention to what's going on? Haven't you been listening? This isn't about mind's eye crystals or Sterling Silver or being King! There is something else going on here, something infinitely more complex and devious. The Gorse is simply using us—Kallendbor included—to get what it wants. It spent a lot of time getting free of that box, and it wasn't happy about being put there in the first place! Think about it!"

Biggar's beak clacked shut. "What do you mean?"

Horris leaned forward. "For a bird possessed of enhanced intelligence, you can be awfully dense. Revenge, Biggar! The Gorse wants a healthy measure of it, don't you see? There are old debts to be paid for injuries suffered, and the Gorse is doing all this to collect on those debts. It practically told us as much. Landover for us, it said, and the fairy mists for itself—remember? I didn't realize what that meant then, but I do now. We have always followed a very sound rule of business, Biggar, and it has served us well. If there isn't any money to be made, we get out. Well, there isn't any money involved in the revenge business, and it's time to fold our tent and get while the getting's good!"

"But there *is* money, Horris," the bird insisted. "That's just the point. There's all kinds of money, just across that lake, just inside those walls. If we can hang on for a few more days, we have a chance to take a good chunk of it with us. The Gorse can help us—maybe without even knowing it. Let the beast have its revenge, what do we care? What we need is what's inside those walls. That, and a way out of Landover. Or have you forgotten we're trapped here? The Gorse can give us both."

"What it can give us is a quick trip into that box with Holiday and the others." Horris shook his head stubbornly. "You saw what it did. It dispatched Holiday like a child. Down into the Tangle Box and out of Landover in the blink of an eye. No more King. It'll do the same with us when it's ready, and I don't think that time is too far off."

Biggar hopped onto the end of Horris Kew's boot. His claws dug in. "Maybe we should hedge our bets a bit, Horris. Suppose you're right. What we need is a little something to keep the Gorse from harming us. Like the box."

Horris blinked. "The Tangle Box?"

"We slip away right now, tonight," said the bird. "We can reach the cave on horseback and return before morning. Take the box and hide it. Use it as a lever to make certain we get what we want." The sharp eyes gleamed.

Horris stared at the bird for a moment, then he shook his head in disbelief. "You've gone round the bend, Biggar. You really have. Threaten the Gorse? What does it care if we have the box or not? We don't even know how to use it!"

"We know the words," the bird whispered. "We know the spell. What if we were to say it again?"

There was a long, terrible silence. Horris wished he had never opened the box in the first place, never spoken the words that released the Gorse, never returned to Landover at all. He wished he had taken up some other less-stressful profession, like leatherworking or weaving. He was suddenly and inescapably fed up with magic in all its forms.

"Come on, Horris, let's go!" Biggar urged. "Don't just sit there. Get up!"

Biggar couldn't see it, of course. Perhaps it was due to the fact that even with enhanced intelligence there was still only a bird's brain inside that tiny feathered cranium trying to sort it all out. Or maybe he simply didn't want to see.

"If we do this," Horris Kew began softly, "if we decide to challenge the Gorse, if we actually go back to the cave and steal the Tangle Box . . ."

He couldn't finish. He couldn't bring himself to speak the words. He slumped back against the tree, his bony frame collapsing in on itself like a deflated balloon.

Biggar hopped back and forth between the other's boot and the tree trunk, hissing like a snake. "You coward! You worm-body! You ridiculous excuse for a wizard! All talk and no action wimp-head! How I ever let myself become involved with the likes of you is more than I can comprehend!"

Something moved behind the tree trunk, barely noticeable, a silent bit of shadow and nothing more, but neither of them saw it.

"Biggar, Biggar, you are not thinking . . ."

"I *am* thinking! I am the only one who's thinking!" Biggar puffed up to twice his size, turning himself into a ferocious black porcupine. "Go on, then! Lie there like a rag doll, a collection of sackcloth sewn up with sawdust brains! Go on!"

Horris Kew closed his eyes and put his hands over his face.

"I'll not spend another moment with such a coward!" raged Biggar. "Not one, single, further, disgusting—"

A grimy hand reached up from behind the log on which he perched, clamped itself over his beak and neck, and dragged him from sight.

After a moment, Horris Kew opened his eyes again and peered about. No Biggar. Just like that, he was gone. Horris sat forward, puzzled. A single black feather lay rocking on the log.

"Biggar?" he called tentatively.

There was no answer.

The hour approached midnight.

Abernathy sat quietly at the edge of the woods and watched the last of the revelers nod off, leaving a sprinkling of fires and the distant, vague shapes of Kallendbor's sentries. The darkness deepened all about. Sterling Silver was a vague bulk against the horizon, almost entirely empty of light. Overhead, the sky was clear and bright with several moons and thousands of stars. It was warm and pleasant and under other circumstances might have assured everyone a good night's sleep.

As it was, Abernathy did not dare even think about sleep, worried sick already over the length of time that had passed since Fillip and Sot had left his side in search of Horris Kew. There had been no outcry, so he didn't think they had been spied, but he was uncomfortable with having them gone this long nevertheless. There were too many ways for that pair to get into trouble, too many missteps they could take before they realized their mistake. He wished he had gone with them. He chided himself for trusting them to go alone.

He had just about made up his mind to go look for them, to slip down into the camp and steal a concealing cloak and search them out, when they abruptly reappeared. They popped up out of the shadows almost in front of him, causing him to start in spite of himself.

"Where have you been?" he asked, irritated.

The G'home Gnomes smiled, showing all their teeth. They looked exceptionally pleased with themselves.

"Look what we have," said Fillip.

"Come, take a look," said Sot.

Abernathy tried to look, for he could see that they did indeed have something—something that appeared to be moving—but they brushed past him without slowing.

"No, no, not here," Fillip said quickly.

"In the dark, away from the camp," Sot said.

So they trekked back into the woods, well away from the meadow and its campers, until there was no one anywhere about but themselves. At this point Fillip and Sot turned back to Abernathy once more, and the former proudly held out his hands.

"Here!" he announced.

Abernathy stared. It was the bird, the myna or whatever it was, the one that belonged to Horris Kew. It was clutched firmly in the Gnome's grimy hands, its neck grasped none too gently, its beak clamped shut so that it could not cry out. Its wings fluttered weakly, but it appeared to have spent itself thoroughly.

Abernathy sighed in despair. "I told you just to look, just to find the bird's owner and come back to me. I did not tell you to take the bird! What good is the bird to us!"

"Much good," insisted Sot, undeterred. He prodded Fillip eagerly. "Show him."

Fillip dropped his fingers below Biggar's beak and gave a small shake. "Speak, bird."

The bird did not speak. It hung there limply, pitifully. It looked half-dead. Abernathy felt a throbbing in his temples and sighed.

Fillip glowered. He bent down close to the bird's face. "Speak, stupid bird, or I will wring your neck and eat you," he said, and he tightened his clawed fingers meaningfully.

"All right, all right!" the bird snapped, coming suddenly alive. Abernathy jerked back in surprise. The bird's head twisted wildly. "I'm talking, okay? What do you want me to say?"

Fillip held the bird out proudly. "See?"

Abernathy bent down for a closer look. "Well, well," he said softly. "You talk a lot better than you pretend, don't you?"

"Better than you, furball," Biggar sneered. "Tell these mole people to let go of me right now or it will be the worse for you."

Abernathy reached out and poked the bird. "What is your name again? Biggar? Well, Biggar, guess what?" There was unmistakable satisfaction in his voice. "It took awhile, but I remember you now. It was a long time ago, wasn't it? You belonged to the old King's wizard, to Questor Thews's brother. One day, you were simply reported missing. What happened? Were you dispatched to Ben Holiday's old world— just like Horris Kew? No, never mind about that. It hardly matters now. Just tell me what you know about the High Lord's disappearance, hmm? And don't leave anything out."

Biggar closed his beak with a sharp clack. But it was too late for stonewalling. Fillip and Sot had overheard most of his conversation with Horris Kew and dutifully repeated it now to Abernathy. They got their facts confused a few times and failed to interpret all the words properly, but it was clear enough for the scribe to figure out what had happened. The Gorse was some sort of monster. It was using Horris Kew and Kallendbor. The mind's eye crystal's were its cat's paw against the throne. Most important, Ben Holiday's disappearance had come about through use of a powerful spell that would some-how have to be reversed. That meant finding the Gorse's cave and the Tangle Box hidden within it.

Abernathy turned his attention back to Biggar. The bird had said nothing since his first outburst, withdrawing into si-lence for the entirety of the time that Fillip and Sot had re-vealed his secrets. Now he glanced quickly up at Abernathy as the scribe bent down close to look at him.

"Polly want a cracker?" Abernathy coaxed maliciously.

Biggar, despite being firmly held, snapped at his nose.

Abernathy smiled and showed all of his teeth. "You listen to me, you worthless bag of feathers. You are going to lead us to this cave—tonight. When we get there, you are going to take us inside. You are going to show us this Tangle Box, and you are going to teach us the words of the spell. Do you un-derstand me?"

Biggar's bright eyes fixed on him. "I'm not doing anything. They'll find me missing and come looking for me. The Gorse, particularly. Wait until you see what it'll do to you!"

"Whatever it does," Abernathy replied pointedly, "you will not be around to see it happen." There was a long, meaningful silence. "The fact of the matter is," he continued, "if you do not show me where that cave is right now, I am going to give you to my friends and tell them to do whatever they like with you as long as they assure me that I will never, ever see you again."

He kept his gaze and his voice steady. "Because I am very angry about being tricked. I am even more angry about what you have done to the High Lord. I want him back, safe and sound, and I expect you to help me if you have any hope at all of living out the night. Has that penetrated your little bird brain?"

There was another long silence. "Say something quick," Abernathy urged.

Biggar's voice came out a croak. "The cave is west, beyond the Heart." Then he recovered. "But it won't do you any good."

Abernathy smiled and gave the bird another look at his teeth. "We'll see about that," he promised.

Biggar's Last Stand

While Fillip kept tight hold of Biggar, Sot was dispatched to find horses for the journey west, the word *find* being understood to be a euphemism for the word *steal* by all concerned. Beggars could not afford to be choosers, and the G'home Gnomes were thieves by nature and habit and would readily interpret *find* as *steal* in any event. The hard part of all this was not in reconciling moral principles, but in accepting that horses must be used. Neither Abernathy nor the Gnomes had any particular love for horses, and in truth horses didn't much care for them either. It was one of those inbred hostilities that could not be overcome by either reason or circumstance. But the distance involved required at least a good day by foot and only four hours by horseback. Since time was running out for Questor Thews and Sterling Silver—dawn, after all, would find Kallendbor and the black-cloaked stranger working hard to discover ways to shorten the siege—necessity ruled and horses would have to be tolerated.

If only barely.

Sot was back in record time, leading two haltered and blanketed horses, one a bay, the other a sorrel, that he had quite obviously removed from a picket line. He had not thought to acquire either saddles or bridles, which complicated matters. The horses were already shying and snorting with distaste at the small, ragged, dirt-encrusted rodent who led them. In lieu of saddles, Abernathy decided to leave the blankets in place, trimming them with Sot's hunting knife so that they did not hang below the horses' flanks and securing them as best he could with a makeshift girth strap woven out of the pieces trimmed. It was a sad-looking job, but there was no help for it.

They mounted up then, Abernathy aboard the sorrel, which was the more rambunctious of the pair, and Fillip and Sot atop the bay. Fillip held the halter rope and Sot the bird. The horses were dancing and huffing by now, beginning to realize what was in store for them and being none too happy about it. Abernathy had them walk the horses at first, anxious to get as far away from the encampment as possible in case they chose to bolt. This was accomplished with a minimum of fuss. When they were several miles off and well up into the hill country west, Abernathy kicked his mount in the flanks gently and they were off.

At a dead run. Both horses leapt away as if on command and tore through the trees and over the hills like creatures possessed. Abernathy tried to rein his sorrel in, but the horse was having none of it. Free of the constraints of bit and reins, it simply took command. Abernathy gave up trying to do anything but hang on. Behind him, he could hear the Gnomes howling in despair. If they were thrown, they might lose the bird. If they lost the bird, they were finished. He gritted his teeth and resisted the urge to shout back useless advice.

Eventually the horses wore themselves out, slowed to a trot, and finally a walk. All three riders were still aboard and in possession of their faculties, although they felt as if their bones had been rearranged. They had come a very long way in a very short time, as it turned out, and before they knew it they were at the Heart and passing west. Abernathy called back from time to time for directions from Biggar, and the bird grudgingly supplied what was required. The moons shifted languidly along the horizon and overhead across the sky as night eased toward morning. The countryside changed its look as the trees thickened and the forests grew more dense. Soon they were forced to proceed at a careful walk in a woods that offered no trail and allowed no misstep.

It was little more than an hour later when they reached the cave. They dismounted at the top of a steep rise, tied the horses to a tree, and maneuvered their way down the slope to a tangled thicket below. The descent went slowly, as all were stiff and sore from the ride. The Gnomes complained loudly and incessantly, and Abernathy gave thought to gagging them. At the base of the slope, they turned back through a gathering of brush and found themselves up against a huge, flat stone into which intricate symbols had been carved. Abernathy could neither read nor understand the symbols.

"What do we do now?" he demanded of Biggar.

The bird was looking somewhat the worse for wear, having been held tightly by the legs during the entire ride, often upside-down as Sot struggled to keep his seat atop the bay. Feathers were sticking out everywhere, and dust coated the once-sleek black body.

"I don't know that I should tell you another thing," he snapped in reply. "When are you going to let me go!"

"When I see the High Lord safe and sound again!" Abernathy was in no mood for argument.

Biggar spit disdainfully. "That won't happen. Not if I help you get into the cave, not if I show you the box, and not if you speak the spell. It won't happen because you're not a wizard or a conjurer or anyone else capable of summoning magic."

"This from a bird," Abernathy replied testily. "Just get us inside, Biggar. Let me worry about the rest."

The bird sniffed. "Very well. Have it your way. Touch these symbols in the order I direct." And he proceeded to repeat the procedure for opening the cavern door as he had memorized it from watching Horris Kew.

A moment later, the stone swung back, grating against its rock seating, yawning into a black hole streaked dimly with a silver phosphorescence. The little company stood staring uncertainly into the uninviting gloom.

"Well?" Biggar sneered. "Are you going to stand out here all day or are you going in? Let's get this over with."

"How far back does this cave run?" Abernathy asked.

"To its end!" the bird snapped. "Sheesh!"

Abernathy ignored him. He didn't like caves any better than he liked tunnels, but he couldn't risk sending the G'home Gnomes in alone. No telling what might happen. On the other hand, he wasn't anxious to walk into a trap.

"I will go first," Fillip volunteered, providing a solution to the problem.

"I will go second," Sot offered.

"We don't mind tunnels and caves."

"We like the dark."

That was fine with Abernathy. He was content to bring up the rear. The better to keep an eye on everyone. Besides, if there were any traps the Gnomes would have a far better chance of spotting them than he would. Too bad his nose worked better than his eyes, but such was his lot and there was no point in bemoaning it.

"All right," he agreed. "But be careful."

"Do not worry about us," Fillip advised cheerfully.

"Not for a minute," Sot added.

Fair enough, Abernathy allowed. Not that he was inclined to do so in any case. "Just keep a tight grip on the bird," he ordered.

They stepped cautiously through the door, easing their way out of night's darkness and into the cavern's. The phosphorescence gleamed in dull streaks along the corridor walls ahead, like candlelight seen through a rain-streaked window. They paused in the entry, casting about. The air within was surprisingly warm. The silence was immense.

A sudden, terrible thought struck Abernathy. What if the Gorse had come here ahead of them for some reason and was waiting? The idea was so frightening that for a moment he could not move. It occurred to him suddenly that he was in way over his head. He had no weapons, no magic, and no fighting skills with which to protect himself. The Gnomes were worthless in a fight; all they would do was burrow to safety. This whole enterprise was fraught with danger and riddled with the possibility of failure. What had he been thinking in undertaking it in the first place?

Then the momentary fear passed, and he was able to calm himself. He had done what he must do, what was necessary and right, and that was enough to justify any risk. High Lord Ben Holiday depended on him. He did not know how exactly, but he knew that in some way it was true. He reminded himself anew how he had aided and abetted the Gorse and Horris Kew in their efforts to subvert the people of Landover and undermine the throne. He reminded himself of the debt that he must pay for his foolishness.

"Well, then, let's proceed," he announced bravely.

The Gnomes, who had been watching him work his way through his hesitancy, eased through the doorway. Abernathy took a deep breath and followed.

Instantly, the door grated shut behind them.

Abernathy jumped, the Gnomes yelped, and for an instant there was complete pandemonium. Abernathy threw himself instinctively against the door to force it open again. Both Gnomes raced to help and ran into each other for their trouble. As they collided, Biggar pecked as hard as he could on the hand grasping him, and Sot let go.

Biggar broke free instantly, flew up into the air, and in the blink of an eye streaked away into the cave.

Within the Labyrinth, Ben Holiday worked his way slowly through the mist, the talisman of the medallion held carefully before him. Strabo and Nightshade trailed, silent wraiths following his lead. They had all been transformed inwardly since the revelation of their identity, but outwardly each was crippled in appearance and capability and bore the weight of their imprisonment like chains. There was the sense now that they walked their last mile, that if they failed to get free this time they would be trapped forever. There was within them a growing desperation.

None was more acutely aware of it than Ben, who carried in his hands their only hope. The medallion did not speak to him; it did not give off light or provide direction. He walked like a blind man, seeing nothing of the trail he needed, knowing only that the medallion had taken him through the fairy mists before and must somehow do so again if they were to survive. For survival was the issue here, though the word went unspoken. If they remained within the mists, they would eventually go mad. Madness was a certainty they could see as clearly as their desperation, a pall as inexorable as the Haze arising when they were threatened. But unlike the Haze, it came not to protect but to destroy them. It did so gradually, an eroding of confidence, hope, and will. It worked against them as surely as a sickness against health, wearing them down so that in the end death was all that remained.

But it would not have them yet, Ben whispered in his mind. Finding Willow again, even in his dream, even for that briefest of moments, finding her and knowing that she depended on him, that she waited for him somewhere beyond the entangling mists of the Labyrinth, she and their unborn child, was enough to strengthen his determination to live. He would find a way out. The medallion would give them their escape. It must.

"I see no change in anything." Nightshade's cold voice drifted up from behind.

In truth, she was right. They seemed to be making no

progress, though they had been walking for hours. Shouldn't they have been clear by now if the medallion was working? How long must it take? Ben peered ahead through the gloom, trying to see some difference in the texture and viscidity of the mist. He did not slow, thinking that if he did they might stop, and if they stopped they were lost. Movement gave hope, movement of any sort.

"There is a lessening of the dampness," Strabo said suddenly.

Ben glanced down. He was right. The ground on which they walked was firmer than it had been at any time since they had come into the mists. Perhaps this was a sign. He took it as one and picked up the pace. Ahead, the trees seemed less dense. Was this possible? Hope blossomed within him. He grew flushed with its brightness. The trees were giving way, opening into a clearing, the clearing opening in turn into a passageway, a hollowed-out tunnel through massive old growth that ran on into a distant dark . . .

"Yes," he whispered aloud.

For it was a recognizable trail they approached now, one familiar to all who had passed through the fairy mists into Landover. They hastened toward it eagerly, even Nightshade brightening perceptibly at the welcome sight. They entered the tunneled gloom in a knot, hurrying down the forest trail. It was the link they had sought, the way back from where they had come. There were no fairies here, no sounds, no movement, no hint of life of any sort save the trees and the brush and the fog that shrouded them. They were still within the fairy mists of the Labyrinth. Yet somewhere close, somewhere just ahead, the door leading out awaited.

But suddenly the gloom closed tightly about before them, turning as dark as ink, becoming a wall that rose and stretched away without end. They slowed as they came up to it, baffled that it should be there. They stopped as they found it would not allow them to go further, touching its surface and finding it as hard and immovable as stone. They walked its perimeter in either direction for a distance and then retraced their steps. The wall offered no doorway leading through. It allowed no passage out.

"What is this madness?" Nightshade hissed in fury.

Ben shook his head. The medallion would neither part the mists nor show them a way around. This wall, whatever it was, was impervious to the magic. How could that be? If the fairy mists imprisoned them, then the medallion should be able to take them through. The medallion gave passage through all of the mists.

Then suddenly he recognized what it was that he was seeing. This black wall was not formed of the fairy mists. It was the confinement of the Tangle Box itself, a different form of magic than the mists, a final barrier against escape. And the lock for this door, he feared, did not lie within their prison. It lay instead without.

He stepped back in frustration and despair. He had been able to pass from the mists of the Tangle Box in his dream, but he could not do so while awake.

"What are we supposed to do now?" Strabo asked quietly, hunched down at his elbow, anger seeping into his voice.

Ben Holiday did not have an answer.

It took Biggar only moments to reach the back of the cavern, the chamber where the Gorse had concealed the Tangle Box. Biggar swooped down to where the box sat on a rock shelf far back in the shadows, landing on an outcropping just above. Now what? He had given no thought to anything but escape up until this point, and now that he had achieved his goal he wasn't sure what to do next. There was only one way out of the cave and that was back the way he had come. There were runes carved in the rock above the door, different than those that opened the door from without, but he knew the required sequence. All that was needed was to lure the dog and the ferrets away long enough to let him trigger the release.

He could hear them coming already, the scratching of their claws on the rock, the whine of their voices.

"Here, birdie, birdie," one of them called.

Biggar sneered. Birdie, birdie, indeed.

He waited patiently in the near dark until they came into view. They materialized out of the gloom like hairy pigs, sniffing and snuffling their way about the cavern floor. How pathetic! It was the ferrets or whatever they were, creeping about, earthbound imbeciles who had about as much chance of catching him as they did of mastering physics.

"Come here, birdie," one of them repeated patiently.

"Here, stupid bird," the other snapped.

Must be the one he pecked, Biggar thought. He would have smiled if his beak had allowed it. He hoped he had hurt the wretched little monster plenty. He hoped the beast developed gangrene and dropped dead. Precious little concern he'd shown for Biggar, after all. Carrying him slung down on that horse! Beating Biggar's head against his leg as he tried to keep his seat! Well, they'd soon see what messing around with him would get them!

He lifted off his perch and flew back across the chamber. They saw him instantly, eyes sharper than he would have thought, and leapt to catch him as he whizzed past. Hopeless, of course. He was twenty feet off the floor and twice as quick as they were. He was past them and speeding for the entrance while they were still clutching at air. Maybe the dog had come hunting, too. Maybe.

But he hadn't. The dog was stationed directly in front of the stone barrier, waiting. Biggar banked hurriedly, narrowly avoiding the dog's outstretched hands and bared teeth. The dog was smarter than the ferrets. He wasn't about to let Biggar escape so easily.

"Come back here, you little . . ."

The dog's shouted epithets died away into echoes that bounced off the rock as Biggar flew back toward the main chamber. So it was a standoff. They were all trapped in the cave. Biggar's mind raced. The trick now was to lure the dog away from the stone slab, to bring him back into the cavern just long enough for Biggar to slip past and trigger the lock. Once he was outside the cave, they would never catch him. Then the Gorse could deal with them. He wondered suddenly if there was any chance that the Gorse would come back to the cave that night. Perhaps Horris would go to it with the tale of Biggar's disappearance. Perhaps. But that was giving Horris more credit for brains than he deserved. These days, Horris was too stupid to figure out how to tie his shoes. Since the Gorse had been released, Horris was scared and confused and generally useless. Biggar was thinking that maybe it was time for a new partner. What did he need Horris for anyway? He was the real brains of the pair. Always had been.

He lifted toward the ceiling as he approached the back chamber, but even so he just narrowly avoided Sot as the Gnome leaped down from a rocky promontory he had gained high up on the wall to one side. The Gnome plummeted past him, hands grasping, and dropped to the cavern floor. Biggar listened to him hit, a dull thud, then heard him groan and start to mutter. Good.

"Nice try, rodent-face," he called out gleefully, and then he ducked as the other ferret threw something past his head. A metal pan or plate, some piece of cookware that Horris had carried in. He squawked angrily and rose up as far as he could go. Time for evasive action.

All sorts of things started flying at him now as the Gnomes attacked in earnest, trying to bring him down. They threw everything they could lift, yelling at him all the while, calling him "stupid bird" and worse, growing angrier by the moment. That suited Biggar just fine. Anger caused mistakes, and he was counting on one from them. They had not seen the Tangle Box yet, and he made a point of staying away from it. Wheeling, diving, soaring out of reach, he teased and taunted them unmercifully, calling them names back, daring them to catch him. Total idiots that they were, they just kept yelling and leaping about and trying to hit him with stuff. Fat chance.

On the other hand, he was growing a tad weary with all this dodging about, and he still didn't have a plan for getting the dog away from the door. He needed a distraction that would bring the dog running, something the dog couldn't ignore. He wondered suddenly what would happen if he spoke the words to the spell that had imprisoned Holiday and the others. Nothing good, he decided and discarded the idea quickly. That box was too dangerous. Besides, suppose it released its prisoners? Better to leave it where it was for now. He scanned the cavern again for another avenue of escape, hoping that maybe he had missed an air shaft or fissure. But there was nothing to be seen.

Below, the G'home Gnomes began pulling blankets off Horris Kew's makeshift bed and tying them together to form a net. Come now, Biggar smirked. He flew at them while they worked, distracting them, taunting them further. He could see the gleam of their yellow eyes as they ducked and hissed up at him. They were really angry, the both of them. Served them right. They completed their net, the whole of it riddled with escape holes—Idiots!—and began trying to maneuver him into a corner where he could be trapped.

"Fatheads! Toads! Stupid groundhogs!" he called down to them, easily evading their pathetic efforts.

He swooped down and picked up some of the lighter implements that had been thrown at him, carried them aloft, and dropped them on the Gnomes' heads. The Gnomes screeched and howled. Maybe that would bring the dog, Biggar thought hopefully. But the dog still didn't come. Not enough noise, maybe. Biggar tried again with something slightly heavier, a wooden ladle. He dropped it squarely on Fillip's head, and the Gnome lost his balance on the perch he had gained some ten feet up and fell headfirst to the floor. It must have hurt terribly, but the Gnome was back on his feet at once. Heads of iron, Biggar thought. No brains to encumber their thick skulls.

The game continued for a time, the Gnomes swinging their net at Biggar, Biggar avoiding the snare and calling out names. No one could gain an advantage. Biggar called the dog names as well, but there was no response. He darted back down the tunnel to where the dog kept watch, trying to draw it after him with insults and nosedives, but the dog stayed put.

It was Biggar who lost patience first. He could not bear that these halfwits had kept him trapped for so long, could not stand the idea of being stymied by idiots. He decided to try something to break the stalemate. He streaked back into the far chamber, past the leaping, grasping Gnomes, and across the room to the Tangle Box. Enough of caution. The one thing that would bring the dog was the box—especially if he thought something dreadful was going to happen to it. Biggar would accommodate him, then.

He teased the ferret creatures back toward the entry, giving them just enough hope that they might catch hold of him to keep them coming, then swooped back across the chamber to the Tangle Box. He landed squarely on top of the container, dug his claws into the crevices where the symbols of power had been carved, secured his grip, and lifted off. It was not easy doing so. The box was heavy and cumbersome. He watched the Gnomes race toward him, yelling more wildly as they realized what he was doing. They were incoherent, however, not yet yelling "Tangle Box" or some such, so the dog still didn't come. Clacking his beak with the effort, Biggar rose into the gloom, the box secured in his claws. His wings flapped madly to keep him aloft. His pinions strained. Below, the ferrets were leaping wildly for him.

He struggled and flapped his way into the highest reaches of the chamber, the Tangle Box bobbing in his grasp. His plan was to carry it about for a few more moments and then drop it. One act or the other was bound to bring the dog.

"Stupid bird, come down!" one Gnome howled.

"Why don't you come up?" he snarled back.

"You'll be sorry for this!" the other shouted.

"Care to see what will happen if I let go of this?" he teased, letting the box jiggle wildly. "I don't think I can hold on much longer."

They shrieked like banshees at that, racing about below him like scampering mice routed out of their nest. He was really enjoying this. He angled from one side of the chamber to the other, drawing them after, a pair of ridiculous, hopeless pawns.

But still the dog didn't come.

He lost patience for the last time. Fine, if this was how they wanted to play it, fine! He was all worn out anyway. He banked away from them to the highest point in the chamber and released the Tangle Box.

Unfortunately, one of his claws caught quite firmly in a seam as he did so.

Down went the Tangle Box, plummeting to the cavern floor, and down went a hapless Biggar with it. The bird struggled wildly to break free, scratching and scraping at the weight about its foot, but it was held fast. Up rushed the stone floor. Biggar shrieked and closed his eyes.

The expected did not come to pass, however. There was no skull-smashing stop on the stone, no splatter of box and bird. At the last possible moment Sot threw himself across the floor and caught both in the cradle of his gnarly, hairy arms.

Biggar had just enough time to open his eyes before a grimy hand closed tightly about his unfortunate neck.

"Got you now, stupid bird," the Gnome whispered.

Abernathy stood at the cavern entrance and listened as the tumult in the inner chambers died into sudden and unexpected silence. He waited for it to resume, but it did not. The silence lengthened and deepened. Clearly something had happened, but what? He could not leave his post to find out. He knew that Biggar would slip past him and escape if he did. The bird had been trying to lure him away for the past hour, waiting for his chance. Abernathy had sent Fillip and Sot in after the troublesome creature, thinking as he did that they were best suited for the task in any event. He did not know how they would ever manage to catch the bird, but there was little choice other than to allow them to try. The extent of their efforts had been evident from the sounds of their struggle, a continuous, relentless cacophony that suggested all manner of unpleasant happenings.

And now everything was still.

"Fillip?" he called tentatively. "Sot?"

No answer. He waited anxiously. What should he do?

Then finally a pair of dim, but familiar shapes appeared out of the phosphorescence-streaked gloom, bearing between them an intricately carved wooden box. Abernathy's heart leapt with expectation.

"You found it!" he exclaimed, restraining the urge to dance a bit.

The Gnomes trundled toward him, looking somewhat the worse for wear.

"Stupid bird tried to drop it," Fillip said grimly.

"Tried to smash it," Sot embellished.

"Hurt the High Lord," Fillip said.

"Maybe kill the High Lord," Sot said.

They stroked the wooden surface of the Tangle Box lovingly and then passed it carefully over to the dog.

"Stupid bird won't do that again," Fillip said.

"Not ever," Sot said.

And spit out a well-chewed black feather.

Dead Reckoning

The sunrise over Sterling Silver was a blood-red stain on the eastern horizon that promised bad weather for the day ahead. Questor Thews was back on the ramparts of the castle, looking down over the waking encampment of Kallendbor's professional army and the ragtag collection of villagers and farmers that had preceded it in the quest for the phantom collection of mind's eye crystals. Night's darkness was receding reluctantly west, edged back by the crimson dawn, and the light washed over the huddled forms of the besiegers like blood.

Hardly an auspicious omen, the wizard thought.

He had been up most of the night scouring the countryside with the Landsview in search of Ben Holiday. He had traveled the length and breadth of Landover, north to south, east to west, and found no trace of the High Lord. He was tired and discouraged from his efforts and frankly at his wit's end. What was he supposed to do now? The castle was under siege, two-thirds of the population were in open revolt, and he had been left alone to deal with all of it. Not even Abernathy was to be found, a new and unwelcome source of irritation. Willow hadn't returned yet either. If people kept disappearing, the monarchy would soon run out of responsible leaders and collapse like a deflated balloon.

Bunion moved out of the shadows and stood beside him, looking down at the congregation stirring on the meadow. For once, the kobold didn't offer his toothy smile. Questor sighed, reached down, and patted the gnarled little fellow reassuringly on the shoulder. Bunion was exhausted and discouraged, too. It seemed as if they all had run out of options and must now simply wait to see what would happen.

They didn't have to wait long. As the sun began to rise and the camp to stir, the black-cloaked stranger appeared out of the forest gloom and made his way toward the far end of the meadow where heavy thickets fronted the face of a bluff. No one was camped in this space, the ground rough and uneven, the brush studded with thorns and itchweed, the light veiled, and the shadows thick. Questor watched the stranger move away from the besiegers. No one went with him. No one even seemed to notice he was there. He did not move furtively, but with a purpose that defied intervention from any quarter. Questor glanced back across the broad stretch of the meadow. There was no sign of Horris Kew or his bird or even of Kallendbor.

Keeping clear somehow of the brambles, the black-cloaked stranger eased through the lingering shadows. What was he up to? Questor Thews didn't know, but he was convinced he would be better off if he did. He kept thinking that he ought to be doing something, but he really had no idea what.

Bunion chittered quickly, urgently.

"No, wait here," Questor advised. "No swimming the moat until we know what he's up to. No heroics. We've lost enough people as it is." And he wondered again where Abernathy had gone.

Kallendbor had come into view now, trailed by his officers and retainers. Most were armored and ready for battle. War horses were being saddled. Weapons were being brought down from the heights in wagons and foot soldiers were lining up to receive them. Questor's mouth tightened. Apparently Kallendbor was growing tired of the siege already.

Scarlet light swept over Sterling Silver and its encircling lake and spread across the meadow. It reached the bluff face where the black-cloaked stranger had stepped out of the shadows. It began to climb toward the woods beyond.

Questor squinted against its glare. The stranger had moved well out into the open and was facing the bluff.

"What is he up to?" the wizard muttered suspiciously.

In the next instant the stranger's arms lifted beneath his concealing cloak, his body went rigid, and lines of fire arced downward into the earth. The wizard started. The stranger was using magic! He exchanged a worried glance with Bunion. There were shouts now from the central part of the meadow, where others had seen the flames. Kallendbor was atop his charger, shouting order at his officers. Men were milling about, not certain what it was they were supposed to do. Lines of soldiers afoot and on horseback were drawing up into formation. Farmers and villagers and their families were caught between fleeing and sticking around to see what would happen.

Had they possessed sufficient foresight, they would have chosen flight. There was a deep, ominous rumble from within the earth, and the sound of stone grating, as if an enormous door had swung open.

Uh, oh, Questor Thews thought belatedly.

The bluff face seemed to rip itself apart, torn like shredded paper, obliterated behind the sundering of the air in front of it. Scarlet dawn light poured into the black hole that was left, filling it with shifting color and smoky shadows. Thunder boomed, shaking the earth and those who stared open-mouthed from both the meadow and Sterling Silver's ramparts. The hiss of monsters mixed with a clash of armor and weapons. Everything rose to a shriek that sounded of things dying in terrible agony.

Questor went dry-mouthed. Demons! The black-cloaked stranger had summoned demons!

A fierce wind whipped across the meadow, flattening tents and standards and causing horses to rear in terror and men afoot to drop to their knees. Kallendbor had his broadsword out, holding it forth like a matchstick against a hurricane.

Demons emerged from the rent, their armor bristling with spikes and jagged edges, all blackened and charred as if burned in the hottest fire. Their bodies smoked as they leapt from the gap onto the meadow floor, steam leaking from their visors and the chinks where their armor was fastened by stays. They were lean and misshapen beings, all bent and twisted like trees on a windswept ridge stripped bare and turned as hard as iron. They rode beasts that had no name and lent themselves to no description, things out of nightmare and horrific fantasy, creatures out of shadowy netherworlds.

Out from the darkest recesses of Abaddon they came, spreading right and left about the solitary figure of the black-cloaked stranger, sweeping from lake to bluff rise and filling up every inch of ground in between until they covered the far end of the meadow. The dawn's blood hue settled over them so that they had the look of coals on which a bellows had been turned, the heat etched into the fissures and cracks of their black forms like fire burned into metal.

Questor Thews felt his heart move into his throat.

When the black-cloaked stranger turned to face him from across the lake, he knew that real trouble had arrived on his doorstep.

"**Y**ou ate the bird? You ate him?"

Abernathy stared in disbelief at Fillip and Sot, who stood crestfallen before him, the satisfied smiles slowly melting from their faces.

"He deserved it," Fillip mumbled defensively.

"Stupid bird," Sot muttered.

"But you didn't have to eat him!" Abernathy shouted, furious now. "Do you know what you've done? The bird was the only one who knew how to get us out of here! He was the only one who knew how to open the box! What are we supposed to do without him? We are trapped in this cave and the High Lord is trapped in the box and we cannot do anything about either!"

The G'home Gnomes looked at each other, wringing their hands pathetically.

"We forgot," Fillip whined.

"Yes, we forgot," Sot echoed.

"We didn't know," Fillip said.

"We didn't think," Sot said.

"Anyway, it was his idea," Fillip said, pointing to Sot.

"Yes, it was my . . ." Sot stopped short. "It was not! It was yours!"

"Yours!"

"Yours!"

They began shouting at and then pushing each other, and finally they rushed together kicking and biting and fell to the cave floor in a tangle. Abernathy rolled his eyes, moved over to one side, and sat down with the Tangle Box on his lap. Let them fight, he thought. Let them pull out their hair and choke on it, for all he cared. He sat back against the cave wall, pondering fate's cruel hand. To have come this close and be denied was almost too much to bear. He watched the G'home Gnomes battle across the cave floor and into the shadows. He still couldn't believe they had eaten the bird. Well, maybe he could. Actually, it made perfect sense, given who he was dealing with. For them, eating the bird was a natural response. He was mostly angry at himself, he guessed, for letting it happen. Not that he could have anticipated it, he supposed. But, still . . .

He ruminated on to no discernible purpose for a time, unable to help himself. The minutes slipped by. From back in the dark, the sounds of fighting stopped. Abernathy listened. Maybe they had eaten each other. Poetic justice, if they had.

But after a moment, they emerged, cut and scraped and disheveled, their heads downcast, their mouths set in a tight line. They sat down across from him wordlessly, staring at nothing. Abernathy stared back.

"Sorry," Fillip muttered after a moment.

"Sorry," Sot muttered.

Abernathy nodded. He couldn't bring himself to tell them that it was all right, because of course it wasn't, or that he forgave them, because of course he didn't. So he didn't say anything.

After a moment, Fillip said brightly to Sot, "Maybe there are still crystals hidden back in the cave!"

Sot looked up eagerly. "Yes, maybe there are! Let's look!"

And off they went, scurrying away into the darkness. Abernathy sighed and let them go. Maybe it would keep them out of further mischief. More time passed—Abernathy didn't know how much. He thought about using trial and error to figure out the rune sequence that would open the door but there were dozens of markings about the door and he had no hope of finding the right combination. Still, what else could he do? He set down the Tangle Box and started to rise.

Just as he did, the locks on the cave door triggered, and it began to open. Abernathy froze, then flattened himself against the wall to one side. The door swung slowly inward, grating and squealing as it went, letting in a faint twinge of reddish-gray light from the approaching dawn.

Abernathy caught his breath. What if it was the black-cloaked stranger? He closed his eyes involuntarily.

"Biggar?" a familiar voice called tentatively.

Horris Kew's plow-nosed face shoved into view as he waited for his eyes to adjust to the gloom. Abernathy stayed perfectly still, unable to believe his good fortune.

"Biggar?" the other called once more, and came inside the cave.

The stone door began to close behind him. Abernathy moved between the door and the conjurer, and said, "Hello, Horris."

When Horris turned, Abernathy leapt on him and bore him to the floor. Horris shrieked and tried to break free, struggling mightily. He was all bony arms and legs, and Abernathy couldn't hold him. Horris squirmed out from under his attacker, dragged himself to his feet, and reached for the door. Desperate to hold him, Abernathy fastened his teeth in the other's worn supplicant's robes and braced himself on all fours. Horris tried to pull free, but couldn't quite manage it. Abernathy growled. The two struggled back and forth in front of the door, neither able to gain an advantage.

Then Horris Kew caught sight of the Tangle Box, shrieked anew, tore himself free with a mighty rip, and snatched up the box. He was making for the door and safety, kicking out at Abernathy furiously, when Fillip and Sot charged out of the darkness and catapulted into him, knocking him from his feet and flat on his back where he lay gasping for breath.

Abernathy took back the Tangle Box, started to give it to Fillip, and thought better of the idea. Using his free hand, he hauled Horris Kew back to his feet and shook him so hard he could hear the other's teeth rattle.

"You listen to me, you troublesome fraud!" he hissed angrily. "You do exactly as I say or you will regret the day you were born!"

"Let me go!" Horris Kew pleaded. "None of this is my fault! I didn't know!"

"You never know!" Abernathy snapped. "That's your problem! What are you doing here, anyway?"

"I came looking for Biggar," Horris managed, swallowing

his fear in great gulps of breath. "Where is he? What have you done with him?"

Abernathy waited for the other's breathing to slow a beat, then brought them nose-to-nose. "The Gnomes ate him, Horris," he said softly. Horris Kew's eyes went wide. "And if you do not do what I tell you, I am going to let them eat you as well. Do you understand me?"

Horris nodded at once, unable to speak.

Abernathy moved back a fraction of an inch. "You can start by opening the cave door and getting us out of here. And do not attempt any tricks. Do not try running. I shall have a good grip on you the entire time."

He propelled Horris back to the entrance, Fillip and Sot following close behind, and waited while the terrified conjurer worked the rune sequence and triggered a release of the locks. The door opened ponderously, and conjurer, scribe, and Gnomes stumbled back out into the light.

Abernathy swung Horris Kew back around to face him. "Despite what you think, this is indeed all your fault, Horris, everything that has happened, so I do not want to hear you say anything else. You have one chance to set things right, and I suggest you take it. I want the High Lord set free. I want High Lord Ben Holiday back in Landover. You put him in the box; now you get him out!"

Horris Kew swallowed, his Adam's apple bobbing, his cheeks and mouth making a sucking noise. He looked like a scarecrow left out in the field long after its usefulness has reached an end. He looked like he might collapse into a pile of straw. "I don't know if I can do that," he whispered.

Abernathy gave him the meanest look he could muster. "You had better hope you can," he replied softly.

"But what will they do to me once they're free? Holiday might understand, but what about the dragon and the witch?"

"You will have bigger worries if you do not set them

free." Abernathy was in no mood to bargain. "Speak the words of the spell, Horris. Right now."

Horris Kew licked his lips, glanced down at the G'home Gnomes, and took a deep breath. "I'll try."

Abernathy, without releasing him, handed over the Tangle Box and moved around behind him. One hand clamped about the conjurer's skinny neck. "Remember, no tricks."

Dawn was a red glare through the shadowy mass of the forest about them as it chased the darkness slowly west. Abernathy did not like the look of it. Bad weather was moving in. He was already thinking about the trip back to Sterling Silver, about the siege, about Kallendbor and the black-cloaked stranger. He gave Horris Kew's neck a sharp squeeze. Horris began to speak.

"Rashun, oblight, surena! Larin, kestel, maneta! Ruhn!"

And the top of the Tangle Box disappeared instantly in a misty swirl of wicked green light.

Ben Holiday saw the crack appear in the blackness of the wall before him and turned toward it instantly. It glimmered as he raced for it, Nightshade and Strabo a step behind, then broadened as if the entire wall had been split apart. Fairy mist spun wildly, drawn to the brightness as if become a living thing. Ben flung himself into the breach, heedless of the consequences, knowing only that an opening of any kind offered a chance to get free. The light seemed to suck him up, to draw him into a vortex that twisted him about like a feather in a great wind. He was conscious of the witch and the dragon being drawn along with him, all three of them caught up in a whirlwind of motion. The gloom and the mist disappeared below him. The Labyrinth faded away. Above, the light took on a greenish glow, and there were shadows that swayed and rippled—tree branches and leaves, he realized—and sky, still dark with night's departure, and the smell of earth and moss and old growth, and the coppery taste of something like sulfur, and the sound of voices crying out . . .

And then he was spit out into the forest gloom of Land-over, come back once more into the world from which he had been taken. He found himself standing less than a dozen feet from Abernathy, Horris Kew, and Fillip and Sot, all of whom stared at him wide-eyed and openmouthed.

Then Nightshade appeared as well, become herself once more, the power of her magic radiating off her body in small sparks and glimmerings. She flung her arms skyward, a spontaneous gesture, the white streak in her black hair gleaming like frost on coal, the cool edges of her sculpted face lifted toward the red glow of the dawn.

"Free!" she cried with joy.

Strabo exploded out of the Tangle Box behind her, returned to his dragon form, scaly black body uncoiling, wings unfolding, rising skyward with a huge burst of fire that rolled from his maw, hammered into the cave door, and then burned upward through the trees. Steaming and glistening, all spikes and edges, the dragon gave a huge, booming cough and rocketed away into the departing night.

"High Lord!" Abernathy exclaimed in greeting, the relief evident in his voice. He snatched back the Tangle Box from Horris Kew and hurried over. "Are you all right?"

Ben nodded, looking around, making certain that in fact he was. Fillip and Sot were making small squeaking sounds in his direction while cowering away from the black form of Nightshade. Horris Kew appeared to be looking for a place to hide.

Ben took a deep breath. "Abernathy, what is going on?"

The scribe drew himself up. "Well, actually, quite a lot, as it happens . . ."

A burst of acclaim from the G'home Gnomes cut him short.

"Great High Lord!"

"Mighty High Lord!"

Fillip and Sot were hugging each other and jumping up and down in glee, apparently convinced that it really was him after all. Ben gave them a tentative smile. What were *they* doing here?

Abernathy tried to continue, but Nightshade had spotted Horris Kew and was starting forward in a rush of black robes. "You!" she hissed in undisguised fury.

Ben stepped quickly between them. "Wait, Nightshade. I want to hear from Abernathy first."

"Get out of my way, play-King," the witch ordered venomously. "We are no longer in the Labyrinth and no longer subject to its rules. I have my magic back, and I can do as I please!"

But Ben held his ground, reached into his tunic, and brought forth the medallion. "We are both who we were. Do not test your strength against mine. I will hear from my scribe on what has been happening in our absence before I make a decision about Horris Kew."

Nightshade stood frozen in place, livid with fury. "Start talking, Abernathy," Ben advised quietly.

Abernathy did. He told the High Lord all about the Tangle Box and Horris Kew, the mind's eye crystals, the black-cloaked stranger, Kallendbor, and the siege of Sterling Silver. Ben listened without comment, his eyes fixed on Nightshade. When Abernathy was finished, Ben stepped back to stand beside Horris Kew. "Well?"

"My Lord, I have nothing to say in my defense." The conjurer seemed totally defeated. His tall, skinny frame was hunched over in submission. "The stranger is a fairy being come out of the Tangle Box—my fault, as well—a thing of great magic and evil called the Gorse. It plans revenge of some sort against the people of the fairy mists after it conquers

Landover. I am sorry I did anything to help it, believe me." He paused, swallowing. "I would say in my behalf that I did help set you free."

"After you trapped us, of course," Ben pointed out. He looked at Nightshade. "I'll have to keep him with me for a time. I may have need of him in dealing with this fairy creature."

Nightshade shook her black-maned head. "Give him to me."

"He is not the real enemy, Nightshade. He never was. He was used as thoroughly as we were, if not as badly. Put aside your anger. Come with us to Sterling Silver and confront the Gorse. Your magic would be a great help. We worked together in the mists; we can do so again."

"I have no interest in your problems!" Nightshade snapped. "Solve them on your own!"

She stared at Ben challengingly. Ben took a deep breath. "I know that what happened in the mists, what passed be-tween us . . ."

"Stop!" she shrieked with such fury that Fillip and Sot scattered into the trees and disappeared. She was white with rage. "Don't say a word! Don't say anything! I hate you, play-King! I hate you with every bone in my body! I live only to see you destroyed! What you did to me, what you pretended . . . !"

"There was no pretense . . ."

"No! You cannot speak to me!" Her cold, hard, beautiful face was a twisted mask. "Take the conjurer! I want nothing to do with either of you! But . . ." Here she fixed Horris Kew with her gaze as a pin might a butterfly. "If I should ever see you again, if I should ever catch you alone . . ."

Her gaze shifted back to Ben. She gave him a withering glare. "I will hate you forever!" she whispered, the words a curse that hung in the following silence like razors waiting to cut.

Then she lifted her arms in a sweeping motion, brought

smoke and mist about her in a rush, and disappeared into the dawn.

Ben stared after her, mixed emotions running through him as he considered the impact of her anger. It seemed strange that it should be like this after what they had shared—and at the same time inevitable. He wondered briefly if there was any way it might have been avoided and decided there was not.

"High Lord!" Abernathy cried urgently, and grabbed at his sleeve.

Ben turned.

A huge shadow fell over them, and Strabo descended once more out of the sky, snapping off branches and stirring up dust and debris as he settled his great bulk down upon the forest floor.

"Holiday," he rasped in friendly fashion. "We are not finished yet, you and I. Is this the one responsible for what was done to us?"

Ben shook his head. "No, Strabo. The one we want is back at Sterling Silver, engaged in further mischief."

The dragon's great horned head swung about, and the yellow eyes gleamed in the half light. "We started this journey together, though we did not choose to do so. Shall we end it together as well?"

Ben smiled in pleasant surprise. "I think we should," he agreed.

When they had gone from the clearing, Holiday, Abernathy, Horris Kew, and Strabo, the men flying off atop the dragon, and when enough time had passed that it was clear that Nightshade was gone as well, Fillip and Sot emerged from hiding. They crept out of the trees and stood peering about guardedly, ready to bolt at the slightest sound. But there was only silence and the faint, lingering smell of dragon fire where it had burned the trees.

"They are gone," Fillip said.

"Gone," Sot echoed.

They turned toward the cave, measuring the distance that separated them from its opening. The door stood ajar now, knocked off its hinges by Strabo's blast of fire, the locks smashed. Steam rose from its blackened surface in delicate tendrils.

"We could go inside now," Fillip said.

"Yes, we could look for crystals," Sot said.

"There might still be some," Fillip said.

"Even though we didn't find them before," Sot said.

"Hidden in a clever spot."

"Where we didn't think to look."

There was a long pause as they considered the prospect. The dawn's coloring had penetrated the forest gloom and was turning everything crimson. Birds had stopped singing. Insects had stopped chirping and buzzing. Nothing moved. The silence was oppressive.

"I think we should go home," Fillip said quietly.

"I think we should," Sot agreed.

So they did.

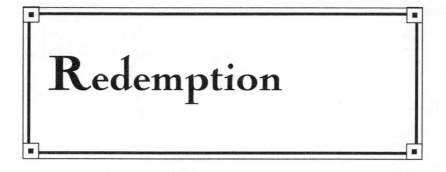

Redemption

As he looked down from his perch atop Strabo, flying high above Landover, Ben Holiday found himself pondering on how quickly things could change. An hour earlier he had been imprisoned in the Tangle Box, as far removed from this world as the dead from the living. A day earlier, he had not even known who he was. He had believed himself to be the Knight, a King's Champion, a personification of the Paladin that was in fact his alter ego. Nightshade and Strabo had not existed; his companions had been the Lady and the Gargoyle, and they had been as lost to themselves as he was. Together they had formed an odd company, bereft of any real knowledge of their past, forced to begin life anew in a world about which they knew almost nothing. Thrown together by a common mishap, compelled to share a life filled with unknowns and false hope, they had reached an understanding during their travels that bordered on friendship.

More than friendship, he amended carefully, where Nightshade was concerned.

Now all of it was gone, stripped away with the recapture of their identities and return to Landover. It was as if they had been made over twice, once going into the Tangle Box, once coming out, stripped each time of life's knowledge and forced to learn anew, strangers first in an unknown world, familiars second in a world all too well known. It was the second that would allow no part of the first, the second that demanded that everything from the first be given up because it had all been acquired and nurtured under false pretenses. It made Ben sad. He had shared a closeness with Nightshade that would never be there again. There had been a mutual dependence that was ended forever. Things would be different with Strabo as well. He carried them now to Sterling Silver to settle accounts with the Gorse, but once that was finished he would be gone. Ben harbored no illusions. There would be no further talks as there had been between the Knight and the Gargoyle, no sharing of fears and hopes, no common effort to understand the workings of life. They would go their own ways as they had done before being lured into the Tangle Box, and the time they had spent together in the mists would fade as surely as a dream on waking.

Ben resisted the urge to look back at Horris Kew, who sat immediately behind him and ahead of Abernathy. The instrument of their misfortune, he thought darkly—yet too foolish and misguided to be held responsible. The Gorse was the real enemy. How was he going to deal with this creature? It had a formidable command of magic and would not hesitate to use it, especially once it discovered that Ben, Nightshade, and Strabo were set free again. Why had it imprisoned them in the first place? What sort of threat did they represent that compelled it to place them in the box? Or was it simply a matter of expediency and nothing more?

Whatever the answers to his questions, there was one chilling certainty. In order to deal with the Gorse, he would once again be forced to become the Paladin, the King's knight-errant, the creature he feared he was becoming in fact. His fear had made him see himself as the Knight within the Tangle Box, and he had barely survived what that had initiated—the destruction of the townsfolk, the River Gypsies, and very nearly the Gristlies. His fear of his dark half had worked to destroy him within the fairy mists, but he had escaped. Yet now he must become his dark half if he was to survive. And once again he must worry how much of the Paladin's identity he assumed and how much of Ben Holiday's he gave up with each transformation.

Ben watched the Heart pass away beneath him, white velvet rests outlined in pristine bars against verdant green grasses, the flags of Landover's Kings a swirl of bright color in the wind. A part of him was anxious for the change, eager for the transformation. It had always been so. It was this that frightened him most.

Horris Kew was thinking as well, and his thoughts were not pleasant ones either. A confrontation between the Gorse and Holiday was only moments away, and no matter who won he was in big trouble. Both would hold him responsible for anything the other had done or had tried to do or even had planned to do. Both would want to exact punishment of some sort. In the case of the Gorse, Horris did not want to consider too carefully what that punishment might be. Certainly it would not be pleasant. Holiday might be the better choice. He wished Biggar were there to consult. He found, oddly enough, that he missed the bird. They had shared a common attitude toward life's opportunities and misfortunes, and it was too bad the latter had caught up with Biggar a little earlier than either of them had expected. Horris felt keenly the loss. If nothing else, perhaps he could have blamed some of what had happened on the bird.

He sighed. Thinking like that led nowhere, of course. He shifted gears and tried to decide what he could do to salvage matters. He would have to do something quick. Already Sterling Silver's bright ramparts were coming into view. Take sides with Holiday then, he decided. His chances were better with Landover's King, a fellow human being, than they were with the Gorse. So what could he do to help himself? What could he do that would put him in a better light when it came time to determine his fate?

Ahead, the dawn was a crimson stain all across the horizon, a strange and terrifying sight. The red was so pronounced that it seemed to have seeped into the earth itself, to color grasses, trees, brush, rivers, lakes, roadways, fields, towns, farms, and the whole of every living thing for as far as the eye could see. Clouds were forming all about them. They hadn't been there the previous day; there had been no trace of them last night. They appeared as if by magic, masking the morning skies west to east, threatening to swallow the rising sun, the harbinger of a storm that was quickly approaching.

Strabo started down, a gradual descent out of the retreating night. The approaching sun momentarily blinded the dragon's passengers, and they squinted against its glare. The castle's polished battlements and towers gleamed redly, reflecting the strange light. The portcullis was down and the gates closed. The bridge running from the island to the mainland was shattered. Shadows clustered darkly across the meadow that fronted the castle gates, and the sluggish movement of armies massing was visible. Ben Holiday started. Battle lines were being drawn up between opposing forces. There were Greensward soldiers at one end of the meadow and Abaddon's demons at the other.

"High Lord!" Abernathy exclaimed in horror.

Ben glanced over his shoulder and nodded back. Demons from Abaddon—the Gorse must have brought them out to aid him in his plan. What had he promised them? What lure had he used? They would not have come if they thought the Paladin would be there to stop them; they had always been terrified of the Paladin. So the Gorse must have promised them that with the King gone from Landover, there would be no threat from his Champion. With Nightshade and Strabo dispatched as well, there was little to fear from anyone.

Ben's mouth tightened. Now he must face both the

Gorse and Abaddon's demons. Even with Strabo to aid him, he did not much care for the odds.

"Strabo!" he called down to the dragon. A wicked yellow eye locked on him. "Take us down! Land right between them!"

The dragon hissed sharply, flattened out his approach, swept the battlefield once in a high, broad arc so that all could see him, and then settled slowly into the center of the meadow.

Ben, Horris Kew, and Abernathy scrambled down. It was like descending into a bizarre painting, a horrifically rendered version of Hell on Earth. The reddish dawn gave the whole of the grasslands a surreal look. Even the Bonnie Blues were turned to blood. Men, women, and children clustered at the edges of the trees and across the ridgeline north like the ghosts of the dead.

Ben turned toward the demons and exhaled slowly as he took in the size of their army. Too many. Far too many.

"My Lord, I think that maybe I have—" Horris Kew began, and was cut short as Abernathy's hand clamped tightly about the back of his neck.

Ben turned to his scribe, who still clutched the Tangle Box tightly beneath his free arm. "Take the box and Horris and move to the lake," Ben ordered his scribe. "Call for Questor to bring the lake skimmer and have him ferry you both across. Hurry!"

Abernathy hastened away, dragging a protesting Horris Kew after. Ben glanced at the demons anew. The Gorse had moved into the forefront of their ranks, black-cloaked and featureless even in the strange light. Ben moved out from the shadow of the dragon to face the demons. He reached into his tunic and held forth the medallion of Landover's Kings. At his side, Strabo widened his maw and coughed sharply, an explosive sound. There was movement all up and down the clustered black ranks, an uneasiness, a hesitancy. It was one thing to face a Lord of the Greensward and his army. It was something else again to confront Holiday and Strabo as well.

"Kallendbor!" Ben called over his shoulder into the ranks of the Greensward army.

Almost immediately there was the sound of a rider approaching from behind. Ben turned. Kallendbor, armored head to foot with only his face showing beneath his lifted visor, wheeled to a stop atop his charger.

"High Lord," he greeted, his red-bearded face pale, his eyes darting nervously to the dragon.

Ben stalked to meet him. "I know of your part in all this, Kallendbor," he said curtly. "You will have to answer for it when this business is done."

Kallendbor nodded. There was no apology in his piercing blue eyes. "I'll answer if I must and if we are both alive at the end of this day."

"Fair enough. For now, let's concentrate on finding a way to dispatch the demons back to where they belong and the black-cloaked trickster with them. Do your men stand ready to fight?"

"We are at your service, High Lord." There was no hesitation.

"Ride back then and wait for my signal," Ben ordered.

Kallendbor saluted and galloped away. Unrepentant to the last, Ben thought. Some men refused to change.

He turned back toward the Gorse and the demons. A huge black rider had moved out in front of the others. The Mark. The others would follow its lead into battle. The demon leader stopped and stared across at Ben and Strabo.

The dragon's crusted head swung about. "Call up the Paladin, Holiday. The demons grow edgy."

Ben nodded. He was resigned to what must happen now, but despaired of it as well. Once again, he must summon the Paladin to do battle for him. Once again, there would be killing and destruction, and much of it would come at his hands. Another terrible battle, and he was powerless to stop it, helpless to do anything other than participate and hope that somehow he could find a way to shorten it. Faint hope, born of desperation and lack of choice. He felt Strabo's eyes watching him. The Gorse was responsible for this and should be brought to account, but how could that be done? How powerful was this fairy creature? Very, he guessed, if the fairy people had gone to such extremes to lock it away in the Tangle Box and keep it there.

"Holiday!" the dragon rasped impatiently.

Lock the Gorse back into the Tangle Box—that was what he should do. Lock it away for good. But how? What magic would it take?

There was no time to wonder about it further, no time to decide what help could be found. The demons had begun to advance, coming across the meadow in a dark mass, slowly, deliberately, inexorably.

"Holiday!" Strabo hissed furiously.

Paladin's sword and dragon's fire—would they be enough to save Landover?

Ben Holiday reached for the medallion that would give him his answer.

Horris Kew was practically beside himself with frustration. He stood glumly next to Abernathy at the water's edge, watching the approach of Questor Thews in the lake skimmer, thinking that his last chance to save himself was about to be taken away.

He had tried to tell Holiday, but Landover's King did not have time for him. He had tried to tell Abernathy, but the scribe had heard all he wanted to hear. He considered telling Questor Thews when the wizard arrived to convey them back across to the comparative safety of the castle fortress, but he was reasonably certain that he would find no help from that quarter either. No one wanted to listen to Horris and that was the hard truth of the matter.

Except that for once Horris had something important to say.

He shuffled his size-sixteens, hugged himself like a rag doll, and tried to remain calm. But it was hard to stay calm knowing what was going to become of him if the Gorse and the demons prevailed over Holiday. If Holiday won, his circumstances would still be precarious, but acceptable. If Holiday won, he had a reasonable chance of staying alive. But if the Gorse came out of this the victor, Horris Kew was stew meat. It didn't pay to dwell on exactly what recipe would be used, but the result would be the same. The Gorse had seen him standing with Holiday and the dragon; it had seen him quite plainly. The inference was obvious. Horris had joined the enemy. There could be no forgiveness. No excuses would be allowed. The Gorse would grind him up and spit him out, and that would be that.

Horris recalled how the creature had made him feel when they first started out together in this hateful venture. He remembered the silky, dangerous voice and the lingering smell of death. He could still feel its power threatening to strangle him with invisible fingers. He did not relish experiencing any of it again. The tic was gone from his eye for the first time since he had set the Gorse free. Here was his chance to keep it from coming back.

Thunder rolled out of the west, building on itself where the clouds massed. The heavy bank was spreading rapidly toward the sun, swallowing up its light as it came, turning everything black. Wind whipped across the meadow and over the confronting armies. Horses shied, and armor and weapons clanged. The air began to smell of rain.

Horris had been thinking about the Tangle Box. How had the Gorse been put into it in the first place? Surely the renegade fairy had not gone willingly—no more so than Holiday, the witch, and the dragon. Twice now, Horris had been called upon to speak words of power that released captives of the box.

Could the spell be reversed?

He thought about the way that Holiday and the others had been dispatched. The Gorse had constructed an elaborate net of magic upon the spot to which his three victims had been lured. Then Horris had appeared with the Tangle Box, spoken the words of power, triggered the net, and the trap had been sprung.

Simple enough. It would seem at first glance then that a similar approach would be necessary to snare the Gorse. Except that something was nagging at Horris Kew. Wasn't the Tangle Box constructed for that particular purpose? If so, then the entrapment of Holiday and the other two was an unnatural use of the box, an aberration of that for which it was intended. Besides, if the Gorse knew this was how the magic worked, how had it allowed itself to be trapped in the first place? And if it didn't know then, how had it learned since?

And what about this? The Gorse had known the words that would free it, but couldn't speak them. It had been necessary to manipulate Biggar through the Skat Mandu charade to have Horris speak the words instead. Didn't this suggest something? Didn't this mean that the Gorse found the words anathema for some reason and so required that another use them?

Didn't it mean, Horris wondered, that the same spell—the spell that the Gorse was so careful to avoid using himself—might work both ways?

The more he considered the possibility, the more sense it made. The fairies, having built the Tangle Box, would have employed a special, customized magic to trap the Gorse within, a magic that it could never use to effect its own escape. And it would not be a magic that would trap away others—

like Holiday, Nightshade, and Strabo—so that, to subvert the purpose of the box, something different would be required to ensnare them. And perhaps, in the bargain, to protect the Gorse from being recaptured. Hence the carefully conceived net of magic the Gorse had employed.

Sure, it was a stretch. But Horris Kew was desperate and his conjurer's opportunistic mind was grasping at straws because that was all that was left him.

They should listen to him, he believed. Holiday, Abernathy, Questor Thews, all of them. They should try his suggestion out. What harm could it do at this point? But he might as well be asking to be made King. No one was going to try any idea he suggested.

Thunder rolled once more, a long, booming peal that shook the ground on which he stood. In the meadow's center, Kallendbor had ridden back to his army and Holiday was turning toward the Gorse and the demons. The Mark had moved to the forefront of his horde and was beginning a slow advance. The dragon had lifted itself into a crouch and was venting steam through its nostrils as the fire built in its belly. Horris glanced over his shoulder. Questor Thews was almost ashore. Abernathy had turned to meet the wizard, his back momentarily to Horris.

Biggar had always accused him of indecision. He hated to think that the bird had been right.

Horris Kew swallowed, his throat dry. Now or never, wasn't it? He glanced again at Holiday. Landover's King had removed the medallion of his office from within his dark tunic and was holding it up to the light.

Do it!

Horris yanked the Tangle Box out from under Abernathy's arm, then lowered his shoulder and knocked the astonished scribe backward into the lake. Then he ran as fast as his long legs could carry him toward the Gorse. He was thinking he had gone mad, he was a fool, he had just made the worst mistake of his life. Shouts rose up as he was sighted. Angry cries assailed him from every side. Out of the corner of his eye, he saw the dragon's black-horned head swing quickly about, and he envisioned himself encased in fire. A moment more, he thought. One moment more.

The Gorse had not moved. It was watching him come, thinking he was bringing the Tangle Box back again, an unwitting pawn to the end. The demons shifted like shadows in the enfolding black of the storm. Weapons glinted darkly. Horris Kew tried not to think about them. His gangly body was shaking, and his scarecrow limbs were flying out all over the place. He was sweating and gasping from the strain of his flight. He had never been so terrified.

He heard Questor Thews shout his name. A bolt of ragged fire zipped past his ear. He dropped to one knee in a panic and set the Tangle Box on the ground before him. He looked across the meadow at the Gorse, and he could see in its terrible eyes that it recognized the truth at last. The monster's black cloak billowed as it charged toward him in rage.

Quickly, Horris began to chant.

"Rashun, oblight, surena! Larin, kestral . . ."

Ben Holiday stood frozen in place, the medallion still clutched in his hand, momentarily forgotten. He had not seen Horris Kew until just a moment ago. Questor Thews was pulling Abernathy from the lake, both of them shouting angrily and gesturing. Strabo was uncoiling his huge, dark length, spreading his wings, and preparing to lift off. Fire leaked from between his jagged teeth.

All of them too late to intercede, Ben thought in frustration and despair.

Mist blossomed in a dark cloud from the Tangle Box, the lid disappeared, and the tunnel back down into the Labyrinth opened anew. Wicked green light shot forth to mingle with the red glare of the sun and the dark of the approaching storm.

Thunder boomed, and a scattering of raindrops began to fall. The meadow had gone suddenly still, the clamor of the opposing armies disappearing into a hush of expectancy.

Out from the Tangle Box appeared a swarm of shadows, misty forms that twisted and writhed in the strange mix of light, dark specters set free. They rose in a cluster and then shot across the meadow toward the demons. The Gorse cried out, a terrible wail of despair. Webs of protective magic spun from its hands, encircling its black form to ward off its attackers. The shadows went right through the webs, seized the Gorse, and dragged it into the open. The Gorse thrashed and tore futilely. It spit like a cat. It fought with every ounce of strength and every weapon of magic it possessed. But the shadows were relentless. They hauled the renegade fairy back across the meadow to the box. They wrapped it about with their cloaking forms and pulled it down.

Down into the prison it thought it had escaped forever.

Down into the frightening darkness of the fairy mists.

They disappeared inside, the shadows and the Gorse, and the lid to the Tangle Box closed for good.

The wind broke loose across the meadow in a howl. Airborne, Strabo passed over the box and Horris Kew like death's shadow, but then flew on to descend instead upon the demons of Abaddon, breathing its fire into their midst. Dozens disintegrated. The rest, bereft of the promised protection of the Gorse and its magic, had no interest in a fight. Led by their Mark, they turned back toward the bluff out of which they had come, back into the rent in the air that had given them passage into Landover, and descended down again into their netherworld home. In seconds, the last of them had gone, and the space they had briefly occupied in the world of light stood empty.

Strabo swung back toward the army of the Greensward, hissing in triumph and challenge.

Standing at the center of the meadow still, the rain falling into his face in sheets, the wind ripping at his frozen body, Ben Holiday exhaled slowly and slipped the medallion of the Kings of Landover back inside his tunic.

Green Eyes

Willow came awake in the faint, gray dawn light, the dampness of the Deep Fell seeping through her naked body. She was lying on the ground, curled into a ball, the baby resting in the crook of her arm. At first she wasn't aware of it. She blinked against the sleep that still clouded her mind, trying to remember where she was. Then she felt the baby move and looked down at it.

Her child.

She studied it for a long time, and tears came to her eyes.

She remembered everything then—coming out of the fairy mists into the Deep Fell, transforming into her other self, forming the pod, drifting into sleep. She cradled the child to her, giving it what warmth she could, lending it the small shelter of her body.

Then she rose, slipped back into her clothes, and wrapped the baby in her cloak. It was sleeping still, not yet hungry enough to wake, not disturbed by its surroundings as Willow was. The Deep Fell had not been her choice for where the baby should be born, and she did not intend to remain there any longer than necessary. Mist rolled through the branches of the jungle trees and snaked down along the trunks. Silence blanketed everything. Nothing moved. It was a dead world, and only the witch who had made it so belonged here.

Willow began to walk, moving toward the light—east,

where the sun rose over Landover. She must get clear quickly, before she was discovered. She was weak still from giving birth, but mostly she was fearful. She was not so frightened for herself as she was for her child, the measure of her life with Ben, the culmination of their bonding. She peeked down at it again through the folds of the cloak, making certain she had seen it right on waking, that nothing had changed. The tears came anew. There was a tightness in her throat. She wanted to find and be with Ben, to make certain he was all right, and to let him see their child.

She walked for what seemed a long time, but probably was not. Her body ached in strange ways—a dull, empty pain in her loins, a constriction in her chest, a soreness that laced the muscles of her arms and legs. She did not know how much to attribute to the birth and how much to sleeping naked in the chill of the Fell. Movement helped ease the pain in her arms and chest, loosening muscles that were cramped and tight. The pain within her loins persisted. She ignored it. She could not be too far from the wall of the hollow, she told herself. If she just kept moving, she would get free.

She came out of a stretch of old growth laced with mist and gloom, entered a clearing, and stopped. Nightshade stood before her, wrapped in her black cloak, drawn up as straight and immutable as a stone statue, her red eyes gleaming.

"What are you doing here, sylph?" she demanded softly.

Willow's heart sank. Having been forced to give birth to her child in this forbidding place, she had wanted only to escape without encountering the witch, and it seemed she was to be denied even this.

She managed to keep the fear from her voice as she answered. "I entered through the fairy mists and by mistake. I want no trouble. I want only to depart."

Nightshade seemed surprised. "Through the fairy mists? Have you been imprisoned, too? But, no. You were elsewhere in his dream, weren't you?" She stopped talking, collecting herself. "Why would you come out here? Why would you come out at all, for that matter? The fairies release no one from the mists."

Willow gave a moment's thought to lying, but decided against it. The witch would know, her magic strong enough here in her lair to detect another's deception.

"The fairies were forced to release me when the High Lord came to me in his dreams and set me free of their magic. They released me from the mists. They did not tell me where I would come out. Perhaps they sent me here as punishment."

Nightshade's gaze lowered to the bundle she cradled in her arms. "What is that you carry?"

Willow's arms tightened about the baby. "My child by the High Lord, newly born."

Nightshade took a quick, harsh breath. "The play-King's child? Here?" She laughed. "Fortune does indeed play strange games with us. Why do you carry the child about so? Did you carry it into the mists as well?" She stopped abruptly. "Wait, I have heard nothing of this child. I have not been gone that long from Landover. I should know of this. Newly born, you say? Born where, then?"

"Here," Willow answered softly.

Nightshade's face twisted into something grotesque. "Born here, in my home? Holiday's child? While I was locked in the fairy mists with him, trapped in that cursed box? Trapped with him, girl—did you know? Together for weeks, drained of memory, made over into creatures we did not even recognize. He came to you in a dream? Yes, he told me so. It was the dream that released him from his ignorance, that led him to divulge the truth about both of us."

Her voice was a hiss. "Have you seen him since his return?" She smiled at Willow's reaction. "Ah, you didn't know he was back, then, did you? Back from his other life, a life with me, little sylph, in which I was his charge and he my protector. Do you know what happened between us while you were carrying his child?

She paused, her eyes gleaming with expectation. "He bed me as if I were his—"

"No!" Willow's voice was as hard as iron, the single word a forbidding that cut short the witch as surely as a cord about the throat.

"He was mine!" the witch of the Deep Fell screamed. "He belonged to me! I should have had him forever if not for his dream of you! I lost everything, everything but who I am, the power of my magic, the strength of my will! Those I have regained! Holiday owes me! He has stripped me of my pride and my dignity, and he has incurred a debt to me that he must pay!"

She was white with rage. "The child," she whispered, "will satisfy that debt nicely."

Willow went cold. She was shaking, her throat dry, her heart stopped. "You cannot have my child," she said.

A smile played across Nightshade's lips. "Cannot? What a silly word for you to use, little sylph. Besides, the child was born in my domain, here in the Deep Fell, so it belongs to me by right of law. My law."

"No law condones the taking of a child from its mother. You have no right to make such a claim."

"I have every right. I am mistress of the Deep Fell and ruler over all found here. The child was born on my soil. You are a trespasser and a foolish girl. Do not think you can deny me."

Willow held her ground. "If you try to take my child, you will have to kill me. Are you prepared to do that?"

Nightshade shook her head slowly. "I need not kill you. There are easier ways when you have the use of magic. And worse fates for you than death if you defy me."

"The High Lord will come after you if you steal his child!" Willow snapped. "He will hunt you to the ends of the earth!"

"Silly little sylph," the witch purred softly. "The High Lord will never know you were even here."

Willow froze. Nightshade was right. There was no one who knew she was in the Deep Fell, no one who knew she had returned from the fairy mists. If she was to disappear, who could trace her footsteps? If her child was to vanish, who could say it had ever existed? The fairies, perhaps, but would they do so?

What was she to do?

"Someone will discover and reveal the truth, Nightshade," she insisted desperately. "You cannot keep such a thing a secret forever! Not even you can do that!"

The witch gave a slow, disdainful shrug. "Perhaps not. But I can keep it a secret long enough. Holiday's life is finite. In the end, I will be here when he is gone."

Willow nodded slowly, understanding flooding through her. "Which is why you want his child, isn't it? So that he will leave nothing of himself behind when he is dead. You would make the child yours and wipe away all trace of him in doing so. You hate him that much, don't you?"

Nightshade's thin mouth tightened. "More. Much, much more."

"But the child is innocent," Willow cried. "Why should the baby be made a pawn in this struggle? Why should it suffer for your rage?"

"The child will fare well. I will see to it."

"It isn't yours!"

"I grow tired of arguing, sylph. Give the child to me and perhaps I will let you go. Make another child, if you wish. You have the means."

Willow shook her head slowly. "I will never give up my

baby, Nightshade. Not to you, not to anyone. Stand aside for me. Let me pass."

Nightshade smiled darkly. "I think not," she said.

She was starting forward, arms lifting within her black robes, intent on taking the child by force, when a familiar voice spoke.

"Do as she asks, Nightshade. Let her pass."

The witch stopped, as still as death. Willow looked around quickly, seeing nothing but the trees and misty gloom.

Then Edgewood Dirk stepped into view from one side, easing sinuously through the heavy brush, silver coat immaculate, black tail twitching slightly. He jumped up on the remains of a fallen tree and blinked sleepily.

"Let her pass," he repeated softly.

Nightshade stiffened. "Edgewood Dirk. Who gave you permission to come into the Deep Fell? Who gave you the right?"

"Cats need no permission or grant of right," Dirk replied. "Really, you should know better. Cats go where they wish— always have."

Nightshade was livid. "Get out of here!"

Dirk yawned and stretched. "Shortly. But first you must let the Queen pass."

"I will not give up . . . !"

"Save your breath, Witch of the Deep Fell." A hint of weary disdain crept into the cat's voice. "The Queen and her baby will pass into Landover. The fairies have decided, and there is nothing more to say about it. If you are unhappy with their decision, why don't you take it up with them?"

Nightshade shot a withering look at Willow, then turned to face the cat. "The fairies cannot tell me what to do!"

"Of course they can," Edgewood Dirk said reasonably. "I have just done so for them. Stop fussing about this. The matter is settled. Now step aside."

"The child is mine!"

Dirk gave one paw a short, swift lick and straightened. "Nightshade," he addressed her softly. "Would you challenge me?"

There was a long pause as witch and prism cat faced each other in the half light of the Deep Fell. "Because if you would," Dirk continued, "you must surely know that even if I fail, another will be sent to take my place, and another, and so forth. Fairies are very stubborn creatures. You, of all people, should know."

Nightshade did not move. When she spoke, there was astonishment in her voice. "Why are they doing this? Why do they care so about his child?"

Edgewood Dirk blinked. "That," he purred softly, "is a good question." He rose, stretched, and sat back down again. "I grow anxious for my morning nap. I have given this matter enough of my time. Let the Queen and the child pass. Now."

Nightshade shook her head slowly, a denial of something she could not articulate. For an instant Willow was certain that she intended to lash out at Dirk, that she would fight the prism cat with every ounce of strength and every bit of magic she possessed.

But instead she turned to Willow and said softly, "I will never forgive this. Never. Tell the play-King."

Then she disappeared into the gloom, a wraith simply fading away into the shadows. The baby woke, stirring in its mother's arms, blinking sleepily. Willow glanced down into the cloak's deep folds. She cooed softly to her child. When she looked up again, Edgewood Dirk was gone as well. Had he been with her all the way? The fairies had sent him once again, it appeared, although with the prism cat you could never be entirely certain. He had saved her life in any case. Or more to the point, saved her child. Why? Nightshade's question, still unanswered. What was it about this child that mattered so to everyone?

Cradling the baby in her arms, she began to walk on once again.

It was nearing midmorning by the time Ben Holiday reached the country just south of the Deep Fell. He would never have gotten there that fast if Strabo had not offered to trade him a ride for possession of the Tangle Box. The dragon had wanted the box from the first, but Ben had refused to give it up, not convinced that it should be in anyone's possession but his own.

"Let me have it, Holiday," the dragon had argued. "I will keep it in a place no one can reach, in a fire pit deep within the Wastelands where no one goes."

"But why would you want it at all?" Ben asked. "What would you do with it?"

The dragon had flown back from his assault on the demons. They were alone in the center of the meadow. Horris Kew slumped on the ground some yards away. Questor Thews and Abernathy had not yet reached them.

The dragon's voice was wistful. "I would take it out and look at it from time to time. A dragon covets treasures and hoards precious things. It is all we have left from our old life—all I have left, now that I am alone." Strabo's horned head dipped close. "I would keep it hidden where it could never be found. I would keep it just for me."

Ben had interrupted the conversation long enough to intervene between a sodden, angry Abernathy, who had just come rushing up, and a terrified Horris Kew, and assisted by Questor Thews had restored some small measure of peace between them. The conjurer had saved their lives, after all, he reminded his much-distressed scribe. He went on then to dismiss Kallendbor and his army, exacting an oath from the Lord of Rhyndweir to appear before him in one week's time for an accounting of his actions. He ordered his Guard to disperse those people who had come looking for mind's eye crystals and found a great deal more than they had bargained for, back to wherever it was they had come from.

Then he remembered Willow. He went immediately to the Landsview and found her just as she was climbing free of the Deep Fell. Nightshade's domain, he thought in horror, and no place for the sylph. He was thinking of Nightshade's parting words to him. He was thinking what the witch might do to Willow if she were given half a chance.

It was a two-day ride to the Deep Fell—far too long under the circumstances. So he struck a bargain with Strabo. A ride to the Deep Fell and back in exchange for the Tangle Box, if the dragon promised that no one else would ever set eyes on it and no one, including the dragon, would ever attempt to open it. Strabo agreed. He extended his firm and unbreakable promise. He gave his dragon's oath. It was enough, Questor Thews whispered in a short aside. A dragon's word was his bond.

So off Ben went aboard Strabo, winging through the storm winds and rain, finally passing out of black clouds and into blue skies. The sun shone anew on the land, spilling golden light across the grasslands and hills running north, cutting a swath of brightness through the fading dark.

"She is there, Holiday," the dragon called back when they grew close, its sharp eyes finding the sylph much quicker than Ben's.

They swooped down onto the crest of a hill, a scattering of woods running right and left. Willow appeared from across a meadow of wildflowers and Bonnie Blues, and Ben ran to meet her, heedless of everything else. She called to him, her face radiant, tears coming into her eyes once more.

He raced up to her and abruptly stopped, the bundle in her arms a fragile barrier between them. What was she carrying? "Are you all right?" he asked, anxious to be reassured that she was well, eager just to hear her voice.

"Yes, Ben," she answered. "And you?"

He nodded, smiling. "I love you, Willow," he said.

He could see her throat constrict. "Come see our child," she whispered.

He came forward a step, closing the small distance between them, expectation and disbelief racing through him. It was too quick, he thought. It was not yet time. She had not even looked pregnant. How could she have given birth so fast?

The questions vanished in the afterglow of her smile. "The baby?" he said, and she nodded.

She parted the folds of her cloak so he could see. He bent down and peered inside.

A pair of dazzling green eyes stared boldly back.

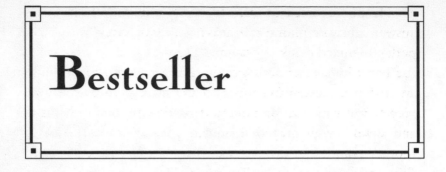

Bestseller

The interviewer sipped a pineapple-strawberry smoothie in the living room of Harold Kraft's palatial Diamond Head home and looked out across the vast expanse of lanai and swimming pool to the only slightly vaster expanse of the Pacific Ocean. It was late afternoon, and the sun was easing westward toward the flat line of the horizon, the gradual change in the light promising yet another incredibly beautiful Hawaiian sunset. The granite floors of the living room and lanai glittered as if inlaid with flecks of gold, the stone ending at the pool, one of those knife-edge affairs that dropped into a spillover as if falling all the way to the ocean. A Jacuzzi bubbled invitingly at one end of the lanai. A bar and cooking area dominated the other end, complete with hollow coconut shells used for tropical drinks at the frequent parties the author gave.

The home was conservatively valued at fifteen million, although the price of real estate is always subject to what the market will bear and its measure is not an objective exercise. Homes around it had sold for ten million and up and lacked both the extensive grounds and the unrestricted view that took in most of Honolulu. Bare land went for five million in this neighborhood. The numbers were unimaginable for most people. The interviewer lived in Seattle in a home he had bought fifteen years ago for somewhat less than what Harold Kraft earned in a month.

Kraft wandered in from his study where he had gone to answer a private phone call, leaving the interviewer to sip his perfectly mixed drink and admire the view. He strolled over to the bar with a brief apology for taking so long, fixed himself an iced tea, crossed the room to the couch where the interviewer was patiently waiting, and sat down again. He was tall and slender with graying hair and a Vandyke beard, and he moved like a long, slow, elegant cat. He wore silk slacks and shirt and hand-tooled leather sandals. His tanned face was aquiline, and his sandy eyes were penetrating. There were rumors of reconstructive surgery and a rigorous training regiment, but that was fairly commonplace with the rich and famous.

"Good news," he announced with a smile. "Since you're here, I can share it with you. Paramount just bought rights to *Wizard*. Two million dollars outright. They want Sean Connery for the title role, Tom Cruise for the part of the Prince. What do you think?"

The interviewer smiled appreciatively. "I think you're two million dollars richer. Congratulations."

Kraft gave him a short bow. "Wait until the merchandising kicks in. That's where the real money is."

"Do you write your books with an eye towards movie sales?" the interviewer pressed. He wasn't getting nearly enough out of Kraft to satisfy either himself or his magazine. Kraft had published three books in two years and dominated the bestseller lists for most of that time, selling more than five million copies in hardcover. But that was practically all anyone knew about him. For all his notoriety and success, he was still very much a mystery. He claimed to be in exile, but he wouldn't say from where. He claimed to be a political refugee.

"I write to be read," the author replied pointedly. "What happens after that is up to the consumer. Sure, I want to make money. But mostly I want to be happy."

The interviewer frowned. "That sounds a bit . . ."

"Disingenuous? I suppose it does. But I've done a lot of things and been a lot of places, and I don't have much to show for any of it. What I have is myself, and my writing is an extension of myself. It is very hard to separate the two, you know. A writer doesn't just punch a clock and go home at the end of the day. He carries his work around with him, always thinking about it, always polishing it up like the family silver. If you're not satisfied with it, you have to live with your dissatisfaction. That's why I want to be happy about what I do. More important to be happy than to be rich."

"Doesn't hurt to be both," the interviewer pointed out. "You've had an amazing string of successes. Do you ever think about what it was like before you were published?"

Kraft smiled. "All the time. But I sense an attempt at an end run. I have to remind you that try though you might, you won't get me to talk about my earlier life. Ground rules for this interview, right?"

"So you've said, but my readers are quite curious about you. You must know that."

"I do. I appreciate the interest."

"But you still won't discuss anything about yourself before you were published?"

"I made a promise not to."

"A promise to whom?"

"A promise to some people. That's all I intend to say."

"Then let's discuss your characters and try coming into your life through the back door, so to speak." The interviewer harbored hopes of publishing a book himself one day. He fancied himself very clever with words. "Are they based on real people from your old life? For instance, the misguided King of your magic land, his inept court wizard, and the snappish dog who serves as his scribe?"

Kraft nodded slowly. "Yes, they exist."

"How about your protagonist, the renegade wizard who saves the day in each book? Is there some of you in him?"

Kraft cleared his throat modestly. "A bit."

The interviewer paused, sensing he was finally getting somewhere. "Have you ever dabbled in magic? You know, played at conjuring spells and the like? Has that been a part of your life?"

Harold Kraft was lost in thought for a moment. When he came back from wherever he had been, his face turned serious. "I'll tell you what," he said. "I'm going to make an exception to my rule of never talking about my past and tell you something. There was a time when I did play about with magic. Small stuff, really—nothing serious. Except that once I did stumble quite inadvertently on something that turned out to be very dangerous indeed. My own life as well as those of others was threatened. I survived that scare, but I made a promise to certain people that I would never use . . . that is, dabble, in magic again. I never have."

"So the magic in your books, the conjuring and the invocations of spells and the like, has some basis in real life?"

"Some, yes."

"And the tales you weave, those spellbinding stories of monsters and elves, of mythical creatures and wizards like your protagonist—do these have a basis in real life as well?"

Kraft slowly raised and then lowered one eyebrow. "A writer writes what he knows. Life experience enters in. It usually takes a different form than the reality, but it is always there."

The interviewer nodded solemnly. Had he learned anything from this exchange? He wasn't sure. It was all rather vague. Like Harold Kraft. He covered his confusion by checking the tiny tape recorder sitting on the coffee table. Still spinning. "Would it be fair to say that the adventures you write about in some way mirror your own life?" he tried again.

"It would be both fair and accurate, yes."

"How?"

Kraft smiled. "You must use your imagination."

The interviewer smiled back, trying not to grit his teeth. "Do you have other stories left to tell, Mr. Kraft?"

"Harold, please," the author insisted with a quick wave of his hand. "Three hours together in the journalistic trenches entitles us to conclude our conversation on a first-name basis. And to answer your question, yes. I have other stories to tell and some time left to tell them, I hope. I'm working on one now. *Raptor's Spell* is the title. Would you like to see the cover?"

"Very much."

They rose and walked from the living room down a short hall to the study, which served primarily as Kraft's office. Word processors and printers sat at various desks, and books and paper were piled all over the place. Framed book covers hung on the walls. A koa-wood desk dominated the center of the room. From the stacks of writing on the top of this desk, Kraft produced a colored photo and handed it over to the interviewer.

The photo showed a bird that was all black save for a crown of white feathers. The bird was in the act of swooping down on a malevolent being that resembled a mass of thistles. Lightning streaked from the bird's extended claws. Dark things fled into a woods at the bird's approach.

The interviewer studied the photo for a moment. "Very dramatic. Is the bird representative of someone from your earlier life?"

Horris Kew, who now called himself Harold Kraft, nodded solemnly. "Alas, poor Biggar, I knew him well," he intoned with a dramatic flourish.

And gave the photo a nostalgic kiss.

About the Author

TERRY BROOKS was born in Illinois in 1944. He received his undergraduate degree from Hamilton College, where he majored in English Literature, and his graduate degree from the School of Law at Washington & Lee University.

A writer since high school, he published his first novel, *The Sword of Shannara*, in 1977. It became the first work of fiction ever to appear on the *New York Times* Trade Paperback Bestseller List, where it remained for over five months. *The Elfstones of Shannara* followed in 1982, and *The Wishsong of Shannara* in 1985. *Magic Kingdom for Sale—Sold!* began a bestselling new series for him in 1986. THE HERITAGE OF SHANNARA, a four-book series, concluded with publication of *The Talismans of Shannara* in 1993.

The author was a practicing attorney for many years, but now writes full-time. He lives with his wife Judine in the Pacific Northwest and Hawaii.